PRAISE

"A rakish, often hilarious series of erotic and platonic misadventures interspersed with a fair amount of from-the-heart philosophizing . . . the hero is irresistible: romantic, respectful, and cheerfully dirty-minded—sometimes all at once." —*Kirkus Reviews*

"*Neva Hafta* is more than just another book about dating, relationships and love gone wrong, it's a story about life. . . . The message is simple yet provocative—marry for love and never settle for anything less." —*Black Issues Book Review*

"Edwardo Jackson's *Neva Hafta* is tailor-made for fans of the author's *Ever After*." —*Essence*

PRAISE FOR *EVER AFTER*

"This is a new millennium romance. . . . Amusing and smart."
—*Black Issues Book Review*

"Jackson pens some entertaining scenes that present an African-American spin on 20-something relationships." —*Publishers Weekly*

"A very believable love story." —*Booklist*

"In this funny and heartwarming debut, newcomer Edwardo Jackson gives us a fresh take on the male broken heart. . . . Jackson has a great ear for dialogue and a knack for truthful, uncompromising story-telling. . . . Be ready to laugh out loud." —*The Dallas Weekly*

"*Ever After* is fraught with the uncertainty of young love and the delicious promise of new beginnings, while taking you on a soul-searching journey that will remain etched upon your heart . . . ever after."
—TRACY PRICE-THOMPSON, author of *Black Coffee* and *Chocolate Sangria*

Edwardo Jackson is a writer with something to say and the skills to say it. The search for true love may never be the same!"
—PEARL CLEAGE, author of *Some Things I Never Thought I'd Do*

**STRIVERS ROW**

During the 1920s and 1930s, around the time of the Harlem Renaissance, more than a quarter of a million African-Americans settled in Harlem, creating what was described at the time as "a cosmopolitan Negro capital which exert[ed] an influence over Negroes everywhere."

Nowhere was this more evident than on West 138th and 139th Streets between what are now Adam Clayton Powell and Frederick Douglass Boulevards, two blocks that came to be known as Strivers Row. These blocks attracted many of Harlem's African-American doctors, lawyers, and entertainers, among them Eubie Blake, Noble Sissle, and W. C. Handy, who were themselves striving to achieve America's middle-class dream.

With its mission of publishing quality African-American literature, Strivers Row emulates those "strivers," capturing that same spirit of hope, creativity, and promise.

*Neva Hafta*

# Neva Haffa

A NOVEL

# EDWARDO JACKSON

STRIVERS
ROW

VILLARD

NEW YORK

2003 Strivers Row Trade Paperback Edition

Copyright © 2002 by Edwardo Jackson
Reader's guide copyright © 2003 by Random House Inc.

This work was originally published in hardcover by Strivers Row/Villard Books,
an imprint of The Random House Publishing Group, a division of
Random House, Inc., New York, in 2002.

Library of Congress Cataloging-in-Publication Data

Jackson, Edwardo.
Neva hafta : a novel / Edwardo Jackson.
p. cm.
ISBN 0-375-75774-0
1. African American men—Fiction. 2. Dating (Social customs)—Fiction.
3. Terminally ill parents—Fiction. 4. San Diego (Calif.)—Fiction.
5. Mothers and sons—Fiction. 6. Journalists—Fiction. I. Title.

PS3610.A35 N48 2002
813'.6—dc21
2002022979

Villard Books website address: www.villard.com
Printed in the United States of America
246897531

Book design by JoAnne Metsch

*To Mom and my future wife—*
*thanks for waiting on me;*
*I'm still waiting on you.*

**CARDINAL RULE TO DATING NO. 1:**

*Never date someone from a health club.*

**CARDINAL RULE TO DATING NO. 2:**

*Never date someone with whom you work.*

**CARDINAL RULE TO DATING NO. 3:**

*Never date someone from class.*

**CARDINAL RULE TO DATING NO. 4:**

*Never let an ex back into your life.*

**CARDINAL RULE TO DATING NO. 5:**

*Never date a neighbor.*

**CARDINAL RULE TO DATING NO. 6:**

*Never date a married woman.*

*The saga continues . . .*

*Neva*
*Hafta*

**W**ANTED: SINGLE BLACK *Female, 20–30. No, scratch that. SBF, 25–35. Better. Nonsmoker, nondrinker, tall, and athletic. Honesty and intelligence are preferred, but if you can fake both of those convincingly, you're in there. Oh yes, must have a love of the arts, especially drama. Cultured. Worldly. Renaissance. MUST LOVE SPORTS. Oh, hell yeah. Must be able to appreciate quality cable programming such as ESPN's SportsCenter. Must have a sense of humor. If you cannot comprehend the humor in a show like* South Park *or in movies like* Happy Gilmore *or* White Men Can't Jump *then THIS AD IS NOT FOR YOU. Must be sexually adventurous. Can I write that? Hmm . . . Okay. Must be sexually liberated. Shoot, might as well be straight up about it— must be a freak. No, I can't write that. Well, I just did. Damn. Forget those whole few sentences. Umm . . . a romantic. YES. Should be creatively romantic as well as receptive to romantic creativity. Was that just redundant? Values intimacy. AFFECTIONATE. Most definitely. Cannot have any hang-ups about Public Displays of Affection. PDA, in my book, includes hand holding, light kissing, and making goo-goo eyes at each other so sweetly until your teeth rot. Independent. Assertive. Confident. A woman who knows what she wants out of life and goes after it. No wallflowers, no shy girls. A*

*twenty-first-century woman. A woman of the new millennium. Am-*
*bitious. Career oriented. Future housewives, golddiggers, and pro-*
*fessional pretty girls need not apply. A woman into commitment.*
*Players and playettes—see ya! Wouldn't want to be ya. No children,*
*please. I know I'm asking a lot at this point, finding a thirty-year-old*
*woman who has never been married and has no kids, but that's what*
*I want. I can just see Khalilah right now spinning her huge eyes in*
*that little head of hers telling me I'm being too picky. She can kiss*
*off—let her make her own ad. Should like to travel, be a decent*
*cook . . . Wait a minute. This is a little more than twenty-four words,*
*isn't it?*

**WITH THAT THOUGHT,** Nick stopped typing. He assessed his
mock ad, generated on his brand-new laptop computer, a gift to himself for having successfully moved to San Diego. There was no way
Nick would ever send in the ad to the *Union-Tribune,* even in a more
edited, concise form. But it was fun to dream, wasn't it?

Casually clicking to save his document, Nick peered out at the
world through amber-colored, reflective sunglasses. He could not
have crafted a better-looking day than this. Resting in his lawn chair
on the beach, Nick's toes tickled the grainy warmth of the sand below.
The clean, sea-blown air made his skin tingle. Seagulls lazily traced
swooping arcs and parabolas of flight against a blue, cloud-smeared,
Impressionist sky. The sun shone brilliantly yet with only the moderate warmth San Diego was so famous for. Perfect weather, perfect
atmosphere, perfect day. Nick knew that this was going to be a memorable birthday.

Twenty-nine years old today, July 24. The last memorable birthday
he could remember was . . . *Jasmine* . . . his twenty-second, when he
had bought his first Toyota 4Runner. *Jasmine* . . .

Okay, that was the last time he was going to think about that name.
This was his birthday. Dwelling on ex-almost-fiancées was not the
order for today, his special day.

Which was why he was at the beach. Laid out in his lawn chair
on the sand, in only a pair of soccer shorts, Nick's athletically toned,
walnut-brown body was on full display. After years of working out,
Nick was now a specimen. His abs were veritable cobblestones of
muscle, his chest was so cut it was almost square, and his arms had

more hills than San Francisco. At a solid six feet, 210 pounds, Nick was a very attractive man.

Or at least that's what women told him on occasion. Nick was no fool. He knew they were checking out his body and not his broad-lipped, wide-nosed, average-looking face. His hair was cut simply in a plain, even-Steven, low-but-not-bald style that he trimmed and lined himself with clippers. His face was not a detriment in the least, but Nick had never pulled women back in high school the way he did now. It had to be the body, he convinced himself. In an ironic way, Nick was comforted by the fact that women were every bit as shallow as men. They were just a helluva lot more sly about it.

Including her. Underneath a wide straw hat and a pair of loopy-looking sunglasses, she watched him. Stole furtive glances, was more like it. Her sunglasses were of a greenish-blue hue and fully penetrable. The steely wall of his reflective lenses hid his own admiring eyes. Since she was giving him "eye candy"—Mal's phrase, not his—Nick responded obviously by shifting his head in her direction. If she couldn't tell he had been checking her out, she could now.

So now it was on. Quickly, Nick surveyed her person for any sign of a natural deterrent. Hmm . . . any stretch marks? *Cardinal Rule to Dating No. 7:* **Never date a woman with a kid.** Ready-made families were not the move for the young, single, and black. Nick wanted a family of his own someday. He wasn't ready to start playing Daddy to some kid he didn't even know. In many respects, he was still a kid himself. When Nick met a woman with a child, no matter how fine she was, he ran like she had the plague.

The next check was for the wedding band on the left-hand ring finger. None.

Next came the debate. To speak or not to speak. That was the dilemma. The woman was certainly attractive. She was a short, compact, thick-looking, darkskin sista. Her modest one-piece failed to disguise her black, womanly curves. Nick pegged her age at about thirty. If he pulled her number, Nick figured she would be a great birthday present to himself. But if he didn't . . .

Too much thinking. That was a sign right away that he wasn't interested enough. When Nick wanted something, or someone, for that matter, he went after it. If he thought about it too long, he would basically think himself out of his motivation. Still, that didn't stop him from flirting with the woman visually before leaving. As he gathered his things, Nick thought with a smirk, *We'll be seeing each other again.*

**A SAN DIEGO** resident for all of two weeks, Nick was still overwhelmed with a sense of adventure. Although his previous home, Chicago, was definitely larger in scope and people, Nick's four and a half years there had left little to be discovered. It was the same when he was in Atlanta: By the time he was a graduating senior at Morehouse College, Nick felt as though he had conquered that city. It was time to move on.

With the windows down and the moonroof open on his brand-spanking-new Limited Edition Toyota 4Runner, Nick reveled in the moderate San Diego summer. About this time in Chicago, he would be sweating a hole through his shirt.

His birthday, a Thursday, marked the second-to-last weekday Nick would have to roam free. On Monday, he started a temp assignment at Bank of America. His MBA had garnered him the temporary position, which was to last several weeks. The pay was *okay*, considering he was going back to an hourly wage for the first time since college, but it was a far cry from the $70,000-plus salary he'd been making at Harris Bank back in Chicago. Nick had come out to California because of his second master's degree, an MFA in acting. He was going to be an actor.

So, for now, until Nick saved up enough money to get his feet under him a bit, he would deign to work hourly for this temp agency. But as soon as he could, he would break away from the agency and try acting full-time. As it was, he planned on going up to LA on weekends and evenings to see what auditions he could get in his spare time. Khalilah, an old friend from his hometown of Seattle, worked for some kind of international business firm in Los Angeles. As infuriatingly platonic as their friendship was, Nick at least had a place to rest his head in the entertainment hub of the universe, less than two hours away.

Reveling in his last few days as a free man, Nick drove the truck along Interstate 5 toward Fashion Valley, San Diego's trendiest outdoor mall. Ever since Nick had arrived in San Diego, he had been on a bit of a shopping spree. He was not rich and actually owed the federal government about ten thousand dollars in student loans, which he had deferred. Nick had been continually rewarding himself after frugally saving from his job at Harris Bank, and after having come in under his moving budget.

Less than ten minutes removed from his car, Nick already toted two bagfuls of stuff he didn't need. Hiding behind his metallic shades, he generously surveyed some of San Diego's finest. There were a lot of white women in San Diego, a switch from the predominantly black cities of Chicago, New York, and Atlanta, locales that had been his homes throughout the past decade. But the Latinas helped make up for a lack of sistas.

Fashion Valley, replete with earth- and magenta-toned Southwestern colors and architecture, reminded him of Atlanta's truly upscale Phipps Plaza mall. In more than half the stores, Nick could not afford the air to breathe, much less their clothes. The shoppers around him were largely jobless rich kids out from school and the independently wealthy who had nothing better to do than to shop. As he strolled into J. Crew, Nick reflected that from the beach to the mall to the weather, he had enjoyed a wonderfully relaxing twenty-ninth birthday so far.

"*Omigod! Is that you, monsieur?*"

That could only be one person. Arms extended, Nick hugged his old high school friend. "Ro-*bair*!" Nick gushed in a faux French accent.

"*Neeco-lah!*" Robert responded, with an even more dreadful Gallic accent. By the time senior year had rolled around in high school, Robert had been Nick's only steady white friend. At a school overwhelmingly minority anyway, just blocks away from Nick's house, cool white kids had been hard to find. Robert was a tall, slim, pale transplant from Michigan's Upper Peninsula (replete with Canadianesque accent and all), new to Franklin High School when they had both been juniors. They had bonded over long, philosophical talks, discussions on current events, and a mutual love for *Seinfeld*. Some of their best conversations had been about that TV show's overlying theme—nothing. You know you have a cool friend when you can sit for hours and talk about nothing.

"Man, what's been up with you!" An octave higher and Nick's

voice would have been a squeal. He had not seen the man in eleven years.

"Oh, it's been quite a long and strange ride, *Nicolas,*" said Robert, still teasing Nick with the French accent. "Come. I was just about to go on my lunch break. We can go over to the food court and talk."

"Cool."

As Robert got himself together to leave, Nick looked around curiously. A men's clothing store. Yeah, that seemed like Robert. Due to his moderate finances, the man hadn't been a walking fashion statement but he'd always had an eye for clothes and ensembles.

Robert led the way to the food court. He bought a Caesar salad from some typically Californian vegetarian place while Nick indulged in a healthy hamburger from Blueberry Hill.

*Eleven years!* Seated and eating away, both men grinned at each other. With the exception of the slight maturation of his face, Robert looked exactly the same. His once curly, crazy dark mane was now cut stylishly conservative, with only the wavy top hinting at his hair's natural curliness. But Nick was a whole different person altogether. Upon graduating high school, Nick had been an inch shorter than Robert's six-one and had weighed only 170 pounds. Now, Nick was two inches shorter than Robert's six-two but a cock-diesel 210 pounds.

They spent the next fifteen minutes catching up. Robert indulged in gossip about old classmates and the like. That was one of Robert's most amusing qualities: The man could be so catty. Naturally, Nick glossed over the whole Jasmine affair, omitting the fact that he had once proposed to his former girlfriend over four years ago, only for her to say no. Once they got caught up on the past, Nick inquired about Robert's present.

"Well, enough about other people. What's been up with you? How long have you been in San Diego?"

"I've lived down here for a couple of years," Robert answered. "I really like it. The weather is so nice and temperate. It's really good for my skin."

"So you're working here full-time?" Hardly the glamour job, if you asked Nick. "I thought you were an artist."

"I still am. I got a master's in drawing from the Philadelphia Art Institute. I've sold some drawings and occasionally I draw commercial sketches for ad agencies. But the whole field can be so hit-and-miss. I still do a lot of drawings at night. But during the day, bills have to be paid."

"I hear that," acknowledged Nick, shuddering at the thought of working an eight-to-five on Monday.

"A lot has changed with me, Nick," Robert said with an impish smile, finishing up the last of his salad.

Polishing off the remainder of his fries, Nick said, "Well, of course. I mean, it's been eleven years, right?"

"Well . . . I've changed more than you know," Robert teased, restraining the urge to laugh. He was clearly enjoying his moment in the sun.

Stuffing his face with fries, Nick mumbled, "Surprise me."

"I'm gay."

Midfry, Nick looked at him. His eyebrows scrunched. The fry just dangled there from his mouth, as if he were the Marlboro Man. "I said 'surprise me,' not 'choke me'! For real?"

Beaming from ear to ear, Robert said, "Yep."

Nick consumed the fry and shrugged it off. "Uh, what does one say to this? Congratulations? Happy Coming Out? When did you realize this?"

"Oh, I knew back in high school, but I fought it. I was still closeted. Remember when Allie Praeger threw herself at me and ended up asking me to go to the prom with her?"

"Yeah, I remember that. How did it feel to have my leftovers?" Nick grinned with male-conquesting bravado.

"I wouldn't know. That whole time I had to fight her off," Robert confessed. "And during prom night . . . she was like a dog in heat."

Finishing up his meal, Nick looked incredulously at his new—and first—gay friend. "You tellin' me that on prom night, she was down and you didn't get *any*?"

Robert started making fake sign-language signals while enunciating slowly, "Read . . . my . . . lips. I . . . am . . . gay."

Nick chuckled, tossing a fry in his direction. "As the breeze?"

Robert lobbed his plastic knife at him. In a low tone, he retorted, before laughing, "As a *blade*!"

**THIS WAS TURNING** out to be a great birthday. After Nick's impromptu lunch with Robert, he cruised around San Diego some more. He drove over the high, picturesque Coronado Bay Bridge to the upscale town of Coronado. Glittering waves of the Pacific winked at him as he drove by a stretch of beach called the Silver Strand. Nick could not get over how palm trees were everywhere. A guy could get used to this kind of living.

By the time he got home from exploring parts of the South Bay, the sun had just set. Pink, gold, and silvery blues and whites receded gently toward the horizon. Nick didn't have much of a direct view of the sunset from where his house sat, but fortunately, he lived only a few blocks from the beach. After several snowy winters and balmy, humid, oppressive summers in Chicago, the mild, humidity-free temperatures of San Diego seemed heaven-sent. This truly had to be paradise found.

Once comfortably arranged on the couch, TV channel on his favorite show in the world, ESPN's *SportsCenter,* Nick heard the phone ring. He figured it was Mom, calling to offer her birthday wishes, as Grandma had done on his answering machine. Instead of Mom, it was someone infinitely more outrageous.

"Whassup, mark! Happy birthday to yo' punk ass!" Malloy!

"Thanks a lot, trick," Nick shot back evenly. "Whassup?"

"Loungin', god. I wanna know what the birthday boy's been up to! I swear, you lucky I'm not over there to give you your birthday beat-down!"

"Yeah, yeah, yeah. Whateva," Nick dismissed him casually. The last birthday he had spent around Nick, Mal had administered the annual nonsensical, perpetually male tradition of punching out the number of years of the birthday boy *into* the birthday boy. Bearing down on thirty, Nick was not sure if he could have survived this year's beatdown. "I've been coolin' out, doc. Gettin' used to this place. You should come out here sometime, hoss. It's pretty tight."

"Yeah, I bet. I bet them bodies are pretty tight." Mal had heard about how everyone was gorgeous and in shape out in California. All part of the plasticity of its glamour.

"Look at you. Supposed to be all married and stuff now and you *still* talkin' shit like a player," Nick accused playfully.

"Hey, you can take the player out the game, but you can't take the game out the player," Mal ghetto-philosophized. "I bet you twenty bones that if we went to a club together, I'd come out with more numbers than you."

"Get the hell outta here!" Nick chortled. "With your old married ass? I'll take you up on that one. I bet you wouldn't even know how to holla to these single ladies. Especially after being whipped for . . . How long's it been? Two years?"

"Two years, eleven months, and nine days," Malloy recited smartly. "*Sir.*"

"Ha-ha, look at you," Nick gloated. "That's just the time you've been married. You been whipped a *long* time before that!"

"Don't be a hater just 'cause you ain't experienced the joys of marriage, kid. Don't hate because you haven't found the woman you want to spend the rest of your life with," Malloy taunted.

"Hate?" repeated Nick incredulously. "*Shiiiiiit,* I am *cool* on marriage, dawg. I ain't in no kind of rush to get married. If you've been paying attention the past year or so, Captain Commitment is dead. Gone. And even before then, he hasn't been in full effect. If it happens, it happens. If it don't, it don't. *Especially* after Jasmine . . . shoot . . . I *neva hafta* get married. I'm cool on *all* that."

"Maybe," Malloy granted, "but you sure was a Captain back in the day. 'I wanna be *sa-ved*!' "

"I'm not savin' any more hos," Nick declared. "So you can check that shit at the door. If a good *woman* crawls outta the woodwork, we'll see what happens. But my days of being Mr. Relationship, Mr. Commitment—"

"Captain—" Mal adjusted.

"Boy, if you don't shut up . . ." Nick warned. "But my days of going out for a relationship are over. Like marriage—if it happens, it happens. Right now, I'm single and loving it. I'm young, black, single, educated, and living in one of the finest cities in America. I'mma be alright."

"Make sure you holla at some of them Mexican honeys south of the border for me. Hook up with a Latina or two," Mal counseled.

"Don't you worry about me, dawg. Just keep laying pipe to your wife and don't worry about The Kid," Nick returned.

"You going to that wedding next weekend?"

"Wedding?"

"C'mon, son, I know you didn't forget?" Mal's native New York accent oozed all over that "son."

"Loq! That's right! I almost forgot. Hell yeah, I'm going. A wedding back in the ATL? I'm definitely 'bout it." Going back to Atlanta, the black mecca of the United States where he had spent four glorious years in undergrad, was always a positive, culturally grounding experience.

"You got your ticket, cuz?"

"Yeah, I got it. It's somewhere in here among all my files. You bringin' Mia?"

"Naw," Mal said, somewhat evasively. "She doesn't really know the bride nor Loq too well."

"True," Nick supposed. "Anybody else gonna be there?"

"All the crew," Mal crowed. "The rest of them are gonna be in the ceremony. We'll be the only ones of the crew not in it."

"That's fine with me. My head's still spinnin' from the move."

"I feel you, dude. I feel you," he agreed. "Well, I'mma bounce, playboy. Just checkin' in on you. Seein' how you feelin' after the big move."

"I appreciate it, partna. Glad you could take time outta your busy married schedule. Say, when am I gonna be a godfather?" Nick was taking shots now.

"Forget you, fool!" came Mal's immediate response. "Don't rush us. You can't put no timetable on that."

"Aw'ight, brotha. I'll see you next weekend in the ATL . . ."

". . . where the playas dwell," finished Mal. "Holla."

"Holla." Nick hung up. Almost immediately, the phone rang again. Flush with good spirits, he picked up. This had to be Mom. "Hello?"

"Hi, Nick." He heard the deep, masculine voice of Mom's husband, Harrison. As far as stepdads went, Harrison was cool. He and Mom had dated for well over a dozen years before they had married more than a year ago. Nick's natural father had never really been around for him, and he preferred not to talk about him. Usually, Harrison's voice was the kind that would shake a room with its mirth, its love for life. He was the kind of guy who instantly transformed himself into the life of the party. His voice was devoid of all of that today. "Happy birthday."

"Thanks . . ." Nick trailed off cautiously. Something was wrong. "Is Mom there?"

"Nick," Harrison began, in the type of tone which always precedes bad news, "your mom's in the hospital."

Instantly, Nick's soul hit the carpet. He could not remember the last time his mother had seen a hospital. She was not the most physically fit person in the world, but Mom was a trooper. Hospitalization could only mean something serious. "Why? What's wrong with her?" he inquired with a suddenly dry mouth.

Harrison took a breath. *Shit.* This was the kid's birthday, and he had some god-awful news to tell him. Within the silence between Harrison's pause and when he actually began to speak, time elongated itself, long enough for Nick to fear the worst. When it came to women in his life, Mom was it. She was the only one. Harrison could sense the kid's anxiety, but went ahead and said it anyway. "Nick . . . your mom's being treated for breast cancer."

Nick's eyes began to water but he stopped them cold. "Where is she?"

"Harborview Medical Center. They're taking great care of her."

The hell they were. "I'm coming up there."

"Alright, but I'm—"

"No 'buts' about it, Harrison," Nick snapped with amazing finality. "I'm on the first flight out tomorrow. I'll call you when I know the details."

"Alright," his stepdad said solemnly. "Take care."

"Uh-huh." Nick hung up the phone. His mind raced too quickly to indulge in tears. His next call was to arrange a flight. The call after that was to Harrison. Nick would be at Sea-Tac airport in Seattle tomorrow on the first thing smoking from San Diego. Next, he quickly packed a gym bag and tossed it onto the futon couch. Then he walked down to the beach a few blocks away, sat out on the edge of Ocean Beach Pier, absolutely alone, and watched the waves bob and crash in the darkness of night.

## 2

**"H**ELLO THERE, HANDSOME."

Nick gently moved a stray piece of hair from her forehead. His mother was a beautiful woman: always had been, always would be. She had put on a few pounds as she had gotten older, just enough to make her look a little heavy. In that sterile, white hospital bed, Nick could already see she had lost some weight due to her illness. Mom wasn't totally hung out to dry. She just looked a little weary from having undergone her first experience with cancer treatment.

Mom lay in bed, wires and tubes hooked up to her with that persistent ping of the EKG reminding them both how precious her life was. There were so many questions Nick wanted to but dared not ask, so many fears he had yet to confirm.

"I'm going to be fine, Handsome." Mom did not sound too reassuring as her voice cracked and collapsed into a hailstorm of coughs. "I've known for about six months now. I didn't want to bother you with it, since you were graduating and going through your actor's showcase and all. And . . . as silly as it may sound . . . I thought I could beat it."

Nick grabbed her hand, holding on to it fiercely. "You still *can*, Mom. You still can."

Mom grinned at Nick, that obvious little grin parents did to humor their naive, hopeful children. "Thank you, Handsome. Thank you."

Nick just stared at her pitifully, helplessly, as she drifted off to sleep.

SOMEHOW, NICK MADE it to work on Monday. He worked Downtown in some faceless, nameless building on a floor whose number he could not remember. As far as Nick was concerned, he could care less about where he was, what he was doing, and how he was doing it. Seeing his mother lying in a hospital bed fresh off chemotherapy had kind of rearranged his priorities. Right now, Bank of America was not one of them.

Dr. Karen Willis, a short, blond-haired, wrinkle-free woman in her midthirties, with everything to live for, had told Nick that even with the best cancer treatments available, Mom would only have two years to live. Realistically, Dr. Willis gave her only eighteen months. *Eighteen months.* That staggered Nick. She was only fifty-nine, the most important woman in the world to him. Of course, Dr. Willis had been quick to offer up tales of miraculous recoveries, unexplainable phenomena, and comebacks that must have been spurred on by an act of God, but Nick wasn't buying it. He was losing his mommy.

For the life of him, Nick could not remember what transpired in his first two days on the job. Mindlessly interacting with his officemates, passively acknowledging their attempts to talk to him, and indifferently approaching his work, Nick let the time slip by. Even the perpetually sunny, pleasant weather began to annoy him in its constancy. Nick wanted to curl up in a ball and cry to his mother, a woman who was probably undergoing some medical test or enduring another bout with chemo at that very moment.

On Thursday Nick was forced to take on some sort of sense of purpose again: The next day he was to leave San Diego's Lindbergh Field for Loq's wedding. Nick dispassionately ran some errands after work, from picking up his suit at the cleaner's to buying a gift certificate as a wedding gift. Even the prospect of going to Atlanta, a place he and his boys affectionately called the "Dirty South," did nothing to alter his mood. All his friends from college, his *boys,* were going to be there and Nick was not excited in the least.

Come Friday, Nick went to work early, left early, and boarded a plane at four in the afternoon for the four-hour flight to Atlanta. He might as well have been going to a funeral.

———

## " 'SUP, PIMP?"

Well, if it wasn't the groom himself, grinning ear to ear. Loq was the same age as Nick, lightskin, thin, but shorter. The man wore thin glasses that alluded to his Morehouse accounting degree and trade as an investment banker, but did not convict him of being a nerd. Loq gave Nick dap, a quick, sliding handshake, along with the kind of hug true boys gave each other.

Nick forced a smile as he felt the onrush of warmth. "You finally doin' it, huh? I'm happy for you, man."

Loq broke the hug and looked at him. "You don't sound so happy, playa."

"Really, I am," Nick said honestly, but lacking the emotional conviction of his sentiment.

A mischievous smile surfaced on Loq's face. "Don't tell me you still salty for me stealin' yo' girl?"

"My girl?" protested Nick incredulously, laughing. "She was hardly ever 'my girl.' "

The "girl" in question was Loq's bride, Desiree. Nick had met Desiree during Freaknik, Atlanta's annual informal black college festival, three years earlier. She had come down with one of Loq's relatives and some of her female classmates from South Carolina State. Desiree and Nick had enjoyed a flirtation that was never consummated. He had been attracted to her tall, thick, brownskin body as well as her mind, which had earned her a degree in computer science a year ago. Now she worked for Coca-Cola in Atlanta in some computer-related capacity, while Loq was just starting to clock major dollars at his on-line investment firm. The happy couple seemed pretty much set. Nick looked forward to one of the more extravagant weddings since he had embarked on his friends' wedding tours three years ago. It seemed to Nick, formerly Captain Commitment, that the members of the crew, players like Malloy, Loq, and—to a lesser extent—his boy Craig, were getting married in the reverse order of their marriageability.

"Well, she ain't my girl yet either." Loq grinned. "At least not tonight. You know where we're going, right?"

"Bachelor party, right?"

"Even better," Loq beamed. "We takin' the fellas over to Magic City."

"Oo." Straight from the airport to the strip club. Watch hijinks ensue. Finally, against his will, Nick cracked a dog of a smile. "Lead the way, brotha."

**THE GANG WAS** all there. Competing with the obnoxiously loud bass music, the ten members of Loq's bachelor party acquainted and reacquainted themselves in the smoky, raunchy seediness of the Atlanta strip club. Nick knew almost everyone, including Brandon, Loq's cousin from his native South Carolina; Loq's boys Marvin, a happily married tax attorney; and Tank, once a notorious womanizer, now also tamed and heading down the same path. It had been just three years ago that the lot of them, Loq included, had been riding out on Peachtree Street, stuck in traffic, hollering at and macking down every woman in their path. Craig, the happily married man he was, grinned at Nick from in front of the stage, where he stuck a five in Caramel Ecstasy's G-string. Originally from Chicago, Craig had befriended Nick during their days at DePaul University. He had just moved out to San Diego a week after Nick with his half-Latina, half-white wife, Olinda. Craig, half black himself but favoring his Irish heritage, and Olinda made a uniquely striking couple. Two nondescript cousins who barely introduced themselves rounded out the entourage. Except for one.

"NICK!" Malloy hollered. A crushing, I-ain't-seen-you-in-*years* hug followed. Dap just would not do. "*Whassup,* son!"

Nick and Malloy were best friends. Their camaraderie extended a decade, back to freshman year at Morehouse College. Although from two different sides of the country—Nick from Seattle, Mal representing New York City to the fullest—they found enough in common to be the tightest of boys. Thanks to their uniform, darkskin complexions, similar heights, and easygoing gaits, many mistook the pair to be brothers. The biggest difference between the two, besides wildly varying accents and terminology, was that Malloy had always been the ladies man. That is, before he had gotten caught up and married. Marriage aside, no one, absolutely *no one*, had a better time when he went out than Malloy.

"You got it, man," smiled Nick in response, with unexpected pleasure. A guy like Malloy would never let you feel down around him. "How long y'all been here?"

"About an hour too long, 'cause I'mma 'bout to go *broke* tippin' this shorty right *here*!" Mal gleefully gestured toward a caramel-colored woman, wearing next to nothing at all, finishing up a table dance a few tables over. Wiping the bored expression off her face when she saw Mal, the woman lit up. Mal mock-shivered with excitement. "Her name is *Tootsie Roll,* dawg. *I* wanna see how many licks it takes to make *her* Tootsie pop! 'Na mean?"

Nick laughed in spite of himself. "How many drinks you had, Mal?"

"Just three," Mal slurred, holding up four fingers.

As he and Nick sat down, Nick kept shaking his head. Mal was having enough of a good time for the both of them. "God bless you, brotha."

"You actually gonna have a *drink* tonight, dawg? Or you still gonna fuck around with that same ole bullshit?" Mal dared him.

"Same ole bullshit," Nick said, ordering a Sprite and orange juice from the scantily clad waitress. "Eh, somebody get Craig back from the stage before that boy loses his mortgage money tippin' that girl."

"Shit, you need to be up on it yourself, my nigga," beamed Mal drunkenly. "It's yo' boy's *bachelor party*! Let it loose, dawg! Tip the chicks, man. Tip the chicks!"

What *was* he doing here? He was in a house full of sin, replete with drunken males, naked women, and booming bass music that threatened to drown them all out, like Celine Dion's *Titanic* song. People he called his friends, his *boys,* were out there making fools of themselves—dancing with butt-naked dancers, ordering table dances, and pitching small talk at the purveyors of flesh (who had heard it all) in a vain attempt to sleep with them. Despite the decidedly hazy, worn, and black atmosphere in Magic City, money flowed like water—down a one-way street. Nick had been to strip clubs a couple of times before and the experience had always left him feeling cheated. His clothes would smell like smoke and marijuana, he would be out sixty dollars, and he would *still* wake up alone. Oh yeah, and the whole male-oppressive, misogynistic factor played upon the kid raised by a strong black single mother, too. What would Mom, in her weakened state, think if she could see him now?

"Y'all niggas ain't hittin' on *shit*! No tip, no strip! You betta tip the pussy!" exhorted the admonishing, disgusted voice of the club DJ. "Twenty more bones and Ecstasy will take it *awl* off! I thought we had some *playas* up in heah. Some *ballas*! Tip the pussy, gotdammit! Tip the pussy!"

As if he needed any more badgering/encouragement, there was Mal, straightening up to go give Caramel Ecstasy a hard-earned ten dollars. "C'mon, Nick. You know we gotta put these girls through med school!"

From out of nowhere, Nick erupted into a great big, giddy, unexplainable laugh. Mal, with all his drunken bravado, insisted upon having a good time. Loq, the groom, who was being serenaded with a special two-song lapdance in his honor, was having a good time. Marvin and Tank had snuck over to the bar with Loq's cousins to have a good time. Craig, just about out of cash, was surely having a good time. Even Brandon's quiet ass, with the trophy model wife at home and everything, slid a dollar into Tootsie Roll's G-string—with the grin of a man having a good time. It occurred to Nick that he was the only one not allowing himself to have a good time. This was a bachelor party, for crying out loud. If this was what Loq wanted to do the night before he got married, at the expense of *everyone* having a good time, then . . . Well, hell. All his problems aside, Nick determined that he was going to have as good a time as anybody.

He walked up to the stage and gave Caramel Ecstasy the requisite ten dollars that brought it all off. Mal and Craig tipsily dapped up and high-fived Nick. After all, they had to put these girls through med school.

**AS NERVOUS AS** he was, it seemed Nick was the one getting married. He was merely one of 250 onlookers in the tightly packed, medium-sized, suburban Atlanta church. The setting was wedding elegant yet not extravagant, with enough white-and-lavender-themed decoration to relay the grandeur, gravity, and giddiness of the event. Even though this was his fourth wedding, Nick still experienced the rush of excitement, happiness, and sentimentality associated with the event for him. Having known Loq for more than ten years, it was as if he were watching a brother getting married, even though Nick was an only child. The whole prospect of a wedding, two people committing themselves to each other for a lifetime, thrilled Nick, even if he wasn't one of those two people.

Once he had been, though. Or at least he had been ready to take that step. Now, he simply lived vicariously through his friends. They were all getting married off, one by one, with Loq the latest casualty of love. Upon graduation seven years ago, hell, even just *three* years ago after their notorious Freaknik funfest, of all of the members of the crew—Nick, Mal, Craig, Loq, Tank, Marvin, and even quiet little Brandon—Nick had always considered himself the most marriage-ready. Mal had been a notorious player since some stupid chick back in undergrad had broken his heart. Craig had been all about the "hotties." Loq, Tank, and Marvin were a South Carolinian cartel of playerism. Now all but Nick were hitched. Unbelievable.

Sure, Nick was jealous, but he was happy for them in the most supportive way. Especially for the bride. Desiree was a beautiful woman. She was exactly Nick's type—tall and tight—which explained why they had enjoyed a harmless flirtation years ago. She was as tall as Loq, at five-nine, and had agreed to wear flats in the ceremony so she wouldn't tower over her husband. Her tight white dress and flowing train beautifully accented her naturally Southern curves. Loq was outfitted in a sharp gray tux with tails, a delicate white rose on his lapel. All the groomsmen were fitted the same way, while the bridesmaids wore satiny, shimmery lavender dresses. Both Tank and Marvin, along with the two cousins from the night before, were in the ceremony. A matching pair of helplessly adorable five-year-old kids, one boy in a gray suit and one girl in a lavender dress, rounded out the wedding party. Nick could not stop smiling throughout the ceremony.

He sat next to Craig and Mal, who observed all with detached marital chagrin. Babies cried during parts of the ceremony. People walked in after the three o'clock start time. Mal and Craig exchanged looks that mirrored their oh-*hell*-no expressions. Neither of their wives would have allowed such ghetto CP time lateness. At both of their weddings, their brides had made sure the doors were *locked* on the dot. Their knowing, snarky smiles seemed to suggest, *If only you knew what you're getting yourself into, brotha.* But, somewhere inside them, they were genuinely happy for Loq. And Desiree looked simply gorgeous.

Despite warnings from the professional photographer about guests taking pictures, flashes galore went off when Loq and Desiree said "I do." In keeping with the finest of African-American wedding traditions, the happy couple jumped the broom, laid out by one of the cousins. Then came their stroll down the aisle, followed by the bridesmaids and groomsmen.

This was as nice a wedding as Nick had been to since Malloy's almost three years ago. Every last detail was so elegantly planned and executed, from the lavender matchbooks with Loq's and Desiree's names and the date on them to the small bottles of bubbles the ushers had handed out to the guests to blow upon the married couple.

But the fun did not stop there. After a good hour of posing privately with the family for the professional photographer, Loq and Desiree caught up with the rest of their guests at the reception in a Hilton hotel ballroom. Craig, Mal, and Nick stood by the welcoming table, accepting the gifts for the newlyweds, arranging them strategically on the large table, and depositing the cards into the card box. Nick shook his head softly as he accepted what had to have been his hundredth card for Loq and Desiree. They certainly had their work cut out for them in thank-you notes.

Craig noticed the subtle shaking of his friend's head and commented, "What's up, kid? You having a good time?"

Nick, mentally recharged in spite of his depressing secret, smiled. "Yeah, man. This wedding is tight."

"I feel you, dawg. My wedding didn't even look this nice," Craig conceded. "See this? They're handing out mints *with their names on them.* That's cool. I wish I hadda thought of that."

"Well, Desiree planned the whole wedding, from what I heard. Even down to folding the napkins and setting the place cards for the dais table," Nick informed him, gesturing toward the long table at the head of the room where the couple, members of the wedding party, and close family and friends sat.

"Wow. She's a cool motherfucker then. I could *never* imagine Olinda doing some shit like that for our wedding—or anyone else's," Craig said of his wife.

"Yeah, this whole thing is amazing. I'm sprung," Nick openly gushed, his eyes a little glazed. "Hell, *I want* one."

Craig laughed oddly. "You're kidding, right?"

"I want one," Nick said with a trace of a smile. "I mean, this wedding has been really, really beautiful. When the right girl comes along . . . I want one."

Mal nudged his boy playfully. "Listen to this dude. Just a few days ago, he was talkin' 'bout how he 'neva hafta' get married. And now look at him. Look at you. The only brotha I know who wants a wedding just to have one."

"Yeah, dawg, it don't work like that," Craig chimed in. "Find marriage material first."

"I know, I know," Nick said. "I gotta find the right girl. But still . . . I want one."

The reception was lighthearted and fun. A generous buffet of soul food kept everyone happy. A middle-aged, overweight black man was their energetic and lively MC. He kept things light and moving, leading the guests through the couple's entrance, the cutting of the cake, and the traditional first dance. At that point, everyone gathered around to watch Loq and Desiree dance to an R&B song, all the while blowing bubbles in their direction. Nick found the whole thing terribly romantic.

When it came time to toss the bouquet, grown women elbowed and jockeyed for position behind the bride. A smugly smiling Desiree observed the wrestling match with amusement. After she turned her back, she counted down from three and heaved the bouquet over her shoulder. A fortyish, heavy-set woman went into a flat-out dive to catch the bouquet but missed. She made quite an impressive belly flop, though. Ironically, the bouquet ended up in the hands of the smallest, most ineligible bachelorette there—Desiree's five-year-old cousin, LaMicah. The sepia-toned girl smiled a big, toothy smile, not really knowing the full implications of what she had just won. How adorable.

Next up: the garter. The gathering of single malehood pretended not to know it was their turn. At the MC's frothy insistence, Nick trudged off to the dance floor, where all the other single men had begun to mill about with uneasy, half-cracked smiles. Mal and Craig smirked uncontrollably. Among the eligible bachelors were a few teenage kids, some college students, and a guy who had been divorced twice, literally *praying*, quietly, that he would catch the garter. Nick stood around, nervous, not knowing a single soul in the twenty-plus gathering of men.

Loq was ready. With the MC commenting the entire time, the garter went up, with bachelors trying to avoid it as if it were a medieval disease. The garter bounced around a few times, even eluding the grasp of the desperate, two-time divorcé. And just guess where that sucker landed.

Nick stared blankly at the off-white garter. Men he didn't know dapped him up and slapped him on the back. Loq and Desiree giggled in delight. It took all of Mal's self-control not to let his hysterical laughing violate Craig's personal space. Craig just stood there, shaking his head in denial. And little LaMicah stood about three feet below, looking up at him, anticipating her dance. Nick had caught the garter. That *had* to be a sign.

LaMicah and Nick made quite the photogenic couple as they enjoyed their ceremonial dance as the recipients of the bouquet and the garter. With Nick leaning over to engage his partner, the pair redefined cuteness. Bubbles floated in and around their dance. Mal made sure to get a close-up picture of the two.

Once Nick's dance was finished, he retreated to Craig and Mal's table, heavy one bridal garter. Good-naturedly, he absorbed all the requisite ribbing and then some. Nick was still fascinated by the superstitious symbolism of it all. He had to be the next man at this wedding to get married. There had to be something to that.

"Of all people to catch the garter, it had to be the guy who wants a wedding just to have one," joked Craig. "That's hilarious."

"It's gotta mean something, Craig," Nick insisted.

"It means that now, no woman is safe! Captain Commitment is out savin' 'em again!" declared Mal with a laugh.

Nick rolled his eyes at the thought. But, nevertheless, he realized something *was* at work here. With a playful grin, he offered, "You never know when you might meet that woman who will turn your life around, dawg. You never know."

"That's right," Craig chimed in. "Anyways, what are you guys doing this evening? We know what Loq-Dawg is doing."

"No doubt," seconded Nick. "He's gonna be gettin' his in *Jamaica*."

"Now, that's what I call a honeymoon," agreed Craig. "But we can't worry 'bout him. He's going into lockdown for the first time tonight. He won't be no good for about at least half a year. But *I* wanna know what's going on for tonight."

"Check it out, playas: I've got an idea," Malloy piped in. "Get some cheese together and let's head out to Mississippi and go on one of them gambling boats."

"You mean go to a casino? You gonna drive six hours to go gambling?" asked Nick incredulously.

"No, *we* are going to drive *five* hours," corrected Malloy, "and it's not just all about gambling. Have you ever been?"

"Gambling? No," Nick admitted somewhat sheepishly. Gambling was one of the few privileges allowed to those over twenty-one that he had never indulged in. All Nick knew was that money spent gambling went to finance the electric bills for the casinos' ridiculous, gaudy lights.

"Then you should ride out with us," encouraged Mal. "See what it's like. You *might* actually enjoy yourself."

"Don't be afraid to lose a little money," Craig grinned. "It's all in good fun, kid. You'll enjoy yourself."

Tag-teamed by Mal and Craig, Nick found his mind had been made up for him. "Alright, alright. I'm in. Let's do it."

"TRY NOT TO marry anyone on the way to the craps table, Garter Boy," Mal quipped as the trio stepped away from the cashier's booth flush with betting chips.

Nick grinned wildly. After four and a half hours inside a rented Hyundai Elantra driving through the depths of the South at night, Nick was more than ready for the glamour and glitz of the riverboat casino in Biloxi. It was about what Nick had expected, only a lot brighter. Lights were *everywhere*. Even though it was well past midnight, the place was packed, and bright as day. Tourists from all around, sticking out with their t-shirts and shorts covering sunburned

skin, waddled around with buckets full of coins and chips in one hand
and free drinks in the other. A casino is a loud place, with persistent
chatter, the endless clanging of men and women slot-machining away
their spending money, and the occasional scream from someone hitting it big on the roulette wheel or losing his house at the poker table.

Sauntering around like a gambler extraordinaire, Mal led the group
between several gaming tables. While Nick and Craig smiled, infected
by the lively atmosphere, Mal kept a stiletto-sharp cool. Such cool-
ness was mandatory in order to step up to the game-of-all-gaming
tables—poker. As Mal sat down at the twenty-five-dollar-minimum-
bet table, Craig and Nick hung back, watching with sheer awe and
adoration. Twenty-five dollars a bet was big money to them.

In short order—fifteen minutes—Mal blew $125 and was reduced
to observer status. Now it was Craig's and Nick's turn in the spotlight. Craig ran off to the roulette wheel—a decision that baffled Mal
(roulette was *purely* luck, no skill involved)—while Nick camped out
at the blackjack table. His goals were modest. This was a five-dollar-
minimum-bet table. At the moment, having not yet received his first
paycheck and with his moving money running out, five dollars a bet
was big money. But the dealer was a very attractive darkskin lady
named Evelyn, so the decision to play at this table was never in doubt.

Evelyn was all business, as were her customers. Her detached, dis-
passionate expression was in direct contrast to Nick's wide-eyed joy.
When a seat came open, Mal sat and side-coached Nick, a gambling
and blackjack novice. Both Nick and Mal hated losing, especially
Nick, when it was with his own money. Evelyn, the cold professional
she was with her flurry of card-dealing fingers and cryptic dealer hand
signals, even offered visual assistance. On a count that was advisable
to stick, she would give him a visual squint as a warning. Even as a
tall, stockily built white guy with a name tag reading "Lucky" pa-
trolled the area for patron and dealer improprieties, Evelyn still took
pity on the hapless newbie who had already lost twenty dollars to the
casino. The old adage held true: The house *always* wins.

After struggling to draw even after several hands, Nick noticed
Craig slink over to his table. Dejectedly, Craig plunked down in the
other empty chair opposite Nick. "Whassup, dawg?" asked Nick cheerfully, happy to be even again.

"I'm out, kid. I lost sixty bucks on the craps table. That's it for me," Craig declared with finality.

"I feel you," commiserated Mal, though not as miserably, now involved in bringing along his protégé at the blackjack table. "Take a hit, dawg."

"Hit," Nick obeyed robotically. He received his card and smiled. Then everyone flipped over their cards.

"Twenty-one! *Pay* me!"

Mal and Nick both gave him a pound—a slight tap of the fist—for his win. On the five-dollar bet, Nick received a meager, five-dollar chip from the dealer. An old, gray-haired, smoking man sitting at the end of the table, flush with stacks of ten-dollar chips, chuckled sarcastically. He had just dropped fifty on that last hand but didn't even bat an eyelash. The new, small-time winners were always more emotional than the veteran, big winners.

After Nick won another hand on a five-dollar bet, Mal acted as his financial manager. "Aw'ight, playa. Put half in your pocket. Every time you win from here on out, put half in your pocket."

"But I can double my stakes," protested Nick.

"You can also double your loss, kid," warned Craig.

"In the pocket," instructed Mal.

With a sigh, Nick obeyed. Nevertheless, he was having fun. As the night wore on, Nick was up a hundred dollars on the five-dollar tables alone. Craig, now seated next to him, grew nervous. "Don't you think you should quit while you're ahead?"

Nick, now betting ten bucks a hand, grinned playfully. "Why, when I'm having so much fun?" As if to back him up, the next hand he was dealt was blackjack.

As the dealers did their half-hourly exchange between tables, Craig commented upon the wedding. "You know, that was a cool wedding. It was really nice."

"Except for those people who came in late and that baby that kept screamin'," objected Mal. "How you gonna come late to a wedding? *Blacks,* man! Friggin' *blacks!*"

Nick laughed. "Yeah, but everything else was tight. Even them bridesmaids."

"True," Craig crowed in acknowledgment. "Did you see the bridesmaid with Brandon? The darkskin one? Now, *she* is what I call a hottie!"

"I'll do you one better, bruh," said Nick, jogging his memory. "Remember the one with Tank? The lightskin one? The shorty?"

Craig nodded stiffly and Mal just smiled strangely.

Nick continued, undaunted. "Did you see the way she wore that dress! My god! There oughta be a law against lookin' so good! I mean, her chest, her butt, her . . . "

Craig and Mal just looked blankly at Nick. "What?" Nick asked, a bit unnerved.

Mal, cracking a smile, said, "There *is* a law. Dawg . . . that girl was only fifteen."

Craig burst out laughing.

Nick shook his head adamantly. "Naw . . . no *way*!"

Craig just laughed uncontrollably, drawing the disapproving glare of the dealer.

"Get the hell outta here!" Nick dismissed. "That girl was at *least* twenty-three."

Mal simply shook his head.

"C'mon! Twenty-one!"

Mal shook his head again.

"Eighteen?" offered Nick hopefully.

"Guess again, chief," Mal said, doing his best not to laugh.

Nick's head hit the table, coinciding with his losing that hand at blackjack. "Fifteen?" he croaked.

"Believe it," affirmed Craig, regaining his composure. "I asked Tank about her after the wedding. He said that's Loq's cousin from South Carolina. She goes to Airport High School in Columbia. She's going to be a sophomore. *Going to be*."

"Fifteen'll getcha twenty!" hollered Mal.

"Damn, I feel old," muttered Nick miserably.

"Would you like a drink?" an attractive white waitress with a Southern drawl piped in.

"Hell yes! Bourbon, straight up," declared the nondrinker Nick.

"You got it, honey," she said, and smiled before disappearing.

Mal raised his own free, half-empty drink, a Cosmopolitan. "Here's to growing old gracefully."

Craig raised his cup. "To lost youth!"

Nick, after receiving his drink and tipping the waitress, added, "To officially being horny old men!"

"Hear, hear!" they toasted in unison.

**AT THE AIRPORT** the next evening, Nick and Craig dapped up Mal at his gate with the smooth, sliding half-handshake. Mal was on a flight to New York, where he worked as a computer-programming executive for a Fortune 500 company in Manhattan. His wife, Mia, a longtime acquaintance of Nick's, owned a women's clothing boutique in the city. The two lived fairly comfortably in a Brooklyn brownstone they owned.

One concourse down, Nick and Craig found their gate for the return trip to San Diego. Nick was sure glad for the company on the nearly four-hour ride. Their flight did not take off for another hour, so they bided their time people-watching from the stiff, plastic airport seats.

Nick could barely contain his glow. He had definitely needed this trip. It had to rank among one of his top-ten weekends of all time. He had been surrounded by friends, his people, his community—three influences that were always refreshing and grounding. He felt invigorated.

And the wedding. More than ever, Nick wanted one. This was an odd position, seeing how just more than a week ago, he had announced to Mal, with no small amount of male bravado, that he never had to get married. But having seen Loq and Desiree's elegant yet not audacious affair, Nick began to get that feeling. His psychological clock was ticking. He could remember himself as a college freshman, having projected his marrying age as between twenty-six and twenty-eight. His twenty-ninth birthday had just passed. Not only was his clock ticking, but so was his mother's.

That's when he saw them. They were a young couple—black, beautiful, and boldly in love. The man was dressed in a sharp, light Italian wool suit and the woman in a dress of shimmery red satin. You could tell they had just gotten married from the gleam in their eyes and her ring, along with their endless fawning over each other.

As the attendant at the gate called out the row numbers for boarding, Nick found himself strangely staring at the cooing, kissing couple. They, too, were in their own little world, where seat assignments and boarding etiquette did not matter. The couple was so young—both of them could not have been older than twenty-five—that Nick stood there, entranced by the ferocity of their feelings for each other, the strength of their legal and emotional bond. Craig began nudging Nick. "C'mon, dawg. Let's go."

The couple did not move and neither did Nick. Their love, their commitment, fascinated him. To know at such an early age whom you were going to spend the rest of your life with boggled him. It also made him envious. He envied their happiness. He envied their love. Nick wished *he* could be married by now. For all intents and purposes, *he* should be married by now. He was overdue. He deserved a wife. His mother deserved to see her only son with a wife. She would die without seeing her only son get married.

"Final call for boarding on Flight 203 to San Diego, California. All rows, all seats."

Craig grasped Nick a bit more firmly by the arm this time. "Let's dip, dawg. I'm not missing this flight because you've fallen in love with a married woman."

Nick snapped out of it, but only because the couple itself (they were indeed a singular entity, joined at the lips) headed toward the passenger ramp. While the spell was broken, the idea remained. Nick was getting married.

# 3

**WANT TO** get married."

Craig stared blankly at Nick. He shrugged. "Okay."

"No, I *really* want to get married," Nick insisted, a little louder now to compete with the hum of the DC-10 they were on. "In a year."

"Whoa, slow down, dawg," chuckled Craig nervously, hands up for emphasis. "That's a pretty tight timetable. You're a young guy. What's the rush?"

Needlessly, Nick swept his eyes around the rest of the plane. Theirs was a fortuitously empty flight to San Diego that Sunday night. Although they had bought tickets two seats apart from each other, they now conferred by themselves in relative obscurity near the back of the plane. "No rush," Nick lied uneasily. "It's just about time. That's all."

The logic escaped Craig. "Do you at least have someone *in mind*?"

A sheepish smile invaded Nick's face. "No."

"Then *why* do you want to get married? Just to be married?" Craig shook his head incredulously.

Nick shifted closer to his friend, as if to share a secret. "I won't front: I want what you have. I want what Loq has. I want what Mal has. If someone would've asked me three years ago who would've gotten married first of the four of us, you, Loq, and Mal most certainly wouldn't have been at the top of the list."

Craig grinned his toothy, childlike smile, one of the features that had attracted his wife, Olinda, in the first place. "Jealous, huh, boi?"

"Oh, I won't even deny that," Nick admitted. "I'm jealous as hell. The whole crew is getting married, and I feel like I'm on the outside looking in at some great big wedding reception."

"Just because *you want* to get married doesn't mean you *need* to," Craig rationalized. "People just don't wake up one day and *decide* to get *married*. It just doesn't work that way."

"It used to. People used to get married for lineage or convenience."

"But it wasn't some haphazard decision and this isn't precolonial China," Craig rebutted. "Why now? Why the sudden rush? Did all the sentimentality of the wedding get to ya? You're acting like you just went to your first wedding."

"That's just it. I've been going to *too many* of these things. When will it be my turn?"

"Soon enough, dawg, soon enough. But definitely not in a year."

"And why not?" argued Nick. "Why can't I fall in love in a year?"

Craig chafed at his friend's illogical insistence. "Why does it have to be a year? Why so soon?"

For the first time since he had learned of it more than a week ago, he slowly revealed, "My mother has breast cancer."

Craig let slip a hushed, solemn, "Wow."

"The doctor gives her eighteen months, two years tops."

Craig reached out for Nick's hand. "I'm sorry, man. Really, I am."

Nick grasped the hand tight. "Thanks." He paused to compose himself and arrange his thoughts. "I am an only child, my mother's only son. Several years ago, it looked like I was on the marriage track, but things didn't pan out. Now, I'd like to get married before my mother dies. I don't care what the doctors say. I figure I have a year to marry someone, or at least find someone who is marriage material. If I can get engaged in a year, that's fine, too. The wedding can take place within six months, before my mother is critical. But I want my mother to see her only son get married before she dies."

After Nick had finished, Craig released his grip, sinking back into the seat. For several minutes they sat there wordless, motionless, only the hum of the airplane engines to keep their thoughts company. As far as he was concerned, Nick was done talking for the trip.

"Do it," Craig said a half hour later.

Nick had almost slipped into unconsciousness. "Huh?"

"*Do* it," Craig repeated, face solemn, belying a hint of a smile. "If you can do it, find a wife in a year."

Knowing his friend's penchant for deadpanning jokes, Nick rolled his eyes before saying, "Quit messin' with me."

"I'm not messin' with you. If you really feel strongly about this, then do it." Tantalizingly, Craig added, "And, if you're interested, along the way you can make some money."

"Huh?" he said for the second time that night.

Craig shifted his body so that he faced his boy. "Check this out, dawg. Check this out. Remember that Hispanic paper both me and Olinda were supposed to start working at tomorrow?"

"*El Mexicano* or something. Right?"

"*Sí*. Anyways, I'm not working there anymore."

"Hold up, hold up, *hold up*. How you gonna get fired from a place before you've even *worked* there?"

"Guess my reputation preceded me," Craig grinned it off. "Actually, they decided that they weren't comfortable enough with my Spanish-speaking ability to hire me on as a full-time editor."

"Well, being able to speak *Spanish* would be crucial to editing a Hispanic newspaper," Nick funned.

"Forget you, boi! I was learnin'." The impish smile resurfaced. "Well, so Olinda, who is still hired on and already in high regard with the newspaper, made a few calls for me. One of her calls made a call for her. And the next thing *I* know, I have a job offer at the *Reader*."

"For real? The free weekly in San Diego?"

"The very same, my friend. I'm like some sort of assistant editor of the entertainment section. But don't expect that to last too long. I was a full-time editor back in Chicago. They've got some fresh-faced, twenty-three-year-old just a year or two removed from college running that section. I've read some of his stuff. He's good, but I'll be better."

"What? Craig with an ego? When did you grow this?" Nick loved Craig for his confident yet rarely cocky manner. Even when they played basketball together, the man would talk trash just to talk trash. Sometimes he would back it up and play well, but when he didn't, he laughed it off as just having fun with the game. He wasn't the type to seem too openly serious about anything, which was why his marriage to Olinda a couple of months ago had come as such a shock to Nick.

"Ha-ha-HELL," Craig rejoined playfully. "I'm serious about some things, dawg, especially when it comes to my career."

"Well, you are the prototypical entertainment critic. You're *the* most serious brotha when it comes to movies and music. I swear, you don't like anything or anybody."

"That ain't true. I just enjoy everything with a *critical* eye," Craig countered. "Besides, music and movies today are awful in general. Rarely an original thought or idea in the whole business."

"And your sharp criticism is here to save them," mocked Nick.

"Yes, but that's beside the point," Craig deadpanned. "As I was saying, they made me associate editor for the arts and entertainment section of the paper. I get to do some promotional pieces and stuff but, most importantly, I get to have a column every week."

"Cool deal. But I fail to see where *I* will be making money out of any of this."

"This is a crazy idea. I know this," Craig prefaced. "But I want you to write a column for the paper every week."

"About what?" Nick screeched. He might be a lot of things, but a writer he was not. "I don't write."

"Yes, you do, Nick. You think I wasn't watching that time three years ago when we were driving back from Freaknik? You wrote for something like three hours straight."

"Well, I had something to say," Nick replied modestly.

"Right. And I bet it was because of that chick you saw while we were down there. She had you all rattled on the inside, it totally spoiled your Freaknik, and you had to get it out. When it comes to women, Nick, you could probably write a novel."

That much was true. "So what do you want me to write about? Hell, what am I *qualified* to write about?"

"I want you to give the paper weekly updates on your wife search. We can call the column 'One Year for One Bride,' or something corny like that. I think San Diego would eat it up like cotton candy."

"I hate cotton candy."

"But kids love it. And that's how this column would make some of the readers feel—like kids. We'll tell the public our goal, keep your real name and the real reason you're doing this private, and then have, like, a weekly chronicle of a black man on the dating scene in San Diego. It would be great. Like a cinéma-vérité thing, only on paper," Craig visualized.

"But what if it doesn't work?" asked Nick fearfully.

"What, the search? Well . . . that's part of life, too. It could turn into a human-interest piece," Craig spinned. "Either way, *no one* will know who you are, to protect your identity as well as the journalistic integrity of the piece. Not even my boss will know who you are. I'll make that one of the stipulations of the deal. All you have to do is what you do best—date and write."

Nick cushioned the impact of such an offer by resting his head against the airplane seat. This made no kind of sense, was totally crazy. Not only did he want to find a wife in one year, a seemingly impossible task if he wanted it done right, but now he had to consider *documenting* all this for entertainment purposes? Even if Nick wanted to, *could* he write effectively enough to pull all this off? Was he a writer and didn't know it, just as he had been an actor before and didn't know it?

"How much will I be paid?"

"Give me a writing sample and we'll figure it out. But I will be pushing for a dollar a word," Craig declared. "For a five-hundred-word piece."

"*Every* week?"

Craig nodded. "Every week."

Nick smiled and dapped his boy up. "You got yourself a deal."

---

**ONE. ONE STINKING** message tarried on his digital answering machine. Nick had been gone a whole weekend and only one person had bothered to call. Actually, according to his Caller ID, a few people who were "Out of Area" had called, but had not left messages. But one of the calls, listed as "Los Angeles Call," had.

"Hello, Nick. This is Shelby Townsend from Townsend Talent Agency. I hope you are all settled into San Diego by now so I can put you to work. I have some wonderful audition opportunities for you this week, so give me a call when you receive this message. I hope you're liking Southern California. Call me."

Click. Shelby Townsend was Nick's acting agent. She was based in

Los Angeles. Nick had met her during a performance showcase in LA put on by the graduating theater students at DePaul a couple of months ago. Although several agents and producers and casting people attended the showcase, Nick had been the only member of his graduating MFA class to have been signed by an agent. He had been so relieved that his acting gamble had paid off, he'd snatched up that agent's offer like Cookie Monster did chocolate chip cookies.

Some "wonderful audition opportunities," huh? Hmm. Shelby had also mentioned "this week." That could be a problem. Nick was supposed to work that week at Bank of America. It was not as if he particularly enjoyed the job but it certainly paid the bills.

Craig's offer jostled around in his mind. Five hundred a week. Compared with what he was making now, five hundred a week sounded like minimum wage. But with monthly expenses of just over two G's, Nick could squeak by on that, if he downsized his budget a bit and got some acting work from Townsend Talent. Hmm again. With that thought in mind, Nick pulled out his laptop.

**A FEW DAYS** later, Nick sat at his desk at work. He was supposed to be working, but his mind was on autopilot. Like a teenager in puppy love, he gazed across the aisle at the back of his coworker, Serena. She was a tall, beigeskin Hispanic woman with jet-black hair and ruby lips. Intellectually, she was top shelf, with undergrad and master's degrees from San Diego State and the University of California San Diego, respectively. Nick loved the delightful way her face would contort and frown when she laughed as if she enjoyed a joke but was careful not to enjoy it too much. With the way she turned her thick Spanish accent on and off like a light switch depending on whom she dealt with on the phone, Nick could tell that she was holding back a lot inside.

And were it not for that aisle and the water cooler, Serena would not even know Nick was alive. One of these days, it would be Nick's goal in life to get her out on a date. As it was, half the red-blooded males in the office hit on her. Nick did not fancy the idea of taking a number to be shot down with the rest of the kamikaze pilots. Somehow, he would have to distinguish himself.

His phone rang. In the instant between the first and second rings,

Nick hesitated. He had been avoiding Shelby since receiving her message Sunday night. She wanted Nick to come up to LA to audition for some roles but Nick had to work. Audition never equaled job. When Nick had accumulated enough wealth to be able to coast for a few months, then he would try this acting thing for real. Shelby knew his number at Bank of America and about his affiliation with the temp agency. In fact, she had even encouraged it. His temping gave her some time to get the ball rolling for him in the acting circuit. But Nick was not quite ready to roll—nor to give up the security of a guaranteed paycheck a week from now.

The number that came up on his phone was a San Diego number. It belonged to Craig's work phone. "Whassup, boi?"

" 'Sup, dawg."

"I got some good news for ya. That writing sample you gave me? The kid loved it."

"The kid?" Nick was confused.

Craig sighed over the phone. In a monotone, he said, "My boss."

"Oh. Better."

"Anyway, I had to edit your piece a little bit. Not much, I just tweaked it a little. *The Reader* pushes the envelope but even we have our limits. But the dude *loved* it. You've got a job—if you want it."

Looking around at the medium-paced boredom that was the financial institution Bank of America, Nick said without hesitation, "I'll do it."

"We're going to call the column 'Marriage Minded.' Your first piece will be in next week's *Reader*. That means you have until next Tuesday to come up with a five-hundred-word commentary on dating in San Diego. Which means your sorry ass needs to find a date. Think you can handle that?"

Nick stared at the back of Serena. Five hundred dollars a week was nothing, but it would allow him to leave this soulless job and concentrate on acting full-time. It was a gamble, but one Nick had to take. And his leaving the bank would afford him a different angle from which to approach Serena. With a gentle grin, Nick said, "I'm all over it."

"**OKAY, ROBERT.** I need your help."

Robert flashed his dark eyebrows at Nick. "Do tell."

"I have a date tomorrow night."

"Who's the lucky guy?" grinned Robert mischievously.

From across the bin, Nick tossed a pair of socks in his general direction. They were at Robert's job, J. Crew. A few midday shoppers milled about, but no one needed help. Robert was free to gossip and advise. "Fuck you, Robert."

"Oh, *Nicolas* . . . I'd just turn you out," he smiled sunnily. "Now, why are *you* asking *me* for advice? Men are more my purview."

Nick began browsing through some dress shirts. "True. And so are men's fashions. Help me pick out something to wear."

"What kind of a date is this?"

"A date date."

Robert rifled through the rack with him. "A rendezvous where two people will be interacting socially, most likely in the evening over a meal, with the possibility of romance?"

Nick rolled his eyes. "Something like that."

Picking through the expensive shirts, Robert asked casually, "How much do you want to invest in this date?"

Nick steered him over to some shirts in his financial hemisphere. "Not *that* much."

"I'm talking about *emotional* investment, *Nicolas,*" he clarified. "Tell me about this girl."

"*Woman.*"

"*What*-ever." It was Robert's turn to roll his eyes.

"Well, I met her on the job—"

"Throw her back," tsked Robert. "Job relationships never work out." He was right. Cardinal Rule No. 2.

"I'm leaving the job tomorrow."

"Okay. This one?" Robert held up a nicely printed polo shirt that actually worked for Nick. With a bemused smile, Nick nodded.

"Continue."

"Well, she's incredibly smart. Has her master's and everything—"

"So do you," Robert pointed out.

"That's beside the point." Nick gritted his teeth. "Are you gonna let me finish telling you about her?"

"I just don't want you in *awe* over the girl. You're no lampshade yourself." Robert winked at Nick.

Nick, suddenly confused by Robert's gayness, was stuck with a contorted look on his face. Robert channeled the need to laugh uproariously into a head-back, silent-laugh affair.

"Forgive me. I love messing with the heterosexuals. Do tell me about this lovely *girl*." They were over by the pants now.

"She's beautiful. I mean, she has to beat men back with a stick on the job. It gets pretty ridiculous."

"Sounds like a harassment case waiting to happen."

Nick iced him over with one hard glare. Robert flashed up his palms as a peace offering.

"She's Latina, twenty-seven, bilingual, has a delightful little smile, and all her own teeth," Nick rushed before Robert could interrupt him again. "There."

"Sounds like you've given her a lot of thought," mused Robert, sifting through pairs of pants.

"Oh, not really," Nick lied offhandedly; the man-hours lost to daydreaming about Serena that week had surely reached double digits. "I'm an actor. I'm a student of human nature."

"Well, Mother Nature, I think the best thing for you to do is not to approach the date too seriously."

"Meaning?"

"Meaning don't come to the date with any expectations. Don't go out with her thinking, 'Omigod, she could be The One.' "

*Little does he know* . . . "Of course not. Not on the first date, at least."

"Not on *any* date, Nick. Play the field! Date early and often! Sample all of what San Diego has to offer!"

"Well, aren't you just the poster child for promiscuity."

"Please, *Nicolas*. We are young, able-bodied men. We weren't meant to be saddled down with *commitment* in the prime of our lives! Life is to be seized and savored!"

Nick held up a pair of pants against the shirt they had picked out. "Sounds like someone's been making up for lost time. Trying to make up for all those years of repressed homosexuality, huh?"

"That's a crude way to put it," muttered Robert.

"Well, I've been secure in my sexuality all my life so I don't feel the same need to 'seize and savor.' "

"Why are you even asking me for dating advice *anyway*? *Hetero*," Robert hissed.

"To be honest, I don't know. It's just . . . I haven't done much *dating* lately."

"You? Really?"

"I haven't had a girlfriend or significant love interest in more than a year."

Robert was floored. "Wow. That's impressive for a serial monogamist."

"Who you tellin'."

"Why the long absence?"

"I just haven't been inspired to really date someone. Moving didn't help either."

"And now *this* woman inspires you?" Robert sounded skeptical. He held up their two selections.

Nick gave him visual approval of the outfit. "I have my own inspiration these days."

"Be careful," Robert warned, leading the way toward the register. "People are disappointing enough as it is. When you project your expectations upon them, you can really let yourself down."

**A MESSAGE WAS** waiting for him when he got home: "Nick, I have a job for you."

Shelby. In the past couple of days as he prepared to switch careers, Nick had totally forgotten about Shelby Townsend. Most agents, to Nick's limited knowledge of the business, were not as persistent as Shelby. Now that his schedule had freed up considerably, he felt bad for ducking her. After all, were it not for Shelby, Nick never would have grown the brass ones to come out here.

"I have a trade show for you to work this weekend up at the LA Convention Center. It's hardly glamorous work but it pays twenty-five bucks an hour and you can see some of your peers and competition. I know you came here to be an actor, not a model, but this can help put some money in your pocket for now while I get you out there. So give me a call back at the office tomorrow. The show runs Saturday and Sunday. 'Bye, sweetie."

Nick shook his head slightly. Everyone in LA called each other "sweetie" or "darling." Just what had he gotten himself into?

It was evening, the late summer sun lingering well past eight o'clock. Outside his door was the sound of waves crashing on the beach, a few blocks away, as the tide rolled in. It was too late to call Shelby back. Besides, his mind was too wrapped up in his date tomorrow night to call her now. But there was one call he would make.

"I'M BEGINNING TO have second thoughts about all this."

"Cool out, dawg. I'm on top of things," Nick reassured Craig, via phone. Having gotten cold feet, Craig had called Nick, frantic, worried that he just might have taken a leap off the career cliff with their far-fetched scheme. Of course, Craig *had* to call right before five o'clock, just as Nick was finishing cleaning up his desk for the last time. It did not help that Serena waited for him across the aisle, feet propped up on her desk, bemused, flirty smile on her lips. With a teasing flash of the eyebrows, Serena tapped her watch. God, she looked so sexy. Damn Craig for delaying his date!

"Are you? Do you have anything written yet?"

"The weekend is young, my friend."

"Do you even have a date?"

Nick snorted with machismo. "Who are you talking to here?"

"Right. Of course you have a date." Craig exhaled for the first time in their conversation. "I'm feeling better."

"You should. She's tight." Nick stared Serena right in her flirtatious, dark eyes. He was all packed and ready to go. Serena stood— with her sexy self. This woman was *born* ready.

"Don't fall in love now. I expect at least a few months' worth of material out of you." Craig wasn't sure if he was kidding or not.

"Actually, that's the point of this whole experiment, is it not?" Nick sighed in exasperation. "Are you done, sire?"

"It's officially the weekend now. Where are you in such a hurry to get to?"

Nick smiled as Serena swished her way past his desk and toward the elevators. Before he hung up and followed her, Nick murmured one word into the phone: "Research."

---

**THE DRIVE TO** LA was quite pleasant and short. On a weekend morning, traffic was virtually nonexistent, and in a mere hour and a half Nick was within the city limits. The Pacific Ocean lay flat out to his left like a never-ending shiny blue quilt. Nick drove with his moonroof open, wearing a pair of shades. The sun was bright and warm. This was the first time he had made the 120-mile trip, but certainly not the last.

When he showed up at Khalilah's door, he was a little surprised at the modesty of the house. She lived in Westwood, a nice neighborhood that housed UCLA. With her alma mater being USC, that was akin to Trojans living among the Greeks. But Westwood was a decided step up from USC's South Central roots. Nick was surprised at the size of the house only because his friend had always insisted on a certain lifestyle; he guessed she wasn't there yet. But the place had a den that doubled as a guest room, so Nick was not one to complain.

She came to the door just as Nick emerged from the 4Runner. Khalilah was a woman three years Nick's junior. He had known her since their days as civic crusaders for the Seattle NAACP Youth Council. Although she was a tasty shade of chocolate with an equally appetizing figure to match, Khalilah was off limits. Theirs was a relationship that never dared rise above what Nick called The Land of the Glorified Eunuch: the platonic friend. The one time he had raised the issue, she had clubbed it like a baby seal. Nonetheless, they were good friends, and she was happy to see him.

"Nick!" she squealed as he reached the porch, lugging a gym bag.

"Koko!" He received a warm hug.

"Come on in. Welcome to my humble abode."

Any earlier thoughts he had had about this being a modest little place were blown out of the water. The interior was *laid*. Art from about five different continents, by Nick's estimation, adorned the walls. A Japanese screen added instant class to an otherwise unimportant corner. African masks lined a hallway leading to the bedrooms. An authentic German beer mug sat on her coffee table. Spicy, exotic incense burned lightly out of Nick's vision.

Plopping his bag down on some kind of authentic Oriental rug in the living room, Nick examined something he suspected to be a hand-crafted West African stool. "Nice trinkets."

Lugging his bag toward the back, Khalilah shouted "Thanks!" over her shoulder. When she returned, she said, "You're lucky I'm here."

Engrossed in evaluating a wall full of diverse figurines from many different cultures, Nick snapped out of his trance. "What?"

"When you called Thursday night. Lucky I'm here. I had *just* returned from Spain half an hour before you called. I *love* Spain." Khalilah was not gloating. Spanish was her favorite language of the six she knew.

"What was in Spain?"

"Same reason why you're here. Business." The woman shifted gears. "And speaking of which, when's your thing?"

Nick tore himself away from Khalilah's private museum. "Two hours. I gotta start getting ready. You have an iron?"

"Sure." Suppressing a smile, she asked, "How was your date last night?"

Nick's face soured quicker than the Bulls after Michael Jordan. "Don't ask."

"Too late. Just did."

Nick shook his head.

"That bad?"

Nick nodded.

Khalilah sighed as she began to retrieve the iron. "Guess I'll just have to read about it."

Nick froze. Read about it? Could he have been so careless as to share with Khalilah his super-clandestine plan to find a wife? Was telepathy Khalilah's seventh language? How could she have known? "Read about it?" Nick asked weakly.

"Yeah. You know, in your memoirs. After you hit it big." She smiled that supportive-friend smile and disappeared in the back.

He nearly collapsed under the weight of his own breath.

⸻

**OKAY, I'VE HAD** *just about enough of this.* Nick vacated his post.

"I'm taking a break," he tossed over his shoulder as he strode past his booth partner. Before she had a chance to protest, Nick was off the exhibition floor.

Slamming quarters into the overpriced soda machine, Nick silently cursed his present fate. Suited in his best double-breasted navy-blue ensemble, Nick was the picture of professionalism. One look at him and surely you would want to buy a home theater system. The sad thing was that Nick was fairly interested in home entertainment and the cutting edge of electronics. But after the fourth hour of turning on and off the same audio/video system and giving the same five-minute monologue of meaningless jargon, the whole affair had somehow lost its appeal. His feet hurt from standing, his head ached from talking entirely too much, and, worse yet, he was bored. If he could help it, he would never do this type of thing again. More than anything, it was a sign of good faith to Shelby. He would have a talk with her on Monday in her office.

Shamelessly, Nick sank his behind down on the carpeted floor in the snack area with his tart, carbonated drink. He was outside the main hallway and away from the exhibition floor, so he was done being a model for the moment. Even if someone did see him, he didn't care. Most of the emaciated models he had met at the show were vapid, self-interested white girls who could care less about meeting one of their peers. The prevailing mood among the "talent" there was one Nick would soon find among many other actors and models in LA—self-preserving narcissism. Later on, Nick would also find out the reason why.

A pair of black-shrouded ankles in heels passed Nick's bowed head. The clink of quarters in the machine alerted him that he was not alone. Head snapping up, his eyes met hers. He was too tired, too unpretentious, and too un-LA to care about how he looked. She smiled.

"Hey. Didn't see you down there."

"Hey yourself," Nick smiled, evaluating. The first sista model he had seen there (and a pretty one at that), this lovely stranger was a sight for *any* eyes. Her shade of brown was just as walnut brown as Nick's. Her dark hair was pulled back into a simple yet beautiful bun and she wore a long, elegant red skirt. In the face of such beauty, Nick started to get up.

"Oh no. Don't get up on my account." She beamed him a radiant smile. "In fact, I think I'll come down and join you."

Gracefully, she slid down the wall next to Nick. The sweet fragrance of Tommy Girl preceded her. "Nice to see someone around here not too wrapped up in how they look."

Nick grinned. Extending his hand, he said, "I'm Nick."

"Miss Joanna Whitley." She shook Nick's hand firmly.

Nick laughed. "Don't have to be so formal around me, Ms. Whitley."

That elicited a smile. "Anna. And it's 'Miss,' " she corrected. "You never know whom you could meet in this town. George Lucas got the *Raiders* script from a waitress who was serving him."

"Is that right?" This was Nick's first exposure to bona fide entertainment-industry lore.

"Oh, I don't know. That's just what I heard." Anna emitted a typical LA smile, flashing perfectly white, straight teeth. "You hear a lot of things in this town."

"Well, you could hand me a script to the next *Star Wars* and I wouldn't have the slightest idea what to do with it. I'm new to Southern California," Nick admitted.

"Don't feel bad, Nick. No one in this business is actually *from* here. Where are you from?"

"Seattle, by way of Atlanta, New York, and Chicago. And, quite honestly, I don't even live in LA."

"Me neither. It's too hectic up here."

"Really? Where do you live?"

"You first." Anna was teasing—he thought.

"Uh, San Diego." Nick was not sure if that was a good or a bad thing.

"That's not so bad, Nick. I live in Orange County. San Juan Capistrano."

His brow furrowed. "Where's that?"

"Well, if you came up here from Daygo, then you probably drove right through us. I-5 plows right through it. It's up in the hills, about fifty minutes north of San Diego."

Nick was still lost. "Oh," he managed.

"Seattle, huh?"

"Beautiful city. One of the most beautiful cities in the country." Before she could even speak the inevitable, he read her mind: "And not as rainy as people think."

Another smile. "So what's with your many moves? What's the story there?"

"I went to undergrad in Atlanta, worked in New York for a couple of years, and went to grad school in Chicago."

"Wow. I think you're a bit overqualified to be an actor, Nick," Anna teased.

"No kidding. I'm over five feet nine."

"For real!" she chimed in. "Do you know how hard it is for me to get a date in this town?"

Eyeing her discreetly, Nick snorted, "I seriously doubt that."

A charming smile. "All the men in the biz are short."

"And how tall are you?" His vantage point from the floor did not allow him to size her up.

"Five-nine," she announced proudly, as well she should. She was tall enough to do runway and print modeling. Lord knows she was attractive enough.

"Not bad," downplayed Nick. As far as he was concerned, she had the height requirements to be the mother of his children. Nick had always been attracted to tall women. For as long as he could remember, he had always wanted to marry a tall woman so he could breed long and lean track and basketball stars. "Are you from San Juan Capistrano?"

"I told you, Nick, nobody's actually *from* here. I'm from New York."

"No accent," he observed.

"Upstate."

"I see." They sat in silence for a moment. "Do you act, too?"

"That's why I'm in LA. If I wanted to model, I would've kept my butt in New York. You don't come to LA to model, believe me."

"Yeah. You come to LA to struggle and starve."

"Exactly." Anna glanced at her watch. "Damn. I've gotta go back to my booth."

"Aww . . . Do you hafta?" cooed Nick cutely.

"Afraid so, *mon frère.*" Anna stood.

He brightened as he stood. "You know French?"

"Just what a Haitian boyfriend taught me once."

"I'd hate to lose you so soon after meeting you, Anna. You know us black folk gotta stick together. Especially in this industry."

"Oh, no doubt. Come by my booth before the day is over and we'll exchange information."

In an instant when she wasn't looking at him, Nick's eyes went heavenward briefly. At this rate, a year was too *much* time. When their eyes caught again, Nick quickly regained his composure. "So, what are you selling?"

Anna frowned briefly. "Jet skis."

"You don't like to jet-ski?"

"Actually, I've never been on one. Sounds fun. I just don't like promoting something I can't afford to actually use. I feel like I'm misleading my customers."

"Hey girl. I'm just here making twenty-five an hour," said Nick, playfully indifferent.

"That's it?" Her mischievous smile was back again as she turned her head, gliding back toward the exhibition hall. "See you later, Nick."

Underneath his Anna-induced haze, Nick curdled. He was *definitely* going to have a talk with Shelby on Monday.

## MARRIAGE MINDED
*by Anonymous*

*In an ongoing effort to make this the best free weekly reader in the country, the Calendar editors are bringing you a new column about serious-minded dating in San Diego County. This is the first column from our single "man on the scene," who is dating not only to provide information for this column but also out of a determination all his own. His name has been withheld to protect the integrity of his reality-based experiences—and his dating future.   —(Ed.)*

I will let you know right now, in no uncertain terms, what the goal of this column is. By August 14 of next year, I fully intend to have found someone I care about enough to marry. You, my free-weekly friends, shall be unseen witnesses to my yearlong, *Hobbit*-like quest.

Unusual? Yes. Call it vigilante dating. Taking love and a holy sacrament into your own hands. My reasons are purely selfish and personal, and they shall remain mine. All you need to know, dear San Diegans, is that I am on a mission and I will *not* be denied.

First, a few things about me. I am new to your fair city. But I must say that I like what I have seen in my month here. I am an actor (don't hold that against me). That makes finding someone real and self-effacing in Southern California nearly impossible. I am also a black male, and finding an African-American fiancée may be all the more challenging. Although I do prefer sistas, I will let all of San Diego know that I am open to all qualified comers.

Which is a nice segue into what the qualifications are for potential Mrs. Anonymouses. She must be smart, preferably college educated, since I have postgraduate degrees myself. Although I am only six feet tall, I'd like her to be fairly tall. I'm trying to breed basketball players here. Or, if she's short, she should have great legs. Must have a sense of humor, be honest, romantic . . . Oh, the hell with it. You all will find out my desired qualities as we take this long, strange voyage.

Believe it or not, I have already had my first interview. My first date en route to the Holy Grail was terrible. On the surface, everything was perfect. My date was a beautiful woman with whom I worked, an object of my desire from the moment I started working with her. We did the ever-so-dull "dinner and a movie" thing. The conversation was fine, the dinner was fine, the movie was fine. Actually, the movie was the highlight of the evening.

I say all that to say this: While everything went smoothly, there was something missing. There was a hollowness to the evening. Like after having eaten a vat full of cotton candy or watching *Saturday Night Live* now, when it sucks. I came away from the experience *empty*. I realized that my lust for her was purely surface material. I hated the pedestrian-ness of it all. There simply were no sparks.

To see her again would be a waste of my time and good column space. If I am to continue on this quest, it must be with a woman who makes me more . . . **Marriage Minded.**

# 4

NCE AGAIN, CRAIG buzzed in his ear like an anxious gnat. "Whaddaya mean you're still in Los Angeles!"

From Khalilah's living room couch, Nick fielded the question coolly. "The trade show lasted through yesterday, and today I'm meeting with my agent."

"Do you have to be there to do it?"

"Of course. She's based out of LA, so why waste a trip?"

In an effort to calm himself, Craig breathed with the gravity of a yoga instructor. "Have you even *written* anything yet?"

"Yes."

"Yes?" Hope returned to Craig's voice. "Is it finished?"

"Pretty much. Save your editing expertise, of course," Nick added, if, for nothing else, to appease his boss.

"Cool! So when can I have it?"

"Don't you guys have some sort of way I can send it to you electronically? Email or fax or something?"

"Yeah, you can email it to me at the *Reader*. My first initial and last name '@sdreader.com.' Just like that."

"Got it."

"Making any progress?" Craig actually cared if his friend found a wife. He just didn't want him to find her too soon.

Nick grinned. "I'll let you know Tuesday."

**SHELBY TOWNSEND WAS** an empire in her own mind. Once a successful agent for Creative Artists Agency, one of the largest in town, she had bolted the second one of her clients landed a multimillion-dollar contract in a big-budget action movie. Within six months, Shelby had constructed Townsend Talent Agency, 80 percent of her clientele shamelessly stolen from CAA. Once that movie premiered and played to movie theaters several months later, however, her client, and the movie, bombed horribly. In Hollywood time, Shelby was instantly forgotten.

Understandably, she was hungry. Nick, of course, did not know any of this when he entered her office on the sixteenth floor of an office building on Wilshire Boulevard in Beverly Hills. Directed into a seat in the lobby by a preternaturally tan, formidably large, and unnaturally blond male receptionist, Nick slid onto a plush black leather couch. Large, blowup pictures of some of her more famous clients adorned the walls, to stroke Shelby's ego more than to impress anyone else. Her current A-list stud was a guy named Fredo—no last name (or would that be first name?), just Fredo. He was currently playing some brazen young doctor on *The Young and the Restless* to a formidable female, Internet fan base. Dark and ruggedly handsome, he smugly mugged at Nick from across the room.

"Shelby will see you now."

Nick hustled into the office to see the flame-haired Shelby Townsend on the phone, barking instructions to someone who seemed like he or she wasn't getting it right: That's right, a double-wide trailer was requested by such-and-such and if what's-his-name didn't get it, he would mysteriously come up with an ankle injury on his next day of filming. Seated across from her desk with Wilshire Boulevard behind her through the window, Nick was a little fascinated, if not disgusted. *Just get me a* part, *bump a trailer!*

After five agonizing minutes of haggling and bitching, during which Nick examined every single Industry-related artifact to be found on her desk and shelves, Shelby mercifully hung up. When she wasn't opening her mouth, she was actually a pretty attractive woman of thirty-six. "Welcome to LA, Nick."

"Thanks. How've you been?"

A roll of the eyes. "Ridiculous. Listen . . . we've got to get you working."

"I have no problem with that." He hesitated. "But I'd like to be doing some real work, you know what I mean? Not just posing in front of cars at a car show or something like that. I want to *act*."

"You and every second person in this town, Nick. I know the feeling." Shelby smiled a sincere smile that seemed instantly less than sincere simply because she smiled it. A woman like her didn't have time to smile. "But the reality of it is, until you nail some auditions, you're going to have to make a living. We've gotta start getting you on some sets."

"What did you have in mind?"

"Well . . . first of all, we're going to have to get you some new pictures. While your headshot is pretty good"—she waded through the shallow pool of talent on her desk to find his—"still, it is not Industry standard. These days, people in this town are going for the three-quarter look. You know, something that shows off not just that killer smile of yours, but also that bod. About waist high or so."

"Uh-huh." When it came to the film industry, Nick was a self-admitted rube. He had no choice but to listen.

"And before we send you out on auditions, we need to have different looks for you. Like, for example, if you're going out for a McDonald's commercial, we need that all-American, clean-cut, commercial look. Clean shaven. Big smile. Gotta lose the goatee."

Protectively, Nick stroked his goatee.

"Then you need what they call a theatrical shot. Real serious. Screams thespian. Or evil. Here, look at this guy."

Shelby slid a headshot across her desk at Nick. A lantern-jawed white guy with steely eyes, wearing a turtleneck, visible only from the neck up, stared down the barrel of life and dared you to pull the trigger. Badass.

Once again, Nick reluctantly nodded, absorbing. The cash registers going off in his head had him weak in the wallet. Something told him that this was not going to be for free.

"And then we need to get you a zed card."

"What's a zed card?"

"A comp card."

Nick shot her another quizzical look.

"It's a composite card, one photo on the front, four on the back, all different poses. Makes you more commercial for modeling."

Nick shook his head. "Uh-uh. No modeling." He wanted no part of the weight-paranoid, cocaine-snorting, backstabbing, sexually liberal demimonde he had heard about.

"Alright, alright. But may I submit you for commercials?"

"Of course." A nationwide commercial was every starting actor's dream. The residuals alone over the course of a year could pay for a Lexus.

"One concession, though. I want you to just go by Nick."

"Huh?"

"On your new headshots, I want you to just go by Nick. Kind of a modeling thing, but it makes you stand out. I mean, your name is ordinary, yet not. It will stand out just from the simple fact that someone had enough gall to go by just their first name, one as simple as Nick." She seemed positively excited about her little idea.

Nick shrugged. "You're the agent."

"Good. So take care of those headshots, and we'll get you in some auditions in no time."

Now time for the *real* question: "How much is this going to cost me?"

Shelby fielded the question like it was an afterthought. "Cost? Well, we'll hook you up with one of our photographers. He'll only charge you five hundred."

Nick tried not to choke on his tongue. "Five hundred dollars?" *American?* he wanted to say.

"He usually charges eight hundred for a portfolio shoot. He'll even throw in your zed card. I mean, to make you more attractive to commercial casting directors, you'll need to have a zed."

Thinking about his mother lying flat on her back in a Harborview Medical Center hospital bed, Nick sure thought about several better uses for five hundred dollars. He was also reminded that time is short on this earth. "Whatever. Set it up."

Shelby made some scribblings on a pad of paper. "I'll get you in there day after tomorrow at eleven. His name is Blake Davis. Brad Pitt once used him. He's quite good."

"Great. Anything else?"

"And there's one other piece of business. We have to get you your SAG card."

The Screen Actors Guild was the largest union for actors in film media in the country. Entrance was tough, seeing how SAG required a speaking part in a movie, TV show, or commercial—as well as almost $1,400 in initiation fees. He had heard of some actors getting initiation-fee waivers in productions, but even those were hard to come by if no one wanted you that badly in their flick. "And how do we do that?"

A big sigh. Shelby was prefacing something. "I know it's not exactly what you came out here to do, but . . . "

Nick braced for the news.

". . . extra work."

"Extra work?"

"You know, background crosses, atmosphere, filling in busy scenes or crowd scenes. Stuff like that." Nick did not like the sound of that at all. Just three months ago, he had been Macbeth in a large Downtown Chicago theater. "Hey, it'll get you a chance to get on the sets, see how things work differently from theater, and you can pick up your three SAG vouchers to become eligible for the union."

Nick adjusted quickly to the proposal. Joining the union would definitely be a plus. He had heard the minimum pay for a speaking part was six hundred dollars. *A day*. "How do I get my SAG vouchers?"

"Until I can get you on some gigs, I suggest you find yourself a call-in service that scouts out extra work for nonunion extras. I have one in mind for you who can put you on a job as early as tomorrow. They will work you as often as you want—every day, if you want—and you will put yourself in a position to get SAG vouchers. You need three SAG vouchers, and the initiation fee, to join the union. If I don't get you a speaking part first, maybe you can bust your hump to get into the union."

"Well, if I'm on the set on a nonunion voucher, how do I get a SAG voucher?"

"You gotta be lucky and memorable. They require a certain amount of people on each set who have to be union. Hope someone gets sick or doesn't show. Cozy up to an AD who has the power to give out

SAG vouchers. You know, impress them—like you impressed me."
Another sincerely insincere smile.

"AD?"

"Assistant Director."

"Oh." One little meeting with Shelby was certainly an education.

She handed him another slip of paper from her pad with the name
and number of the call-in service. "They charge thirty-five a month,
but they can work you all month. They're worth it."

"Thirty-five *hundred*!?!" Nick screeched.

Shelby erupted into a fit of laughter, uncontrollable, hysterical
laughter that instantaneously made him feel worse than stupid. It may
have been the most genuine moment from her the entire meeting.
"Thirty-five *bucks,* honey. Thirty-five dollars." An amused grin. He
had so much to learn.

Sheepishly grinning off his own embarrassment, Nick nodded
stiffly. Boy, didn't he know it.

---

**NICK SCURRIED PAST** the passersby along the Third Street
Promenade. His hurried, disturbed visage contrasted sharply with those
of the tourists and independently wealthy who lollygagged along the
thoroughfare. As he passed yet another contortionist twisting himself
this way and that, Nick checked his watch nervously. He was late and
it just would not do.

Parking had been a bitch but wasn't it always in Santa Monica?
Diners, moviegoers, street vendors, homeless people, all passed by
in a blur until Nick arrived at the end of the world-famous Santa
Monica Pier.

There she was, standing with her back to him, facing the ocean, the
sunset, the future. Waves lapped quietly some thirty feet below. Seagulls traced parabolas in the sky in lazy competition with one another.
The setting sun, stubbornly being dragged toward the horizon, emitted its protest in dazzling hues of orange, red, pink, and gold. As she
turned her dark brown face over her shoulder, she smiled a warm, familiar invitation to him, the way old lovers did to each other. She
looked perfect.

"You're late," Anna grinned at him.

Palms outward, Nick could not fight it, could not fight her, did not want to fight the moment. Every ounce of his body slackened to her comely features. At that moment, Nick was certain that the Santa Monica Pier had simply been an invention of the lovely Joanna Whitley in an attempt to subdue his will to hers, without her having to say a word. If that were true, this setting was much more successful than an attempt.

"I'll forgive you," she smiled generously.

Nick slid in next to her at the railing. Their hands meshed like melted Hershey's chocolate bars. A bold maneuver, for sure, but Nick figured a few long, positive phone conversations had afforded him as much.

Without a word, she withdrew her hand slightly, not enough to offend but just enough to reclaim her own appendage from this audacious, yet attractive, stranger.

Nick was undaunted. "So you wrapped early, huh?"

"No, it was an early call," Anna yawned. "Three A.M. Thirteen hours."

"Dang, that's tough."

"Hardly, honey. You'll see," she grinned again. "How was your first day of extra work?"

"Boring. Made background crosses for six hours," Nick informed her, making a face.

"Don't be surprised, Nick. Extra work is a waste of your talent."

A roar erupted from the passengers on the roller-coaster behind them. "How do you know I've got talent to waste?"

"You've gotten this far with me, haven't you?" she half-smiled. Anna had this amazing way of balancing her lips between a smile and a smirk yet still keeping it remarkably sexy.

"So would this be considered a *date*, Miss Whitley?"

Anna studied the melting sun. "I haven't decided yet."

Nick reached for her hand again, only to watch her take it away—again. "Is something wrong?"

"I'm just not there yet."

"Holding your hand? Am I moving too fast, Anna?" Nick tried to be charming in the face of defeat.

"No. I'm moving too slow." Now it was her turn to offer a smile. "Sorry. Had a bad relationship. You know how it is."

*Boy, do I,* thought Nick, betraying no expression. "You never really answered my earlier question."

"You mean are we dating?"

Nonthreateningly, Nick piped, "Yeah."

She drew a half stride closer to him, armed with her patented smile. "I'll consider it."

---

**NICK CAME HOME** to find a note on the living room table from Khalilah. It was right by the remote, where he wouldn't miss it. She was gone to North Africa for a couple of weeks. Be good and water her plants. Nick grinned ruefully. Now he knew why they had always been incompatible romantically: the girl was too busy and gypsy-blooded to entertain a regular relationship.

After turning on the tube to *SportsCenter,* Nick made a few calls. One was to his extra call-in service. Although he had been unimpressed with the day's work, he hoped that this was an isolated boring experience. He was to work on the set of a new African-American firefighter show called *Blackdraft* the next day. His next call was to check his messages at home. Just one, from a perplexed-sounding Serena, who wondered where Nick had been hiding since he quit the bank temp job (and, subsequently, their date). And then Nick made his favorite call.

"This Mal."

"Whaddup, mark?"

"What up, Trick Fabulous." All these years, and their intro had rarely changed.

"I'm in LA, man. Had my first day on set. A hospital show."

"Word? They have you changin' bedpans?"

"Ha-ha-HELL. You're a funny bitch," said Nick. They could playfully insult each other for hours.

"You holla at any stars?"

"Naw, man. They pretty much keep us separated from the principals."

"The who?"

"Principals. People with speaking parts," explained Nick. "They get their own trailers. We're huddled together in a holding area like inmates around the last pack of cigarettes."

Always about the bottom line, Malloy asked, "How's the pay?"

"Shitty. You don't make any real money until overtime."

"Yeah, that sucks, dude." Mal grew quiet.

"How's the wife?"

"She straight." Mal had a sudden edge to his voice. Usually, the man could talk for hours about his wife.

"You straight?" asked Nick, concerned.

"No doubt," said Mal.

In the stale, uneasy silence, Nick was unconvinced. He felt so pressed to fill the space with *something* that he flirted with the idea of telling Malloy about the wifehunt. A reformed player like Mal would never understand it, though.

Luckily, Mal saved the convo for them. "Eh, remember your boy Carlton? The one from Seattle who went to Morehouse with us?"

"Of course. That's my boy."

"You hollered at him since you moved down?"

"Naw, I haven't. Good lookin' out, kid."

"Yeah. That fool probably knows some hos for you."

**"YEAH, I GOT** hos for you, dude."

It was two days later and Nick and Carlton were seated at Seau's, a restaurant in San Diego's Mission Valley, next to the Mission Valley Center shopping mall. Seau's was a restaurant established by life-time San Diego Chargers football player Junior Seau. His place was a sports-bar-cum-restaurant, overloaded with giant-screen TVs that trumpeted ESPN, ESPN2, Fox Sports Southwest, and various other sports channels nonstop. Stepping into the place was an assault on the visual senses.

It was a Friday night, the place was hopping, and the waitresses were lovely and skimpily clad in their tight black tops and short black tennis skirts. As another tanned, firm-legged waitress passed by their table, Nick, eyes still following the talent, said, "I don't want hos, dude. I want *women.*"

"Whatever, janky dude. I got some of them, too." Carlton was Nick's boy from high school. He stood about five-ten, with medium-brown skin and a black-bearded face. Originally from Louisiana, he had grown up in Seattle alongside Nick. C-Town, as Nick called him, was a year older and had graduated from Franklin High and Morehouse a year earlier than Nick.

This was their first meeting since Nick had moved down to San Diego. Last time he had checked, Nick heard that Carlton was working for Costco Wholesale Club, on the corporate side. It had been that job that had made Carlton migrate from The 206 (Seattle) to the warmer climes of SD (San Diego). Nick was just grateful to have another friend in the area, especially one with access to women. With extreme curiosity, Nick had noticed Carlton clutching a copy of the *Reader* as he sat down. Nick's first "Marriage Minded" column had come out the day before and he had not gotten a copy of it.

Ignoring his own curiosity, Nick asked, "So how you livin', C-Town?"

"Man, I can't call it. You know how I been workin' for Costco for somethin' like five years, right?"

"Yeah."

"Well, I'm about to quit that shit. I'm planning a career change."

A victim of a recent career change himself, Nick leaned forward with interest, as well as to compete against the noise of the TVs and the diners chattering and clattering. "To what?"

A somewhat guilty smile surfaced. "Sportscasting."

"Get the fuck outta here."

"I took a year's worth of on-camera classes at City College. I've been training with Channel 2 for two months now. They think I'm ready."

Nick felt betrayed. He had never known about this passion of his friend's. "So how did you even get an interview? What are your credentials?"

"Communications degree, and being a former baseball star at Morehouse."

"We only had a baseball team for two years," Nick pointed out.

"And I starred both years," Carlton smiled. "Look, everyone lies a little on their résumés. I just lied my way into a job."

Still suffering from shock, Nick dapped him up. "I'm proud of you, my man. I never knew you had that in you."

"Same could be said for you and this acting shit, nigga. When did *that* happen?"

"Four years ago, when I first moved to Chicago. I had some free time on my hands outside of work and my MBA classes, so I took an acting class. As they say in the theater world, the acting bug bit me."

"Yeah, yeah, yeah. That's the storyline I heard. I just wanted to hear it from you face-to-face." Carlton studied his friend's features. "Just like me . . . I guess you're serious about this career change."

"Serious enough to walk away from a seventy-thousand-dollar-a-year job in Chicago to make minimum wage as an extra serious," Nick deadpanned.

"Yeah, that's pretty serious, nigga."

"So where would I take a young lady on a date in this city of yours, Big Pimp?"

"A female or a ho?"

"A *lady*."

"Oh. Try Ocean Beach Pier."

"We've already done a pier," denied Nick.

"Aw'ight, janky dude. Try Embarcadero Park. It's over there by Seaport Village."

"Where? What?"

"Another bomb first-date spot. It's on the waterfront, right off Downtown and Seaport Village, a nice, touristy little hangout. A cool way to kill an afternoon," Carlton elaborated.

"Good lookin', C-Town."

"Always, playboy. Always."

NICK WAS SPLAYED out on his futon couch, absorbing his first professionally written piece in the *Reader,* when the phone rang. His cordless with Caller ID informed him it was Craig.

"Whassup, dawg?"

"It's all you, kid. You peep the new edition of the *Reader*?"

"I'm inhaling it right now." Nick scanned the article for what must have been his hundredth time. "You didn't change much."

"Not much to change. You're the talent in this endeavor. My editing won't move papers," Craig smiled impishly.

"And it's yet to prove that my column will either."

"Gotta keep the faith, playa, gotta keep the faith. We won't know until the mail comes in on Monday. But tell me something. How's the roster check?"

"Well, there's this girl I'm talking to that I met at some LA modeling show or something."

"Naw, kid. I need you to speak to me in terms that I can understand."

"Aw'ight, aw'ight. I've got this one off guard, kind of timid and would rather hand the ball off to someone else instead of looking for her own shot."

"It's like that?"

"Yeah. But she seems coachable, though. I'm setting up a tryout for her tomorrow night. Although she plays for a visiting team in Orange County, she's gonna take the team bus to play a game down in San Diego and work out for Coach."

"Ah . . . home-court advantage," breathed Craig. "Continue."

"Um . . . that's it, I guess."

"That's it?" Craig was disappointed. "You ain't met any honeys on set yet, kid?"

"Naw, man. I've been so focused on what's going on around me, I haven't even thought of meeting anyone on set. Besides, they're all actresses. How real could they be?" rationalized Nick.

"Kid, we need you to date. Date date date date date!" Craig implored. "Are you sure you're even gonna have enough material for the column due on Tuesday?"

"Look, I will *always* have enough material for the column," Nick assured him. "Believe that."

"Alright now," Craig said warily. "You're not the only one with a lot riding on the outcome of this column."

"Believe me, I know," sighed Nick sadly. "I know."

NICK AND ANNA had spent the previous three hours talking, laughing, simply enjoying each other's company on the same park bench. Without noticing, they had been party to the sun's daily, spectacularly colored retreat beneath the horizon. Their conversation was open, nimble, and unforced, allowing them to span a variety of subjects. They talked about past loves, past lives, past experiences that had molded and shaped their presents. Anna's trademark reserved friendliness was thawing out into adoration for this brownskin individual from Seattle. Her best efforts to fight him were now going ignored. Nick was winning her over.

No fool, Nick could sense it, too. Therein lay the dilemma. If he won her over, charmed her to the point of submission, later on, she might deem the whole relationship adversely, feel that she had rushed into things "too quick" with him. God, did he know about falling for someone so fast, so soon. As much as it pained him, Nick was going to have to measure out his charm in doses that the lovely Miss Whitley could handle.

That thought was uppermost in his mind as he sat on that park bench with her in Embarcadero Marina Park, nightfall all around them, just the occasional jogger, rollerblader, or strolling couple invading the privacy they publicly claimed as their own. Nick studied her eyes intently, dark rounded marbles of obsidian so bright, so black, that instead of letting you penetrate them and see inside, they merely reflected your own image. Knowing full well he was staring too long into her eyes, Nick reveled in the voyeurism, forcing the New Yorker Anna to say something.

"You're staring."

"I'm enjoying the view."

"It is nice, isn't it?" she teased.

"I'm sure it gets even better."

There was a moment there. Their heads had been, ever so subconsciously, leaning in toward each other. Anna's breathing had become slow and expectant. Her lips were parted just barely, as if she were about to whisper the letter O—or to be kissed. Half closed, her eyelids primed themselves for the visualization of the actualization of a kiss.

Nick's body was tense and ready, too—but no kiss. Gracefully, he let the moment pass.

Anna, never one to be caught at a disadvantage, recoiled slightly, managing spin control in the only way that she could. "You didn't kiss me."

"Pardon?" That was another unexpected, point-blank statement from Anna.

"There was a moment there . . . and you didn't kiss me."

"You're right. There was a moment there," Nick quietly agreed. "Why? Did you want me to kiss you?"

"Perhaps" was her coy response.

*I've got her,* thought Nick confidently, silently celebrating his victory.

"But yet you did not," she continued, intrigued. Anna did not want to ask the next, most obvious question, having put herself out there this far. So Nick took the liberty of answering it for her.

"Sometimes you have to let a moment pass you by."

He did not need to say any more—and he didn't. Pleased with his answer, Anna snuggled up against Nick, placing her lovely head against his solid chest. As a crescent moon cast down its light upon the reflecting waters of San Diego Harbor, Nick and Anna watched the waves bob and dance themselves throughout eternity.

## MARRIAGE MINDED
### *One man's quest to get married in a year*
### *by Anonymous*

Restraint. For us feeble men, this is not a quality that comes easy. When you have spent your entire life being taught, molded, and instructed to be the initiator, the aggressor, the breadwinner, how do you explain restraint to a man?

Sometimes, we men move too fast. No, I'm not talking about those of us who move at the speed of a Tomahawk cruise missile to get all up under a woman's skirt. I'm talking about "fast" socially, in the way we socialize with women. I mean, yes, there may always be that latent sexual urge for women who attract us (friends and otherwise, I might add), but I'm talking about the way we approach the whole dating/mating process. Granted, with my quest to get married in a year, I am not the best example of day-to-day restraint. But a recent experience showed me the value of such a quality, the value of patience and restraint.

I recently had a date with an attractive, charming woman in an all-too-romantic, makeout-ready environment. I'm talking about a nearly empty park, at night, by the water, just the two of us talking for hours on a park bench. I couldn't have picked a better location had I written it myself.

So we're talking, enjoying each other and everything, when there is a moment. Guys know what I'm talking about. That is the moment when you must decide to fight your traditional, if not biological, male upbringing to pursue the woman, or use your dating socialization to "play it cool." Do I kiss her and conquer, or tease her and make her wait?

Eight times out of ten, guys will take the first option, to plunge right in and conquer, usually en route to something stimulating like good, hot sex. That, my friends, is not what I, nor this column, is about. In that moment with my lady friend, I choose the latter option, if for no other reason than to build up anticipation for the first time we actually *do* kiss.

Sometimes it's just better to let a moment pass you by. Life is made up of many, many moments, special and otherwise. Although carpe diem is a valuable philosophy to uphold, when it comes to love, those moments in time that we miss will replicate themselves if they are truly meant to be. If this woman is to be the one who will make me quit this column, then there will be more moments in the future when the time will be right to kiss her. One thing my zealous brethren must remember is that there are no easy paths in life, or in the course of wooing a good woman. If you want a good *woman*, and not just some overgrown girl with morning breath who you find in your bed the next day and have no idea how she got there (or why she's *still* there), then you must exercise a trait that flouts all that we have been trained to become as Y-chromosomes in this society. It may be a struggle at first to wrap your mind around this thinking. But remember, the end goal, a wife, will make all that restraint worthwhile.

When it comes to love, remember this one truism: There are no shortcuts to win that heart most worth winning.

# 5

**N**ICK WAS ALMOST paralyzed with shock. The mailbags were so gray and big. All of it was mail. All of it was for him.

As Craig gleefully began to wade through one of the three bags in the living room, Nick gingerly opened up a letter. "Dear Anonymous, I think it's wonderful that a man is so commitment oriented these days. Good luck to you on your search. All the best, Candice."

Nick looked up at Craig. "That's sweet."

Craig opened up a small, padded envelope. With a pencil, he extracted a pair of purple, grape-scented panties. Craig took a sniff. "So are these. Edible."

Rolling his eyes while Craig guffawed his head off, Nick continued swimming. "What did your editor say when the mailbags came?"

"He cursed several times and then went back to making my job miserable." Craig beamed broadly. "The little fucker didn't know what to think. Two months, kid, and his job is *mine*."

"Dear Anonymous," read Nick from another letter.

Hey there. I'm a 5'8", 135-pound half-white, half-Latina redhead from Chula Vista. I'm 28 years old with a finance degree from the University of San Diego and a master's in business administration from UC–San Diego. I don't smoke, don't drink, have no kids, and have never been married. I am looking for a guy like you: old-fashioned, into commitment, and who values the institution of marriage. We are looking for the same things. My number is below. Call me—if you dare meet your soulmate.

"That one doesn't sound half bad," commented Craig.

Wordlessly, Nick showed him the picture that came along with it. The photo boasted a naked, bronzed female, flat on her back, legs over her head, with her butt and vagina for all the world to admire.

Amazed, Craig said, "I did not know a coochie could do that."

Big sigh from Nick. "I have my work cut out for me."

---

## "MAYA T. PATTERSON."

"My-T Love."

Nick's 4Runner screamed up I-5 toward LA near the beach resort town of Oceanside. As far as Monday mornings went, this one was beautiful, the sun glistening off the Pacific to his left causing Nick to wear darkly tinted shades. He was on his way to work, making his weekly trip up to LA. At seven o'clock, Maya T. was already at work.

A hint of surprise caught her voice. "Hey, Nick! What's up?"

"You." Nick had missed her Texas accent. "Haven't heard from you in a grip, stranger."

"Yeah, I'm sorry about that, Nick. I've been so busy with the campaign and everything. We're comin' down the home stretch, ya know." She sounded so grown-up. Nick had known her since he was in college, and to see Maya T. blossoming and handling things over the past few years was a beautiful sight. Maya T. was the campaign manager for the mayor of San Francisco, up for reelection. "November's just two and a half months away."

On his own countdown, Nick said, "Don't I know it."

"I'm sorry I haven't called since you moved. It's just been mad hectic around here." Her voice sounded rushed and impatient. "Had you not called so early, you would've missed me for the day."

"Busy, busy woman. I like that." Nick's mom had always told him to date someone who was busier than he was, so she wouldn't be clingy and overdependent. "Just don't get too busy for your friends."

Maya T. sucked her teeth. "Nick . . . I could never be too busy for you."

Nick glowed internally. What he and Maya T. had could best be described as an advanced friendship. Expanding their original penpal-ship via letters and the Internet, Nick and Maya T. had enjoyed a "friendship with privileges," with him coming out to San Francisco about every other time after she would come out to see him in Chicago. Now that he was on the West Coast, he hoped that perhaps their "friendship with privileges" might be extended into something more permanent. "I'm gonna hold you to that. I'm coming to see you."

"When?" her voice perked.

"If I can get a cheap seven-day-advance ticket, next weekend."

"Ooo," she cooed. "Are you bringing the—"

"Yes."

"And the—"

"Of course."

Nick could almost see her lips curl up appreciatively. Their last rendezvous was so legendary, it had nearly gotten her evicted. "I gotta go, Nick. But definitely, *definitely* bring your sexy tail up here and han'le up. Ya hear?"

Nick grinned. He heard.

---

**BLACKDRAFT WAS A** UPN-network show produced by Warner Bros. and, hence, filmed on the WB lot. Nestled on the other side of a giant hill from LA in The (San Fernando) Valley, the home of the WB campus was in Burbank, with sprawling studios on the north side of a man-made creek known as the Los Angeles River. Nick parked in the extras lot on the south side of the river, made his way across Forest Lawn Drive, and entered the movie studio lot, past security. Although it was just background work, it blew his mind that he was here, ready to go to a movie set, about to be a part of a major-network program that would be seen all over the country this fall. Had anyone asked him four years ago if he could ever have seen himself in this position, Nick would've laughed in their face.

As Nick ambled down the private streets on the WB lot, he reflected on his last call home. Mom was going into surgery that afternoon at two-fifteen. Doctors were going to try and stop the spread of the tumor. Nick had stopped Harrison right there; he didn't want or need any more details. Ever since that fateful night of his birthday, Nick had begun coming to grips with the idea that the only parent he had known was going to die on him. Until someone could tell him affirmatively that she had been cured somehow of a disease that kills hundreds of thousands of women a year, Nick would not entertain false hope for a second.

Nick checked in with the Second Assistant Director before grazing by the craft service table for breakfast. He was early. Now no longer a neophyte to a set, Nick knew to expect free meals when working, one of the few perks of being the lowest on the entertainment-industry food chain. He made himself a breakfast of donuts and Rice Krispies and settled into a folding chair in the holding area for extras.

*Blackdraft* was UPN's great black hope. The network was trying to cash in on the recent spate of cable minority dramas, and was hyping this predominantly black drama, the only one of its kind on network TV, to kingdom come. Of course if the show failed, it would be because it was a black show, and appealed to too narrow an audience that did not include Iowa corn farmers with Nielsen boxes. But if it succeeded, it would be because of the foresight of the studio execs. Little to no credit would go to the writers or the actors, or simply to the fact that a black drama's time on network prime-time TV had more than already come.

Because of the hype, Nick noticed that this set was a tad more stressed than others. The ADs, the inevitable carriers of stress and tension from the director, were professional and cordial but still ridiculously authoritarian. Last time he had been on set, their annoyed, frantic, disgusted, and widely ridiculed refrain of "Be quiet!" to the background talent had been chanted more times than a hooker did Hail Marys after confession. With only a thirteen-episode order to start instead of the usual twenty-two, everyone involved realized that they had to perform well—and perform soon.

As the other extras filed in, Nick examined the background talent closely. The set they were to be working on today was the hospital set, where there was an assortment of men and women to act as hospital staff and passersby. As usual, the women were *foine*. A chocolate sister so dark and so delicious she put the Crunch in Nestlé strutted through Nick's vantage point, when his unannounced fashion show was interrup—

"Whassup, black!" A reddish-colored brotha with long brown dreads plopped down in the chair next to him. Like Nick, he was dressed in black shoes, white socks, navy-blue pants, and a white t-shirt—another firefighter extra. He thrust his energetic hand at him so quickly, Nick nearly lost a donut.

Recovering, Nick dapped him up cautiously. "Whassup now."

"Ayinde, brotha."

"Nick."

"You worked this set before?"

"*Blackdraft*? Yeah. I'm a regular extra."

"Looks like you savin' lives, too, B!" Ayinde grinned boisterously. Nick had heard that accent before. "Where you from, kid?"

"Brooklyn, baby! Bed-Stuy 'til I die, black!"

Nodding sagely, Nick approved. "I used to live in Crown Heights."

"Stop lyin'! My auntie stays out on President Street!"

"So did I."

"Small freakin' world, B!" Ayinde dapped him up again. "So what's your angle, black?"

"I don't follow."

"What's your hustle? What else are you into? Nobody's an extra just to be an extra. Unless they have some real low self-esteem or no kinda ambition, 'na mean?"

"I feel you," nodded Nick.

"Most of us got three or four different hustles. What's yours?"

"Well, I used to be a credit analyst for a couple of different banks, but now I do some freelance writing when I'm not acting. I just moved out here from Chicago."

"Yeah, I heard that. I've been out here for six months. Most people who do extra work have just moved out here from somewhere, or they use it to fill in the gaps between real gigs," Ayinde explained. "That's why I'm here."

Most Hollywood extras had aspirations far beyond their current status, and were quick to point out that Brad Pitt and Eriq LaSalle had both started out as extras.

"So what're you into?" asked Nick. "What's your hustle?"

A sheepish grin dissipated into a secret-sharing smile. Ayinde leaned in conspiratorially close. "Porno."

Nick's eyes widened. "Porno?"

Offering a shit-eating grin that only a man could give, Ayinde affirmed with, "*Porno.* I have a day job with this porno company called Straddle Me Entertainment. It's off the hook, son."

Nick could barely contain his laughter. "Straddle Me Entertainment?"

" 'From the people who brought you *Cum Close* and *Cum Closer.*' " smiled Ayinde brightly, reciting his company's tagline.

"Just what the hell do you do for them?" Nick took a moment. "Are you . . . uh . . . *acting*?"

Ayinde guffawed at the notion, which quickly brought him the visual ire of the Second AD, who was checking in more extras. Quieting down, he said, "Naw, B, naw. I'm not talent. But I sure have seen some, word is bond!" Reveling in the memory, he almost laughed. "I just do some clerical work in the production office, that's all."

Enjoying a grin of his own, Nick said, "But the fringe benefits . . ."

". . . are off the meter," Ayinde finished. "They have some parties that will blow your mind!"

"Is that all?" funned Nick.

The two of them laughed and dapped up. "Black, if only you *knew* . . ."

Ayinde stopped talking long enough to observe a pretty, café au lait lightskin sista with more butt than a little bit sit down on the opposite side of holding. "Dang, that booty is Mos Def!"

"Huh?"

"You know, Mos Def, the rapper? The song 'Ms. Fatbooty'?" he elaborated. " 'Had so much booty you could see it from the front!' "

Nick laughed. "No doubt, man. No doubt." He had to give the man dap on that one. Right then and there, their unholy alliance was made.

⁓

**CRAIG MADE HIS** way into the *Reader* offices around ten o'clock. He should have been there by nine, but, out of blatant disrespect to his *Tiger Beat*–aged boss, he showed up anytime he damn well felt like it. Armed with a cup of piping-hot Starbucks, Craig crashed into his cubicle, getting ready for another long day of work. Time to check the email.

What the . . . His box had 126 messages! Was this a virus of some kind that kept spamming him email or something? The first message was from his wife, sent shortly after she had gotten to work. The second advertised hot teenage sluts in convents. Tasty. And then 124 had something or other to do with responses to Anonymous' column. He never thought this many people would respond to his email address at the end of the column.

Unbelievable.

With a wry, smug smile, Craig picked up the phone. It was time to get Nick his very own *Reader* email address.

**IT HAD BEEN** a long day. Pushing fifteen hours, Nick struggled to stay attentive while standing on his mark. He could swear that they had been shooting the same scene for two *hours* now. Every possible angle for the scene had been covered with multiple takes, including a few Nick never even knew existed. The star, a preternaturally unflappable, dapper brotha of thirty-two named Wendal Love, was impatient and tired. His younger costar, Wesley Harper, kept flubbing his lines or otherwise messing up his scene. It was obvious to more people than Nick that this was Wesley's first prime-time TV series as a regular. Perhaps the pressure from the studio and production staff had somehow trickled down to the actor.

As Nick zoned out the scene's rehearsal for the umpteenth time, he checked his cell phone, whose ringer was turned off. Messages. Both of them from Anna. Listening to the messages, Nick's smug smile returned. She did not want them to "let another moment pass them by."

Ayinde ambled over to Nick's mark, cheesing. "Squarin' your plans for tonight, B?"

"More like tomorrow," whispered Nick, folding the cell phone and pocketing it. "How many more times do we have to do this dang scene?"

"Just think of the overtime, black."

"*You* think of the overtime. You're union—overtime for you is worth your time. I'm still messing with Kibbles and Bits."

"You gotten a voucher yet?"

"Not yet."

"Keep comin' back and doin' a good job, you'll get a voucher. While you at it, never hurts to snuggle up next to the ADs," Ayinde suggested. "Joke with them, call them by their first name, get them to remember you. And always leave a headshot with one of them."

Nick nodded, taking it all in. "They should call you Background Yoda."

"Lock it up now! Picture's up!" screamed the AD.

Retreating to his mark, Ayinde grinned, "Just don't call me Late for Dinner!"

---

**THIS TIME, THEY** did not let the moment pass them by. Nick lay in Anna's arms, the result of a passion-filled hour of kissing, petting, grinding, and moaning. They had not had sex but had come damn close. Nick was convinced that he could not find his wife by having sex with her instead of making love to her. Both of them were fully clothed, save Anna's black Victoria's Secret bra, which was scattered somewhere on her living room carpet. And she held him, a touching little maneuver that Nick could fully appreciate.

Anna's was a nice, modest townhouse in a suburb filled with nice to very nice homes. Everything in her house belied her middle-class background and sensibilities, from a bookcase full of literature to her diploma from SUNY-Purchase sitting on the fireplace mantelpiece. Little motivational computer printouts lived in some of the oddest places. A printout on the refrigerator would proclaim "Guest Starring JOANNA WHITLEY," while the printout on the bedroom closet announced a "Special Appearance by JOANNA WHITLEY," and the printout on the door to the bathroom read "Introducing JOANNA WHITLEY." All in all, hers was a well-maintained, neatly organized, amply decorated piece of buppie-hood.

After working background on the set of *ER* that day as a med student and miraculously getting released early, Nick had called Anna up to see what she was doing. She had been taking it easy, having just returned from a three-day shoot in Miami for a music video. Her rent had been paid for the next month, and she was simply lounging. He wanted to bury his pain in her warm, affectionate arms.

News had come to him in the form of a message on his cell phone while cameras had been rolling. Despite hours of surgery that had stretched into late last night, little progress had been made. The operation had failed. The tumor was too enlarged at this point to remove and their efforts to stop its spread had been minimal at best. Yep, it was official: As much as he would like to deny it, Mom was still scheduled to die.

He had needed someone, anyone, a woman; a woman who was not his mother so he could cry on her bosom about his mother. After he had received that message in between shots, nothing on the set had mattered. The angles, the camera directions, the harried ADs trying to place and move him had all meant nothing. Nick had zombied his way through the last few scenes and had bolted from the set as quickly as his weakened legs could carry him.

Nick had cried all the way down to San Juan Capistrano.

And here he was now, wrapped up in the arms of a woman he barely knew, using her as a surrogate for a substantive relationship. She had no idea why Nick's face had been so crushed, its expression involuntarily betraying an inner sadness her warm greeting simply could not alleviate. But she had accepted his quiet, monotone self into her arms. They had begun kissing with a ferocity and familiarity they had never shared before. He had melted into her open arms and she had graciously, generously accepted him.

Although on her home court, Anna still did not feel entirely at ease. She had her own demons to hide. The emotional nature of this evening had almost allowed the carefully controlled Joanna Whitley to allow those demons to have wings. It was far too soon for all that, she decided. It was far too soon.

Nick reached for her. She allowed it. Their tongues merged inside the on-ramp to her soul. Bodies shifted weight, shifted gears. Appendages grew, hardened, slickened, made their presences known. They rolled off the couch onto the floor to better accommodate her body on his. His hands found their way under her blouse once more. Nick enjoyed the tactile sensation of the hardness of her nipples. Her lower regions throbbed and radiated from the warmth of his. Before she knew it, her blouse was open, her ebony bosom dangling, the hardened, erect raisins that were nipples sliding in and out of his mouth. Everything about him, this moment, this feeling, looked so right, felt so natural, seemed so perfect. . . .

"Hold on." Too perfect.

Nick reluctantly released the nipple from his teeth. "What's wrong?"

"We need to stop. I need to stop."

"Don't worry, Anna. I'm not going to make love to you," Nick assured her, nuzzling back up to her breast.

Anna recoiled. "It's not that at all. I just . . . I just can't."

Nick straightened, making eye contact with her, watching her retreat to the couch. Her blouse had somehow buttoned itself back up. Feeling even more vulnerable than he was from his prone position on the floor, Nick feebly asked, "What's the matter?"

Seemingly withdrawn into a different dimension, Anna said, "It's not you, it's me."

"That's a cliché, Anna."

"It's the truth." She actually sounded genuine.

Ditching his problems for a moment, Nick slid onto the couch next to her. As her body reacted with a subtle shift to his movement, Nick was careful not to touch her. Not now, not yet. He wanted to know why. "Talk to me. Please."

It was as if her spirit had burrowed away, packed up, and gone into hibernation for the winter. "It's hard for me to explain."

"Try." Nick would not let up. He was concerned. "For me."

"I . . . I just have a hard time opening up to people sometimes."

"You were 'opening up' just fine to me a minute ago."

"It's hard for me to trust."

"Is this because of your ex-boyfriend?"

"No. That was six months ago."

"Then what is all this about?" Nick earnestly sought her avoiding eyes. They were making such progress in their conversations, their interactions, in their romance. Why was she bringing all of it to a screeching halt?

Gingerly, she gave him her eyes. "I . . . I . . . I don't want to talk about it."

"**WOO-WOO, WOO-WOO! RED** flag! Red flag!" howled Malloy from New York.

Nick had to take the phone away from his ear to avoid going deaf. Seemingly in better spirits, his boy was back to his old, rambunctious self. "That's what I thought, too."

"Yo, this chick got *issues, son!*" he proclaimed. Under a pleasant, summer-night breeze that merely remixed the cocktail of heat and humidity in the air, Mal sat on the stoop of the brownstone he and his wife owned in Brooklyn, cordless phone in hand. "I say go Hot Boys on her ass and 'drop her like she's hot'!"

Stretching out on Khalilah's couch, Nick soaked up his counsel. *SportsCenter* relayed the in-progress baseball scores to Nick's oblivious demeanor. "But she's the one decent candidate I've met since I've been out here."

"Candidate for what? This broad running for office?" snorted Mal. Nick had already decided once and for all to keep his wifehunt secret from his best friend. "One thing there is plenty of in this world is air and pussy. You don't need to stress over either one."

"C'mon, Mal. You know I ain't like that. While I know my last year or so has been kinda freewheeling since I was with Queen, I want something of substance now, you know?"

"Freewheelin'? Nigga, please!" Mal cracked up. "Dude, there is not an ounce of player in you. Not an ounce, not a speck, not a *drop.*"

"And who's the married one?"

Mal bristled. "They don't make me no more, dawg. I was *born* a playa. Marriage only changes the game, it don't stop the game."

"You cheatin' on Mia?"

"Bitch, don't make me reach out and touch someone," Malloy threatened. "Hell naw. How that gonna look, me cheating on my wife? All I'm sayin' is I got more game *married* than you have *single.* I *still* got interns at work throwin' they panties at me."

The roll of Nick's eyes was prodigious. "Whatever, dude. Whatever."

"But back to this chick with emotional and intimacy problems," refocused Mal.

Nick sighed. "I won't even lie. Sometimes I envy what you have."

"As a connoisseur of fine women, I am a firm believer that no matter what one is into, he should make time in his life for creatures that are soft, rounded, and pleasant-smelling. Girls are fun. This by no means is to be interpreted as 'make her your girlfriend.' You must take my advice as a man under the age of thirty who has an exclusive relationship," Mal advised. "Deal with this chick, but deal with others. Don't put all your sperm in one ho."

"What!"

"Aw'ight, aw'ight. Don't put all your eggs in one basket," Mal amended.

Despite considering the source, Nick knew he was right.

---

THE WEEK WOUND down quickly. Nick continued to work on *Blackdraft* for a couple of days before heading down to San Diego late Friday night. He would have stayed up in LA for the weekend, especially considering Khalilah was still in Africa, but that was contingent upon Anna acting right, which she was not. She had flaked out on a date with him and hadn't returned a phone call from three days ago. A little dismayed at her shadiness, Nick turned down an invitation from Ayinde for one of his porno parties and made the trip back home to San Diego.

There was something refreshing about coming back to his house up the hill from Ocean Beach. Nick derived an indescribably immense amount of pleasure walking into his house in the relative calm of San Diego. LA had such a busier, faster pace than SD that Nick reveled in the 180-degree change in attitude he experienced when I-5 entered San Diego County.

On Saturday, after a quick canvass of his married or otherwise occupied friends, Nick struck out for San Diego's best-kept secret—the swap meet. A weekend staple for God knows how long, Kobey's Swap Meet in the San Diego Sports Arena parking lot always packed 'em in on weekend mornings. Anxious for the latest mix tape and a new pair of cheap sunglasses, Nick found himself in the middle of the bargain-hunting throng, in the shadow of the dullest, ugliest stadium he had ever seen. A mere dollar had gained his entrance, and nearly every tented vendor maintained his interest.

It was at the African bead and oils tent that he saw her. Mal's playeristic advice from earlier in the week had repeated in his head like a bad refrain from a Britney Spears song. This woman was young, no older than twenty-five, Nick imagined, with grapefruit-sized breasts that fought against her tightly packed, floral-accented sundress. Her skin was swathed in a pretty color of brown so rich and dark, she was one ninety-five-degree day away from being truly black. Long, obviously weaved hair was a few shades darker and straightened, framing the sides of her pretty but not spectacular-looking face. The pleasant protrusion from her backside put the "bum" in Bonita Applebum. She had to put him on.

Rifling through the stack of fake Gucci sunglasses, she did not notice Nick sidle up next to her. Not a name-brand guy anyway, Nick dug in the same box of sunglasses as she did. He offered a genial smile. "How you doin'?"

"Fine," she replied, with the hint of a smile.

How he hadn't noticed her friend, who hovered just behind her, Nick would never know. "Kisha! Whatchu takin' so long fo'?"

"Hol' on, trick. I'm lookin' fo' somethin'." Both their accents were ghetto fabulous. Normally this might be enough to deter Nick, yet he decided to forge ahead. Shame on him for even contemplating stereotyping the young lady just from the way she talked. There might be some substance to her—might. Either way, he thought he would take a page from Mal's playbook: different styles for different types of women.

"What's your name, shorty?"

This time, she gave him more of her attention. "Kisha."

"Nick." He fought his home training to shake her hand. Didn't want to come off too bougie or sophisticated in case he truly was dealing with a ghetto superstar. "Y'all headed to the beach today?"

"Why you ax?" she questioned.

"I don't know. It's hot, I'm new to San Diego . . . I don't know what y'all do to kick it out here on weekends. Just go to the beach, right?"

She giggled. "Yeah, you new. Man, white people go to the beach. Do I look white to you?"

*You look like you should be melted and poured all over my body,* Nick internally salivated. "So what're y'all 'bout to get into?"

"Barbecue. We finna get our grub on at dis barbecue at Balboa Park."

"Is it a family thing?" asked Nick. He wanted to go, but he didn't want to intrude.

"Naw, my church is throwing it," she said, attention returning to the sunglasses. "But there'll be music and stuff there."

"Kisha!" screamed her impatient, ghetto-volumed little friend. "Come *on*!"

"Sounds like fun," said Nick, simply to say something.

Attention still diverted, she said to him, "You should come."

*Don't have to ask me twice.* "Aw'ight, then, shorty. I'll follow y'all out."

Surfacing from the box with a pair of gaudy gold-colored mirrored faux Guccis, Kisha modeled them for the vendor and Nick before paying for them. "Cool."

"Kisha!"

**"YOU CAN'T SAY** that I'm not equal opportunity," opined Nick over dinner. Carlton and Nick debriefed at Seau's again, their background lit up by a multitude of TVs and multimedia.

Nick's pseudo-date had gone shockingly awry. The barbecue had become a ghettofest of epic proportions. Everyone had been behaving themselves for the most part—early on. A bewitching brew of beef, pork, and hot dogs had accented the air. Kisha and Nick had flirted famously while partnering up against her cousins to play spades. Until her ex had showed up.

"So you're tellin' me that nigga was wavin' a gun around?" inquired Carlton, astonished.

"*And* he was drunk."

"Beautiful."

"Then he tried to take a swing at me with the pistol."

"Like he was trying to pistol-whip you?"

"Exactly," Nick affirmed. "I ducked, he missed, and he fell down ass first onto the huge tray of potato salad."

"Well, damn. Party over, then. Cain't have no picnic without the potato salad. So what happened to Kisha?"

"Fuck if I know! Any woman with baggage like that does *not* need to be on my team." Nick drank in a long swig of pink lemonade.

Carlton laughed as Nick chopped and sliced at his spicy Cajun chicken breasts voraciously. While the episode did sound funny on one level, it disgusted Nick on an entirely other one. *Cardinal Rule to Dating No. 8:* **Just say no to the ghetto.** Ghetto Woman had been an utter waste of time. Although he would have tried to mess around with her back in his younger, more naive, less commitment-oriented days, Nick now did not have time to waste. It was almost September.

The local news played on the centerpiece Jumbotron screen facing them. Carlton tapped Nick excitedly, trying to steer his attention away from his food.

"Check it out, playboy! This is a piece I did an hour ago from the Padres game, right after it got done. Check me out."

Nick stared at the TV version of Carlton—smooth, professional, and geared up in a nice, light Ralph Lauren suit—looking nothing like the tank-topped, khaki-shorted individual seated across from him now. C-Town chatted easily, glibly almost, with Padres institution Tony Gwynn, posing questions, nodding his interest to Gwynn's responses, bantering lightly with him. As Carlton grinned his achievement at the big screen, Nick cut away from the screen to watch the eyes of his friend, then back to the screen, transfixed. He really was doing it. Carlton was every bit a sports reporter.

An inner envy that Nick could barely explain grew with every bite he took. His friend had made the leap of faith from the practical to his passion. Successfully. Just what the hell was *Nick* doing? Extra work? He was proud of his friend yet envied his success. It was time for Nick to pull off the warm-ups and get into the game.

**NICK SAT IN** Shelby's office Monday morning, the picture of career determination. As he patiently waited for Shelby to cut the umbilical cord from her phone and her ear, Nick formulated an aggressive attack plan in his mind. Although he did not want to alienate his only professional link to the Industry, Nick also was extremely cognizant of the fact that he did not move out to California to make somebody's background cross.

The second Shelby was off the phone, Nick said firmly, not rudely, "This background shit has got to stop."

"I agree." She was not shocked or offended at all—complete agreement.

"How are we going to stop it?"

"I have an audition for you."

Nick breathed. "Thank God."

"Don't consider this the end-all, be-all, though, Nick," Shelby warned. "There are ninety thousand unemployed SAG actors in this town. Not to say that you aren't special, because you are, but you still have to put food on the table. If you have to do some extra work to do that, then so be it."

"I got a check for $55.18 on Saturday for one day's work. If that's gonna put food on the table, then I'm on Slim-Fast."

"Your audition," said Shelby, blithely changing gears, "is tomorrow at eleven in Hollywood. Here's the address."

Shelby pushed a slip of paper at him, allowing him to scrutinize the address. "The project," she continued, "is an independent-film spoof of the slasher-pic spoof *Scary Movie*."

A spoof of a spoof. *There's Oscar material,* Nick thought. "And the role?"

"A dayplayer role . . . One day, maybe two days tops. Drug Dealer #2."

Nick almost choked on his pride. *"Drug Dealer #2?"* There was more than one of them?

Shelby snatched a page off her fax machine and read the description that accompanied his lines, called sides. " 'Works in conjunction with Drug Dealer #1 and Drug Dealer #3 to sell weed to the slasher, in hopes of getting him too high to kill people. Slasher ends up helping them move product, hilarity ensues. Broad, physical comedy.' "

*Macbeth, Macbeth . . .* Hand out to receive his lines, Nick swallowed his self-respect. "My sides, please?"

**NICK WAS EARLY.** About a half hour early out of sheer nervousness, Nick sat in the waiting area for auditionees out in the hall. The audition was being held at the production offices of a small production company Nick had never heard of and was sure never to hear from again.

Certain he had overprepared, Nick uselessly studied the lines before him one more time. He had three lines, none of them funny, one of them downright coonish, which challenged his integrity as a black man. He was torn between having a shred of dignity and not getting the part, or slapping on the proverbial blackface and putting on a show. Nick took little solace in the fact that multimillion-dollar film star and fellow alumnus Samuel L. Jackson had once played a pimp and a crackhead on film. When you gotta eat, you gotta eat.

Surveying the competition, he recognized that at least he had come dressed for the audition. First of all, Nick wore no black, red, or white—colors that show up bad on camera, according to Shelby. That eliminated two of the brothas waiting with him. Second, Nick looked the part. Ridiculously outfitted with a bandanna, Timberland boots, oversized jeans, with black Calvin Klein underwear waistband protruding above the waistline, and a gaudy fake gold chain, Nick looked the part of a Caucasian casting director's drug dealer fantasy. So that eliminated two others in the waiting area with their collared shirts and their shiny black dress shoes. They were too damn pretty to be drug dealers. So Nick was up against just one other dude, a brotha with jeans sagging so far, they nearly slipped right off his hips when he stood up. *Drug Dealer #2 is* mine!

The casting assistant poked her head out of the door. "Next up is Nick."

Nick bounced up, affected his most (pathetic) B-boy swagger, and sauntered into the audition room. Thanks to the cloud of his false drug dealer bravado, he could not hear the snickers behind him.

"I DIDN'T GET Drug Dealer #2."

Nick could almost hear Anna's eyes rolling on the other end. "I'm sure you're crushed."

"Quite. But not as much as I was when you stood me up yesterday," Nick stated pointedly.

"I didn't mean to," Anna protested lightly. "Something came up."

"We had a *date*, Anna," Nick reminded her.

"It was an audition."

"Coulda called a brotha."

"You're right."

The conversation lapsed into an awkward lull. As could be expected, Nick busted them right out of it. "Are you avoiding me?"

The bluntness of the truth can cut through bullshit like a hollow-point bullet. "Huh?"

"Are you avoiding me? I haven't seen you since I came over last week," Nick pointed out. "You've canceled one date, stood me up on another . . . I just get the distinct impression that you're avoiding me."

Anna was silent. Anything on her part could only be an indictment of her guiltiness. That's because she was as guilty as O.J.

"I really like you, Anna. I thought we were making progress, getting to know each other, getting to like each other. And all of a sudden, you just put on the brakes. What's goin' on?"

"I . . ." Her voice trailed off, the disappointment in herself evident. She settled with "I like you, too, Nick."

"What can I do, Anna?" asked Nick, his eyes scanning the darkened horizon of the Pacific as his car flew down I-5 South. He was approaching San Juan Capistrano and wanted to stop by—but not for bullshit. "What can I do to let you like me more?"

Reticence tainted every word, impugned her every syllable. "Just give me some time, Nick. I'll come around. Just give me some time."

As Nick's 4Runner passed the last exit for San Juan Capistrano—Anna's exit—Nick reluctantly accepted her answer. He had no choice. But with his mother ailing in a bed at Harborview Medical in Seattle, time was a luxury he simply did not have.

**HIS FLIGHT FROM** San Diego had taken all of an hour and fifteen minutes, if that. Nick had no idea because he was knocked out. A week at the dizzying pace of LA's entertainment community could do that to you.

As Nick deplaned in San Francisco International, he saw the woman who had been his closest friend for almost a decade. Maya T. Patterson seemed an ethereal, Nubian mirage in a desert of Asian and whiteness. She stood a striking five-eleven in her flat brown sandals, with her cute white shorts and matching ribbed V-neck t-shirt contrasting with her rich, dark brown, Colombian-coffee-beans-before-they-meet-the-grinder skin. Looking every bit the professional black woman, with her cute, retro-twenties Billie Holiday wavy hair and arched eyebrows, Maya T. greeted him with a sophisticated, business-like air. Her hand was extended formally.

"Nice to see you again, sir."

They shook hands. "Likewise, Ms. Patterson."

"How was your flight?"

"Quick."

"And your landing?"

"Smooth." They stood there, face to face, restraining grins that would break them out of their fabricated moment. Nick would be the one to do it. "Permission to kiss you. Ma'am."

"Granted." Their mouths disappeared into a long, unapologetic search for loose fillings. When Nick finally let the woman come up for air, her familiar Texan accent surfaced, along with her smile. "On behalf of the mayor, the City of San Francisco welcomes you."

Nick gave her another peck. "Gotta love that Bay Area hospitality. Hope I didn't salt all your game here in the airport."

Maya T. scoffed, linking arms with him. With a mischievous gleam in her eye, she said, "Let's get outta here."

AS USUAL, THE weekend with Maya T. went by in a whirlwind. She took them by some of the haunts they favored whenever Nick was in town. They lazily rode bikes through Golden Gate Park, meandering their way down to the zoo and back along the Pacific Coast Highway before trekking back to Maya T.'s Outer Sunset home. After seeing a movie, the two wandered around the beautiful, upscale homes of the North Beach area, enjoying the view of the bay just as much as its residents. Continuing to stun Nick with her development as a woman, Maya T. dragged him along to Sonoma County one evening for a wine tasting. A nondrinker, Nick was happily surprised at how fun the somewhat bougie affair was. And to top it all off, they took a boat cruise around the bay from Fisherman's Wharf, almost a ritual every time Nick came into town.

With Maya T.'s long, charcoal frame ensconced in his, Nick leaned against a railing on the boat, his arms savoring her, keeping her, protecting the moment. A shimmering sun gleamed its way toward a dinner date beyond the Golden Gate Bridge and the horizon. Alcatraz pouted in the distance, an aging reminder of a once unique purpose long since gone. As he breathed in the bewitching brew of Calyx on her neck pulse points, Nick sighed, contentedly. What was to keep them from doing this forever?

"I'm still sore," she grinned, staring off into the tessellating pattern of the dancing waves.

Nick pulled her backside tighter against him. "Are you complaining?"

"Yeah. Obviously, I don't get it often enough."

This elicited a smile from Nick. "Well, maybe you need to come out and see me more often."

"With you in California now, that can be arranged." A warm glow took hold of her face as well.

Gently, without any innuendo or real purpose, outside of curiosity, Nick asked, "Do you ever think about marriage?"

He could feel her body shift like a fault line. Those same six words had been what had gotten him in trouble with another woman not even five years ago. Nick scrambled for damage control. "Not to me, silly. Just in general."

"Yeah, I do," she replied. "My parents have been together for more than twenty-seven years. Marriage means somethin' to me."

"Mmm. Me, too."

"When I get married, it's only gonna be once."

"True."

"He's gonna be my lover, my best friend, my everything. I am still young enough, and naive enough, to be able to believe that."

"There's nothing wrong with that," Nick whispered softly in her ear. God, she said all the right things. Could his search be over before it had really started?

"I take marriage so seriously that I know I couldn't possibly get married before thirty-five."

Nick turned rigid—and not sexually, either. The woman was only three years his junior, at twenty-six. "Why so long?"

"I'm a busy woman, Nick. You know I be out here han'lin' up," Maya T. asserted with a smile. "What have I been telling you these past few years is my goal in life?"

Nick rolled his eyes silently. She turned to face him, glowering playfully. "Say it," she ordered.

"Total and unequivocal worldwide domination," Nick recited reluctantly, in unison with her.

"Dat's right—worldwide domination, baby," she crowed, accent flowing freely. "It's time these fools out here started to recognize all that Maya Treasure Patterson has to offer! I'm gonna be runnin' thangs in a few years, Nick! I'm gonna be the head of the largest political consulting firm ever known to *wo*-man!"

"And you can't do that being married?" inquired Nick meekly. When Maya T. got started on what she was going to do and how she was going to do it, Nick stepped out of the way and watched her roll.

"Naw, Nick! I got moves to make, chile!" she declared. "I mean, how am I gonna be a good wife, a good *parent*, if I ain't never there? These next nine years or so, I'll have to be mobile, unattached, free to roam around the world, makin' things happen. That's why I don't have a man now. Don't have no time for one."

"So, basically, you just want to be an international player," Nick simplified.

"I didn't say all that, suga," she smiled. "All I mean is I have to be available to make moves now, while I'm young and unattached, and *then*, someday, when I'm able to provide for my family, I'll settle down. For me to be good at what I do, I have to be free. Know what I'm sayin'?"

Nick would not allow Maya T.'s dark eyes to pierce his mask of defeat. When Nick had been in his marriage-neva-hafta mode, Maya T.'s manifesto had been so wonderful, so welcoming, so convenient. Now, it was merely another disappointment to throw on the pyre of his love life. He still cared for her, deeply, but could see that she was on a far different timetable than he could afford. Nick surrendered a peaceable smile. "I know."

"I like what we have, Nick."

"Me, too."

"I mean, a friendship with privileges. It's really quite adult of us."

"Can you believe it?"

"I like it. I mean, we are friends first and foremost. I will always care for you in that way . . . and more."

With people a short distance away on the deck of the boat Maya T. slid a hand down to Nick's zipper, shielding it with her body. As she began to massage and stroke the region to stony life, she said, "But don't think I couldn't use more of this in the near future." Her hand found its way past the feeble guard of the zipper. She found warmth inside, in contrast to the cold of the boat on the bay at night. "I'll come down to visit you in San Diego when you least expect it. I like spending time with you. We play well together, Nick."

With his body readily agreeing to her sexually charged will, Nick acknowledged that they did play well together—they were just playing on different teams.

## MARRIAGE MINDED
*One man's quest to get married in a year*
by Anonymous

There are no instruction manuals for interpreting women. Likewise, there are no primers on how to conduct yourself as a man.

Being a man means acting as one part hero, two parts provider and conqueror, and one part mind reader. The hero plays role model for the family and for society. This only reinforces the demigod-man myth every man craves in order to thrive. The provider/conqueror role is well entrenched in our male-dominated society. The mind-reader part comes in mostly when we are dealing with women, for not only are men expected to be the aggressors, the initiators, but also we have to be able to read a situation (i.e.: a woman's mind) and be able to make smooth, suave adjustments to it.

So I ask the question, ladies of San Diego County: What the hell do you all want??? Recently, my wife search has taken a slight turn for the bizarre. I'm with a woman, a beautiful woman with whom I have great chemistry and interact extremely well, and with whom I enjoy spending time. When we start to make the natural progression to the physical level—not even sex yet—she balks. Stones me. This has happened on several occasions, sandwiched around her standing me up a few times. Then the clichés start spewing: "It's not you, it's me."

Ladies, I don't get it. A man is a perfect gentleman, an attraction is there, and then you *run* from it. And in case some of the cynical were wondering, no, I was not giving off the I-have-to-get-married-in-a-year vibe. I have actually been very indifferent. Funny how the more you act like you don't care about women, the more they are supposed to want you.

Explain this phenomenon to me, ladies. How is it you all jump on TV shows like Oprah and Sally Jessy Raphael, cry about how there are no good men—especially good *black* men—out there, and then go running around after all the bad ones? Then you all *end up* on shows like Jerry Springer and Jenny Jones, whining about how Derron cheated on you six times with your mother, your sister, your stepmother's play cousin Nay Nay, and the family dog.

It's sickening. All my life, women have passed over perfectly good men for players, the guys who end up hurting them. Good men, loving men, **marriage-minded** men are too often relegated to the role of the dreaded F-word—friend.

Let me tell you this: Friends get none. Once you are classified as a friend, you might as well be a prison inmate, without the possibility of parole. The longer you are in the Friendship Prison, the less of a chance of a pardon from the Governor. Death Row inmates have a better chance at an appeal than a male friend does. In short, seniority sucks.

So how do I get past this and find a loving, friendship-based relationship that will last "as long as we both shall live"? That is a good question. That is a question that confounds all of my various male roles—the hero, the protector, the conqueror, and the mind reader—all at the same time. So until there is an instruction manual on how to give women what they want, I will have to stay indifferent and aloof, yet somehow **Marriage Minded**.

# 6

**"R**OSTER CHECK."

Nick relaxed in a deck chair poolside with Craig. Craig shared a two-level stucco home on a hillside in Point Loma with his wife, Olinda. On a clear day, they could see all the way to the naval shipyard in the harbor. Today was a picture-perfect day, straight out of the San Diego Chamber of Commerce visitors' guide—temperature in the high seventies, low humidity, and a gentle breeze, occasionally washing over their half-naked, outstretched bodies. Olinda was off somewhere inside, absorbing the air-conditioning while reading an article she had to edit. The boys had their bonding time.

"Normal or expanded?"

"Expanded *is* normal."

Nick gazed heavenward, eyes wrapping around a wayward nimbus cloud. "Alright, fine. Maya T. Patterson, twenty-six, five-eleven, power forward."

"School?"

"Oh, right. San Francisco State. A veteran for Team Nick, Maya T. has shown remarkable instincts with the ball—"

"Ball*sss*," Craig laughed.

"Want me to do your roster check?" threatened Nick. "Olinda, five-three, twenty-seven, University of Chicago, point guard. *Lifetime, long-term contract as team captain.* Shut it up."

Craig held up his hands playfully in surrender, a gold band gleaming on his ring finger.

"A natural captain," Nick continued, "Maya T. seems to play for her own team. Will get in the game, but only in spurts. Not ready—or willing—to lead this team. But definitely has potential."

"Potential's good," Craig said, just to say something.

"Potential sucks," appraised Nick decidedly. "Not unless it's realized."

"Let's keep this update moving. Next!"

"Anna, twenty-seven, five-nine, SUNY-Purchase, small forward."

"Why a small forward?" Craig asked.

"She sure as hell ain't aggressive enough to be a power forward," Nick explained. "Anna is in my starting five, getting the majority of playing time right now. However, when the game is on the line, when she has the opportunity to prove her true star power, she chokes in the clutch. Pulls herself right out of the game. Coach is considering relegating her to the bench."

"Next."

"That's it."

"That's not a roster, that's your column's obituary!" Craig crowed. "What about Khalilah?"

"On the bench indefinitely. No, check that—not on the team at all."

"Serena?"

"Cut."

"Your ex-girlfriend Queen?" He sounded desperate.

Nick shook his head.

"Damn, Nick! What's the matter? You work in *the* most socially gratifying industry there is! Where are the hotties? Bring me hotties!"

"Don't you think I want to?" objected Nick. "No one wants to get married more than I do. Believe that. It's the middle of September. We have until next August. It's just gonna take me some time."

Craig lent a sympathetic yet not totally believing eye.

"It's gonna take me more time than I thought."

**"I NEED MORE** pressure!"

The message was relayed. "More pressure!"

"More water pressure!"

Savin' lives, savin' lives; Ayinde and Nick were, once again, savin' lives. The thirteenth floor of an office building was totally ablaze. Lieutenant James Donovan hollered once again behind him for more water pressure as he aimed the flow of water from the head of the hose. Six men outfitted in firemen's battle gear, complete with yellow hats, clung to the hose behind Donovan. On cue, a beam from the ceiling crashed to the floor, aflame.

The lieutenant's eyes flitted from side to side. Danger lurked within. If they didn't put out this fire right now, the whole building could go. The heart of the fire lay on the other side of a burning doorway. Shucking off danger, Lieutenant Donovan flung himself through the doorway. He tugged on the hose behind him for Jamrock to follow.

He did not. He would not. The burning doorway held Jamrock back.

Donovan glared back at his probationary officer. "Come on, Proby!"

Jamrock shook his head with fear.

"Come on, Rock!" Donovan's eyes seethed with anger.

Once again, utter fear.

"CUT!"

"God-dammit!" Wendal/Donovan hurled his helmet to the floor. Instantaneously, the flaming set extinguished itself. The hose was dropped, people started chattering, and some audacious grip pulled out a cigarette and began smoking on set. Wendal stalked over in the general direction of Wesley/Jamrock, the heat from his glare also smoking. The director, an aging white man with thinning hair, thankfully intervened, redirecting Wendal, and his glare, to a neutral corner.

But the director was not done. "Wesley . . . I'd like to speak with you in the hallway for a moment."

The Second AD came over to Nick and Ayinde, diplomatically stage-whispering, "You guys can go back to holding."

"Dang, he gonna catch it, B!" Ayinde observed brightly to Nick en route to the empty fire station set.

"Doesn't he get a stuntman for that?" Nick asked. "I mean that shot did look kinda dangerous."

"Shoot, Wendal did it. It's a controlled fire on a *firefighter* show. Your boy needs to knuckle up and just do that work."

"Controlled or not, fire is fire. If that was my ass, I'da had a stunt-man," scoffed Nick. He vamped a pose. "I'm too pretty to get burned."

Ayinde gave him a playful shove as Nick checked his cell phone. "Negro, please!"

The cell phone beeped. There had been a message left during the shooting of the last scene. Nick wandered away from holding to get a better signal.

"Hey, homie. It's Telly." The lovely Spanish trills of a West Side Chicago accent jarred him instantly into a smile. Chantel.

Chantel Mojica was the best woman he could never have. Half Latina and half black, Chantel defined sexiness and was easily accepted in both worlds, crossing them seamlessly and at will. A former coworker of his at Harris Bank, Chantel had gone from just another beautiful woman Nick lusted after to something of a big sister, always safeguarding his heart, especially when he was too stupid to do so.

"I need to ask you a favor, *ése*. I know it's only been a couple of months since you left Chicago, but I want you to come back for a visit. Call me. You know the number," she trilled invitingly.

Without hesitation, Nick called her back.

"Harris Bank, Chantel Mojica."

God, how he had missed the lyrical quality to her voice. "Whassup, Ms. Mojica."

"Hey, baby boy," she gushed warmly.

"Sounds like you've been sleeping," Nick observed.

"Naw. Just working."

"Same difference."

"Ordinarily, I'd smack you for that, *ése,* but I'm too happy to hear from you. How've you been?"

"I'm good," he lied. No sense in weighing down her mind with his life. "So what's goin' on?"

"It's time you came back to Chicago," Chantel announced decisively.

"So you miss me?" inquired Nick, with no small amount of innu-endo.

"I want you to come visit," she hedged, not giving in to the insinu-ation.

"You miss me," grinned Nick, as he briefly fantasized.

"Can you come next weekend? Not this one coming up, but the following weekend?"

Although excited, Nick was also suspicious. "Two months I've been gone and you can't live without me, Chantel? What's up?"

"Just consider this as doing me a favor, alright? I'll pay your airfare and everything," Chantel bargained.

"So that's what they're calling it these days? Doing someone a favor?"

"Shut it, homie," she snapped reflexively. Instantly, she softened. "I've gotta go. I'll call you this weekend with details. Make sure you bring a nice suit."

"Will do," whistled Nick, blessing his good fortune.

"Be a good boy," she sang.

"Or be good at it," he sang back.

" 'Bye, *ése*."

Nick caught his breath. What just happened here?

After filing away his cell phone, Nick nearly ran over Wesley.

"Oh shit! Sorry, man," Nick apologized. Wesley hadn't even noticed him. A glower was engraved on his young face. "You alright, man?"

Wesley Harper was a young cat. No more than twenty-five years old, Wesley was a five-year veteran of filmed entertainment. He had started off doing theater in his hometown of Cleveland before turning out for an open call for a Spike Lee movie that changed his life. Since then, Wesley's caramel skin, crème-de-cacao face, and curly bush of dark hair had graced the screen in seven feature films and a few commercials. And thanks to doing a film with a WB-network teen-drama star, Wesley's mug had been plastered in more than his fair share of black teen magazines. His was a star on the rise, with *Blackdraft* being his first role as a series regular on TV. Like everyone else, he, too, had a lot riding on this show. "Naw, man . . . Naw."

"What's wrong?" Nick was earnest. "Seriously."

He exhaled a torrent of frustration, studying the stage floor as if the answer lay within it.

"My bad," Nick excused himself, beginning to back away. "I know extras aren't supposed to talk to principals."

"No, it's alright." Wesley snorted. "What a divisive piece of shit."

"Agreed."

Wesley searched the floor, then himself. "Got a cigarette?"

"Don't smoke."

"Neither do I," Wesley mugged sheepishly.

"This job will drive you to it, huh?" offered Nick sympathetically.

"I used to smoke. Talk about your bad habits. But training for this one role got all that bullshit outta me."

"So what went on back there?" asked Nick gingerly. He didn't exactly have a right to know, but he was curious. "Looked like a job for a stuntman to me."

"For real!" Wesley chimed in. "I mean, the director wasn't even set up on the reverse side to catch my face, so what's even the use of risking me for that shot? German piece of commercial-directing shit."

"And then Wendal wants to punk you. That ain't right."

"Hell naw, it ain't. He ain't shit, though," Wesley dismissed. "He likes to throw his little TV-star persona around like he's somebody. I've worked with bigger guys than him. I ain't trippin'."

"Yo, I gotta hand it to you," Nick said, dapping him up, "I appreciated your work in *Angels of Percy* and *Player to Be Named Later.* I thought I was about to cry when you had to leave your father."

"Thanks a lot, man. That means a lot," Wesley said, genuinely appreciative. "But I have to hand it to my costar. He did all the work."

Nick leaned against a set door, enthralled. "What was it like working with Denzel?"

"Oh, man, he was totally professional. A very cool cat. Even cooler in person than on screen, if that's possible. And you shoulda seen the types of women tryin' to holla at *him* . . ." Wesley dapped Nick up for the memory. "*Man,* you wouldn't believe the kinda—"

"First team in! Light up the set again!" came the First AD's voice.

"Yo, man, I'll have to get at you later." Wesley dapped him up again. "Thanks, though. Thanks for being there to listen."

"No doubt, man. No doubt."

"What's your name, anyway?"

"Nick."

"Alright, Nick. I'm Wes. I'll holla at you later." He trotted off to set.

Nick smiled. His first real brush with Hollywood.

**DODGER STADIUM WAS** a sight to behold. Nestled up in the mountains sharply jutting north of Downtown, Chavez Ravine, home to the Los Angeles Dodgers ever since their infamous move from Brooklyn in the fifties, afforded a spectacular view of smog-oppressed LA. It was that very view Nick took in from behind the safety of a guardrail at the edge of the parking lot plateau.

Craig came up behind him, draping an arm over his shoulder. "What's up, kid?"

"You, kid."

"Way to come through, kid."

"No doubt, kid."

"Where are we sittin', kid?"

"C-Town got us tickets behind the plate, kid."

"Stop lyin', kid!"

"Ain't lyin', kid!"

"Kid!"

"Kid!"

"Kid!"

"Kid!"

"We at Dodger Stadium, about to see a Dodgers game for free from behind the *plate,* kid!"

"Life is good, kid."

Nick and Craig looked at each other and burst out laughing.

"Let's bounce," Nick said. "Kid."

Twenty minutes later, Nick and Craig sat six rows behind the plate, each saddled down with enough popcorn, fries, and Dodger Dogs to kill a vegan. On the field, position players warmed up by tossing the ball around the diamond. Carlton, the benefactor of their good fortune, strolled around near the visiting-team dugout, interviewing several San Diego Padres. With typically late-arriving LA crowds, the stadium was only half full under a sun-drenched sky. What a great day for baseball.

And for business. "That last column you did got a lot of response."

"Oh yeah?" Nick said nonchalantly, biting into a Dodger Dog. "Like what?"

"Most women *hated* it, kid!" laughed Craig. "One chick said, 'What the hell we want is an end to whiners like you.' "

"Great," shrugged Nick. " 'Marriage Minded's' first hate mail."

" 'Men aren't victims,' said one woman," Craig recited from memory, "while another wanted your 'shriveled-up penis nailed to a cross' like her heart was when her fiancé stood her up at the altar."

Nick gulped down his bite of the Dodger Dog. He stared oddly at the ketchup-covered wiener in a bun. "Dang."

"Yeah, they were pissed."

"Pissing women off wasn't my intention. A brotha just gets frustrated, you know?" explained Nick honestly.

"I don't care if you piss 'em off or pander to them. Advertising estimates we moved about twenty-three hundred more copies last week."

"Stop lying!"

"Man, get used to it," cheesed Craig. "You're a hit."

As if on cue, a foul ball flew back forcefully into the metal screen protecting the fans, making a sharp, clanging sound. Both guys jumped back as if the ball could hit them. Then they both turned to each other and smirked viciously in Carlton's direction. Life *was* good. Kid.

---

**NICK CAME BACK** home to San Diego that Friday morning. Having not received a call for either an audition or an extra gig the previous night, he decided to come back that day before the Friday-afternoon rush gridlocked the 405 into a sea of metallic statues.

A surprise was taped to his front door. A yellow notice for a package waiting for him at the post office. Without even going inside the house, Nick snatched up the notice and drove off to the post office. Twenty minutes later, he opened up a mysterious package without a return address in the comfort of his air-conditioned living room.

How odd. One of those popular bobblehead dolls in a Seattle SuperSonics jersey bobbled its way from the depths of Styrofoam peanuts. A slip of paper with writing in black Sharpie marker lay inside the box. It read, "I'm sorry. Anna."

Awww . . . Nick, quirky, soft-hearted smile stamped on his lips, instinctively reached for the phone. Imagine his surprise when the thing rang right as he touched it. "Uh, hello?"

"Whaddup, Cletis?"

"Whaddup, Herb?"

Malloy laughed uneasily from his desk at work. His was an office on one of the middle floors of a Manhattan building that was home to Morgan Stanley, where he oversaw the Management Information Systems Department. "I ain't heard that one in a minute."

"Surprises keep a relationship fresh. But you know that, of course, being *married* and all," Nick sniped playfully.

"Whatever, dude," Malloy grumbled dismissively. "So what's the deal, son?"

"Chillin'. Marinatin'."

"Just marinatin' in the sauce, fo' sheezy?" picked Mal in his best, affected, West Coast/Bay Area accent.

"You know, just marinatin' befo' it start crackalatin' and I be poppin' my collar on these fools who don't be smellin' me, fo' sho'," fired back Nick, à la Bay Area rap star E-40.

"My brotha, do *you* even know what the hell you just said?" quizzed Mal.

"Hell naw. But it sounded authentically West Coast, didn't it?" smiled Nick.

"But for real, son, what's up wit you? What're you doin' home on a Friday morning? I thought I'd have to call your celly next."

"Naw, man. Didn't get called. No work today."

"So you a movie star yet? When do I get to start seein' your grille on some commercials and shit?"

"I'm far off, brotha. I'm far off," conceded Nick sadly. "I am doing background work on a new TV show for Paramount called *Black-draft*. It's a firefighter show. Should be pretty hot."

"Pun intended, right?" Mal snickered. "What's background work?"

"Extra work. I'm one of those ebony-colored blurs you see in the background, behind the main characters."

"Oh. Do you have any lines?" Mal seemed a little disappointed. He had never paid attention to anything else on TV besides people with lines.

"No lines."

"Dang." Mal brooded for a moment. He studied the paper clips on his desk as if they were an SAT. "Nick . . . dawg . . . are you happy?"

Asking Nick if he was happy these days—with thoughts of his mother lying on a hospital bed after a bout of chemotherapy fresh in his mind—was a loaded question. Of course, there was no way Mal could know this. Combined with the near-absurdity of what he was doing in trying to find a wife on a timetable, Nick couldn't quite bring himself to come clean to his best friend. "You mean doing what I'm doing?"

"Yeah. With your job. The direction of your life."

Nick hesitated. Mal sounded so serious, so unlike his normally exuberant self. "I guess I'm happy enough. I mean, I'm by no means where I want to be in my new career, but I'm just starting. Success doesn't happen overnight. But the main thing is that I'm following my passion, doing something that I love."

"Wow." Malloy chewed that one over. "Following your passion."

Nick sensed something was wrong, but didn't want to push it. If Mal had something he wanted to share, he would do it on his own timetable. Instead, Nick stretched out on his futon couch and fumbled for the remote. Switching gears, he said, "Speaking of following your passion, I was just about to call Anna when you called."

"Not the chick with emotional and intimacy issues!" Mal howled. "What the hell for, my nig?"

"Well, she sent me a gift. And it *has* been over a week since I last talked to her," added Nick.

"Good. Don't call that broad, player. Let her sweat you out, like the big-pimpin' Morehouse Man you are," Mal advised.

"Is that right."

"Trust me on this one. Hos are like trains, dude. There's always gonna be another one comin' every fifteen minutes," Mal declared. "Especially when it comes to this chick with emotional and intimacy issues . . . It's best to wait until her train gets on the right track."

"But she did send me a gi—"

"Uh-uh. Players aren't moved by small material shows of remorse. Players are only moved by *obese* material shows of remorse. And even then, we're not moved very much. Leave her wantin' more, god. Leave her wantin' more."

"If you say so," said Nick, just to put a capper on the subject.

"Ah, but if this concept eludes you, I shall be out there to offer a full tutorial to you, my brotha."

"You're coming out to Cali? You?" Nick was incredulous. East Coast Mal in West Coast Daygo? "When?"

"Two weeks from today, if you don't mind puttin' me up."

"You know I got you, brohamme," gushed Nick excitedly. "How long are you staying?"

"A week? Two weeks, if you can stand me," offered Mal timidly.

"Bump that. You're my boy, Mal. Stay as long as you want," Nick invited. "I've been thinking lately about staying close to the crib anyway. I'm tired of driving up to LA for only three hundred bucks a week. Hey, is Mia coming, too?"

"Naw. She's too busy at work. It'll be just you and me, just like back in the day. Fire up the PlayStation and take your ass-whuppin' like a man."

"Whatever, man. You couldn't beat me in no PlayStation game if your name was Massa and my name was Toby!"

"Ah . . . how quickly they forget," breathed Malloy arrogantly.

"I do remember this, though: I made you retire them damn Knicks," Nick recalled smugly.

"But I gotta play with the Knicks! They're my squad," he said sheepishly.

"Whatever, man. It'll be cool just to kick it again."

"No doubt, playa. No doubt," agreed Mal. "Well, don't let me hold up your day now. Some of us people work for a living."

"Forget you, herby dude. Herby Love Bug."

"I'll holla at you later, Cletis."

"Peace."

———

"*THIS IS WHAT* you call a favor?"

"Hear me out, Nick. Hear me out." Chantel piloted her sporty BMW Z3 along I-55, heading toward the North Side. Nick had flown into Midway, the cheaper of Chicago's two main airports. Downtown Chicago stood tall, guarding the inland sea of Lake Michigan with its distinctive, cloud-grazing skyscrapers. As it was almost October, the wind had picked up off the lake to accompany the rain. It was a week later, and Nick was back to the scene of the crime: the city where he had spent over four years recovering from a severely broken heart.

"I'm listening," Nick said, focusing on the clouds that obscured the top of the sleek, black John Hancock building in the distance.

"I mean you're an actor, right? All I'm asking you to do is . . . act." Chantel looked magnificent, as usual. Her naturally bronzed face bore little makeup, allowing the tight-fitting black leather pants, V-neck red angora sweater, and silver jewelry to set off her beauty pyrotechnics. Inheriting flawless, creaseless, ageless black skin, the lovely five-foot-two Ms. Mojica looked every bit of twenty-two, instead of her recently turned age of thirty-two.

"You told them I was your *fiancé*! Small role I'd be playing!" Nick hissed. "How you gonna go and tell a lie like that to your family, anyway?"

"You don't understand," Chantel grimaced, gripping the wheel. "In a family like mine, everyone is married with children by the time they're thirty. Shoot, my thirty-three-year-old cousin is gonna be a grand*mami* in January. At *thirty-three*! And on top of all of that, my cousin's wedding is this Sunday and she's only twenty-two. . . . The pressure was getting to me."

"Pressure? What pressure? Sounds to me like you're too chicken-shit to stand up to your family and defend your lifestyle."

" 'Defend my lifestyle'?" she shot back. "It's not like I'm a lesbian or something. I'm just single, and it's getting to be a little much for my extended family to take. They want little cousins from Telly."

"No prospects?" Nick asked incredulously as he looked around, becoming refamiliarized with the city of seven million people.

Chantel gave him a look. "If I had any, you think I would've called you?"

Nick was not sure if that was a compliment or not.

Twenty minutes later, they sat on a park bench facing the vastness of Lake Michigan. The rain had slowed to an inconsistent light mist. For the moment, the lake-driven wind was behaving itself. Low-hanging clouds obscured the lake's horizon, lending an eerie, dream-like atmosphere to the area.

Chantel stared off into the lake while Nick watched her. "When my father died last year, that's when grandchildren really started to matter to Mami. My being an only child doesn't help. I think she wants to be able to spend time with her grandchildren before she dies."

Nick could relate to that. Carefully, he studied her face. She was such a strong woman. Always had been. Nick could remember many a time when the older Chantel would envelop him in her motherly ways and tend to a heart so oftentimes broken it could not remember how to put itself back together again. Throughout the course of their near-five-year friendship, ever since Nick had moved from New York to Chicago, Chantel had been a confidante, a counselor, a resource. Tough, smart, and funny, Chantel Mojica rarely appeared to need all three of those in someone else. One time had been when a fiancé of hers had broken her heart years before she knew Nick. Another was when her father had died last year and Nick had comforted her. He could see that this was one of those times. She needed him.

"My father." She laughed, giving the Hispanic lilt in her voice full play. "Papi could've waited until I was fifty to have kids. The man didn't admit his daughter was having sex until I was *twenty-five*! If he were still alive, I don't think Mami would be so pressed about this." A gulp of air. "But he's not."

Nick inwardly sighed, outwardly projected nothing but loving eyes and support. "So what is my role?"

The liar bit her lip. "Well . . . your name is Jorge. We've been dating off and on for about a year, but you just proposed to me about three weeks ago. You're originally from the Dominican Republic, hence your dark skin."

"I am half Panamanian, you know."

"Well, for *this* role you're Dominican," Chantel stressed.

"My Spanish sucks," Nick confessed.

"Don't worry. I told them you were raised in the States by an over-achieving Dominican family who emphasized English as the language in the home."

"You've thought this out some." Nick was mildly impressed. "How did we meet?"

"You work for Harris Bank, International Affairs. That explains why you're never in town when they want to see you, because you're away on business," she explained. "In fact, you spend more time living in your second apartment in New York than you do in your house in Highland Park."

"Highland Park?" Nick whistled. "Jorge's a baller."

Chantel shrugged. "I had to make it far enough away so that they couldn't bug me about visiting him."

"How does your mother feel about you dating someone who is always out of town and never has much time to spend with her daughter?"

"She loves it because she loves people who are driven for success. People who are hard workers. As long as he's payin' the bills and taking care of her Chantelita, Mami wouldn't care what he did."

"So what does Jorge like to do? Play golf in Tokyo? Polo in Paris? Cricket in London?"

She lost a brief struggle not to roll her eyes. "From there on out, just be yourself. I didn't elaborate too much to them about him . . . you. But I had a feeling you'd be able to come to my rescue—and you did—so I told them a few things about you."

"Like how I once proposed to a woman just for her to say no?"

"No . . . like how you used to make bad women choices until you met me."

"Droll," carped Nick, "very droll. But a question, Ms. Mojica: After this wedding, aren't they gonna want to see more of their future son-in-law?"

"I have an exit plan all mapped out. Since Jorge lives mostly in New York, he's going to move there permanently. So I go follow the man I love."

"You're leaving Harris Bank?" inquired Nick, somewhat amazed. For him, having met her on the job his first year in Chicago, Chantel would always be synonymous with Harris Bank.

"I'm leaving Chicago, especially the bank," she clarified, picking up a rock, examining it, then chucking it. "Shortly after I move to New York, Jorge and I will break up and life moves on."

She paused, reflecting. "I've lived my whole life in this city. I think that it's the greatest city in the world, but it is definitely time for me to expand my horizons and get away from home. Not finding a *real* fiancé here, too, makes this decision a helluva lot easier. I need to move on, Nick. I need to start over somewhere I don't know *anyone*. And maybe, just maybe in the process, I'll get to know myself."

Picking up a rock and chucking it, Nick said solemnly, almost to himself, "I know the feeling. Don't I ever know that feeling."

**EVEN THOUGH CHANTEL** was like a big sister to him, that still did not mean Nick preferred ending up on the couch. Yeah, so what if it was a necessary precaution? He could not help that he was attracted to her any more than Chantel Mojica could help herself from being so damn fine.

After passing an uneventful night on the couch, Nick was awakened early (for a Saturday) by Chantel so they could go shopping. The wedding was the next day and there were several accessories for which she wanted to comparison shop.

Trapped within the shoe section of an Ann Taylor store in the upscale Michigan Avenue Water Tower Place shopping mall, Nick began to drift off into sleep. There were only so many pairs of pumps that could hold his interest (okay, so there were *no* pairs of pumps that could hold his interest). He was in that hazy netherland betwixt wake and sleep when he saw her.

*Oh no, not her!* Nick scrambled up from one of the plush leather chairs men spent the better part of their relationships in when their women shopped Ann Taylor and bounded to the counter, where Chantel was trying to decide which pair of nearly identical-looking shoes to buy. Seeing that the saleswoman was no help, Nick made it easy for her.

"She'll take these," he said, thrusting the pair in Chantel's right hand at the woman.

Less than five minutes later, they were in the relative obscurity of mall traffic, heading in the opposite direction of his sighting. Or so Nick thought. When Chantel stopped to consult a mall directory, Nick started. There *she* was again, verbally bullying some poor guy who was with her like she was his girlfriend or, worse yet, his mother.

Skittish, Nick scurried over to Chantel. "I'm hungry," he lied. "Let's eat."

Nick towed Chantel toward the down escalators, away from the woman who was humiliating her man.

Fifteen minutes later, Nick was safe again in the mob at the food court. In line for some generic Chinese food, Nick felt his stomach silently revolt. Being in Chicago, his stomach knew that if it wasn't fried chicken from Harold's or the tiny White Castle burgers, it wasn't worth eating. His mind was more preoccupied with how to escape this mall without having to run into her.

Too late. As he turned away from the counter with his tray full of food, he nearly knocked her over. Their eyes met. Damn.

Asanti.

"Nick." As frigid as ever.

"Hi, Asanti."

She took a step back to examine him, covering the maneuver with a small laugh. The man still looked good. He was bigger, broader-shouldered than she had remembered. The only thing that hadn't changed was his dark, cool ebony skin.

Asanti was a sight to behold as well. Her short, thick frame still burst with more womanhood than Calista Flockhart could hope for in three lifetimes. With her dark hair pulled back in a ponytail, exposing her creamy, light brown face, Asanti looked like a cover model for *Black Health,* athletic sweatsuit and all. "After all these years, I finally run into you."

"How are you, Asanti?" Nick asked, partly out of curiosity, but more out of common courtesy.

"I'm fine." Forthright as always. Nick's biggest complaint during their one-year pseudo-relationship was her jawbreaker-hard exterior that had effectively warded him off from ever truly knowing her. That was a sad realization to come to about someone, especially after having once been inside her.

"So what've you been up to these past few years?" Nick swore to himself this was his last attempt at polite, nostalgic chitchat.

"I went back to school and got my degree. I'm working on my master's now as I work in Northwestern's admissions department."

Nick almost choked. *Asanti* was getting her master's at *Northwestern*? He had met the woman in a gym. They had been on only one bona fide date. Their illustrious history had been spent more horizontal than vertical—at her request. Asanti was the Big Pun of Single Black Chicago—she wasn't a player, she just crushed a lot. Nick could barely contain his surprise. "Wow. I didn't know you were so . . . uh . . . studious."

"You hardly knew me at all."

Did that sound like an accusation? *We are done here.* "It's been four years. I'm sure a lot has changed."

Asanti snorted sarcastically. "Remember the last thing you said to me?"

Nick winced. " 'I've washed my hands of you'?"

"No. It was 'Have a nice life.' " Nick grimaced. She continued. "And I have. That's my husband over there."

Someone just dropped a brick in Nick's stomach. "Husband"? *As in "Until death do us part"?*

"I got married a year ago."

Nick's world once again seemed out of his control. How did a woman, albeit a fine, peanut-butter-bronzed-skin woman, like Asanti, get married? Four years ago, she couldn't commit to staying through the morning after an all-night tryst, and now she was legally bound to a man in a mutually exclusive relationship? "Great. I'm . . . I'm happy for you."

She observed him with her cold, unflinching eyes. It was as if she was deciding whether to slip into her hardass act of old or to maintain a cool, detached distance. Mercifully for Nick—and the rest of Water Tower Place—Asanti chose the latter. "Thank you. I won't hold you up, Nick. I should be getting back to my husband."

The very words made him envious, disgusted. "It was . . . uh . . . good to see you. I wish you and your husband well."

Asanti started to pass by him when she stopped and leaned into his ear. "The next time you see me . . . don't run."

His shame was prodigious. Somehow, Nick found his way over to where Chantel sat, scarfing down some inferior Mexican food. "Who was that?" she asked innocently.

Nick sat down, solemn, contemplative. "A reason to be jealous."

---

**JORGE AND CHANTEL** made quite the striking couple. Nattily attired in a dark, double-breasted navy Ralph Lauren suit, Nick complemented Chantel's light pink bridesmaid outfit handsomely. Chantel's large, diverse extended family swooned and carried on about Nick before the wedding began. They were all so excited to meet— and to inspect—him that he felt like a racehorse before being saddled up. As uncomfortable as he felt posing as Chantel's soulmate, Nick carried off the act with just as much aplomb.

His second wedding of the year Nick watched with a little more than awe. It was a big Catholic-Mexican wedding, with all the accoutrements. The bride was a vision in white, her fiancé a veritable dark-haired, three-dimensional campaign to be the lead on a *telenovela*. Once again, that pang, that longing for a lifemate struck him as Chantel's cousin and her groom exchanged vows. He had had that once . . . a long time ago. And although he continued his search, his race against time, it felt like he might never feel that way about someone again.

Nick broke out of his self-absorbed cloud in time to see the most important part:

"I now pronounce you man and wife."

At the reception, Nick and Chantel, ironically, ended up catching the garter and bouquet. Or, rather, *Jorge* and Chantel did. Chantel's mother, a short, round lightskin black woman, beamed like a lighthouse.

So they danced. The music was a slow song in Spanish. Nick held Chantel close as they moved gently across the floor under the scrutiny of what seemed like half of Chicago's West Side. They spoke in whispery tones.

"I want to thank you for coming out here, Nick," she said. "You're a really good friend. You didn't have to do this."

"Yes, I did," he responded. "Or else I wouldn't have been a really good friend."

Chantel closed her eyes with a warm smile, allowing the music to carry their thoughts. As her eyes stayed shut, his stayed open—wide open. He drank in everything around him, from the guests to the bride and groom to the cake. No more weddings, Nick decided. *No more until it's my turn.*

"Chantel."

"Mmm?" she purred.

"Nothing."

She opened her eyes and gently placed a hand on the side of his smooth brown face. She cooed, "Whassup, baby boy?"

Nick tried to hide the intent in his eyes. "This wedding is so beautiful, Chantel, just so beautiful. Your family is wonderful, if aggressive. Don't you ever think about having one?"

Almost without realizing it, they exchanged something. As much as Nick had tried to hide it, his true intentions had been found out. Suddenly, Nick worried that he would scare her off. Chantel recognized this, interpreted it, and moved on gracefully. She gave him a generous smile.

"I do," she admitted mysteriously, dropping her eyes from his gaze, closing them, and pitching a tent on his chest. "I do."

"**WONDERFUL JOB, *JORGE*,**" congratulated Chantel, dumping her purse onto the couch when they returned to her condo on the North Side. Her shoes came off next as Nick closed the door behind him. He slipped out of his jacket and shoes before he crashed onto the couch, stretching his body out lengthwise. Chantel sat perpendicular to him, right on his stretched-out lap. "You done good."

"*Gracias.*"

"*De nada.*" Without leaving his lap, she reached toward the living room's coffee table and grabbed the cable remote. She clicked on her stereo and cable box, a steady stream of soft Spanish rock instantly flowing. Involuntarily, her body began to sway.

"You've still got energy?"

"C'mon, let's dance, Nicholito."

"I'm too tired, Chantel," he groaned at what would have otherwise been an enticing invitation. "Misleading a church full of people all day will do that to you."

Chantel smiled. Graciously, she changed the digital-music channel to an R&B station. A soft, sweet Toni Braxton song played. She settled in along Nick's body with her back to him, pulling his arms around her waist, and gazing up at the ceiling with her head propped up against his chest.

They sat in blissful silence for a few minutes, absorbing the supple grooves.

"Why did seeing Asanti yesterday unnerve you?"

"I don't think you would understand."

"I think I would."

Nick sighed. Not facing Chantel made this a bit easier. "I don't know about you, but one of the things I've always wanted was to be married. Not just married but *happily* married. The older I am, the further away from marriage I seem to get."

"I'm thirty-two years old, Nicholito," Chantel said. "I think I would understand *that*."

"But then seeing Asanti . . . It's as if this world is working in re-verse. All these people I never would have pegged for marriage—who didn't even want to be married at first—get married *first.*" Nick bit his lip. "It's as if I feel like I'm doing something wrong. Or there is something wrong with me."

Chantel rolled over so that she faced Nick. Her dark brown eyes churned up heat, an intensity Nick could rarely recall seeing. "There is *nothing* wrong with you, Nick. Don't you ever believe that. You are a wonderful man, a wonderful friend."

Speaking before he could control the emotional rush behind it, Nick said, "Is that why we aren't together?"

The question stunned her. Nick continued. "Is that why we made love that one night, a year ago, and we never dared mention it again? Because I'm 'too wonderful a man,' 'too wonderful a *friend*' to be in your life?"

Chantel recoiled into an upright position. "Not so much honesty at one time, homie," she chuckled nervously. "I might have to start lying to you."

"No. You've been lying to me, to yourself, for a year now," Nick challenged. "What the hell happened between us? What the hell was it that kept us from happening?"

Nick had more questions than Chantel had answers.

"When I met you, you were in a bad patch. When we became friends, I was in a bad patch. When we made love, it was right after I broke up with Queen. If there's never been a good time for us, then when *is* a good time?" drilled Nick. He sat up, alert and edgy. "The attraction is there. We are great friends, with the capacity to be great lovers. I don't see the—"

Chantel flew at him like a sprinter out of the blocks. His body caved in under the ferocity of the woman's attack. Senselessly, inex-plicably, and with a primal energy, Chantel's lips clawed at his face, her tongue seeking his, her skin striving to be one with his own. She ate at him, kissing with such force and desire that it threatened to consume them both. Her breathing was both guttural and sensual at the same time. Nick struggled to keep up, grappling her back and pushing her body deeper into his.

In short order, Chantel's hands found purpose and began tearing at

Nick's shirt and tie. Under a barrage of kissing, she moved her hands south, to Nick's zipper, liberating the hardened, oppressed region. Nick timidly began to unzip the back of her dress.

With all the subtlety of a jackhammer, Chantel jammed her tongue in his mouth, forcing his breath rate to match hers. When Nick massaged the bare skin of her light brown back with tender care, Chantel's tempo suddenly changed. She eased into the kiss, lingered in it, reveled in its wetness and roughness and tenderness. And then she let it go.

She let it all go. Chantel slowly disengaged herself from Nick's mouth, raising herself to an upright, straddling position. As had been the theme of the past few minutes, she now seemed in control while Nick struggled to catch up.

This was an undeniably sexy position to Nick, and Chantel knew it. That was exactly her point. As their heart rates calmed down and reclaimed their normal docility, her eyes transmitted a mélange of hurt, pain, and missed opportunities long past. They also betrayed a yearning, a thirst that Nick knew he alone could not quench. For if they dared dive into the pool of passion, that lake of liberating, all-consuming love, lives would have to change. Dramatically. The distance, the transition of relationships, their wildly divergent career paths . . . they risked tearing their lives apart over this passionate yet unknown commodity called love. Nick knew about the fiancé who had broken her heart. Chantel knew about the would-be one who had broken Nick's. She could not take that chance again, even if Nick could.

"This is why it is never a good time," she said softly, reluctantly removing herself from the couch.

Nick straightened his wrinkled, half-open shirt. Solemnly, he nodded. He understood.

"Thank you." She rewarded his understanding with a gentle, pursed-lip kiss. "Jorge."

---

**WHEN NICK RETURNED** home, it was officially October. As the plane touched down under sun-kissed skies, Nick realized that Southern California had no seasons. October looked the same here as

December and June. Ridiculous. Even Atlanta had enough character to start raining in October.

Returning home was uneventful. A small stack of junk mail awaited him, along with three inconsequential messages on his answering machine. He did notice several "Private Name" calls listed on his Caller ID that did not match up with the people who had left messages. Sitting down at his kitchen table, Nick sifted through the junk to find a letter from Anna. Nick opened it, read it, and was slightly moved—*slightly*. Said she missed him. He reached for his cordless phone. Time for this charade to end.

"Hello?"

"Hi, Anna. It's Nick."

"Hi," she said shyly.

"I got your letter."

"I've missed you."

"I know. Thanks. I just—"

"I want to see you," she said with quiet assertion.

"Well, it's Thursday. I'll be back up that way on Monday—"

"I can't wait that long. There're things I need to tell you . . . want to tell you . . . things you need to hear. I'll come see you."

"When?"

"Now."

"Well, it's kind of a long drive. . . ."

"Would you mind letting me stay the night?" she asked coyly.

Would he! This was almost like a whole new woman! Mal had been right. Logic was like kryptonite to women. A little bit of ignoring a woman went a long, long way. "Not at all."

"I'll see you in an hour and a half."

"Drive safe." Nick hung up, absolutely stunned. That was easy. *Too* easy. Did this make him a slut?

**TRUE TO HER** word, Anna arrived ninety minutes later. They talked on his futon couch. For three hours. The floodgates burst open about her abuse as a child, her reluctance to trust, and the ex-boyfriend who hit her. This was all new information to Nick. He treated her with the utmost respect by just being there to listen.

Anna apologized for how distant she had been. She just wanted to make sure that he was not going to disappoint her. He vowed that he would not. A bond was created, an understanding reached.

They went to bed together. Nick didn't try anything and Anna didn't expect him to. For the first time in a while, she felt totally safe. She cared about him and it showed. Nick was grateful. Maybe all of the paces she had put him through were going to be worth it.

In the morning, Nick awakened to the doorbell. His weary eyes glanced at the clock. Eight-thirty. Since Anna didn't have a gig today and Nick wasn't going to LA for work until Monday, no one was in a big hurry. Careful not to wake her, Nick eased out of bed, quietly leaving the bedroom for the living room. Figuring he was amply dressed for a mailman or UPS delivery person, Nick paddled out to the door in just shorts and a wifebeater. Who else could it be this time of day?

*Maya T.*

Nick's mouth gaped like the Grand Canyon. Dressed in jeans and a sleeveless blouse, Maya T.'s long, lean form stood on his front porch, shocking the bejesus out of him.

"You're gonna let some flies in if you don't shut that thing," she grinned, nodding at his mouth.

Nick searched for words. "It's just that . . . uh, I mean, you're *here*. What a surprise!"

"I know." Maya T. smirked her way past him, shoulder duffle in tow, before Nick could devise an unobtrusive way to stop her. She dumped her bag on the futon couch. "Worldwide domination is nothing without someone to share it with."

Reluctantly closing the door, Nick said, "I don't follow."

"I was thinking about what you said when you came up to see me last month. You said I should come out and see you more often."

Nick could have groaned. "And you said that you would come down to San Diego when I least expected it."

"Bingo," she smiled. "I figured that maybe you were right. Maybe we should try something out like a relationship, see where it takes us. You're in-state now, we can come see each other more often, and we could actually turn our little three-year fling into a *thing*. I could get used to being your girlfriend."

Those were beautiful words to hear from a beautiful lady—if only they were spoken at another time and place.

"Now come give me a hug, suga."

Still formulating an exit plan, Nick embraced her in the middle of the living room, mind frantic.

"Nick," came a groggy voice.

*Shit.*

Maya T. released him from the embrace and turned around. Some chick who was at least two inches shorter than her, wearing just a long nightshirt, waddled into the living room. From the bedroom. Nick's face crystallized in fear.

"Nick . . . who's your friend?" Anna asked innocuously, groggily.

Maya T. whipped her furious, embarrassed eyes upon Nick. "Yes, Nick," she said acidly, melting him with each indicting syllable. "Who's your friend?"

## MARRIAGE MINDED
### *One man's quest to get married in a year*
### *by Anonymous*

Men are simple beings. There is nothing in life that we enjoy more than alcohol, women, and being around each other—and not necessarily in that order. Oh yes, there is one other thing we value highly: privacy.

Yes, we can be difficult, but we are fairly uncomplicated. We enjoy our privacy. We do not have to tell a woman everything that goes on. And, in keeping our privacy, sometimes there will be things that are better left unexplained or, rather, not mentioned at all.

First of all, please *call*. The next time you want to surprise one of us, please *call*. The relationship you save just might be your own.

I recently consoled a friend of mine. We had had stops and starts in the past when it came to getting to know each other. She wasn't exactly forthcoming with information about herself. She had her reasons— very good reasons. Finally, when she did tell me what they were, everything made sense. She stayed the night while I comforted her in the most platonic way. I was being a good friend.

But then, another friend of mine, a female friend who has always demonstrated a lack of interest in pursuing a meaningful relationship, decided to show a bona fide interest in a relationship at an altogether *wrong* time. Her feelings were hurt, my feelings were hurt, and why? Because she *didn't call*.

Think about how men must value their privacy. Do you, Married Woman, think you would have married your husband had he told you every stinking thing about himself and his relationships? Doubtful. Or how about you, Relationship Girl? Do you think your man has *honestly* told you how many women he slept with before you (trust me, it's whatever number he's told you times three, or to the second power—whichever number is higher)? Your man would be stupid to tell you that on occasion he fantasizes about Janet Jackson while making love to you. There are some things women don't need to know.

So my friends did not know about each other. Let's say that they had. What would have changed? Well, Friend #1, the one who spent the night, would never have opened up to me if she knew that I was actively talking to other women (which all guys are, ladies, until you lock them up into an exclusive relationship—and sometimes even then). Whatever bond we had formed that night would never have happened because of some unnecessary bit of information. Friend #2, had she known I was talking to someone else, may not have just showed up at my door *without calling,* but also she would not have ever taken the initiative to consider seeing me and making an effort for a relationship. I never would have known what she was truly feeling for me had I told her the whole, inconsequential truth.

So I say all that to say this, ladies: We are not impractical beings. We censor our words, our thoughts, hell, our *truths* to make your world a safer place to live. While two very good prospects for wifedom have now gone by the wayside, I have only one request of someone who might end up dating me: Before doing anything, *please call.*

## 7

AYUM! I WISH I was there to see that!" hollered Malloy.

Nick drove back from the airport, where he had just picked up Mal, a scant six hours removed from the scene that seemed straight out of a bad movie on latenight HBO. Mal kicked his feet in childlike delight at the thought of it. Focusing on the road, Nick could not share his friend's enthusiasm.

"So did they go at it?" Malloy salivated. "Did they girlfight or something?"

"Please."

"No bitch-hits?" Mal sounded genuinely disappointed.

"Let it go, Mal."

"Dawg, you've got it all wrong. I'm not tryin' to embarrass you over this. Not at all, son. I just gotta hear how the hell you got out of it with your molars intact."

Nick was in no mood for spilling his guts today but figured that an accurate account would be the quickest way to shut Mal the hell up. "Maya didn't say anything after that. She picked up her bag and dipped. As quickly as she came, she left. Took the next flight back to San Francisco."

Mal sucked his teeth, shaking his head from side to side. "That was poor game management, playa. A true pimp would've gotten those broads together and made a sex sandwich."

"Just shut up, alright? You don't know what the hell you're talking about," snapped Nick. "I pissed off Maya T. and confused the hell out of Anna, at a point when *both* were just starting to warm up to me."

Mal observed the passing scenery of Downtown San Diego. "All I'm sayin' is that you did nothing wrong in this scenario, right? I mean, true, you had Ole Girl stay overnight, but you didn't even get so much as a whiff of her panties, right?"

"If you want to put it like that, no, I didn't."

"Right. You've done nothing wrong, then, for Maya T. to be mad at you for the long term." Mal clucked his teeth again. "Shoot, bitch shoulda called."

"She's not a bitch, Mal, she's a lady," Nick retorted. "She's a lady and a friend. She's one of the longest, dearest female friends I've got. She helped me out with some things you wouldn't even know where to begin with, and at times when you weren't around to even try. That's my friend. And I'm gonna have to figure out a way to get my friend back."

"Well, what about this Anna girl? What's her story?"

"She's gone through a lotta shit in her life. She has issues with trust and men, physical abuse. That's why she backed away from me before. She was protecting herself. And then the moment the iceberg begins to thaw and she thinks she can trust someone, here I have some other woman coming into my house and hugging up on me at eight-thirty in the morning." Nick smacked the wheel in frustration. "God, that must've looked so bad."

"Like I said, playa, bad game management. Just bad game management," Mal diagnosed. "You've done nothing wrong, we can get you out of this, and all will be good in the hood. *Shiiiiiit*, I've escaped from worse back in college, remember?"

"Yeah, I remember."

"So don't sweat it, son. I'll have you back on top of these hos—pun intended—in no time. Your game will be so tight, they'll be callin' you Milton Bradley!"

**AFTER DUMPING MAL'S** luggage off at home, Nick took him to Fashion Valley. Why waste time in unleashing Mal upon San Diego?

Next stop was J. Crew. Nick arrived at a time he normally found Robert there, only to find instead some short, preening, blond-haired flack with a badly matted Caesar haircut.

"May I be of assistance?" he lisped.

Mal's titter was cut off by a sharp look from Nick. They needed this lisping fashion emergency at the moment. "Is Robert working today?"

SoCal Caesar frowned. "No, he doesn't *work here* anymore."

Mal gaily swung his hand out, pivoted, and swished his way out of the store. Nick did his best to ignore him. "Do you know where he's working now?"

Caesar looked from side to side to make sure a manager was nowhere within earshot. Conspiratorially, he leaned in and whispered, "He's in the Brookstone downstairs."

Now, was that so hard? Mocking him, Nick leaned in and whispered, "Thanks."

Outside the store, Nick grabbed Mal by the elbow and steered him in the right direction. "I swear, I can't take you nowhere."

"No, you thertainly can't," Mal lisped wildly.

Showing the benefits of a back-massaging recliner to a Medicaid retiree, Robert most definitely worked in the muscle-relaxation and gadget store called Brookstone. When the silver-haired senior citizen escaped the vibrating contraption, Robert sank into the machine in his place, disgusted he could not close the sale.

Nick snuck up behind him. *"Ro-bair!"*

Robert leapt out of his chair. "Geez!" Seeing his old friend, his heartbeat returned to normal. He quickly found his faux-French accent. *"Nicolas."*

"How goes it, monsieur?"

Robert shot Nick a look that would've shouted "Look around!" had it had lips. "Would you care for a vibrating hand massager today?"

"That's quite alright."

"Who's your friend?"

"This is my boy Malloy. Malloy, Robert," Nick introduced.

"Nice to meet you," said Robert, shaking his hand.

"Whassup," Mal said coolly. Drifting toward the walkway, he said, "I'mma be outside."

"So what're you doing here?" asked Nick.

Leaning in, Robert confided, "I got fired."

"For what?"

"Stealing."

"I swear, I leave you alone for a month and you haul off and lose your mind. What's wrong with you?"

"I didn't *do* it," Robert snapped. "A few of the more high-ticket items grew legs, and everyone in the store wants to tag the fag."

Nick could recognize discrimination when he heard it. "Damn. That sucks."

"Like it's my fault they're fashionably challenged while I am fashionably fabulous. Besides, if I were to steal anything, I wouldn't risk losing my job over some Eurotrash *vests*," Robert bristled.

"Who do you think did it?" snooped Nick.

"Smedley. That little closet prick with the Caesar cut."

"That bitch's name is Smedley!" guffawed Nick.

"Doesn't he look like a Smedley?" Robert digged cattily.

"So what've you been up to lately?"

"Oh, just fucking half of the Hillcrest district," Robert announced cheerily. "Mmm . . . I have a date tonight, too. . . ."

Hands on his head, Nick said, "My virgin ears."

"Don't play the innocent, *Nicolas*. It doesn't suit you," barbed Robert smugly. "And, yes, Mommy, I am playing safely."

Nick rolled his eyes at Robert, who rolled his eyes right back. "Really, Nick, the stereotype of the overly promiscuous, sexually irresponsible, HIV-positive gay male is *such* a cliché."

"Fuck you," returned Nick. "Far be it for me to care if your dick falls off. Go sell a foot massager or something."

"Love you, too, Nick. Quit being a bad host and attend to your friend. Don't be a stranger," Robert whistled, turning back toward the merchandise.

"Have fun on your date."

Robert wiggled his fingers over his shoulder.

A mere ten feet from the store as they walked, Mal burst out with "That dude was sweet, wasn't he?"

"Sweet?"

"You know. Sugar in his tank? Light in the ass? A fag?" Mal said all of this without any malice, an observation that disturbed Nick even more.

"Oh, my archaic friend. You mean 'Is he gay?' "

"So he is a fag?"

"You mean 'Is he gay?' Yes."

"I knew it, I knew it," said Mal. "So he *is* a fudge-packer."

"What's up with all the gay hate, Mal?" Nick accused. "Whassup with that?"

"I mean, I'm not a hater. I wouldn't consider myself prejudiced or anything. It's just that that shit's unnatural."

"You mean loving someone? Or being persecuted for loving someone outside of society's norms?" Nick had more than a little experience in both.

"No, I'm talking about ass-pounding, dude. That shit ain't natural! For a man to take it in the ass from another man is *un*natural."

"But you've had anal sex before, right?"

"With a *woman*! There *is* a difference."

"Really? How would you know?" Nick shot back.

Mal was at a loss for words—so he played it off. "Shut up, dude. I can see where you're headed with this. You're gonna try to rationalize it, try and logically justify homosexual behavior to me. Well, I ain't buyin' it."

"You don't buy logic?"

"Humans are not logical beings. We are the only species that consumes all of its natural resources until they're gone without replenishing them. We ain't logical, dawg. And neither is homosexuality. Ain't nothin' another man can do for me."

"But two women getting together . . ."

"Yeah, that's hot!"

Nick shook his head. "You know, you represent all that's wrong with black male homophobia."

"Naw, nigga, you got that the other way around. I represent all that's *right* about black male homophobia," Mal announced proudly.

"You know you're terrible, dude. You know that, right?"

"Nope," his best friend grinned. "I'm Mal."

"C-NICE!" MAL GREETED Craig with dap. "Whassup?"

"Life is good, kid," Craig smiled, laid out on a beach blanket. "Pull up some sand."

Life *was* good at Mission Beach. With the late-afternoon afterwork crowd milling about in the shops that adorned the pathway separating civilization from the beach, a pretty good mix of kids and adults took advantage of the warm, sea-breezy skies.

Nick unfolded two large beach towels for the two of them. Mal took his time making it down to the sand, ogling the various pretty, bikinied women strolling around. "Now that's what I'm talkin' about right here," he shivered.

Craig chuckled. "So how's the wife?"

"She's coolin'. How's your ball and chain?"

"Olinda's doing great. Thanks for asking." Craig yawned. "So what're you guys getting into this weekend?"

"Anna's coming down tomorrow," Nick announced. He missed Mal rolling his eyes. "I'm gonna try and smooth things out with her from this morning by taking her and her girl Frisbee-golfing with me and Mal. And then later on, we're gonna hook up with C-Town and head to Tijuana. Wanna come?"

"You know it, kid." They dapped up.

Nick watched Mal drink in the sights. Talk about a mongoose in a henhouse, but only on a three-thousand-mile leash. "So what do you think of Cali so far?"

"I mean the slimmies are off the *meter*! Check out the honeydip in the red!"

It was Woman on the Beach! Damn, did she look good. Chillin' with her girlfriend, a forgettable-looking lightskin girl, Woman on the Beach had her curvy, coffee-colored complexion on full display in a two-piece. It was unfair. She was such a concoction of sweet chocolate skin and caramel-brown hair, it was as if she were a divinely created Twix bar made in the form of woman.

She caught them all staring, reacted with only a slight start, playing it off so wonderfully indifferent, as women were trained to do from inside the womb. Slowly, they all returned their eyes to their sockets, and drifted their gazes to less obvious targets. Save Nick, who dragged his eyes away from her reluctantly, even slower than the rest, hoping to catch one more glimpse of her face.

He did. In a split second, her eyes flitted up as his eyes were grazing away. She caught the corner of his eye, but that was enough. Recognition. If her girlfriend hadn't been there, he would've walked over to talk to her. *Cardinal Rule to Dating No. 9:* **Never approach a woman with her friends there.** Talk about setting your recipes for disaster. It was pressure enough to know that your boys would be watching (but encouraging), but then to have extra sets of female eyes, all of them wishing, praying you would say something corny and fail, just so that their miserable, lonely, ugly lives would not be made any more miserable and lonely and ugly because the lives of their happier, congenial, prettier friends would be made that much better . . . It was all too much.

So as he had done once before with Anna, Nick let the moment pass.

"**FRISBEE-GOLFING? THAT** shit sounds sorry," stated Malloy honestly.

"I mean, tell me how you *really* feel," muttered Nick.

Keeping with tradition, the boys played sports video games on the Sony PlayStation 2 into the wee hours of the morning. Trash talk was ubiquitous. Male bravado commanded centerstage. They cursed at each other as if it were a second language. Just another night of male bonding between Nick and Malloy.

"You think you're gonna get her back by playin' some kinda Ultimate Frisbee golf game or something?"

"Maybe not, but I have to do something to help offset what happened today." Nick shook his head as he focused on the football game they were playing. "It can't get any worse."

"So she was mad?"

"Hell yeah, she was mad. Wouldn't you be?" posed Nick. "I mean, she had just spent the night before pouring her heart out to me, finally melting the iceberg of a wall she had for her front, just for another woman to show up at my door this morning, overnight bag in hand. My credibility's pretty shot right now."

"It's early in the game, playa. It's early in the game." Mal bolted straight up, his arms erect like goal posts. "Touchdown! *Bi-atch!*"

"Ain't nobody studyin' your black ass. Sit your tail down," groused Nick. " 'It's early in the game.' "

"I don't get it," Mal said, easily kicking the extra point on-screen. "You've known Maya T. for something like a decade, right?"

"Right."

"You wanted a relationship with her before, she said she couldn't, then she comes down here today to start one up, only to see you with another woman, and now she says she wouldn't," summarized Mal. "Right?"

"Basically. She didn't say anything, nor has she returned my calls today. And at this stage, I'd say a relationship is pretty much out of the picture," Nick evaluated.

"True. But you also want to be with Anna, right?"

"Right."

"So what is it with this girl?"

"What do you mean?"

"I mean, what is it with this girl that makes her so special? You told me how you've been courting her for over a month now, but you have not shown me anything that makes this girl special, that makes her stand out from the pack." On the football field, Mal's New York Jets were driving toward Nick's Seattle Seahawks' end zone again. "Just because she likes you is not reason enough."

Nick absorbed every word. No matter their differing worldviews, particularly when it came to women, Mal was always good for some old-fashioned common sense. So he listened.

"There's a lot of hos out there, dude. A whole lotta hos . . ."

"Mal . . ." Nick did not feel like hearing the Players' Anthem from Malloy for the umpteenth time since the beginning of their unholy alliance freshman year in college.

"Listen to me, dude, listen. There aren't a whole lot of *women* around, dawg," Mal philosophized. "One is less populous on this earth than the other. It's like eighty to twenty percent ho to lady. You just don't lie down and open your heart to them. You gotta guerrilla-pimp these hos. You see them old James Bond films? Sean Connery's Bond would never die over no ho!"

Trying to zone him out, Nick grumbled, "It's a miracle you ever got married."

"I'm serious, dude. You haven't told me one thing about this broad Anna that makes her worth all of the bullshit she's put you through. And until she does, *if* she does, *then* you can bleed your heart out to her," Mal instructed. "But until she shows you something special about her, I say drop her like a pair of panties."

"Original," mumbled Nick, focusing all of his energy on the living room TV.

"I'm just sayin', bruh, I've seen some hos leave skid marks on a lot of tight brothas. I don't wanna see that happen to you," Mal emphasized. *Again,* he dared not say.

Another touchdown. Mal jumped up and started doing a ridiculous end-zone dance, pretending to smack an imaginary ass. "That is, unless I'm doing the driving!"

**FRISBEE GOLF WAS** actually a very entertaining affair. Balboa Park, San Diego's large central park, had a course dedicated exclusively to the flying-disc sport. The game was quite the rage, too; all nineteen holes on the course were full with merry bands of "golfers."

Nick, Mal, Anna, and Anna's friend Tauja were one such band. Tauja was a tall, bright-skinned girl with legs and lashes that stretched on like piano strings. With the customary greenish-grayish-brownish hazel "pretty eyes" a woman of her cosmetically applied beauty usually had (contacts, of course), Tauja was a professional model and music-video dancer. While the men lapsed into their competitive natures and actively tried winning the game, the women shuffled along, complained, and generally slowed the game down. After half an hour, they were the only ones at the fifth hole. Even the beer-drinking group of six that had started two holes behind them were now two holes ahead.

As attractive as Tauja was, Mal seemed unimpressed. The man could spot a fake a mile away. "Come along, Ms. Dong Song."

" 'Thong Song,' " she corrected. "I was in Sisqo's video for 'Thong Song.' "

"I know. I just wanted to hear you say it again." Mal and Nick exchanged eye rolls.

"Did you know that Tauja was also in Will Smith's 'Wild Wild West' video?" Anna said. "She was one of the women at the masquerade ball."

"I don't think she got that far down her résumé," muttered Nick under his breath.

"Give her time," smirked Mal evenly.

"You know, I could've gotten you on that shoot, too, Anna," Tauja reminded her. "You really should come on more auditions with me."

"I think I might have to," Anna worried. "I haven't worked in almost a month."

"Sorry to break this up, ladies, but it's your turn to tee off," Nick said. "Miss Whitley."

Anna took a few steps back before hopping forward three times and unfurling her Frisbee. She shanked it—wide left, into the trees. Anna shrugged apathetically. Her score through the first four par-three holes was already in the twenties.

Nick readied for his tee-off, taking a few steps back. As he began his hops forward to release, Anna said, very blasé, "So are you fucking her, Nick?"

His Frisbee went careening into the ravine, far left of the fairway. Tauja attempted to hide her amusement, badly, while Mal instantaneously hated both of them. "Excuse me?" said Nick.

"Are. You. Fucking. Her," Anna clarified, which really didn't clarify much at all.

"What kind of question is that?" stalled Nick.

"A direct one," Tauja snickered.

"Shut up," ordered Mal.

Tauja glowered. Now their hatred was mutual.

Nick began to lead them down the fairway in search of their various Frisbees. "Don't ask me a question you don't want the answer to."

Anna stalked after him down the fairway. "Does she put out? Is that why you're with her?"

Malloy made sure that he and Tauja followed after them at a safe distance. He wanted Tauja to have no part of this lovers' spat.

"I've known you for a fraction of the time I've known Maya T. You said the other night that you're not ready for a relationship. We're not even together. I'm not going to answer to you for anything at this point," Nick responded firmly. "It's early in the game."

*Tell her, dawg!* Mal wanted to say, happy to see his boy grow balls right in front of him.

"So being with me is a game to you?"

"No, it's not. But sometimes it feels like it must be a game to *you*.

Until two nights ago, I didn't see much of the real Miss Joanna Whitley. You'd lead me on, then turn me away. Lead me on, turn me away. I always wanted to be with you, Anna, but you wouldn't let me." Nick bent over and picked up his Frisbee. "Now, I've got options."

Anna snatched her Frisbee from the base of the tree and strode past Nick. "I give you my heart and you give me 'options.' Now *that's* a fair trade."

**NEEDLESS TO SAY,** the rest of the Frisbee-golfing did not go over well. Anna spent the majority of the time mean-mugging Nick with her pissed-off face, while Mal and Tauja exchanged mere civilities, if they spoke at all. Nick ended up winning the round, but it didn't really matter. The rest of their afternoon and evening with them was scrapped when the girls decided to go back to Orange County. Mal and Nick did not even try to stop them. No hugs were traded, just stiff goodbyes.

Nick decided to take Mal down to the Gaslamp Quarter, labeled by a lot of white people as the French Quarter of the West. As usual for a Saturday under warm skies, the whole area teemed with life. They perused the multicolored, multileveled, open-air Horton Plaza shopping center and stopped to get something to eat. Mal had been careful not to say much this far, allowing his friend to simmer. But as they ate, he couldn't contain himself. "I'm proud of you, dawg."

"Why?" Nick knew why.

"With Anna. You handled that situation like a player. Like a man," Mal evaluated.

"Don't patronize me, Mal. She had it coming."

"See what I meant earlier? I don't see that chick lasting too much longer. No broad not your wife should give you that much drama."

"Amen," agreed Nick.

"Now, with that settled, what time do we meet Carlton and Craig?"

"An hour."

"Mexico, here we come!"

**TIJUANA WAS A** twenty-minute drive from Nick's house, if that. *Crossing* the border to Mexico was a whole other issue entirely. On a

summery-type day such as this one, in October, everyone was making
a run for the border. Just sitting in the car waiting to get up to the border guards took forty minutes itself. But once across, nothing could
stop the four of them.

Nick, Craig, Mal, and Carlton found Craig's Jetta a spot several
blocks away from Avenida Revolucíon, the main drag of Downtown
Tijuana. Craig's car was the ride by default, seeing how tales of car-
jacking, kidnappings, and corrupt, greedy Mexcian police had de-
terred Americans like themselves from bringing over a car with
serious market value. They parked under a street lamp and made their
way by foot.

This was Nick's first trip to Mexico. He liked what he saw. For one,
the four of them stood out attractively; Mexican men were shorter
than they were. Their darker skin tones made them more accessible
to the locals than your ordinary American *gringo,* as several señoritas
made eye contact. Mal in particular seemed to enjoy flirting with the
beautiful brown women of the border town. Language did not pose
much of a problem as Carlton was almost bilingual in Spanish, and
Craig had been slowly picking up the language over the past couple of
years, thanks to his half–Puerto Rican wife. The buildings were older
and less sophisticated than those of San Diego's Downtown, and several of the streets were paved with cobblestone. Bustling with activity,
the sidewalks were packed with a good number of American tourists
as they grew closer to the heart of Downtown.

Mal and Carlton hollered at every other attractive female who
dared give them eye candy. Craig would fire off a joke every now and
then, as well as admiring the hotties. Convinced no woman in Mexico
could interest him, Nick laid back in the cut, observing, contributing
to the conversation and banter with an occasional funny story or two.
All of them found time to pick up a trinket, as silver was dirt cheap in
Tijuana. It was just like Nick was back in Atlanta, kickin' it with his
boys after Loq's wedding, or at Freaknik three years ago, the last fun
year before the cops sucked all the life out of it.

After a quick return to the car to stash their booty, the boys headed
back toward Avenida Revolucíon. Nightfall had set in. It was time to
party. On weekends, thousands of Americans flocked to TJ for its
nightlife.

Problem was they were the wrong type of Americans. Packed inside

Club Xtasy, the boys were surrounded by excitable partygoers at least twelve years their junior. Teenagers. Teenage kids migrated to Tijuana every weekend as if on pilgrimage, lured by Mexico's cheap booze and lax alcohol restrictions. So it was no surprise that this club, like almost every other club on Revolucíon, had a playlist that was primarily techno. The teenyboppers would lose their minds when a techno remix of some Jennifer Lopez song would play.

While Nick held up the wall, searching for someone legal to talk to, the others dove right in. Mal was quick to dance with a Mexican honeydip with a short red skirt and an even shorter red tube top. Craig and Carlton hit the bar, content to challenge each other's masculinity by going tequila shot for tequila shot. With the liquor as cheap as it was, not to mention that it was a drink which did not require ice made from suspect Mexican water, the two had at it. In no time, they were both pissy drunk, inviting Nick to join them.

"Nick, get your sorry ass over here, playboy," Carlton hollered at him over the oppressive, thumping techno beat. "We gettin' you drunk tonight!"

Nick reluctantly landed at the bar. "That's alright. I'll watch you two burn off all the taste buds on your tongue."

"C'mon, kid. Have a shot with us," Craig encouraged him, already beginning to slur his speech. "I'm buyin'."

"Naw, I'm good."

"Drink *something*," Craig urged.

The bartender looked at Nick expectantly.

"Orange juice and 7-Up," ordered Nick.

"Bitch, if you don't order something else, C-Town's gonna bust you in yo' eye, ram a shot of vodka down your throat, and chase it wit' some Jack!" Carlton threatened.

Uh-oh. When Carlton began referring to himself in the third person, as the entity C-Town, it was time to do something to placate him. C-Town was different from Carlton. C-Town was a party animal, a Malloy on crack, addicted to having a good time and making everyone around him do so, too. Kind of like Bruce Banner and the Incredible Hulk, C-Town usually came out only when drunk or angry.

Basically, if Nick did not order a drink with alcohol in it, C-Town would do his best to embarrass the hell out of him, even if it required alerting the entire club. A big sigh. "Midori Sour," Nick capitulated.

C-Town and Craig reluctantly turned back to their drinks.

"What a pussy drink," mumbled C-Town.

"I'm a little disappointed in you, kid," said Craig.

"Well, at least it's got some alcohol in it," Nick defended himself. "May even make some of these jailbait specials look attractive."

Drink in hand, Nick turned his back to the bar and scanned the dance floor. Nothing really caught his eye until . . . Wait a minute! She looked over twenty! She looked fine, too! Nick gulped down the rest of his drink and waded onto the dance floor.

Nick tried dancing up behind her, smiling his physical invitation when she turned around. She flashed some teeth and it was on. The woman was Latina, and she seemed to have an American air about her. She wore a tight bebe baby tee and some fitted Iceberg jeans that molded to her round behind. Short, of course, which made dancing with her a challenge, as Nick struggled to come down to meet her low center of gravity. Quite a workout for the legs. But damn if she wasn't worth it, with her high cheekbones, dark, raven-colored hair, and tiny black mole on her cheek. If it were possible to radiate in the dark of the sweaty, techno-saturated club, she did.

Mercifully, the DJ changed to a salsa song. Mal grabbed the woman nearest to him and marched out into the middle of the dance floor, breezing right past Nick. Nick gazed on enviously. The man had no fear.

Nick's partner said something to him in Spanish. Nick shrugged, offering up his palms to indicate he did not understand.

"Let's dance to this song, *chico*," she requested in good, accented English.

"I don't know how to dance to salsa."

"I'll show you real quick." She taught Nick the basic step and they were on their way. He also was careful to study those around him, including the amazingly talented Malloy. By the end of the night, Nick was twirling, dipping his partner, and having a grand time.

**ON THE CAR** ride back, Mal drove while Nick rode shotgun. Craig and Carlton were passed out in the backseat, snoring and slobbering on themselves. Six tequila shots will do that to you. On an ac-

tive night like tonight, the best friends indulged in a typical party debrief.

"So what's the story with Señorita Latina Mas Fina? I saw you
lockin' her up all night."

Nick grinned. He couldn't deny it. "Her name is Esmerelda. Digits,
baby."

"Tight, tight," Mal approved. "That's a phat-ass name. Where
does she live?"

"We didn't get that far. Let's see." Nick unfolded the scrap of paper
with her phone number on it. He frowned. "What kind of area code
is fifty-two then sixty-six?"

"Lemme see that." Mal took the paper and glanced at it. "That's
the country code, dawg. See, fifty-two is the country code, then sixty-
six is the city code. Then the number."

"Ohhhhh, man," groaned Nick. "You mean I've gotten myself a
Mexican girl?"

"What? What's wrong with that?" asked Mal. "From what I saw
of her, not a helluva lot."

"It's just that the border crossings and the long-distance phone calls
are gonna suck. And who knows if she can even come into the country to visit me," complained Nick.

"Just take it one step at a time, son. One step at a time."

"Well, what about you, Mal? Dancing like you weren't married no
more," kidded Nick.

An inscrutable look crossed Mal's face, then quickly vanished.
"Don't hate, congratulate."

"Where'd you learn how to dance like that?"

"Had me this Dominican girlfriend in high school for a minute. We
used to get down at her family picnics to all that good stuff. Salsa,
merengue . . . I didn't realize until tonight how much I missed it."

"Mia doesn't salsa?"

"Mia doesn't do much of anything." Mal quickly changed the subject. "Now, just like in that movie *Swingers,* how long are you gonna
call your girl?"

"Three days?" Nick answered, remembering the movie on LA dating life.

"No, tomorrow. Three days is going on white-boy speed. Who

knows how many numbers she gave out before she met you, son. If you wait that long, another brotha might get to her first," rationalized Mal. "And we don't like him."

"No," Nick agreed. "We most certainly do not."

**SUNDAY WAS A** fairly casual affair. Nick took Mal to a Chargers game at Qualcomm Stadium. The Chargers played the Seahawks in front of another sellout crowd. Even though the Chargers were steaming toward mediocrity in the young NFL season, the stadium was still packed. Although they inexplicably did not have a pro basketball team, San Diegans supported their sports teams.

Nick relished cheering for his hometown Seattle Seahawks. Mal relished shoveling down hot dogs and popcorn while trying to keep his friend from getting killed. The Chargers might suck, but their fans were still passionate.

After the game, they ate at Seau's, Carlton's favorite spot and quite the after-game hangout. The Chargers fans drank their woes away at the bar while Nick indulged in a hearty steak to celebrate the Seahawks' win. Junior Seau himself came out to grab the house mic, commiserating with fellow Chargers fans.

By the time they got home, it was time for Nick to pack up for the week. He was due on set at 10 A.M. for *Blackdraft*. A call from Khalilah on his machine let him know that she was somewhere in Egypt and would not be back for another two weeks. So, basically, Nick and Mal would have the run of her place in her absence. They left for LA at ten o'clock and were safely bedded down for the night two hours later in Khalilah's house. Nick did call Esmerelda before he left. So much for that Other Brotha.

**THE MOOD ON** the *Blackdraft* set was warm. Shortly after Nick had checked in that day, Ayinde delivered the good news. "Guess what, B? *Blackdraft* won its time slot on Tuesday! UPN's picked up the show for a full season!"

With his being entertained by Chantel in Chicago last Tuesday, Nick had forgotten to check out *Blackdraft*'s series premiere! "Well, that's alright," Nick said, smiling as he drifted over by the craft service table. He and Wesley reached for the same donut.

"My bad," said Wesley. Recognition at first, but no name. "You're . . . you're . . . um . . ."

"Nick."

"That's right. Of course you are." Wesley dapped him up. "How's everything going, man?"

"Can't complain, I suppose," said Nick. "Not doing nearly as well as you guys."

Wesley smiled, a bit sheepish. He was proud but still gracious. "That took us by surprise, too. No one expected us to win a time slot. Not in primetime. Not ever."

"Well, here's to proving white America wrong—again."

"Here, here." They clinked Dixie cups full of Ruby Red grapefruit juice. After a sip, Wesley said, "Hey, why don't you come to the party they're having over at Wendal's house in the Hills tomorrow night? It's at seven-thirty and it's gonna be real casual. Just come through if you can. Today's our last day of this episode, we have tomorrow off, and then we'll be back and rolling on Wednesday. It'll give us all a chance to unwind and kick it."

A house party by a famous and successful actor in the Hollywood Hills? *Don't have to ask me twice.* "I'm there," Nick said, grinning.

---

**THIS WAS NICK'S** first Hollywood party. Hell, it was Nick's first California party. A little nervous, he was glad to have Malloy with him, proverbially holding his hand. Mal had been caught off guard with Nick's party invitation late Monday night when he had come back from set, and had had to run out and pick up an outfit that morning. Mal sported a pair of linen pants and a loose-fitting polo while Nick wore dark, ribbed dress pants and a stylish electric-blue collared shirt. This was his "Audition Shirt."

Wendal's house was, of course, very nice. When Nick pulled up in the circular driveway, he felt a small sense of inadequacy as he parked his model-year 4Runner next to an assortment of Beemers and Benz. Mal admired the landscaping as they strolled down a pathway adorned with stone sculptures that were probably Greek in origin. The house was three levels with many windows in either direction, and Roman columns supported a balcony hanging over the doorway. Nick rang the doorbell.

"It's hard to believe a brotha lives here," Mal mused. "This house looks almost as big as my high school!"

"Try not to drool on the carpet. It would probably cost a month of your salary to clean it."

Thanks to a very Jeeves-ish looking butler, Nick and Mal were escorted through the house to a backyard area, a full acre at least, complete with swimming pool and putting green. The party was in full swing, with the various cast members, production staff, and other Industry people with whom Nick was not familiar living it up poolside, in the large hot tub, and milling about in the gazebo area. A long table was set up, filled with nothing but eats. Both men wasted little time gravitating toward the table.

Wesley met them halfway. "Hey, what's goin' on, Nick?"

Nick dapped him up. "Chillin', bro. This here's my man Malloy."

"Whassup, black," said Mal as he dapped Wesley up.

"Wesley, man."

"No doubt. Yo, you were that heat in *Player to Be Named Later*!"

"Thanks, man."

"For real. That's love."

Nick hid an inward smile. It was not every day that he saw the habitually unaffected, cooler-than-an-iceberg-in-Antartica, playa-for-real Malloy fan somebody up.

"So where's Wendal?" Nick asked.

"Cornering the head writer about changing his character," Wesley snorted. "Bump that guy, man. I don't care if it is his party. Go 'head and get you some food. We'll talk."

Mal didn't last long at the food table. Dropping crab cakes to go cozy up to Lisa Nicole Carson, Mal trotted off to stargaze some more.

Nick couldn't blame him. There were a lot of folk there. Morris Chestnut had a flock of attractive ladies all listening to him recount a story. A sullen Ice Cube drank a beer over by the pool, just staring out into the water like his character Doughboy from *Boyz N the Hood*. Taye Diggs hit on some multiracial model-looking woman who was at least three inches taller than he was. Wasn't that bestselling author

Lolita Files giving Nick the eye from the hot tub? Not that Nick would mind. *Wit' yo' foine self* . . .

"Excuse me." The voice was soft, polite, and definitely feminine. Its high-pitched tone reminded him of the late-eighties flash-in-the-pan recording artist Michel'le, only it was sexier. And it was accompanied by the scent of fresh chocolate.

Nick looked up. Lawd-a-mercy! This heavenly creature Fate had thrust before him was flawless. Physical perfection in every way. Dismissing his own theories on perfection as an ideal instead of a person, Nick allowed his eyes to devour this chocolate-scented perfection. She was the dark brown complexion that mahogany furniture aspired to be. Sizing her up instantaneously like The Terminator, Nick figured she was five-eight, no more than 140 pounds. Her waist was enviable and her C-cup breasts threatened to spill over the short, flimsy swath of fabric that clothed her body—but just barely. Even her straightened, shoulder-length hair was all hers. And then her eyes. Her eyes deserved a book all their own, with their astonishing, intoxicating beauty. It was almost as if he had seen them, seen her, before. Impossibly, somehow, those gorgeous dark crystals of soul were fixed upon him.

"Excuse me," she politely repeated.

"Yes?" With his hand clutching a ladle full of potato salad in midair, Nick felt like the world's biggest boob.

"Have you seen the macaroni and cheese?"

Glad to be lobbed a softball for a question, Nick faked composure and put down the stupid ladle. "They ate it already. See?"

He gestured toward a tin of macaroni remains.

"Rat bastards!" She sucked her teeth and then chuckled. "Guess that's what I get for showing up on CP time, huh?"

Her smile was infectious. Nick couldn't help but return it.

"I don't think I know you. I'm Shana McAdams."

*Yes, you are,* drooled Nick's inner child, not fully getting her name. He shook her hand. "I'm Nick."

"So how do you know Wendal?"

"I work on the show."

"Really?" That seemed to pique her interest. "Cast or crew?"

"Uh . . . cast," Nick fabricated. Well, in a sense he *was* part of the cast. Just a silent part. Nick also hesitated because he was unsure of whether Shana's interest was from being an Industry insider or from being a professional pretty girl/self-employed model groupie.

"Well, I didn't mean to hold you up from your dinner," she began her exit gracefully.

*Woman, you could hold up my life . . .* "Not a problem" was the only thing he could think to say.

This woman, who was in a galaxy of fineness *all* her own, continued to be generous with her attention. "Well, it was nice meeting you. See ya around, Nick."

"Pleasure meeting you," Nick squeaked out before she dissipated into a cloud of people far more important than him. Whether she would later admit to it or not, Nick would stake his 4Runner on the fact that they had just shared a moment. The way he knew was because he kept replaying that moment in his mind over and over for the rest of the night.

**THE NEXT DAY** he was on set. Once again, Nick was needed to fill some background in a day full of tame, talky firehouse scenes. He *really* wasn't feeling this. There were just so many pointless, motivationless background crosses one could make sixteen times in a row, with no hope of a spoken line in sight. He had not moved from Chicago to be somebody's background blur.

By the time his scenes were over, Nick stormed back to holding and fired up his cell phone. His call was to Shelby. Naturally, she was not there. She had not been "there" in almost a week. Nick started thinking bad thoughts.

To settle his nerves, he grazed by the craft service table, which was typically filled with every type of candy and snack one could imagine. When he reached for the gummy bear jar, his hand brushed someone else's. A soft hand.

"Excuse me," she grinned. "Have you seen the macaroni and cheese?"

Shana McAdams, in all her eminence, stood right before him. She was dressed in a uniform costume identical to Nick's.

"You know, we really should stop meeting like this," said Nick. "You always catch me eating."

"Good to see you again, Nick."

"You, too. Most definitely." He subtly licked his lips. "Do you work here?"

"Yes," Shana replied sunnily. She scooped up a handful of gummy bears. Before shoveling half of them into her mouth, she mentioned, "I'm cast."

"Imagine that." Nick offered a timid laugh. Then, his brain began to work in overdrive. Shana McAdams, Shana McAdams . . . *that* Shana McAdams! "Why didn't you tell me you were a celebrity?"

Shana laughed. "I'm just an actress. Anyone who has to say they're a celebrity isn't a celebrity."

"Wait a minute. Weren't you in . . . in . . . What the hell was the name of that cheesy flick . . . Ooops, my bad. No offense."

"None taken." That smile on her face seemed to be pretty constant.

*"Boys Club!"* he shouted. "That's what I saw you in before. You're Saya Hamilton! You were *great,* Shana! I mean, the movie sucked, thanks to some formulaic writing and uninspired directing, but your performance really stood out. I enjoyed it."

"Great. Well, I gotta head back to set. We can talk about the movie when we break for lunch. Is that cool?"

"Is it!"

---

**NICK SAT ACROSS** from Shelby's desk, as serious as if he were about to take a life. "Shelby, I'm through."

This caused her to look up from examining some photo-shoot proofs for Fredo. "What?"

"I'm through. I'm gonna take a break from Hollywood."

"Well, don't we have thick skin," the agent commented dryly. At least he had her full attention now. "May I ask why?"

"I've been banging away at this acting thing for two months now, and all I have to show for it are two SAG vouchers and a crick in my neck from reading so much on set." Nick sighed. "I need a break."

"Yes, you do, and you're just one audition away from getting it! You have to hang in there, Nick. Trust me when I say that I'm working for you over here."

He resisted the temptation to roll his eyes. "Don't worry about me, Shelby. Fredo needs you more than I do right about now."

"I don't get paid unless you get paid. That's how it works."

"I doubt my big payday is gonna come from Drug Dealer #2."

"We all have to start somewhere," remarked Shelby, using one of her well-worn Industry platitudes. "So what're you going to do instead? Temp?"

"I'm going to stay in San Diego. Probably do some theater."

Shelby shook her head slightly. "No, no, no, Nick . . . Nobody goes to San Diego to act. That'll be career suicide."

"I figure it'll give you some time to get me an audition that matters," Nick said with no small amount of pointedness. "Something to make me drive 125 miles for."

"I see. Well, I guess you have it all figured out, huh?" That the battle-scarred agent managed to say that without his feeling patronized was a testament to her malleability.

Nick stood, ready to go. This was the first time he had met with Shelby in which the meeting had been ended by himself, instead of by a phone call or her busy schedule or—God help him—*Fredo*. "Happy hunting."

IT WAS ONLY a matter of time before Ayinde said something. Nick came back from the WB commissary, humming a tune and munching on a donut. After Nick plopped down into a folding chair and broke out the sports section, Ayinde finally said it.

"Yo, B. You been doin' a lot of fraternization with the principals, B." Ayinde wasn't jealous—he was just curious. "Especially that girl firefighter."

"She's hot, ain't she? They don't get much more perfect than her."

"Give yourself some time, son. LA's full of perfect-looking women. It's just a matter of time before you see someone you like better," Ayinde predicted. "There will always be someone finer."

"Amen to that," Nick concurred. "I certainly hope so."

"So what're you gettin' into tonight?"

"Nothing, I guess."

Licking his lips, Ayinde cut his eyes to ensure that their conversation was private. "Check it out, B. That porno company I work part-time for, yo, they're havin' a pool party at the president's house. Wanna come with?"

"Stop lying, man!" Nick was thrilled. "Can my boy Mal come? He's from New York."

"No doubt, god, no doubt. Word is bond." They dapped up to seal the deal.

---

**NICK WAS RELATIVELY** disappointed. For a porno party, everyone was pretty well clothed. A gaggle of women lounged by the pool in sarongs, shorts, and bikini tops. Only a few of the hotter-looking women swam in the pool, bouncing a beach ball. There were surprisingly few men at the party, most of them lounging by the patio area, with the female-to-male ratio hovering around four or five to one.

Actually, Nick hadn't known what to expect; he was simply happy to be there. But whatever surprise may have shown on Nick's face Mal kept internalized. His dark globes coolly appraised the scene. One would think that being married, and forced to make love to the same woman for the past three years, would have made Mal *more* excited to see the legion of gorgeous, skimpily clad women at this party.

Ayinde bubbled up to them. "Yo, what's goin' on, B?"

Nick dapped up his boy. "Good lookin' out, kid. I appreciate it. Yo, this is my boy Malloy."

"Yo, peace, black," Ayinde greeted, dapping him up.

"Whassup." Mal continued to survey the wildlife. "There's a lot of cake around here, god. Lot of cake."

"Wait 'til you taste the icing, my brotha." Ayinde smiled. "Come over here by the patio area. We're about to get some women together and play a little drinking game."

Ayinde's "little drinking game" turned into a full-blown lush affair. While Nick, the nondrinker, largely observed, Malloy became the life of the party. Without alcohol in his system, Mal was entertaining enough. Get some liquor and several fine women around him, and he was off the hook. Four drinks to the wind, Mal had soon enticed a small cadre of tanned, buxom women, who draped on and flirted with him shamelessly. Not exactly to Nick's surprise, Mal flirted back. The man was good for making a woman feel good, all right.

Eventually, Nick got bored and wandered off inside the house. It was beautiful, a two-story-view home in Pacific Palisades. Maybe Nick was in the wrong business. Porn paid well.

Nick was trapped in the kitchen with a porn starlet named Valdetta. She was young, pretty, Asian, and the rising star of "only" (her words, not Nick's) *twenty-five* pornos. She blabbered on about how porno was legitimate work, the purest form of artistic expression. Through porn, she helped fill a void in couples' lives. If she, Valdetta, a former bag girl at Safeway, could touch or arouse other people, then she had somehow fulfilled her purpose here on this earth. All of this was said by her with a straight face—and a chest full of more saline than an IV.

A half hour later, Nick escaped her clutches. He never thought he would see the day he would be happy to leave a room full of porn stars.

Knowing he was not supposed to, Nick ambled along the hallways of the expansive house. He observed the medium-priced works of art passively, as he actively thought about his future. Leaving the LA scene had to be a good thing, right? It could only save money to stay put in San Diego for a few months. He had seen in the online version of the *Reader* that there were several auditions for theater around town. It was time to dust off the Shakespeare.

Searching for the bathroom on the second floor, Nick opened a door. Talk about the shock of his life! There was his very married best friend, Malloy, standing with his pants around his ankles and *his* best friend in his hand, about to be serviced by some woman with dirty-blond hair, the Silicone Valley in her chest fully exposed, on her knees, about to pray to the Mandingo god. This may not have been a john, but Nick's friend sure looked like one.

Mal turned his head in Nick's direction. His eyes were bloodshot from too much drinking. He turned on his trademark, charismatic smile. "A little privacy, dawg."

"A little privacy?" Nick spat incredulously. "How about 'You're a little *married*! *Dawg*'!"

"Married?" asked the woman from her kneeling position.

In a tone that did *not* offer any room for dispute, Nick bellowed seriously, "Whore, leave."

The woman scrambled out of the room only after trying to find her bra and her dignity. She found only the bra.

A disgusted Mal began to zipper up. Nick, up in his face, seethed righteous indignation. "What the fuck was that, Mal! I swear, I could just *shake you* right now! How the fuck you're gonna cheat on Mia? How the fuck you're gonna cheat on your *wife*!"

If Mal had been drunk before, he sobered up real quick. With all the solemnity of a pallbearer, he said, "I don't have a wife anymore. Mia and I . . . we're separated."

Mal paused to collect his thoughts. Tears lurked at the corners of his life.

"My wife is leaving me."

## MARRIAGE MINDED
*One man's quest to get married in a year*
*by Anonymous*

At this rate, I'll never get married. That's right, I said it. With the obstacles being thrown in my way from various women, my search for a bride almost seems fruitless.

Last week, an unfortunate incident occurred where two women I was interested in ended up meeting each other *in my house*. Unfortunate, indeed. This has become so "unfortunate" that neither is speaking to me. My best girlfriend prospects, my best wives-in-training, have evaporated—all because of the thoughtlessness of one female, the one who *did not call*.

There's more. It would have been easy enough for the other woman there to ostracize me from her heart and let it be that. But no, she still wanted to see me. For the gentlemen who are out there reading this column, if a woman is mad at you and doesn't want to speak to you, consider yourself LUCKY. If she wants to hang around, be friends, and give herself every opportunity to make discreet and not-so-discreet remarks about your character, then she will ensure that your life is a living hell.

But there's more. When a woman is fed up, she will go ahead and ask direct questions she really does not need, or want, to know the answers to. Be careful when you ask a question, ladies, because we just might give you the answer. Especially when that question revolves around commitment.

True, I am in the market to get married. It's not a

secret. I hope y'all are out there searching for my wife with me. But I still have a shred of male common sense. It says, on page 204, section 12, subheading 69 of the *Male Guidebook,* that a man is not your man until he tells you so. Until he asks you to be his lady or uses some other means to indicate the exclusivity of this relationship, then you are not his girlfriend. And until you reach that vaunted status, a man has no obligations to you. A man is not going to tell you the entire truth. A man is going to see other women.

Until you are a girlfriend, you have no rights, no claims upon the man. Just because you *like* him doesn't mean he's going to give up other women for *you.* Just because *he* likes *you,* he's not going to give up other women for *you.* Consider his dating patterns as protection for the man. To prevent your seriously breaking his heart, the man will have several other women that he's "talking to" in order to offset any potential damage a nongirlfriend could cause. Only after and not before reaching girlfriend status can a woman make demands upon her man.

So when Ole Girl demanded to know, in a very snippy tone, the answer to a question she had no business asking, I did us both a favor by not answering. For a woman not my girlfriend, it truly was none of her freakin' business. I did not lie, but also, I did not tell her the truth.

The truth is, I was very into Ole Girl, and what had happened to make her distrust me was unfortunate. It may take some time in order for her to like me again. In retrospect, the one really good thing I can say is that I never lied to her. But, at these prices, what price honesty?

The cost? It just might cost me my getting married.

# 8

**AN I LIVE** with you?"

It all made sense. The degradation of women. The excessive flirting in Tijuana. The ridiculous advice he dispensed for Nick to "lay his game down." Staggering from the weight of such a pronouncement, Nick had to vacate the room, the house, ending up by the pool. Nick did not know whether to vomit or fall in.

When Nick finally found his voice, he croaked, "You want to stay with me?"

"Can I?" asked Mal meekly. Nick had known this man a third of his life, and he had known him to be anything but meek.

"What happened?" Nick struggled into a deck chair, an effort to avoid tipping over into the pool. His legs felt weak, weaker than when he had first heard Mal was getting married over three years ago. Back then, he had feared losing his best friend to a woman. Now, Nick feared "that woman" was losing his best friend.

"It's still happening, Nick," Mal said gravely, looking his best friend seriously in the eyes. "Ever had a cavity?"

"No."

"Well, it's just like that—the slow, continuous decay of a relationship. It's rotted, bruh. Rotted to the core."

Mal knelt by Nick's side while Nick mulled over the severity of his words. Nick watched the chlorine water in the empty pool ripple peacefully, so much unlike his life right now. "I don't know when exactly it began, but for almost a year now, it's felt as if my wife was drifting apart from me. Ever since she got her master's last year and opened up the shop, I could feel her pulling away. All of her energy was going into the shop. She loves that damn clothing store more than me."

This sounded so unlike Malloy. He was jealous of his wife's boutique? These were grounds for separation? "I don't understand."

"She wasn't the same, man. A husband knows his wife. She'd come home emotionally wasted, romantically aloof, sexually distant. Something was going on at that shop," Mal concluded.

"So you spied on her," Nick deducted, disappointed. When men who did not trust their women resorted to following them around, they became instantly pathetic.

"Yeah, I did," Mal admitted. "Mia's cheating on me."

"Shut up!" Nick verbally slapped him. Had decorum allowed, Nick would have thrown him into the pool. "Don't you dare make an accusation like that against that woman! That is the only woman, and I mean the *only* woman who loves your ass ad infinitum! Considering the amount of hos you done run up in, you better be sure, be sure *on your life,* that what you're saying is true! If you accuse your wife of something that heinous, then you better have ironclad evidence. You're my dawg and everything, but if you fuck up this relationship, this *marriage,* I will personally *beat your ass*!"

Mal swallowed solemnly. "I hear you, man. I'm not joking."

That small admission hit Nick like a Mack truck falling from the sky. His whole expression changed. In a strangled voice, Nick asked, "How do you know?"

"A month ago, I'd skip lunch and leave work early. I followed my wife for a week after I left work. She would close shop around eight every night. The third night, I saw something that changed the whole reality of my marriage. I saw her kiss another dude."

"What?"

"I saw her kiss another man."

"Where?"

"In her shop."

"On the lips?"

"Yes, nigga!" spat Malloy, incensed. "I saw her kiss another nigga, dude! I followed them to this motel in Jersey where she spent *three hours* up in that nigga's room before she kissed him *again* outside the motel room and left. I couldn't *believe* that shit!"

Nick was stunned into submission. He just simply did not want to believe it. In a way, he had overseen their whole courtship from afar. Mal and Mia had hooked up during the time when Nick was in Chicago, struggling to get over the woman he had proposed to, Mia's best friend, Jasmine. As Malloy continued to talk to Mia to keep tabs on Jasmine for Nick, he had also fallen for her. Finally, here was a woman who could match Mal wit for playeristic wit. Mia had had a habit of dating players, thugs, and con artists. So when Mal had stepped to her with his charming-player act, she saw right through it, called him on it, and had his tail whipped for an eternity.

And now it was all stripped away. It was all being tainted, bastardized by marital infidelity, which Nick had never known could exist in the woman.

"Did you confront her?"

Malloy sat down on the pavement and crossed his legs. He stared out into the aquamarine pool, not daring to look at his friend. With his complex range of emotions, he couldn't. "Yeah, I did. She didn't even *deny* it."

Nick wanted to throw himself off the edge of the canyon the house rested on. If Mia no longer loved Mal, then the world was upside down. He felt trapped in an inverted universe. Nick sadly lowered his head. "What did she say?"

"She didn't say shit," Mal said, glaring a hole into the water. "She put on this hurt, guilty expression and did not say a goddamn word. And that was the last time I spoke to my wife. A month ago."

"She left the house?"

"No, but she might as well have. We haven't spoken two words to each other since. She'd leave little notes for stuff she needed me to get done for her, but after I confronted her, we haven't talked."

"What did you do to her, Mal?" Nick accused. "I remember you telling me that women don't cheat unless men give them a reason to. What the fuck did you do to make her go out and cheat on you?"

"You know, if you weren't my boy, I'd have crushed your trachea by now," Mal said in a murderously quiet voice. He took a moment.

"Maybe I worked some long hours recently. Maybe I'd come home from work late and she was missin' me. Maybe she suspected somethin' wasn't right. But it was always work related, I'm tellin' you. I gave her no reason to cheat on me."

Not wanting to see his friend's eyes, Nick gazed off and asked, "Have you cheated on her?"

"No."

"But you were about to."

"You damn right." Mal brooded for a moment. "My marriage is over, Nick. I'm out of my fuckin' mind. I don't know what to do."

"Yes," Nick said quietly.

"Huh?"

"Yes, you can live with me."

**THE NEXT DAY** on set was to be Nick's last. His head was in such a tailspin, it was actually a good thing he did not have any lines to recite. He could wallow in the thickness of his thoughts without much interruption. Ayinde, curiously, was not on set today. The man was probably still reeling from the drinking game last night at the party. Nick was reeling from the fact that he had just gained a new roommate, albeit his best friend, whose heart and head were in a precarious position.

Fridays usually were arduous days because the director would try and cram in everything he could get shot before the weekend set in. A fifteen- or sixteen-hour day would be nothing new to the cast and crew. About three uneventful hours past Nick's early-morning call time, he browsed the craft service table, looking for something to nibble on.

From behind he heard, "Excuse me. Have you seen the macaroni and cheese?"

"Hey, Shana," Nick said, without even having to turn around. Her wonderfully chocolate smell preceded her.

She sidled up beside him. "Hey you." Her eyes could detect something amiss. "What's wrong?"

"Nothing. I just had a lousy night. How're you doing?"

"Don't try and change the subject," she chastised. "We were talking about how *you* are doing."

"I'm alright. Really. Oh, and this is my last day on the show for awhile."

"Why's that?" A hint of disappointment was in her voice.

"This extra work ain't for me. I think I'll start doing some theater or something back in San Diego. You can lose your acting chops being an extra like this."

"I see." Shana turned thoughtful. Then she beamed her million-dollar smile at him. "Well, I wish you success in everything you do. You'll make it. I know you will."

Nick would miss her. Shana was so beautiful, so sweet, and so positive. And she smelled damn good, too. "Thanks. You're a sweetheart."

She gave Nick a hug. "I've gotta go to the makeup trailer. I'll talk to you later."

*As if you need makeup,* Nick thought, reluctantly breaking from the hug. "Take care."

And she was off, leaving behind a cloud of dust that smelled like chocolate.

**THE NEXT FEW** weeks were a period of transition for Mal and Nick. This was the first time they were to actually live together on their own. Seven years ago, when Nick had first moved to New York, he had stayed over at Mal's parents' place with Mal and his sister Tikka, but had soon moved out into his own place. Even though they had been friends since their freshman year in college, they had never been roommates.

Luckily for Nick, Mal was not a slob. He also had not brought a whole lot of personal effects from New York. The man had packed as if he were going on vacation and merely bought a few articles here and there to supplement his wardrobe.

The two coexisted fairly peacefully as both of them sought jobs. Nick continued to secretly pump out articles for the *Reader*—to Craig's glee—as well as to search out legitimate acting work. Nick recruited a San Diego agent, who sent him out on an audition only once a week. The rest of the time was spent going out to every audition advertised in the *Reader*'s "Stage Notes" section, as well as battling Mal in PlayStation sports.

Mal, on the other hand, found work in a couple of weeks. He took a job as an IT specialist through a temp agency for a biotech firm in San Diego's tech-heavy Sorrento Valley. Each morning, Nick would rise to drive Mal down to the trolley station, where Mal would take a complex arrangement of trains and buses to get to where he needed to go.

There were so many questions Nick had about their arrangement that he did not dare ask. What had happened to Mal's old job at Morgan Stanley? Why didn't he stay with his sister Tikka and her husband? What did his parents think about Mal's separation? Did Mia approve of this separation? Did she know he was not coming back? All of these questions swirled about in Nick's head, threatening to leap out of his mouth at any time, but he knew he had to be more tactful than he had ever been in his life. These were complex emotions they were dealing with. His main concern was Mal's well-being, but Mal seemed to be getting along fine.

As far as Nick's love life was concerned, that was another story. Ever since her outburst on the Frisbee golf course, Anna had fallen off. It was a mutual apathy: Nick did not make much of an effort and neither did she. Maya T. was MIA, no matter how often Nick called and left messages. By the third week, he just gave up. She must have been really pissed at him not to return a phone call. As impossible as it might seem, Nick and Maya T. had not had a significant fight over anything in their nine-year, long-distance friendship. He really missed her.

The one woman who showed promise was Esmerelda. They talked a couple of times a week at first, bumped up to four times a week by the third week. Compared with a lot of the phony women he had met on LA sets and the equally pretentious actresses he met out on auditions, Nick found Esmerelda to be a breath of fresh air. She was a student at the local college in Tijuana, premed, and refreshingly naive when it came to the American entertainment industry. She could not tell Julia Roberts from Julia Childs. But when it came to the *telenovelas,* she was an absolute fan. She could rattle on and on about how Marisol nearly cheated on Geronimo, or about her favorite new *telenovela* star, Fredo. No matter how much he tried, Nick still could not escape Shelby Townsend's reach.

Their flirtation grew into a bona fide date. Nick trekked back across the border one weekend afternoon to see her. Esmerelda was stunning in her fashionable, American-style sundress and plunging neckline full of cleavage. Tooling around in the 4Runner, Esmerelda showed Nick her hometown of Tijuana, places she had played when growing up, her old school. Normally, a woman recounting her childhood via a driving tour would have bored Nick, but Esmerelda was so sweet, so engaging, and so beautiful that he listened anyway. After a while, listening to her became endearing.

Around twilight, they ended up at the beach, lying flat on their backs on the sand. His head was right next to hers, but upside down, with his body stretched out in one direction while hers went in the opposite. At low tide, the waves subtly caressed the beach. Nick and Esmerelda, "Ezzy" as he now called her, just lay there, head to head, gazing upward and trying to find the stars against a purplish, darkening sky.

**"NIIIIIICK!" SHE SQUEALED.**

"Koko!!!!" Nick mock-squealed back into the phone. In a more masculine voice, he said, " 'Sup?"

"I need a favor, Nick."

Nick sank back against his futon, twirling his index finger in the air to Mal as a sign to take the game off pause. They were playing PlayStation basketball, the perennial matchup of Nick's SuperSonics against Mal's Knicks. "What's that?"

"There's a PKP convention accompanying the Gold Coast Classic next weekend down in San Diego. I wanted to know if I could stay with you?" Khalilah asked timidly.

Concentrating more on the game, Nick obliged her simple request. "Sure. No problem. It's the least I could do, seeing how you've opened up your home to me in LA whenever I need to come up."

"Oh yeah, and one more thing. Could two of my sorors stay, too?" she asked in a rush.

Now, that distracted Nick. "*Two* of your friends?"

"Yes?" she said hopefully.

"As in a grand total of three females living in my house?" Nick counted, a bit overwhelmed.

Mal smacked Nick on his arm. "Three women up in this piece? Say yes, nigga!"

"C'mon, Nick," cooed Khalilah invitingly. "Wouldn't you like to spend a weekend with three beautiful ladies?"

"Wouldn't I like to spend a weekend with three beautiful ladies," Nick repeated for Mal's benefit. When Mal threatened to smack him again, Nick hurriedly said, "Okay, okay. I'll do it."

"Thanks so much, Nick!" she gushed graciously. That was just for show. There had never been a doubt in her mind that Nick would say yes.

"So when should I expect this shipment of beautiful ladies?"

"We'll be there Thursday night. There's a conference on Friday at the convention center Downtown, a step show that night, the game on Saturday, and parties all that night. We'll be out of your hair by Sunday evening."

"If your friends are cute, they can stay in my hair as long as they want."

"Oh, Nick. You're so *nutty*!" Khalilah was an amazing combination of intelligence, beauty, and corniness. Her love of travel and her gypsy-blooded nature gave her a lexicon different from most of Nick's African-American friends. "Well, thanks again, Nick! I'll call you when we're about to leave."

"Take care."

Nick hung up, firmly refocusing on the game. Mal, of course, was full of questions. "So what the deal?"

"Seems like Khalilah and two of her sorority sisters are coming down this weekend for the Gold Coast Classic."

"What's that?"

"It's kinda like a Bayou Classic–West," Nick explained. "For some reason, two black colleges each November come out to San Diego to put on a football game. And for some reason, half the black people in Southern California turn out for it."

"Who's playing this year?"

"I think it's Howard and Florida A&M."

Malloy whistled. "FAMU and The Mecca! Man, this place is gonna be off the hook!"

"Fa sho'," Nick agreed.

"Did Khalilah and them go to Howard or FAM?"

"Please," Nick snorted. "They're just down here for the Pheta convention that same weekend and the game. Khalilah and all her heads went to USC."

"So Khalilah's a Pheta, huh," Mal sized up. The lovely ladies of Pheta Kappa Pheta were world-renowned for their beauty, brains, and bravado. No one was sexier, smarter, or sillier. To hear them tell it, as the sorority tagline went, "All men dream of loving a Pheta queen." "I bet her friends will be tight."

"I ain't studyin' them," dismissed Nick.

Mal rolled his eyes. "Please don't tell me you're gettin' your heart all wrapped around that Mexican chick."

"I didn't say that. I like her, though."

Mal shook his head disapprovingly. "You'll learn one of these days, you'll learn."

"Learn what?"

"Not to be so easily impressed."

**THE PKPS ARRIVED** with much fanfare—and baggage. Khalilah and her girls quickly employed Nick and Malloy as unpaid valets as they lugged in some twelve bags among the three of them. For a three-day weekend.

Once Nick was able to put the bags down, he assessed his visitors. The Phetas knew how to *represent*! Khalilah's sands (line sister), Kina, was five-three, a toffee-colored woman with a down-to-earth demeanor, as evidenced by her exiting the car wearing a pair of socks and flip-flops. Rail thin, but with pouty lips and catlike eyes, Kina definitely worked with what she had. Andrea was Khalilah's other soror, a five-five, dark-chocolate woman with a full chest and tight, thick legs obscured by knee-high boots. Talk about *sexy*!

Mal and Nick looked at each other and exchanged grins. Three beautiful ladies, indeed!

As the ladies settled in, the boys bent over backward to assist. Mal went to work on Kina, allowing Nick to holla at Andrea. In casual chitchat he found out that Andrea was in her second year of med school, was a native Los Angeleno, and had graduated from Loyola Marymount. This all helped prime him for the real question Nick wanted to ask, as he helped get her situated in the guest room, now Mal's room.

"So what does your boyfriend do?" he inquired, innocently enough.

"Boyfriend?" Andrea laughed uneasily. "I don't have one of those."

*Jackpot!* screamed Nick silently. "That must be by choice."

"Why do you say that?"

"Because the only time a good-looking woman is alone is by choice." And Mal said *he* had more game than Parker Brothers . . .

Andrea blushed. She stopped and started a couple times, almost as if she did not know what to say. "Thank you."

The full-court press was on.

THE NEXT DAY, the boys were to meet the girls down at the San Diego Convention Center, right along the waterfront, after their convention sessions were over. Upon arrival, Nick and Mal found themselves awash in waves of red and green, the PKP sorority colors. Waiting for them at the entrance to the Convention Center was Craig, who loved a good step show as much as the next black man.

Dap was exchanged. "Whassup, kid?"

"It's all you, C-Nice," greeted Nick.

"Whassup, kid?" Craig said to Mal.

"Whassup now," Mal greeted back.

"Where's Carlton at?"

"He ain't comin'," said Nick. "The station stuck him with the Stingrays game at the last minute. We'll have to get our swerve on without him."

Craig took a look around at all manner of beautiful black women streaming in and out of the Convention Center, shaking his head in disbelief. "Now *this* is what I mean by 'bring me hotties'!"

Deep within the burrows of the center, they met up with the ladies and had dinner. Mal discreetly kept Kina's interest while Nick openly kicked game to Andrea. Nick was not entirely sure, but he thought she was feeling him.

Dinner led directly to the step show. It had been such a long time since both Mal and Nick had been to a step show that Nick had forgotten how lively and exciting it was. The main ballroom was packed with some fifteen-hundred-odd boisterous young black folk. Omega

Q-Dogs barked their way around, Deltas oo-ooped, AKAs skee-weed their presence into tone deafness, the Phetas responded with their phee-wees, and the Sigmas and Kappas tried to shout each other down.

As the step show got underway, the scene was raucous. People stood up in their seats and wildly cheered on their affiliations. The Howard and FAMU contingents jostled the atmosphere for screaming space. When the Qs from Howard successfully executed a blindfolded, wrist-tied, flaming-cane routine to George Clinton's "Atomic Dog," the crowd erupted from the stands in applause, overflowing the stage, mobbing the victorious steppers. The step show was effectively over.

Afterward, the six of them strolled from the Convention Center to the adjacent Gaslamp Quarter. The Gaslamp flowed with people from the step show, people from DC and Tallahassee for the game, and the normal Friday-night party crowd. Nick had never seen so many black people in San Diego. It was like a little piece of Atlanta had been imported here.

In the thick of the stream of the street life was Robert. The man had his arm around some strapping, tall, dark-haired guy who held a cup for him, while Robert flailed about, no doubt cattily criticizing something or somebody. He was already three sheets to the wind— whatever that meant.

Nick went up to him. "Robert."

"*Neeeecolah!*" his drunken self bellowed. He reeked of vodka and tonic. At least he wasn't at the slurring-speech stage yet. "What a surprise! What're you doing down here tonight?"

"I went to a step show with my friends. You remember Malloy, don't you?" Nick gestured to Mal, who gave a cursory nod before looking sharply away.

"Quite the socialite, isn't he?" barbed Robert. He detached himself from his male friend and swaggered over to Mal and the women. "It's alright, Mal. Gays don't bite. Unless you *want* us to!"

Mal looked away in disgust. Robert continued undaunted. "Hello, everybody! I'm Nick's token gay friend! I'm Robert!"

Nick's eyes rolled to the very back of his brain. He did not know whether to be embarrassed for himself or for Robert. The ladies and Craig introduced themselves with a minimum of snickering.

"So how long are you ladies here for?" Robert asked.

"Sunday," said Khalilah.

"Out here to have a good time?"

"Most definitely."

"Follow me. I'll show you the best time in the city."

The girls looked at the guys for guidance. Nick shrugged, Mal looked off scornfully. Nick smiled. "Go ahead. It's your world."

*Was this club picked specifically to embarrass Mal?* Nick wondered. The Rainbow Room was an underground, very crowded gay club. A heavy, annoying, techno/drum-and-bass beat saturated the air. Except for the music, and the fact that all the men and women in there were gay, it seemed like a regular club. Even though the girls were having a good time, bobbing to the techno music and sipping on drinks at a table, Mal felt distinctly uncomfortable, telling Nick so at every turn.

"Is that dude lookin' at me, dawg?" asked Mal, not daring to look back in the guy's direction.

"Huh? Which one?"

"The white one with the Kangol on."

"Oh, him?" laughed Nick. "Looks like he likes his meat dark!"

"Aw, shit! I *knew* it! I've gotta get out of here!"

"Relax, homophobe. Have a drink. The ladies are having a good time and that's all that matters."

The ladies were holding their own little conference.

"Hey, Sands, what's the story with Nick? Is that you?" Kina asked Khalilah bluntly.

"No, Sands. Nick's just my friend."

"Mmm . . . with friends like that, who needs a boyfriend?" remarked Andrea, sizing Nick up as he stood next to Malloy. "You sure he's available?"

"Very."

"That's good to know," she acknowledged, still continuing to check him out.

When the dance music changed to techno, the women popped up and waded onto the dance floor. Craig, Nick, and Mal brought up the reluctant rear. Robert was already out there, dancing with reckless abandon, with his nameless wonder from the Gaslamp. Craig respectfully danced with Khalilah. Nick and Andrea started to get into their dance, as she chose to grind herself against his crotch several times. Mal could hardly get loose, afraid that somebody male was checking out his ass.

Nick, Mal, and the girls crawled home about 3 A.M. Mal was shot, having fallen asleep on the car ride home. For the most part, so were the ladies, save Andrea. As soon as they got home, everyone hit the sack, with Kina and Khalilah sharing Nick's queen-sized bed, and Malloy on the couch. Everyone, that is, save Nick and Andrea.

Andrea sat on the steps of Nick's front porch and smoked. It was not until Nick came outside to check on her that he realized exactly what it was she was smoking.

"How does a bright girl in med school end up smoking weed?" chided Nick lightly, easing in for a landing next to her.

Andrea took in a large drag before answering. "It's natural. It's of the earth."

"It also kills brain cells. Never mind," Nick caught himself. "I'm not here to lecture you."

"So why are you out here?" she asked in a way that did not seem standoffish.

"Thought you could use some company."

Andrea smiled, her dark eyes glistening in the moonlight. "I could."

They talked for the better part of an hour. Nick asked as many questions as he could of her, interested to know as much about her as possible. As their time grew longer, and the roach she puffed on dissipated, getting to know her proved to be an easy feat. Andrea was sexy as hell, with her tight black woman's body and scheming dark eyes. But still, one thing bothered him. *Cardinal Rule to Dating No. 10:* **Don't date women who do drugs.** Just being around her right now was illegal.

Finally, her marijuana was gone. Andrea exhaled mightily and inhaled clean ocean air. She stretched her arms out behind her, reveling in the elastic sensation of her body. Inadvertently—or so Nick thought—one of Andrea's breasts grazed his arm as she stretched. And as she stretched in the opposite direction, it grazed his arm again.

Taking her cue, Nick began doing a little stretching of his own, creating enough incidental contact that was anything but incidental. Andrea ended her stationary calisthenics by laying out flat on her back on the porch. Nick copied her, making sure that their arms touched. Then she rolled onto her side, curling up beside Nick's torso, her leg casually draped over his. Nick could feel every hair on his body stand at attention. He was conscious of her every movement, of his every muscle.

That was when liberties were taken. Moving on its own, Nick's free arm reached over to massage Andrea's exposed, ebony arms. That forced his body to meet hers, sideways, and then things happened. Wonderful things. Sexy things. Sexual things. Pants, muffled groans, sighs. Hardenings, softenings, lubricatings. Tongues, lips, hips, fingertips. Massaged, meshed, grated, penetrated. Wetness. Tartness. Roughness. Softness.

As Nick removed his fingers from inside her, he said through his own heavy breathing, "We can't do this."

Struggling to her feet, Andrea said, "Okay. Let's take it inside."

"I just want a kiss goodnight," Nick requested, getting to his feet.

"No."

"No?" Just a minute earlier, he had been inventing new ways for her body to say yes! What the hell did she mean by "no" to a simple goodnight kiss?

"I'm afraid that if I kiss you, I'll want more than that." She wasn't afraid at all. Andrea had made her little admission tantamount to an invitation.

"Don't worry about it. All I want is a kiss," Nick assured her, moving in to kiss her.

This time, she let him. Their kiss was hot and passionate, intense and sloppy, free and rangy. Once her lips had made short work of his, she moved to other regions of his smooth brown face, his neck, his ears. Her hands circled his butt, drawing his pelvis into hers. Those chocolate-coated jugs of womanly flesh slammed into his chest. This kiss would not stop, could not end itself. Between breaths, Andrea moaned, "I want to have sex with you."

Nick, against common guy sense, broke away with "No, we can't *do* this."

With her sparkling dark eyes, Andrea peered up at him from her five-five frame. Her eyes seduced, cajoled, persuaded, and challenged all at once. Although she was high, she still knew what her body wanted. Innocently, she asked, "Why not?"

A sigh allowed Nick to compose himself. "I don't want this to be a one-time thing."

"Well, if it's good, this can be a several-time thing." Her eyes would not be denied.

*Cardinal Rule to Dating No. 11:* **Never turn down sex?** Or maybe that was just simply a guy rule. Either way, for men, there were only so many times a guy could say no to sex. With a beautiful, sexy, assertive, willing partner, a sly woman who had manipulated Nick right into the position where she had wanted him, Nick had not one ounce of resistance left.

Andrea engaged his lips one more time. "I'm going to stay out here and smoke one more joint. You go inside, and I will meet you in the guest room in fifteen minutes."

Although it had not dawned on Nick at the time, she must have done this before. Nick played off his excitement by simply doing as he was told. Careful not to wake anyone in the house, he went about setting up the guest room as Seduction Central. He dusted off the Bath & Body Works Sun-Ripened Raspberry massage oil. Nick unearthed scented candles he hadn't used since Chicago. Completing the scene was the unveiling of the gold-foil-wrapped Magnum condoms.

Nick lay on the bed with the lights down low, in just his boxers, awaiting the inevitable. And awaiting. And awaiting. Nick had almost awaited himself to sleep when Andrea entered with the stealth of an Iroquois Indian. A lopsided grin possessed her face as she silently shut the door behind her. Seduction Central; Andrea approved.

"Lie down," Nick commanded, finally feeling like the man of the situation. Andrea peeled off her top to reveal a black lacy bra doing a poor job of restraining nature's two best blessings. She slid out of her shorts down to her panties, lying down on the bed on her flat stomach.

Nick promptly went to work. A few squeezes of the bottle dropped cold oil on her lower back. Her body shivered in reaction, to Nick's delight. His hands went to work displaying skills he had not employed in many moons. Soon, her whole body was as relaxed as a jellyfish in water. As he molded and shaped Andrea's soft, brown, malleable clay, he accepted the consequences of his actions. *If you're going to do this, Nick, do this!*

And he did. Three times, about five different ways, to three successful conclusions. They were quiet, they were carnivorous, and, most of all, they were good.

**THE GOLD COAST** Classic itself was off the hook. Qualcomm Stadium, where the San Diego Chargers and the San Diego State Aztecs play, was filled only to half capacity, but even that was still an impressive amount of black people. As usual with a black college football game, the best parts of the game had nothing to do with the action on the field. The Howard and FAMU cheerleaders, outfitted in cute, short uniforms, danced, tumbled, and flipped their teams on to glory. A black version of The Wave, called The Sway, started among the crowd, their arms slowly rippling—swaying—around the stadium at a snail's pace to the beat of the amped-up bands. And they *were* amped up. The half-time show was a high-energy musical and dance duel, ending in a stalemate between the Bison and Rattler bands. An appreciative audience danced along with the bands as they played the latest dance cuts.

The gang was all there. Nick, Malloy, Craig, and Carlton accompanied Khalilah, Kina, and Andrea in the stands. Reveling in their blackness, they, too, danced, stepped, swayed, and sang with the rest of the crowd throughout the game. For the Morehouse Men, Nick, Mal, and Carlton, it was like a homecoming.

Nick watched with guarded interest as Andrea shook her rump to Juvenile's ghetto dance classic "Back That Thang Up." The residual visuals from last night's tryst still lingered wonderfully in his memory. Even by his standards, his performance had been legendary. The way that Andrea smiled at Nick all day, without having to say a word about last night, verified it. Only one question skulked at the back of his mind: Would it happen again?

The after-parties were predictably exciting. After Howard won on a last-second touchdown, the revelers spilled out into the parking lot and into nearby clubs. Nick obliged the ladies, taking them wherever they wanted to go. They bounced from club to club, party to party, getting in for free on the strength of the good looks of the PKPs alone.

After dropping off Carlton and Craig, they returned home around three in the morning again. Mal must have been getting old, because he was pooped, promptly passing out on the couch. The girls also headed off to sleep almost immediately. Or so Nick thought.

Nick was only twenty minutes asleep on the futon when a gentle hand caressed his neck. He woke up to find Andrea, in a long night-shirt, hovering over him. "Hi," she whispered, so as not to wake Malloy on the opposite couch. She had sex in the eyes. "Come outside with me."

So as not to disobey Cardinal Rule No. 11, Nick followed her outside, only to watch her promptly light up some bud. Not only was this a flagrant violation of Cardinal Rule No. 10, *again,* but also it was patently unattractive.

"Do you need to smoke in order to have sex with me?" Nick asked, one intonation away from an accusation. If the only way he could be with her was if she was high, then she definitely did not need to be on his roster.

"No, I don't," she smiled, disarming him in a way he had not expected. "Look, I'm in med school. I know the stuff's bad. I just like to smoke it, that's all."

"How often do you smoke?"

"Two, maybe three times a day."

"A *day*?" Nick could have choked. "I hate to break this to you, Andrea, but that makes you an addict."

"Really?" Andrea said, raising an eyebrow as she finished off the last of her joint. "And what if I had to have sex with you two or three times a day? Would that make me an addict? A slut?"

Andrea was now up in Nick's face. As sexy as she was, Nick could barely get past the stench of the marijuana smoke now ingrained in her lips, hair, and clothes. He forced a smile. "It would make you very smart."

Now it was Andrea's turn to produce a smile. "Then shut up and fuck me, Nick." For good measure she added, "Please."

BY SUNDAY AFTERNOON, the girls were gone. Nick could finally breathe (smoke-free and) easy. In their glorious three-day stay, somehow, the women had eaten through two and a half rolls of toilet paper. That was a month's worth for Nick and Malloy. Amazing.

Khalilah had said all the right things, offered up all the requisite thank-yous before hauling the ladies back up to LA.

After their session last night, another wholly satisfying, two-orgasm experience for Andrea, she left Nick's house with only a tepid goodbye. She played into the potential awkwardness of it all by not saying much. Nick could understand and did not press the issue, allowing her to slip into the nether regions of her uneasiness. He did not want to admit it, but Nick felt a bit used.

Too tired to go out and play ball after a weekend of escorting beautiful women around, Nick and Mal ended up in their familiar sanctuary—on the futon couch. The obligatory PlayStation battlefield this time was baseball, an odd choice, considering it was out of season. Nick needed the slowness and methodical nature of the game to decompress his feelings.

It was almost as if Mal could hear the clunkiness of his friend's thoughts. "Let her go, dude."

"Huh?"

"Andrea, man. Let that broad go. Chalk her up to game," Mal advised.

"What are you talking about, Mal?"

"Come on, dawg. You don't have to shit me, aw'ight? I know you hit that, son."

Nick was astonished. "How did you know?"

"I didn't—you just told me," grinned Mal. Nick slapped his forehead at his stupidity. Mal just chuckled it off. "Man, don't sweat her, dude. You have to be more blasé about these chicks you deal with. Not every one of them deserves the honor treatment."

"Whatever, man."

"So how was it? Was she good?" Nick grinned his response. An answer like that did not need any words. "Yeah, she looked like she could put somethin' on a brotha. Well, discard her and on to the next."

" 'On to the next'?" Nick repeated disdainfully. "Just find 'em, fuck 'em, and flee?"

"Worked for N.W.A. Not a bad motto to live by, dude," advised Mal. "Not every girl is The One, you know? You gotta stop lookin' at these broads like they're princesses. You can't treat every one of them nice."

"What kind of advice is that?" screeched Nick. "You just reaffirm what all women say about men right there."

Mal rolled his eyes like a slab of dough. "Treat a queen like a ho, and a ho like a queen, and you'll have her forever. Guaranteed. No matter what these broads be sayin', they don't want a nice guy. They run game as much as we do. They *want you* to run game on them. Broads be just as scandalous as dudes, dude! I'm tellin' you—"

"So what you're trying to say is that Andrea was a one-time thing?"

"Man, I may not have been the best student at The House, but I am a 4.0 student of human nature, especially of the female persuasion. Just the way she looked at you today . . . I could tell something was up." Mal clicked away at the game in silence for a moment. "That's how I knew you smashed that."

"Eloquent as ever, Mal," sniped Nick sarcastically.

"Bruh, that chick was as disposable as a razor. Throw her out and get another one. Now this Esmerelda hottie," evaluated Mal, "has potential. She genuinely brings something to the table. She's got a little substance. And the fact that y'all haven't messed with each other is not to be overlooked, either. Put a little time in on her. She may yield some positive results."

"She's a woman, Mal, not a stock."

"True. But life is short. Time is an investment. You shouldn't have to waste your time on *nobody*."

That really resonated with Nick, stunning him into silence. When Mal was right, he was right.

## MARRIAGE MINDED
*One man's quest to get married in a year*
*by Anonymous*

Here is a new concept for you all—women as sexual predators. Don't pretend like they don't exist. Y'all know who you are. These women exist, and, because of a recent event, I am out to expose them all.

There are three types of female sexual predators:

**The Innocent (*Predatorius victimus*).** Mostly found in innocuous environments like church, school, or the Self-Improvement and Lifestyles section of a bookstore, The Innocent attracts her prey via a series of staged coincidences, subtle, obsequious comments, and well-known contradictory statements that men are forced to interpret and reject in order to understand The Innocent. This predator feigns the utmost innocence while staging more and more situations in which to interact with her prey. Before the prey knows it, he has fallen into a carefully laid trap where said prey is now expected to pursue the coy Innocent, asking her for sex enough times until she may still seem demure, ladylike, and generous in giving in to his demands. In actuality, she is not *giving in to* anything, but only reaping the dividends of her investment.

**The Aggressor (*Predatorius dominatrius*).** Her primary habitats include the bar, the club, and anywhere rich men with loose purse strings can be found. The Aggressor (also subcategorized as *Predatorius golddiggeritus, Predatorius overeager-maritalorius,* and

*Predatorius conquistadorius*) engages her prey head-on, opting to initiate and make the first move. This is not a problem for the male prey, except that The Aggressor tends to have other agendas besides companionship. These agendas include financial gain, marriage for no other reason than to be married, or simply the thrill of the conquest. The usual result of The Aggressor seducing her prey is simple sexual conquest and quick dismissal, then preferring to seek out newer, fresher prey.

And then there is the last type, one I had the (dis?) pleasure of running into recently: **The Detached Manipulator** (*Predatorius calculatorius*). She combines some of the tactics of The Innocent with the assertiveness of The Aggressor. While The Detached Manipulator may exhibit a coy attitude at times, she knows exactly what she is doing. She will set up coincidences and events with the express purpose of seducing you. Once the male prey is in her grasp, she will not play dumb or innocent, but she will tell you outright that she "wants to have sex with you." At this point, many potential prey, excited by the "refreshing" nature of her directness, will submit to her predatory charms. She does just enough to make the prey think that he has done something to get her to this sexually aroused point, but, in reality, she has been manipulating the situation from jump.

The consequences of being seduced by Predatorius Calculatorius? For most men, the effects are minimal. The sexual predator makes his job a lot easier—sex without commitment. But for the **Marriage Minded,** falling for the charms of such a beast is merely a sad diversion, and a waste of the one thing I do not have—time.

## 9

**T**HANKSGIVING WAS A small but friendly affair. Nick had grown closer to Esmerelda, to the point of inviting her to dinner at Craig's. Mal was present, as well as Robert. Carlton had to work.

Tapping into her Puerto Rican roots, Olinda put on a gutfest of traditional American food, Mexican dishes, and Puerto Rican delicacies. Mal, who had once dated a *boricua* as well (there wasn't a race alive that Mal hadn't messed with), eagerly attacked the Puerto Rican food with gusto. Robert ate in between cracking highly erudite jokes, while Craig, as usual, weighed in on everything that was and was not cool (Kid!). Nick and Ezzy enjoyed the food, the company, and each other. For the first time in years, Nick felt at home, part of an extended family.

That didn't stop Nick from putting in a call to Mom from the kitchen during dinner. For a change, Mom was home, walking around and doing fine. Chemo was working for the moment and she felt okay. That gave Nick the heart to continue on with Thanksgiving dinner over at Olinda and Craig's without her. Her well-being constantly lurked at the corner of his thoughts.

Over dessert, Mal remembered why Carlton was absent. "Hey, isn't Carlton supposed to be on the radio tonight? After the game?"

The Chargers were making their first appearance in the NFL's venerable, nationally televised Thanksgiving Day Turkey Bowl game. Carlton was to appear on a local AM sports-talk show directly following the game.

"Yeah, that's right, kid," affirmed Craig. "Turn it to 690 AM."

Mal bounded into the living room to turn on the radio. He turned the volume up for everyone else to hear. After a set of commercials, the broadcast returned to *The Jeannie Rhome Show.*

Nick had heard Jeannie Rhome's show once. Hers was quite an act—abrasive, no-holds-barred, sarcastic, opinionated sports talk. Accountable to no one, it seemed, Jeannie badgered her callers, hounded her guests, and generally intimidated the world. Her motto was "Come hard or don't call at all." With the equally opinionated Carlton on her show, Nick was sure sparks would fly.

And did they!

"We'd like to welcome San Diego's newest addition to the sports-casting airwaves, Carlton Maxey. Glad to have you on the show, Carlton," Jeannie greeted him innocuously.

"Glad to be here," Carlton replied by rote.

"Alright. Now that the pleasantries are aside, I want to know how in the *world* you could call the Chargers a team on the rise after today's debacle!" she pounced on him. "I mean, really. You'd have to be legally *blind* to consider them anything above a JV college rugby team!"

"Ooo!" Nick reacted from Craig's dining room.

"She really broadsided him," Robert concurred, amused.

"Yo, he got lit up, kid!" laughed Craig.

Carlton recovered nicely. "I assure you, Ms. Rhome, my vision is twenty-twenty. If anyone's vision needs to be checked it's yours, especially if you can't see the potential and nucleus of talent in this ball club."

"Call me Jeannie," the host insisted. " 'Ms. Rhome' makes me feel old."

"No, 'Ms. Rhome' is fine," replied Carlton tersely. "And I think that as Johnson matures, so, too, will this team."

"But it doesn't matter how much Johnson matures as a quarterback if his inexperienced offensive line keeps laying down the way they do!"

"Well, I think you can lay that problem at the feet of new offensive-line coach Fritz Snyder," countered Carlton. "Last year, before his hire, the Chargers were fifth in the league in least amount of sacks allowed. Now, three months into the season, they give up more sacks than any other team in the NFL. I bet they're missing the old line coach right about now."

Jeannie was duly impressed. "I did not know that."

"Johnson has been on his back more times this season than a self-employed model during a porno convention."

Jeannie could not help laughing. "And on that note, we'll be back for your calls—come hard or don't call at all—right after these messages of capitalist propaganda by commercial influences."

Once the radio went to commercial, Nick remarked, "That was a nice recovery."

If only they knew how nice. Inside the studio in Downtown San Diego, Carlton had earned the hard-fought respect of one of the toughest sports-talk hosts in the nation—and a lot more. They grinned away at each other like two teenagers in puppy love. Sure, they had just executed an entertaining and professional show segment, but more lay beneath their eager grins. Jeannie liked his spunk and Carlton admired her aggressiveness. This was the beginning of a beautiful friendship.

"I HAVE AN idea."

"I'm listening." Nick adjusted his feet, sitting poolside next to Craig. This was yet another "Marriage Minded" strategy session, conducted at Craig's house on a cloudless, warm, early December day.

"Have you been reading the emails?"

"I try to. I get about twenty a day. Fifty on print days." Nick took a sip of lemonade from his nearby glass. "I'm getting a lot of love."

"Don't front, kid. You're a hit," Craig assessed. "Have you noticed a common theme among the emails?"

"They're mostly from women?"

"And they all want to meet you."

Nick looked askance. "What're you up to over there?"

Craig stole a moment to choose his words carefully. "I think you should meet them."

"*Meet* them?" screeched Nick. "A gaggle of horny, desperate women? What the hell for?"

"It would be the ultimate PR stunt," salivated Craig. "We get a turnout of about a hundred ladies . . . let them ask you questions . . . maybe get a record company or somebody to sponsor it. Give away some free CDs or something. It'd be tight."

"What else would I have to do?" Nick inquired suspiciously.

Craig beamed with victory. "Just show up."

---

**NICK WAS ONE** week away from temping again when he finally booked an acting job. A non-Equity community playhouse was putting on a play written by the owner. Complicating matters, the owner was also *acting* in the play—and the material wasn't very good. But for an additional $200 a week and a chance to exercise his acting chops, this play would be worth it.

The living arrangement with Malloy continued to work out. Thankfully, Mal paid half the rent and utilities, easing Nick's burden during his acting dry spell. Despite the column's popularity in the *Reader*, $500 a week was still $500 a week; it could only go but so far.

Nick also worried a little about his best friend. Understandably, Mal had been a bit of a social recluse since his abrupt move to San Diego. The only times he would go out and be sociable were with Nick. Nick felt responsible for him, so they were almost attached at the hip, socially. Still, this was so unlike Mal. The boy could turn a funeral into Mardi Gras. Social exclusion for him was unhealthy.

All of these thoughts swirled about Nick's mind as he returned from the audition he had just won. Nick had been so good in the callback that they had hired him on the spot. Rehearsals began the following Monday.

Nick entered an empty home. Mal was still at work. The blinking light from the answering machine beckoned him.

"Hi, Nick. It's Anna," began the cautious voice of the first message. Nick rolled his eyes in reaction as the message played. "I just wanted to see how you were doing since I haven't heard from you."

"And you *won't*," Nick spat at the machine. He began to fix himself something to eat in the kitchen.

"Well, give me a call when you get a chance," Anna invited hopefully. "Take care."

"Good riddance," taunted Nick evenly, pressing the delete button. Nick was more than happy to let her trifling self slip into the area of the Industry called the Video Ho-Zone.

"Yo, what the deal, B?" Ayinde! "Eh, man, we've been missing you on set and everything, cuz. There's actually a lil bit of food left at the craft service table."

"Forget you," smiled Nick.

"Anyways, holler at me, B. I'm followin' your example and leavin' that extra ish alone. I done copped me a gig on a movie as an AD. We roll out to Bermuda for a three-month shoot next Tuesday. So holla at a brotha before I skate. Come up and kick it for a minute. You know my number. *Peace!*"

End of messages. Nick picked up the phone. He was ready to call Ayinde and tell him how he would not be able to make it up to LA this weekend when the phone rang.

"Hello?"

"Hi. May I speak to Nick, please?"

"Speaking."

"Hi, Nick. It's Shana."

"No, really. Who is this?"

"It's Shana. Shana McAdams."

Suddenly, Nick was starstruck. *Shana McAdams* was calling up *his* phone?!? "Uh, hi, Shana," he rebounded a bit clumsily. "Uh, how did you get my number?"

The laugh was nervous, sheepish. "Directory Assistance."

Of course. "So . . . uh . . . what's goin' on, Shana?"

"Well . . . you know, we've missed you around set and everything."

Missing an *extra* around set? "Uh-huh."

". . . And, like . . . well, you know . . . some of us were kinda interested in seeing how you were doing and everything."

"Uh-huh." Nick formed the inklings of a smile. For a woman who made her living by speaking clearly, Shana fired off filler words without discretion.

"But that's not why I called." Shana laughed nervously. That helped ease her tension. Her trademark positivity took over. "Actually . . . I have this . . . *thing* to go to on Saturday."

"Uh-huh."

"It's sort of a . . . um . . . celebrity gala–type thing. You know, red carpet, black tie, the whole nine."

Nick could not believe his ears. "Uh-huh," he egged her on.

"And I was wondering if . . ."

"Yes?" Nick could have wet his pants, he was so excited.

". . . if you would accompany me," Shana finished, with all the grace of a football player ballet-dancing on ice.

"As your *date*?" Nick clarified, for the greater benefit of the universe.

"Yes." Shana cringed on the other end of the phone.

Nick held the phone away from his mouth, covered the mouthpiece, and did a little dance. When he returned, he said calmly, glibly, "Shana . . . you had me at hello."

Shana burst into an easy laugh; Nick could almost smell the chocolate.

"So that's a yes?"

"Does Shana McAdams like macaroni and cheese?"

**FOR SOME REASON,** Malloy actually decided to pick up a weight and work out with Nick that evening. In the history of their friendship, Nick could count on one hand the times the medium-heavy, 170-pound Malloy had lifted with him. The two of them were at the Bally's in Mission Valley, a place that Mal had quickly established as having "negative hotties." There was so little talent to look at, all they could do was, regrettably, concentrate on their own workouts and talk to each other.

So they held court in the sauna room. On a Friday evening when the both of them were dateless, they had the hotbox all to themselves. Mal lay out on his back along the wooden bench while Nick sat hunched over, watching his sweat drip.

"So Shana McAdams, huh?" Mal said, eyes closed.

"It's funny that when people talk about her, they always use her first and last names," observed Nick.

"Well, she's done a lot of work. I mean, there's *Family Bonds, The Last Woman on the Face of the Earth,* her crackhead-turned-beauty-pageant-queen in *Second Chances* . . . She's large, man," recounted Mal. "And her turn as Saya Hamilton in *Boys Club* was the shit."

"I know, I know, I know. Who turned you into Roger Ebert?" Nick smiled underneath his sweat. "Shana bitched to me one time on set that, lately, she's been going head up with Nia Long for roles. When Nia passes on a role, they go to Shana."

Mal whistled. "Nia *Long*! Now *that's* not bad company at all."

"And to think when I met her the first time, I didn't even know who Shana was."

"Should that make a difference? I mean, hos are hos. She's just a classier ho, with a lot more money."

Nick sucked his teeth. "She's a nice girl. Genuinely sweet. Cut her some slack."

"I can't, dawg. You've used it all up," Mal remarked. " 'Genuinely sweet.' So is Esmerelda. What's happening with her?"

"We're taking it slow, Mal. I like Ezzy and everything, but weren't you the one who's always advised 'not to get your head all wrapped around one broad'?"

"True. But I don't want to see you give this Shana chick any extra slack just because she's Shana *McAdams.*"

Nick looked over at the closed-eyed Mal. "Are you accusing me of being a starfucker?"

"Huh?"

"Are you accusing me of being a starfucker?" Nick repeated, a little more tense.

"No," Mal replied. "Not yet."

That pissed Nick off. "Well, let's talk about you for a second, *Malloy.* Why aren't you coming up to LA with me? Why do you content yourself with sitting up in my house all the time like Noah on the Ark?"

"Dawg, I'm chillin'," Mal said unaffectedly. "Maintainin'. Besides, you need to go hang out with your boy before he dips to that movie shoot. You don't need me hangin' around like a third leg just to go watch you prance off on some date."

"Negro, I don't *prance.*"

"Whatever, dude." Mal, still sedated, took his hands and "pranced" them along in the air.

"Well, why don't you go out and *meet* some people? Manufacture a social life. This hangin' around the house–type shit ain't like you," Nick remarked. "Meet a girl or something."

Mal bristled, opening his eyes for the first time. "Naw, dude. You know me. Once I'm out there, I mean I am *out there.* Ain't no sense in meeting any new heads right now, especially while I'm trying to sort things out. Besides, in the past, I've cut through more broads than a redwood forest. I've had enough ass for *two* lifetimes. I'm chillin' now. I am still a married man."

"Have you talked to Mia yet?" Nick posed the question with all the care of balancing nitroglycerin on his nose. "It's been two months."

Malloy started to rise but stopped himself. He settled back onto the bench, content to close his eyes.

"No," he said in a tone that effectively ended the conversation.

"**TELL ME YOU** ain't the luckiest sonofabitch on earth!" dared Ayinde. Nick and Ayinde cruised Beverly Hills' notoriously chichi Beverly Center. This was not a place you just came dressed in sweats and some flip-flops. On a Saturday afternoon, Beverly Center was filled with impossibly beautiful people vamping down the walkways with the elegance of movie stars. There was so much talent on a day like today, it was actually hard to distinguish a movie star from anyone else. *"Shana McAdams!"*

"That's the fiftieth time you've said her name today, bruh," mentioned Nick, calmly disguising his own butterflies. "I've been counting."

"Well, make it fifty-one. Shana *McAaaaaadams,*" Ayinde purred ridiculously.

"Shut up, man, and turn in to this tux store with me."

As Ayinde watched him go through the motions of getting fitted for a tux, Nick reflected on what his boy had said about his date tonight with one of the hottest young actresses in Hollywood. He *was* the luckiest sonofabitch on earth!

**SHANA LIVED OUT** in Malibu, where heaven and earth met the water. Although it was already dusk, Nick could tell this was beautiful country. Expensive, modern-design homes dotted the Pacific Coast Highway, which ran alongside, high above the ocean. Canyons and valleys were home both to flora and fauna as well as sparse pockets of civilization. Malibu was a template of how mankind reconciled itself with nature.

They had agreed that Nick would trek out to her home; that way the limo driver could pick them up so they could arrive at the benefit together. To say that Nick was nervous would be like saying that the Berlin Wall was merely a partition. *Let's see . . . movie star. Going to her house. Dressed to impress.* She's *going to be dressed to impress. Red-carpet celebrity benefit. Roomful of people with a lot more money and power than me.* Nervous? Of course he was.

Shana's house didn't help either. Hers was a gorgeous, two-level modern home on a cliff that overlooked the Pacific Ocean. Nestled atop one of the many hills that formed the picturesque canyons along the highway, it was accessible only by a private road. As Nick rang the doorbell and openly admired the movie star's home, he could see why.

She answered the door and did not disappoint. Gorgeous, radiant, flawless. Pick one and it applied to her. Shana was a vision in a red, tight-fitting, Mandarin-style dress which hugged her body like the PCH hugged the curves of the ocean. Her long, dark hair had gentle auburn streaks in it, and was pulled back into a bun with decorative chopsticks holding the arrangement in place. Shana McAdams was a modern-day Helen of Troy: She could conquer nations with just one look.

Somehow, Nick restrained his enthusiasm. "Excuse me. Have you seen the macaroni and cheese?"

"Well, don't you look nice," Shana beamed, giving him a quick once-over. Nick sported a traditional tux—black jacket and white tuxedo shirt, complete with special buttons, cuff links, and black tie. "Come on in."

As Nick expected, the interior of Shana's home was very, very nice. Art from around the world adorned every wall, instantly and authentically giving her home character. She volunteered to give him a tour. The view from the master bedroom upstairs was simply incredible, as it encompassed the darkened Pacific Ocean and the pale, reflecting moon. Four bedrooms, three bathrooms. With the exception of a couple of particularly memorable cast photos and pictures in her den of a few of her friends who happened to be famous, you couldn't tell an actress lived there. Quite a show of narcissistic restraint on her part, Nick noted. As the tour concluded back in the cozy living room, Nick was duly impressed.

"All this is for you?"

"Pretty much. I have the occasional out-of-town guest, but this is all for me," she answered. "And I entertain a lot."

*I bet you do,* Nick did not say. Her king-sized bed had looked like a player's paradise.

The doorbell rang. It was the limo driver. Shana generated a smile that could make men change religions. "Shall we?"

**NICK HAD NEVER** been to a red-carpet affair before. So imagine his surprise when he emerged from the limousine to a blitzkrieg of flashing lights. Once he helped his date out of the car, the intensity of the lights doubled. On a Saturday night, Shana McAdams was on duty.

"Shana!"

"Shana!"

"You look beautiful, Shana!"

"Can you pose for *People,* Shana!"

"Who is your date, Shana?"

"Can we get one of just you, Shana?"

"Can we get one of you and your date, Shana?"

Shana McAdams attractively gripped Nick's arm and held him close to pose for the cameras. Nick, slipping into actor mode, effectively wiped that deer-in-the-headlights look from his face to pose with her.

"Shana! *Entertainment Tonight*! Can we have a word with you?"

Through perfect teeth, Shana said, "I'm sorry. I have to go take this one. Just wait for me here, please."

Shana trotted over to the cameraman and Pat O'Brien, who beamed a telegenic smile of his own as he engaged her with questions.

As for Nick, he did his best not to look how he felt—awkward. The flashbulbs continued popping, Nick kept grinning, and he continued to feel how many women must have felt over centuries, millennia—

like an arm charm. His date was doing her job right now, chatting up the press, while Nick stood there smiling like the village idiot. And the questions that kept coming did not help either.

"Can we get another picture of you?"

"What's your name, Mystery Man?"

"Are you and Shana dating?"

"Are you and Shana sleeping together?"

"What is your name, sir?"

"How did you meet Shana?"

"How long have you two been dating?"

"Are there wedding plans in your future?"

Nick decided to answer one of their questions. Maybe that would shut them up. "My name is Nick."

Furious scribbles slowed down the verbal attack, but only momentarily. Within seconds, the reporters were back in full force, snapping as many pictures as ever. Didn't those cameras *ever* run out of film?

"Are you and Shana sleeping together, Nick?"

"Nick, are you and Shana dating?"

"How did you meet Shana, Nick?"

"Nick, how long have you two been dating?"

"Are there wedding plans in your future, Nick?"

Mercifully, Shana rescued him in short order by slipping her arm around his and leading him into the hotel. She was effusive in her apologies.

"I am so sorry for that back there. A lot of times they want to take pictures of me or interview me about something, and they just want me."

"Don't worry about it," Nick assured her. "Besides, according to the *Enquirer,* there are wedding plans in our future."

Shana smiled. Nick basked in the warmth of her glow.

Once inside, Nick found an ally, Wesley Harper. Wesley bounded over to Shana first and gave her a hug and a kiss.

"Shana! How you doin', babe? You look great," he complimented. Then, doing a double-take in Nick's direction, Wesley asked in disbelief, "Nick?"

"Whaddup, Wes?"

"I almost didn't recognize you, man! You clean up nice!" Wesley teased him. They dapped up into a one-arm guy hug.

"How're things on set?"

"Man, you know Wendal is still *tryin'* to terrorize everybody. But the last two episodes we're shooting before hiatus are gonna be filmed by Jim Cameron."

"James Cameron?" Nick echoed incredulously. "James Cameron is going to film two episodes of *Blackdraft*?"

"Believe it or not. I'd love to see Wendal try and intimidate *his* ass!"

Nick laughed along with his friend. It was good to catch up with Wesley, as well as see a friendly face in this glammed-out affair. The three of them talked a little bit more before Shana and Nick went off to their table.

Three hours later, the benefit began to wear on the both of them. They were bored out of their minds, full, and beginning to feel the effects of "The Itis," that sleepiness that would take hold of you after eating. Shana desperately needed to stay awake for this, as the gala was an important fundraiser for AIDS research and there were cameras everywhere. Despite suffering from The Itis, too, Nick kept them both awake by continually whispering in her ear, telling a joke, or relating a funny story or two. Nick got away with incidental leg and hand contact where he could, noting that she did the same right back to him. They enjoyed each other throughout the gala.

Nick and Shana were knocked out on the ride back to her house. It was late. The benefit had been a success, raising over three hundred thousand dollars for AIDS research. Shana herself had donated two thousand tax-deductible dollars toward the cause. Nick had met several people within the Industry that night, all of whom had his card but still would not remember him the next day. The pair looked so cute, with her head leaned on his shoulder, while his head leaned against hers.

They both awakened to the sound of the car door opening. "Ms. McAdams, you're home," announced the chauffeur.

Shana exited the vehicle, tipped the driver handsomely, and walked in slow motion to her door. Nick, unsure of what to do next, followed at a measured distance. Wasn't this the scene in movies where the woman invited him in for a nightcap? And what the hell was a nightcap anyway?

"Well, thanks a lot for inviting me out, Shana. I had a really great time tonight."

Still somewhere betwixt sleep and wakefulness, Shana said, "It's a pretty long drive back. You're welcome to stay here, if you want."

Nick could have answered in a nanosecond, but delayed it, so as not to appear overeager. "Sure. Thanks."

Shana led Nick upstairs, where she changed in the bedroom and he in the bathroom. Nick felt markedly silly coming out of the bathroom in a pair of tight Vassar shorts and an oversized (for Shana) t-shirt, but it beat sleeping in and wrinkling up that ninety-dollar-a-night tux. Curious about what movie stars wore to bed, Nick was interested to learn that they wore what everyone else wore—a long t-shirt. He was sure there were some panties under there somewhere. If not, he hoped he would find out pretty quick, as Shana crawled into bed, head hitting the pillow like a hammer.

"Uh, where would you like me to sleep, Shana?" Nick was still a gentleman.

"Where would you like to sleep?" came her muffled reply.

"With you?" was his tentative response.

"Climb in," she offered.

Nick had no idea how one got oneself into bed with movie-star perfection, but in under a minute, he was experiencing it. He was now in bed with Shana McAdams. *He was in bed with Shana McAdams!* That thought swirled around and about in his head as he nestled into his side of the bed. Never mind that this was a very big bed. Nick could still tell his boys that he had been in bed with Shana McAdams and *not* have it be a lie!

Eerily, Shana said, "Now you can tell your friends that you slept with a movie star."

Nick laughed nervously. "Now, why would I do that?"

"Because it's the truth." She shifted her body so that now her butt was only a foot away from him. Nick acted as if he, too, were trying to get comfortable, "accidentally" brushing his leg against her rear end. He let it linger there. She let him let it linger there.

In careful, measured degrees, Nick moved from accidental contact into a full-out spoon position with her. Nick was spooning Shana McAdams!

"Does it ever get tired being Shana McAdams?"

She pressed her butt right up against his hardening crotch. "What do you mean?"

Nick stared past her, out the window, into the vastness of the Pacific Ocean in the middle of the night. He was no longer nervous, and just beginning to get over the awe of feeling her perfect body next to him. After all, these limbs and flesh he encompassed in his arms were still just that—a body.

"Do you ever get tired of people seeing you as a movie star, an actress, some untouchable entity, and not ever as just plain you?" Nick wondered aloud. "I bet you probably get that a lot."

"I do. You'd be surprised at how many starfuckers I get who aren't even fans. Very attractive, very handsome men—actors, singers, rappers, whatever—who are simply trying to hang on to their careers or enhance them by dating me because their publicist thinks it would be a good idea, not because they actually like me or we have something in common. . . . It's sickening," she explained matter-of-factly.

"Is that why you chose me?" Nick asked simply.

"For tonight? Yes." Her whole body sighed, relaxing even more into his. "Because you actually seem to like me."

"It's kinda hard not to," Nick admitted. "You're gorgeous, successful, funny, smart . . . I mean, you went to Vassar, for crying out loud. What chance do us poor men have?"

"Flatter me some more," she instructed playfully. "Say more things like that."

"Do you always smell like chocolate?" Nick asked. Shana's trademark scent had lingered all night, and seemed only amplified in bed.

"I read somewhere that it's an aphrodisiac. Pheromones or something. And that's when I started wearing that scented oil." Shana turned to face him, smiling in the darkness. "Is it working?"

"Your smile could power California for a month," declared Nick.

"Well aren't you sweet." Shuttering the smile, Shana turned back into the spoon position.

"Are you sure I'm not a starfucker?"

As his hand cupped the side of her breast, she diverted it, pulling it all the way around, and kissed his palm. "Well, tonight you're not," she smiled.

ON THE WAY back to San Diego the next day, Nick stopped off at Shelby's. In her dropbox, he deposited one of his many headshot prints with a Post-it attached that said, "Remember me?" It was the least he could do since she had not garnered him an audition in two months and Fredo, *again,* had appeared in a commercial for Mexican toothpaste, according to Esmerelda.

Upon returning home, Nick suffered through an extensive debrief with Mal on the Frisbee golf course. As much as Malloy had belly-ached about Frisbee-golfing that first time out with Anna and her Ho-Zone friend, he had secretly become addicted. It was a good source of exercise and a chance to shoot the breeze, and Nick and Mal tried to play about once a week. Mal, of course, was disappointed that Nick didn't "hit that," but prided in his boy climbing into bed with Shana McAdams. Not a whole lot of men could claim that.

The next morning, Nick was awakened at six by a phone call. It was a full hour before he had to drop Mal off at the trolley stop, so he was angered at being awakened so early. "Yeah?"

"Nick, it's Maya T." Her voice was tense and edgy.

"Well, here's someone I thought I'd never hear from again," Nick remarked dryly.

"What are you doing?" she accused.

"Right now? I *was* sleeping."

"No, I mean with Shana McAdams?"

"Huh? What're you talking about?" Nick's mind raced. How did Maya T. know about Shana McAdams?

"I'm talking about you messin' with Shana McAdams. It's on the front page of the Style section up here in Frisco," she informed him.

"What are you talking about? I'm not messing with her. We had one date."

"That's not what I heard. There's a picture of you and her all hugged up on each other. The caption reads, 'Shana McAdams and her newest beau, Nick, were seen together at the Beverly Wilshire Hotel for an AIDS benefit/celebrity gala. When asked if they were making wedding plans, Nick had no comment.' "

"My, you're an excellent reader," came Nick's sarcastic comment. "Do you believe everything you read in the paper?"

"Marriage, Nick? How long have you been dating her? Even longer than you were screwin' me?" she charged.

"No, Maya, we just had that one date on Saturday and it was to-tally innocent. I'm not marrying her; I'm still getting to know her. But would it be such a bad thing if I were interested in marrying her? At least I'd know she was ready for a commitment," Nick said pointedly.

"That's not fair, Nick," Maya T. defended. "I told you what my position was from the get."

"And I told you mine. I'm twenty-nine years old, Maya. I'm not going to be forty-five when I get married. I don't have that kind of time."

"But you had time enough to screw around with that other heffa in your house, didn't you?" she leveled.

"If you would've returned any of my calls or listened to the messages I left you, I told you, nothing ever happened between us," Nick explained. Then he turned sour. "You know, this shit is corny, Maya T. Whatever happened to the old My-T Love I used to know and love?"

"Whatever happened to the Nick I used to know and love, and not this game-playing *starfucker* who prances around with movie stars?" Maya T. shot back evenly.

"What is it with that word!" Nick said, exasperated, about to go off if he heard the word *starfucker* one more time. "And I don't *prance*!"

"You know, I thought we had something special. I thought we had a special understanding."

"We did. But then when I tried to raise the stakes, you folded."

"No. When you tried to raise the stakes, I called your bluff—and you didn't have jack or shit in yo' hand!"

"This is comical. After turning down the idea the first time, you wanna call and flex on me like you're my girlfriend or something?" Nick snapped back. "You know what, this is getting real tired real quick."

"Well, enjoy it, 'cause it's the last you gonna hear from me for a while," Maya T. threatened.

"Speaking of starfuckers, do try and stay vertical now that you got your man elected mayor."

With that last barb Nick lobbed, Maya T. promptly hung up on him. A moment of surprise registered as Nick looked at the phone, daring it to change its tune. Then, with a shrug, he replaced the phone on its hook and went back to sleep.

**A CALL AWAITED** Nick when he returned from his daily morning trip with Mal. Great. It could only be his mom, calling from Seattle in her deteriorating state, wondering how her son ever got hooked up with a successful actress like Shana McAdams.

"Hi, Nick, it's Shelby."

*Wow,* Nick thought. *A little reminder goes a long way.*

"I just wanted to congratulate you on going to that celebrity gala the other night. You and Shana McAdams managed to get a picture on page three of today's *LA Times*!"

*Woo-hoo, great. It was only a date, y'all. I did not walk on the moon.*

"Anyways, off the strength of that appearance, I promptly lined up five auditions for you, including one for *Naval Crossing*, a hundred-million-dollar submarine flick that desperately is looking for a strong black male lead. I got them all on Tuesday and they're all well paying. But *Naval Crossing* is the biggest. Call me and let me know if you can come up for these tomorrow. Take care, hon."

Five auditions for big-budget *speaking* roles? Could he make it? Hell yes!

Nick sat at the dining room table, about to return Shelby's phone call when it struck him. One date with Shana had done more for his embryonic acting career than almost five months of his hustling had. Whether he meant to or not, Nick had just become that word he hated the most.

**MARRIAGE MINDED**
*One man's quest to get married in a year*
*by Anonymous*

*LADIES! MEET Anonymous in the Fashion Valley parking lot by JCPenney on December 17 at 2:00 P.M.!!! First 50 women receive free gifts and prizes!!! Come meet the man who is MARRIAGE MINDED!!!*

Fame. It is one of the most intoxicating, perplexing experiences in life. Those who have it don't want it, and those who desperately want it don't have it. I want to tell you all about a recent experience I had in my quest for marriage with a person who lives inside the curious bubble of fame.

I went to a function with an actress friend of mine (who shall remain nameless in case one of you intrepid souls put two and two together). This was a typical Hollywood celebrity affair: red carpet, black tie, the whole nine yards. One of the more interesting aspects of the night was that my date was vastly superior to me in importance. I was literally shoved aside while paparazzi and media took pictures of my far more famous date. This, however, did not bother me.

What has bothered me is the reaction I have gotten from people I have considered my friends. For some reason, my friends assume that I went out with this person simply based on the fact that she is famous. Never mind that she is tall, gorgeous, has a college degree, a sense of humor, a healthy appetite, dainty feet, long, thin, piano fingers, beautiful eyes, smooth skin, and smells like she was created in Willy Wonka's

Chocolate Factory. All my "friends" can fixate on is the fact that this woman is famous, rich, and, well, *famous*. I had to have some sort of agenda for saying yes to this date (that's right, ladies: She asked *me* out; it's not a crime). It cannot be simply because I find her interesting, engaging, and all of those other reasons listed above.

What my friends don't realize (because I have not told them) is that I am out to get *married*. I have less than a year to do it. I cannot go around and throw away perfectly good opportunities at love just because someone is above or below my station. In fact, I don't think I would even be having this problem of (what seems like to me) outright jealousy from my friends if this woman were Chief Fry Cook at McDonald's. And if she were Chief Fry Cook at McDonald's and I had the opportunity to meet her, I still would have gone out with her. She would be the best-smelling, most intelligent, classiest, most glamorous fry cook in McDonald's history.

The part of all this that kills me is that you're damned if you do, damned if you don't. If you date a fry cook, people will tell you that you're settling. If you date a movie star, then you're being a gloryhound and fame seeker. The clock is ticking, ladies and gentlemen. I have eight months left to find my wife. Right now, I do not have so much as a girlfriend. I cannot bow down to others' criticisms, comments, and petty jealousies when I find someone I genuinely like. For, unlike others, I am still **Marriage Minded**.

## 10

SMERELDA MADE HIM feel guilty without saying a word. The two of them shopped at Fashion Valley that afternoon. Nick needed a blazing new Audition Shirt while Esmerelda was just along for the ride. She was quite the window-shopper, too, ogling the M.A.C. cosmetics store, several shoe stores, and dragging Nick into the dreaded Ann Taylor. When Ezzy tortured him with a twenty-minute visit to Victoria's Secret, Nick felt like the unofficial was almost official—like a boyfriend. It weighed heavily on his mind that his brand-new Audition Shirt bought just half an hour ago at Nordstrom's was for a spate of auditions earned from a dalliance with another woman.

After the extended stay at Victoria's Secret ended, Nick steered Ezzy into the Brookstone store in which Robert worked. The fussy egghead was working, too, as Robert came over to greet them.

"*Hola,* my friends," breathed Robert. "*Qué pasa?*"

"That was pathetic," Nick teased as Esmerelda giggled.

"Nobody asked you," Robert shot back evenly.

"Hello, Robert. How are you doing?" Esmerelda greeted him in perfect, accented English.

"I am fine. Thank you for asking," he replied warmly. "Doing a little shopping, I see."

Esmerelda, a walking billboard for DKNY and bebe, said, "Yes. I just love American fashion."

"You have good taste," the fashion-critical Robert approved. "And so do you, Nick."

Nick wrapped an arm around his lovely companion. "Thanks."

"I meant your tux on Saturday," Robert clarified. "My, you looked sha—"

"Excuse me, babe. I need to talk to Robert for a moment," Nick cut him off crisply. He led Robert several paces away from his girlfriend-in-training. "What're you doing?"

"I *thought* I was giving your ass a compliment," huffed Robert. "It's not every day you dress yourself for a formal occasion *and* I am a fan of the wardrobe."

"Think, Robert, think! This is not the time or the place for that!"

"You mean she doesn't know? She doesn't know you went out with Shana McAdams Saturday night? Just about everyone else does. It's on the front page of the Currents section in the *Union-Tribune*," Robert pointed out.

"I'm sure it is. I guess Mexico has 'real' news to worry about," Nick remarked. "Look, just keep this on the D.L., okay? I'm at a delicate stage with Esmerelda, and I don't want to blow it."

"Well, aren't you quite the player." Robert was enjoying this immensely.

"I'm not playing nobody," Nick whispered. "I'm just keeping my options open. There are some things that don't need to be told to people you're just getting to know."

"Oh, don't worry, *Nicolas*. Your sordid little secret is safe with me—and half of North America." Robert affected a bemused smile. "Besides, I've been too busy these days to spread gossip."

Nick examined Robert for a moment. The man had on an expression Nick could swear he had never, *ever* seen on him before, not even in high school. "Robert, are you . . . are you *in love?*"

Robert nodded his head quickly. *Giddy.* The word to describe Robert was giddy.

"I don't believe it!" Nick gasped. "Who's the lucky guy?"

"His name is Antony."

"Anthony?"

"No, *Antony.* He's Italian. I met him at Bally's," Robert divulged excitedly. "An older gentleman. Still, he has a body straight out of Greek sculpture!"

"You met him at Bally's? Since when did your skinny ass start working out?"

Robert hit Nick lightly. "I don't. But that Bally's in Mission Valley is a hotbed for homosexuals."

*If only Mal had known,* Nick laughed inwardly. "Well, congratulations, I guess. Even Robert can be tamed by monogamy."

Robert took a bow. He jabbed his head in Esmerelda's direction. "Better hurry along. Don't keep your date waiting."

"Just keep your mouth closed, okay?"

Mimicking Mal savagely, Robert said, "It's on the D.L. Playa, playa."

---

**"BIG DAY TOMORROW?"** Khalilah greeted Nick at the door.

Nick slid past her into her living room, plopping down his belongings and himself on the couch. After having shopped with Ezzy, he had had four hours of play rehearsal, most of which had been a table read of the script, twice. With some luck, Nick could squeeze in the five auditions tomorrow, jet back down to San Diego, and only be a half hour late for rehearsal that night. Oh yeah, and somewhere in there, he was sure he would have to eat something. "You better believe it."

"Did any of them give you any sides?" Khalilah had watched her friend struggle through his first few months in the Industry, becoming hip to some of the lingo as he went along. "Sides" were lines.

"Nope. Pure cold readings, all of them."

Khalilah shuddered. How Nick did this at all amazed her. How scary it must be to enter a roomful of powerful people with only a sheet of paper that you were expected to breathe life into, having had it for a scant five or ten minutes prior.

"Has Andrea said anything about me?"

Khalilah grinned. "No. Why?"

"Nothing. Just wondering." Nick made a home on the couch.

Locking the door and turning out the lights, she said en route to the bedroom, "Break a leg tomorrow."

Stretching out on the couch to invite sleep, Nick said confidently, "I will. Five times."

---

**NICK'S MOST PRODUCTIVE** day as a professional actor began with a bang—he walked in on the director and his assistant having sex. Oops! Not the best way to make a first impression. Usually, auditions are very controlled arenas. Sides are put out, talent is herded to a waiting area, names are called, and stars are born. Nick's guessing wrong on a bathroom door ended up with his catching an eyeful of bare, white ass. Although he was even more embarrassed than were the middle-aged, married director and his cherubic, nineteen-year-old assistant combined, Nick still noted that the director took a greater-than-normal interest in his performance. The man studied his reading with the brooding intensity of a William Shatner.

Little did Nick know that this was as good as his day would get. A delay in the auditioning process at the next audition caused him to be late for his third. Since his name was not Matt Damon, Cuba Gooding, Jr., or Denzel Washington, Nick was promptly screamed at. Unnerved, he still went into the audition room like the champ he was and gave a solid performance. What did unnerve him was the nitpicky casting director, who drove Nick to severe second-guessing, decimating his audition with ridiculous direction. Shattered, Nick stumbled into his fourth audition, gave a flat reading, and stumbled out with nary a memory of the experience. To make matters worse, Morris Chestnut wished him good luck on his way out the door.

So this was Nick's mind-set for his fifth and final audition, at a quarter after two that afternoon. Squeezing in a fast-food lunch at Westside Pavilion helped him gather his thoughts, if not his confidence. With this being the audition for the lead in *Naval Crossing,* a big-budget, independent film by one of Hollywood's most successful female producers, Ilene Zimmerman, Nick had to bring his A game. A quick phone call from Shana had affirmed that he would meet her for a cup of coffee real quick before his trip back down to San Diego for rehearsal at six. That would be his reward if, and only if, he had a successful audition.

Nick arrived ten minutes early and signed in. Crossed out six names above his was Blair Underwood. Jeffrey Wright and Isaiah Washington had also been by earlier to audition. Not that this made Nick nervous, mind you; it just gave him an idea of the competition.

He studied the sides for ten minutes, until the lines were fully within his grasp. Overpreparation could be just as bad as underpreparation. Nick put the sides down and started to read the newspaper. He was relaxed, as he should be. This is what he had trained for in graduate school.

"Nick." Surprisingly, Ilene Zimmerman herself emerged from the audition room. She was a thirty-eight-year-old woman with red hair, tan skin, and freckles. Her body was standard Hollywood-player issue: fake breasts, reduced nose, tummy-tucked waist, collagen-implanted lips, and liposuctioned thighs. In short, she looked like a pretty, perfect, plastic doll. She smiled easily. "Come on in."

The audition room was pretty comfortable. Soft leather couches arranged in a conversational fashion took up the center of the room. Ilene invited him to sit down on the couch with her and read his sides, as if he were speaking to her.

Nick read through the lines with her once and she seemed fairly impressed. "Good, Nick, good," she approved. Ilene stood and walked behind him. "Now, you know that nudity is required for this role, right?"

*I do now,* thought Nick. Internally, he shrugged. He had a good body that he was very comfortable with. Taye Diggs dropped trou for *How Stella Got Her Groove Back* and now brothaman was making four million a flick. "Yes," Nick lied.

"Do you have a problem with that?" she asked, placing her hands on his shoulders.

"Not at all." *I do have a problem with your hands being there. . . .*

"Good." Ilene started to massage his shoulders. As casually as if she were ordering a latte, she said, "Take off your shirt for me."

Wow. The woman didn't even *ask*.

There was nudity required, right? The least he could do was show her his chest. While Jeffrey and Blair probably did not have to do this, they had reel to show off their bodies. Nick did not.

Nick unbuttoned his Audition Shirt to reveal a muscular, curved chest, the light outline of six-pack abs, and waves of dark auburn flesh. Ilene took it all in with one look. "Are you wearing boxers or briefs?"

What the hell did that have to do with the price of tea in China? "Briefs."

"Take off your pants."

Nick tried to hide the surprise in his eyes.

"Please," she added, still very businesslike. "We have to have an accurate picture of what your body looks like."

Painfully, Nick slid out of his pants, standing in front of her in just his black ribbed Calvin Kleins, trying his best not to feel like the world's biggest fool. Or whore. Or both.

Her inspection lasted a full twenty-five seconds. Ilene walked over to the couch, sat down with her arms outstretched on its back, and crossed her legs beneath her miniskirt. She was all business.

"Okay, here's the deal: You sleep with me, you get the part."

Nick's face contorted into rage. *"WHAT?"*

"You come over here to this couch, have sex with me, and you will get the part," Ilene explained patiently.

Wordlessly, Nick began to scramble back into his clothes.

"What are you doing?" she demanded.

"I'm getting the hell out of here," Nick shot back, pants back on.

"Nick, you're a nobody. You fuck me, and I will make you a somebody," Ilene pitched. "I *have* condoms."

"Not interested." Nick was surprised he could even manage coherent English at that point, he was so offended.

"What the hell did you expect? Why do you think you got this audition?"

"I dunno, maybe because I have *talent,*" Nick snapped.

"Please. The only reason you got this audition is because you're fucking Shana McAdams," Ilene said. "And now you're passing up the opportunity to fuck me."

"No, I'm not," Nick said, his shirt back on his back where it belonged. "I think I just *got* fucked by you."

With Nick en route to the door, Ilene became desperate. "Come on, Nick. Just let me suck your dick. I *love* big, black dick."

Hand on the doorknob, Nick did not even look at her. "Kiss my ass."

"You'll never work in this town again!" she screamed at the closing door. *"Ever!"*

**NICK'S EMOTIONS WERE** mixed as he waited on Shana at the Coffee Bean & Tea Leaf in Burbank. It was a busy place where a lot of Industry types loped over from the studios to enjoy a latte or two in celebrity obscurity. This was the perfect place for Nick not only to meet Shana, but also to be lost in his thoughts until she arrived. As much as he had enjoyed spending the night with her that one night, Nick was not sure if dating a movie star was worth all the trouble behind it.

Of course, when Shana landed at his table, somehow looking glamorous in a firefighter's uniform, all that changed. She was beautiful and bubbly and smelled like chocolate. He tabled his fears for the moment and concentrated on her.

"Hey you," she greeted, sitting down.

"Hey, Pretty Girl," Nick returned. "How're you?"

"Fine. What're you drinking?" she asked brightly.

"Well, it's not macaroni and cheese, but it'll have to do," Nick quipped. "An ice-blended with vanilla. You want one?"

"Can I share yours?"

Nick hesitated before answering. *Stop being silly,* he told himself. "Sure."

Shana fetched a straw before sucking a bit out of his cup. She gave a shiver. "Mmm . . . so cold. So good!"

"So how's your day been?"

"Same ole, same ole. Wendal went off on an extra today for missing a cue." Shana shrugged it off brightly. "What a monster."

"I take it Wendal's not your type?"

"Believe me, he's tried to get at me before on set. But I don't play that," Shana said in between sips.

Somewhere, Nick could have sworn he had seen a flash, like a camera or something.

"But forget about me. How did your auditions go?"

Nick soured. "They went fine until the last one."

"What happened?"

Nick debated the merits of talking about this. Well, Shana *was* an

Industry insider, a working actress. Maybe she would be able to shed some more light on today's unfortunate incident. "I think I got propositioned."

"Propositioned? Propositioned, how?" The possibility of what Nick implied blew her mind.

"Like a 'come-over-to-my-casting-couch' type of proposition," Nick explicated. "Saying that the role required nudity, she had me strip down to my briefs, right before she asked me to have sex with her."

"Wow. I'm sorry to hear that, Nick." Shana was so supportive. "That's really sad."

"To make things worse, I only got the audition because I was 'fucking Shana McAdams,'" added Nick ruefully. "She only brought me in because she thought I would put out."

"Well, that was crass of her, if not out-and-out wrong," Shana commented. Positive but cautious, she probed with "And how did that make you feel?"

"That she was right. That I never would have gotten these five auditions today if I hadn't been seen with you at the gala on Saturday."

"And you know what? You may be right," acknowledged Shana honestly. "Don't concern yourself with how you get the opportunities. Just make sure that once you have them, you take advantage of them."

"I know. But still, it made me feel like a whore."

"Nick." Shana grasped his hand gently, supportively. "Let me give you a few pointers. One: Even if a role requires nudity, you should not have to take your clothes off at the audition. Two: You did nothing wrong here. She was the one who preyed upon your trust and made a bad judgment call on the type of character you have. That's what she gets for believing everything she sees in the paper. And three: Don't give up on us just because of the fame thing. Being famous is not something I can control. But we *can* control continuing to get to know each other better. Okay?"

God, she made so much sense. They didn't come much better than Shana McAdams, famous or not. She leaned over and gave him a peck on the lips. "Now help me finish your drink before I make you late for rehearsal."

**AFTER A THOROUGH** bitching-out of Shelby, Nick vowed to leave Hollywood alone and concentrate on his craft. Rehearsals became all-important to Nick as he delved more and more into his character. Over the next week, his contact with Shana was minimal as *Blackdraft* scurried to finish shooting its remaining episodes before the winter hiatus.

Everything in life was settling down to normal. Finally, Nick was able to enjoy the regularity of a schedule again, knowing where he was going to be at six o'clock at night five days a week. Carlton and Jeannie Rhome had begun dating as much as their schedules would permit. Mal continued to work and seclude himself. Robert was MIA now that he had a bona fide boyfriend. Nick and Esmerelda talked on the phone every night, giving her the advantage over Shana. He genuinely liked Ezzy and was ready to make her his girlfriend. Life was beginning to find a groove.

Of course, that groove lasted all of one week. Craig left a message for Nick on Tuesday morning, reminding him of Anonymous' appearance at Fashion Valley. Nick could hardly wait. A hundred lonely and pathetic women who actually gave a damn if he found a wife would be there. He didn't know whether to be comforted by that fact or frightened by it.

On his way back from dropping Mal off at the trolley station, Nick stopped at the local Ralph's supermarket. Ready to buy some juice, Nick noticed the new issue of the *National Enquirer* on the news rack as he waited in line. His mouth dropped in horror.

*SHANA MCADAMS' HOT NEW HUNK HURTS HUBBY!!!*

She was *married*?!?

"Do you have your Ralph's card, sir?" asked the cashier.

For the first time in his life, Nick snatched up a copy of the *Enquirer* and paid for it. After handing over his Ralph's card, paying for his items, and fleeing the store, Nick could not get back to the 4Runner fast enough to rifle through the fish wrap of a news rag. Flipping past the cover, which had a picture of him and Shana in their formal wear for the gala, Nick found the offending article on page twenty-six.

This was not good. This was not good at all. Using descriptives like "hunk," "hottie," and "stud," the article painted Nick as movie star Shana McAdams' new boyfriend. Not only had Shana been seen with Nick at the gala, flirting "very closely with him," according to an anonymous gala attendee, but also the couple had been "caught canoodling" at the Coffee Bean & Tea Leaf in Burbank. A picture of Nick and Shana sharing his vanilla ice-blended appeared right above the article.

But there was more. While this was all good and fine for the hard-working Shana McAdams, star of more than four more movies coming out next year, her husband of six years, whom she was separated from, was reportedly "not happy." There was a picture of him, too: a scruffy-looking white guy with long hair and weathered skin. He looked like a trailer park resident, a surfer boy, or both. Nick enjoyed his quote the most: "When I find out who this Nick guy is, I'm gonna knock him upside the head. Doesn't nobody respect the sanctity of marriage anymore, dude?" Rumors about Shana and Nick's wedding plans, once Shana's divorce was final, were neither confirmed nor denied.

Nick sat there in stunned disbelief. Then, like a bat out of hell, he drove toward home.

---

"HELLO, NICHOLAS. IT is your mother. I just got a call from your grandmother, who told me she saw you in the *Enquirer* with some movie star that you're going to marry. Is that true? What is her name? I think you should tell your poor mother who you're marrying. Give me a call when you get this message."

The machine clicked. Next message.

"So that's why you can't return a phone call? You're too busy screwin' around with movie stars, huh? Well, you know what? Don't bother to return this call. I am *so* mad I ever opened up to you." That one was Anna.

"I knew it all along. Holla back at me, you homewrecker!" Wesley.

"Eh, B, what the deal? I'm out here in Miami on a one-day location shoot, and whose mug do I see all up on the front page of the *National Enquirer*? B, I don't care what they say. Hit it, but don't *marry* the broad. Even if it *is* Shana McAdams. I mean, as long as Tyra Banks is still out there, why stop at Shana McAdams?" A waterfall of laughter ensued. Damn Ayinde. "Anyways, I just wanted to mess wit' you. One."

Those were the messages waiting for him when he returned from the store, with only more to come. Frantic, Nick grabbed the phone and called Esmerelda. She was not there. Of course she wasn't; she was in class. Esmerelda used to tell him how she would practice her colloquial and informal English by reading the *Enquirer*. If Esmerelda ever saw that *Enquirer*, it would be curtains for the woman he was going to ask to be his girlfriend over dinner in Coronado that night.

Nick called her repeatedly over the next few hours, all to no avail. So then he finally decided to call Shana.

"Hello?" Shana answered her cell phone.

"Hey, it's Nick. You busy?"

A script rested in her other hand as she sat in her trailer on the WB lot, reviewing her lines. There was an edgy tenseness to Nick's voice that her positive self picked up. "No," she lied. "What's wrong?"

"Why didn't you tell me you're married?"

"I'm not. I got divorced three years ago."

"Well, not according to the *National Enquirer* today!" huffed Nick.

"Do you know how ridiculous that sounds?" laughed Shana easily. "The *Enquirer* has never been known as a bastion of journalistic integrity."

"They have this article in there, with two pictures of us, that makes me look like a homewrecker and makes you look like a wannabe bigamist. There's even a quote from your husband."

"Ex."

"Not according to him. He says that I am not 'respecting the sanctity of marriage' by dating you. They claim that you two are only separated!"

"No, the papers were final three years ago. He's an alcoholic surfer boy who put his hands on me once, so I stepped. I wouldn't be surprised if they paid him for that quote," mused Shana.

"It doesn't matter, Shana. All across America, people are gonna scan the cover of this dishrag of a mag and think I'm this homewrecking, pretty-boy boy-toy," Nick protested. "The headline on the cover says 'Shana McAdams' Hot New Hunk Hurts Hubby.' With *three*, count 'em, three exclamation points!"

"It'll be alright, Nick," she assured him. "You're not a real actor until the *Enquirer* starts making stuff up about you."

"This isn't funny, Shana!" Nick paced around his living room. "I had my mom call me up today and ask me if I was marrying you!"

"Are you?" she quipped.

"No, I'm not. As a matter of fact, I don't think I can continue dating you."

Nick couldn't have crushed her feelings any more if he'd used a compactor. "Wh-wh-why?" Shana McAdams stammered gracelessly.

"I just can't do it anymore, Shana. I mean, I do like hanging out and talking with you. But the reality is you live in LA, you have a crazy life that exists in the public eye . . . and you lied to me."

"I never lied to you, Nick. I may have omitted telling you about my divorce, but that was coming. Most fans know about my ex-husband if they do any kind of research on me. Being married to him just wasn't something I liked to talk about."

"But I wasn't a fan. I was your friend."

"You still are my friend! We're still in the getting-to-know-each-other phase, Nick," she clarified. "Don't let the *National Enquirer* end a wonderful friendship."

"We can still be friends, Shana, but that's all we are ever going to be." Just saying it, Nick felt a whole world better. Although he would miss her chocolate-smelling self, he now had a free conscience to hone in on Esmerelda—if only he could get to her before the tabloids did.

**DINNER WAS A** timid affair. While Esmerelda gawked at being taken out to the Fish Market, a waterfront restaurant in the ritzy suburb of Coronado across the harbor from San Diego, Nick struggled with his conscience. She had not said anything about the *Enquirer,* so why bring it up?

Dinner was finished, the check was paid, and Esmerelda had finished up the last bit of New York–style cheesecake. Their dinner total came to almost seventy dollars. If that didn't make her his girlfriend, Nick did not know what did.

So he decided to do it. To pop the question of sorts. One small step for man, a giant leap for marriage-kind.

Breaking the silence in unison, they both said, "I have something to tell you."

They chuckled nervously.

"You first," she offered in her beautifully accented English.

"No, ladies first," said Nick gallantly.

"Okay." She took a deep breath, reached into her purse, and pushed a piece of newspaper across the table. "It's over."

Nick's jaw unhinged, letting his mouth drop and hang suspended in space like a disco ball at a nightclub. No sound came out.

"I guess we were never together at all. That was the problem. Now I know why," she stated plainly.

Nick did not even have to unfold the article, but he did anyway. There it was: Nick and Shana, sharing an ice-blended. "You were too busy romancing movie stars to be serious about me."

Esmerelda made her point succinctly then let it sit there, weighing down space and time with the truth, like a wheelbarrow's worth of bricks. "No wonder why two and a half months after we met, I am still not your girlfriend."

Nick wanted to tell her how he had cut it off with Shana today. He wanted to tell her that there had been nothing between them. He wanted to tell her how he had only spent one night with her. That did not sound right. The truth, in its pure, crystalline form, was often more complicated than a lie. The truth of it was that he had been playing the field, balancing his options, making sure that Esmerelda was the one he was supposed to be with. That was the *truth*. And that truth would have been easier to 'fess up to had he not been outed by the damned *National Enquirer*. From the second that Esmerelda had found out about another woman from someone else, no matter how truly involved Nick was or was not with her, it made everything that came out of Nick's mouth smell like a lie. To be humiliated through a national medium, of course, made Nick's transgression all the more unforgivable.

All of these complex thoughts leadened his brain, preventing him from uttering a single word. In her simplicity, Esmerelda said more than enough for the both of them.

"I know I am not a movie star. I am only a girl from Mexico whose greatest aspiration is to be a pediatrician." Esmerelda stood, ready to leave. "One of these days, you will realize that there is no difference between me and her. We are both women, with hearts that can be broken just as easily as the next woman's when we have trusted someone. But when she breaks your heart, as she most certainly will someday, I hope she does it not because of what you do, but because of who you are. Because I never had that luxury."

Esmerelda left the still-speechless Nick at the table. She left him with the remains of his pride, the article, and, of course, with a seventy-dollar dinner check.

**NICK DID NOT** want to do this. He was in a foul mood. His two best prospects for a wife had gone by the wayside just yesterday. The last thing he wanted to be was sociable. Yet here he was, pulling in to the parking structure in Fashion Valley at a quarter till two the next day. He had agreed to meet Craig outside Old Navy, near JCPenney.

Craig was ebullient when Nick arrived. "Kid!"

"What up, Craig."

"Yo, you're not gonna *believe* the turnout, kid!"

"What'd we get? Two hundred? Three hundred?"

"Follow me." Craig led Nick around the corner and down the walkway to the parking lot. What Nick saw next blew his mind.

Women. Thousands of them. Stretching on for as far as the eye could see. They milled around the parking lot, a sea of long hair and soft features. A makeshift stage had been built with the *Reader*'s logo on it. Several TV trucks were parked on the periphery of the crowd, while a couple of news helicopters warred for airspace overhead. Camera crews stood as close to the stage as the crowd would allow. They were all here for "Marriage Minded's" Anonymous. They were all here for him.

Nick's will plummeted to the bottom of his bowels. Panic swept over him. He retreated from the edge of the parking lot and into the mall area.

Craig, puzzled, followed him. "What's wrong, kid? You're up in five minutes."

"I'm not going out there," gulped Nick.

"What do you mean you're not going out there?" objected Craig. "All these people are here to see you!"

"And so are all those reporters and cameras and helicopters!" Nick panicked. "I didn't expect to see all that!"

"Okay, the cameras are unexpected. But it's all good pub, kid!" Craig spinned. "Look at all those women out there! Look at them! They all want a piece of Anonymous! Give the people what they want!"

Nick settled into a smile. "Alright, kid. I'll give the people what they want. Go prep them for me."

"That's the spirit, kid," approved Craig. "I'll go introduce you."

Craig started down the walkway toward the parking lot a few steps ahead of Nick. Nick stopped. Panic swept over him again.

"I'll give the people what they want. Everyone loves a magic show."

And with that, Nick disappeared.

## MARRIAGE MINDED
*One man's quest to get married in a year*
*by Anonymous*

First of all, my apologies, ladies. I was unavoidably detained. From what I heard, however, the crowd was quite impressive. Thank you, women of San Diego, for showing your love to a man who has one simple objective—to find the love of his life, on a time frame.

Today's topic is trust. I'm sure I'm not telling you anything you don't already know in today's column. I just want to discuss some recent reminders about the fragility of trust, particularly when it pertains to a woman's heart. I would also like to offer a reversal of an earlier opinion, a recantation, if you will.

It has been said that men are dogs. We are mostly classified as dogs because we see more than one woman at a time, and usually lie in order to cover it up. That is wrong. Not the seeing more than one woman at a time, but the lying part.

Trust is built upon the appearance of honesty and communication from both sides. Without one of those two ingredients, trust is hard to maintain. I experienced this firsthand recently.

Now, there is this woman I was dating. Notice the operative word "was." We are *no longer* dating because I failed to disclose the information that I was seeing other people. In fact, I failed to disclose that information for about two months. The way she found out was from a secondary source. When it comes to hearing truths, it is *always* best to hear them firsthand, not through someone else.

And that, finally, is what did me in—the second-hand truth. I stand before you today, my friends, to tell you that I now have zero—and I do mean *nada*—marriage prospects. We are a scant eight months away from my engagement due date, and I have not a soul I can call my own. The reason why I lost my best prospects? I failed to respect that most important issue of trust.

There is nothing wrong with a man seeing more than one woman, especially if he is in a situation as critical as mine. I am getting married only once; it will be forever. So instead of going through a succession of trifling experiences and relationships one by one, I need to have them simultaneously. I need to separate the wheat from the chaff immediately, so I can find my bride.

The women I date obviously do not need to know this. But had I been honest and up front with these women that I had been seeing *other* women, that they had some competition, I would have at least been able to keep one of them.

What I did was not so much wrong as it was stupid. There was a logical yet truthful way through this whole situation. Unfortunately, I played into one of nature's worst creations—male bravado/ego—and played myself out of my two most worthwhile marital prospects.

The lessons to be learned from all of this? One, it is not wrong to see more than one person at a time. Just make sure she knows about the other. And, two, telling the truth is always better than a lie. For if the truth from that lie ever reaches the person deceived, you can count on spending the holidays alone. Trust yourself, and trust her.

## 11

**T**HE SEARCH WAS on for Anonymous. When the *USA Today* crossed her desk with pictures of a crowd of more than ten *thousand* pathetic women lined up for a glimpse of some *newspaper columnist* in San Diego, she dismissed it as just that—pathetic. She continued to scan the article while her makeup was applied, amused to read about how traffic had ground to a halt on Friars Road by the mall where it had taken place. A free weekly newspaper in San Diego called the *Reader* had staged it all. Interesting. Pathetic. Whatever.

She dumped the paper in the trash and proceeded with the rest of her workday.

---

**CHRISTMAS FOUND NICK** and Malloy in Seattle. The change of scenery did Mal some good, as he was able to feel part of a family for the holidays. That was Nick's main concern for him, knowing that this would be Malloy's first Christmas away from his wife in three years. Harrison was in good spirits as he made sure that everything was festive and gay.

Mom looked weak, having dropped a good thirty pounds due to the chemotherapy treatment. Still, she made every effort to participate in the gift-giving and Christmas dinner that Nick cooked. Nick took every excuse he could to hug her. Seeing her weakened state and being around her, decidedly upbeat in the face of illness, only strengthened his resolve to marry before she died. For a woman who had sacrificed her entire life just to ensure that his would be even slightly better than her own, bringing her a daughter-in-law was the least Nick could do. If the new medicines doctors were developing to combat the disease could hold up, maybe she would even live long enough to see a grandchild.

Malloy watched in awe as Nick's mother shuttled around the house with as much energy as her weakening body could muster, fully participating in day-to-day life. Her joking and playful carpe-diem energy were infectious. They were starting to give Malloy a new lease on life.

His revelation was complete on New Year's Eve. Nick drove the two of them back from just having bought some Ezell's chicken to celebrate quietly at home with Mom and Harrison. Malloy said simply, "I'm back, dawg."

"What're you talking about?" Nick said mindlessly, navigating his way through the Central District.

"I'm *back*, playa!" Mal declared. "I've got my swagger back, dawg! I'm ready to live life again! I'm tired of walkin' around here like somebody done shot my best friend. The playa-for-real is *back*!"

"Is that a good thing?"

"That is a *great* thing, my nig! It's time for me to get back to the Malloy who once had five women in one night! It's time for the Malloy who will drink you under the table then steal ya girl! It's time for the greatest pimp President Street has ever known to *represent*!"

Nick did not know whether all his declarations were a good thing, but was pleased to see some fire in Malloy's belly.

"I have two words for you, playa." Malloy paused dramatically. "Game *on*!"

"I JUST WANTED you to know that I'm still mad at you for that little stunt you pulled," muttered Craig as he drove Nick and Mal back from the airport. Mal was in the backseat, knocked out.

"C'mon, kid. You were right. It was the PR coup of the year," grinned Nick at his editor. "My no-show got those women even more fired up."

"It made me look bad," pouted Craig. "My boss thinks you're a flake."

"It made the paper look great," Nick debated. "The *Reader* had ten thousand people show up for one great big 'sike.' They were mentioned all over the country in other papers and news outlets. You can't buy that kind of free publicity."

All he said was true. Even though he had stiffed the crowd at Fashion Valley, Anonymous' profile could not be bigger. Everyone in San Diego wanted to know who this guy was. Two thousand letters a week poured in for or about "Marriage Minded." The week following the pseudo-event, six thousand emails a day overwhelmed the *Reader*'s website, crashing the server on more than one occasion. The stunt had been so successful that Craig's pimple-faced editor suggested possibly doing another Meet "Marriage Minded" event, only to stiff the women *again*. All of a sudden, Nick and Craig were sitting on the hottest secret in Southern California.

"Maybe, but you need to make it up to them. To your fans," Craig specified.

"You're right, you're right," conceded Nick. "I owe you one. What do you have in mind?"

"I'm not sure yet," Craig mulled, gripping the steering wheel. "When I figure it out, I'll let you know."

"I bet you will."

---

A WEEK OF rehearsals and work kept Nick and Malloy busy. Nick, still reeling from the loss of Esmerelda, kept his mind on his play. They were to open a week from Friday. If he had any flirtatious tendencies, he took them out on his costar, a pretty yet waif-thin blonde with skin that looked sun averse. Theirs was only an onstage romance, although for research they went on a couple of mock dates to develop a more genuine chemistry and rapport. Other than that, Nick was totally absorbed by his rehearsals, working out, and lowering his golf score in Tiger Woods PGA Golf on the PlayStation 2.

Nick and Mal were almost ships passing in the night, with Mal not getting home until Nick was in rehearsal. So that Friday night, the last night Nick would have off before a long, brutal stretch of technical rehearsals known as Tech Week, the boys went out to party at the Juke Joint Café in the Gaslamp Quarter. Juke Joint was, quite possibly, the only spot in Downtown San Diego that was consistently black and the clientele consistently fine. Friday nights were always exciting, with the dance floor in the back playing host to hip-hop and the like.

Bang, bang, choo-choo train, lemme see you do yo' thang! Under the cover of high-energy booty shake music, Nick and Malloy got their groove back! In a joyous, freewheeling mode Nick had not seen since Atlanta, Mal pushed up on three women at once, enthralling them all simultaneously as he worked to freak their backsides. Nick, who had found an Amazonian, six-foot-one sista in heels to dance with, worked her butt like a full-time job. The boys from Ocean Beach represented righteously.

Nick, still dancing, leaned over to Mal, who was in the middle of spanking some poor girl's ass to the beat. "Please, Hammer, don't hurt 'em!"

"You see how these girls just Mal-itate to me? What did I tell you, dawg?"

They looked at each other, smiling wildly. In unison they said, "Game *on*!"

**THE PREVIOUS NIGHT** had reenergized Nick, so he was out at the beach early. Mal, having had one mixed drink too many, was still passed out in his room, probably dreaming of smacking more ass. With his laptop, Nick sat in his lawn chair in the sand, attempting to get a jump on his article due Tuesday. Despite a sunny day, warm for January, and an ocean of limitless possibilities, inspiration escaped him. There was no one on his singles landscape right now.

Nick did a brief review of the past five months. The remains of Serena, Anna, Maya T., Andrea, Shana McAdams (always thought of as two names, never one), and Esmerelda dotted his mind like a graveyard of missed opportunity. Chantel did not count, but she did not help, either. Six women in five months, and not a single relationship to show for it.

Once again, opportunity presented itself. Woman on the Beach trudged onto the sand and set up camp about five yards from Nick. Acting like she did not notice him, she went about reading her book, stretched out on her beach towel. While she still wore her trademark wide straw hat and loopy, greenish-blue sunglasses, this time Woman on the Beach gave Nick more to work with. Her two-piece bathing suit showed him more dark chocolate than a Godiva store. She had a nice, flat, but not quite toned midriff and a dusky incline for a butt you could skateboard on. Woman on the Beach had it going on today.

But so did Nick. Inspired by Mal's "Game *on*!" philosophy, Nick decided this would be the last day she would be known merely as Woman on the Beach. Before courage escaped him, he packed up his laptop and traversed the short distance between them with energy and confidence.

"I am so sorry for taking so long," apologized Nick.

Woman on the Beach looked up from her book. "Taking so long for what?"

"For introducing myself. I've seen you on the beach a few times, but it was never quite the right moment." Nick kneeled to her level. "Hi, I'm Nick."

"Paris." She accepted his handshake.

"Mind if I sit?"

"Make yourself at home."

Nick made himself comfortable. "That's a beautiful name."

"Thank you."

"Do you live near here?"

"Yes."

A thoughtful pause by Nick. Once again, he apologized. "You know what? I apologize again. I apologize for not asking you more unique questions to match your unique personality."

Nick stood and headed back over to his beach towel. Stunned, Paris watched him do it, undecided on whether or not to say anything. How different. How bold. How odd.

"Nick!" she called out to him. He looked expectantly. An intrigued smile surfaced on her face. "Don't be sorry. Come on over."

Game *on*!

"SO SHE FELL for the rope-a-dope, huh?" smiled Malloy.

Paying more attention to his furious button-tapping, Nick said, "I can't believe that old school game you used to kick in undergrad still works."

"It's alright to admit you were schooled at the feet of a master," Mal quipped.

"Master this, *bi-atch!*" howled Nick, knocking in a birdie putt from twenty-five feet. Nick was a little more emotional when it came to PlayStation 2 golf because it was not his premier sport.

"Notice how I keep an even keel, no matter if I'm winning or losing," Malloy pointed out. "You should learn from that. You can apply the principles you learn from these ass-whuppin's to real life. Especially with females."

"Let me guess: Don't get too excited about the women I meet."

"You got it, Big Pimpin'," approved Mal. "For players like us, women are fully replaceable. Take me, for example—"

"What about you, trick-made?" Nick countered. "I saw you get about six numbers last night. How many of them did you call?"

"All six."

"Dang, boy. You don't play."

" 'I'm not a player, I just crush a lot,' " sang Malloy, quoting the late Big Pun.

"Got any dates lined up?" snooped Nick.

"And you know this."

Nick leaned back against the futon couch. He was not sure if he was ready to see his best friend go out and date people not his wife. "What about Mia?"

"What about Mia?" parroted Mal. "Her cheatin' ass wasn't thinkin' about me when she went to that hotel room with some nigga."

"Do these girls know you're still married?"

"That's irrelevant."

"But you're still man and wife."

"I don't wanna hear that," Mal dismissed.

"But you're still *married*," stressed Nick. "I know I'm not the most religious guy around, but it's still a sacrament."

"Look," Mal barked, whipping furious eyes upon Nick. "Go fall in

love, Nick. Fall hopelessly, helplessly in love. Buy your lady a diamond ring. Put twenty thousand dollars on a wedding and invite all
your boys and all her girls to witness it. Exchange vows, my brotha.
Exchange vows that you will protect and keep her, honor and cherish
each other as long as you both shall live, in the eyes of God, until
death do you part. Say all of this in front of your family, your friends,
a priest, and *God*. You say all of this and she vows the same. And
then, three years later, after the two of you have made a life together,
after you have legally and willingly donated your soul to hers, watch
her throw it all away by pissing on that very sacrament of yours."

Mal paused to gather his composure and steady his thoughts.
"Have that happen to you and then *you* will know how to tell *me*
how I should act."

The rest of the game was played in silence. For Nick, silence was
the one thing he did know.

---

**NICK NEVER LIKED** conventional dates. Dinner and a movie
bored the hell out of him. But because of his dress rehearsal for the
play that night, a conventional date was all Nick had time for. Since
Woman on the Beach—er, Paris—was a nurse, she was not on call
until that evening. So they caught a movie at the notoriously teenager-
infested Mission Valley Center—where kids cutting class made half
the movie inaudible—before dining at TGI Friday's.

"So how's the play comin'?" Paris asked in her native Louisiana
Creole drawl.

"It's comin' along fine. We're ready."

"Great. You're not nervous?"

"Nervous-excited, not nervous-scared," clarified Nick. "You're coming to opening night, aren't you?"

"Of course. I'd love to see you act. I just have to find a babysitter,
but I'll be there."

Nick almost choked on his French fry. Did she say *baby*sitter?!?

---

**"SHE HAS A** kid, dawg."

Opening night had been a success. The Play-Right Theatre's three
hundred seats had sold out. Critics from all the major local papers

had witnessed Nick tear it up as the charming but psychotic killer in the woefully underwritten lead role. Nick's acting ability had transcended the material, elevating the performances of his castmates, the play overall, and garnering him a standing ovation at the end.

Now, less than an hour removed from makeup, Nick sat across from Carlton—actually, C-Town—in the bar at Seau's. Not caring to debrief him on his San Diego acting debut, Nick concentrated on deconstructing his date with Paris instead. C-Town was loose because sports-radio woman Jeannie Rhome had dumped him. He was drunk—drunk from libation and drunk from his own sadness and disappointment.

C-Town groaned in nostalgia. "Jeannie has a kid."

"I don't know how you do it, C-Town," Nick marveled, shaking his head. "Ever since high school, you've always dated women with kids. It's like you're a single-mom magnet. How do you do it?"

"It's not calculus, bitch. It's a relationship," growled C-Town. "She's a single mom. She won't let you get too close to the kid at first anyway. If you love the woman, you'll love her life." A pause. "I loved Jeannie's life."

"You were in love with Jeannie?" Nick was incredulous. This was new information.

"Yes," moaned Carlton.

"Have you told her how you feel?" asked Nick.

"I told her last night. That's why she dumped me. I scared her off."

"Stop lying!"

" 'My divorce is finally behind me, my career is starting to take off . . . I don't want to be in love,' " quoted Carlton wretchedly. "She said it all dramatic and shit, like she was Vanessa Williams in that stupid dancing movie nobody saw. What am I supposed to do, my nigga?"

Forced to extract himself from a day that had been devoted to himself, Nick felt for his friend. Although Carlton's emotional investment was only two months, once love hit, not a damn thing else mattered or made sense. "Beg. Grovel. Tell her how you feel," Nick offered sincerely. "There's nothing else you can do."

C-Town polished off another rum and Coke. "I guess, in the end, that's all we can offer these chicks: Just tell 'em how you feel."

Even in pain, the man was simple but profound. Nick took his advice—and anguish—to heart.

---

**"ROSTER CHECK."**

"Just one," reported Nick as he threw a baseball at his friend. Craig deftly caught the ball and returned the favor. "Paris, five-six, University of Houston, twenty-nine years old. So far, so good. Captain material."

"That's it?" objected Craig. "Just her?"

"Plus one. She has a daughter."

"Nick, Nick, Nick, Nick, Nick," Craig tsked. "Where are the hotties?"

"It's winter," Nick shrugged, wiggling his toes on the Ocean Beach sand on a seventy-degree day. "Maybe they're out of season."

"Nick," began Craig, "this is a serious problem, kid. I've received more than three dozen calls from local and national media outlets asking—no, begging—for the identity of Anonymous. There were countless local and regional TV and radio pieces on that ridiculous turnout for you in December. Two articles are coming out, one by the *Union-Tribune,* one by the *LA Times,* both talking about the ' "Marriage Minded" Phenomenon.' You're a *phenomenon,* kid! We've got the hottest secret in San Diego—hell, the hottest *bachelor* in San Diego—and you're trying to tell me he can't get a *date*? Kid!"

Nick fired a strike into Craig's glove. "It's not all about dating, Craig. It's about me finding my wife."

"And how do you do that? By *dating,*" emphasized his editor. "Now that we've got this buzz going, we need you to sustain the momentum. Don't you want to be married?"

Nick held the ball for a moment, afraid he would throw a laser at Craig's head. Remembering some of Mal's comments, Nick wondered why the married criticized the single so easily. Nothing would make Nick happier than to find his soulmate before his mother passed away.

Displaying remarkable diplomacy, Nick said, "Before you met Olinda, you had never even been in love, Craig. The over-under on you was that you would *never* get married. Finding your soulmate is not as easy, or as simple, as dating more people. Do not worry about me. I will *always* have something interesting to write about. I promise."

Craig caught the ball and then jogged it in to Nick. "I'm sorry, kid. I was out of pocket on that one. This is just a very important time, for both you and me. We have a lot riding on this, in both our personal and professional lives. Especially you, man. I just want to make sure this all has a nice, smooth, happy ending for everyone."

"I certainly hope so, C-Nice. I certainly hope so."

**THE REVIEWS WERE** in. Nick was a hit. Everyone from the *LA Times* ("a haunting, devastating performance") to the *San Diego Union-Tribune* ("a charming, charismatic turn") was jocking his performance.

With a week of shows under his belt, Nick allowed himself to celebrate. He and the cast went out to some dive of a bar/club in Pacific Beach. PB was notorious on Friday nights, with dozens of similar dives promoting loud rock and dancing that catered to a predominantly Caucasian crowd. This was not the first time socially Nick had been an oasis of melanin in a Caucasian desert. The few times he had hung out with his hard-drinking, self-absorbed classmates at the DePaul Theatre School, Nick was always the ethnic blip on the social radar. Although he would never subject himself to the racket that pounded their ears in the smoky club by choice, Nick could at least share a drink or two with his castmates.

Or eight. Nick was plastered. Drunk off a steady stream of Midori and Amaretto Sours, Nick was outrageous. He flirted shamelessly with Molly, his flaxen-haired romantic interest in the play. He exhorted everyone to "holla at some women and put yo' thang down!" Nick even gave another female costar a lapdance. He was so drunk, Nick actually grabbed Molly and *danced* to this terrible music. The only other time in his life Nick had been drunk was at Malloy's wedding, three years ago.

Which explained Molly. Nick was all over her. Finding her an equally playful partner, Nick danced (off beat) and grinded into her backside. His hands roamed everywhere, even making a visit to palm her regrettably flat butt. Molly was not a bad-looking woman. But eight drinks later and that white girl looked *foine*!

The rest of the night had been lost in a pleasurable, alcohol-induced haze. Things came and went, events happened, and Nick woke up. With a screaming headache. Naked. In Molly's bed.

Nick's eyelids fluttered crazily. A head roll to the right confirmed his worst fears. Molly, naked, creamy-vanilla white and awake, leaned over and Frenched him.

"Glad you're awake," she purred. "If I had to wait any longer, I was going to wake you up myself. But . . . after last night . . . I don't think I need an excuse. . . ."

Molly crawled on top and started to go down on him. As her lips formed a wonderfully wet seal around him, Nick instinctively stopped her with a hand to her head.

From her kneeling, hovering position over his dark, erect form, Molly asked, "What's wrong?"

*Everything,* Nick did not say. How about their being naked, his being in her bed, the tattered, torn gold foil of a Magnum on the dresser. He internally groaned. Nick liked Paris, had been talking to her regularly, and felt as if he should not be here. Also, Nick had never done this before. He had had one-night stands before, but never a *drunken* one-night stand.

As he peered at Molly's aquiline nose, thin lips, and the light smattering of freckles on her face, Nick's resolve weakened. The damn condom wrapper had proclaimed that the damage had been done. There was no way he could *un*-fuck her. So Nick decided to make the best of a bad situation.

**WHEN NICK RETURNED** home, lugging a hangover and a big ball of shame, he received his second surprise of the early day. He came home to see a woman in just a long t-shirt and panties sitting in his kitchen with Malloy, eating cereal.

*You have got to be kidding me. . . .* "Whassup, Mal."

Mal should have owned the patent to the devilish smile. "What it is, catdaddy?"

"Who's your friend?"

"Oh, my bad, son. This here is Jamilla," Mal introduced. "Remember her from the club last week?"

"Vaguely," Nick responded limply. *There have been so many,* he wanted to say. Not to penalize Jamilla for Malloy's indiscretions, Nick shook her hand with "Nice to meet you."

"So where've you been, bruh?" cheesed Mal. "Looks like you've had a wild night, too."

*Too.* Nick escaped into his room. He wanted no part of this.

Half an hour later, Mal's female companion had left. Malloy sauntered over to Nick's door and knocked. "Eh, dawg. Why you duckin' me?"

Nick emerged from the depths of his room to confront his best friend. "What're you doing bringing that ho back to the house?"

"She's not a ho, she's a *lady,*" Malloy sardonically mimicked Nick.

"Still."

"Still what? Look, I pay half the rent and utilities around here. This is my home, too."

Nick searched Malloy's eyes for a sign, any sign of regret or remorse. What Nick found was shocking. "Don't you love Mia anymore?"

That stung Mal. "I don't know."

With that, Nick retreated into his room. He placed a phone call and left a message. That call was to Mia.

**THREE WEEKS PASSED,** seemingly without incident. Nick continued to romance Paris and block out his and Molly's inebriated indiscretion. He had even met Paris' daughter, a precocious eight-year-old named Nicole. Luckily, the little girl approved, making Nick's job as boyfriend-to-be much easier. The door to the guest room remained a revolving one, as Malloy shuffled them in and out, continuing to see women not his wife. Malloy had turned into a McDonald's—billions and billions served. Nick lost track somewhere after the fifth nameless, soft-skinned creature had entered his not-so-secret sex chamber. So far, Nick had not even received a call back from Mia. He diluted his worry by basking in the warmth of his appreciative theater-going crowds.

Nick and Paris got along famously. Their conversations were easy and unforced, natural and free-flowing, spiritual and silly. Although Nick hated to admit it because of Mal's earlier commentary, he had become easily impressed with the down-home, relaxed attitude of the Louisiana native. She possessed a uniquely Southern charm, one that mixed humor with a heaping helping of good sense. Paris was straight-forward and direct, yet compassionate and sensitive, with a veritable Ph.D. in life. Being a single parent at twenty-one had quickly taught her life lessons a master's could not. With her affectionately calling him the most generic endearment known to mankind ("baby"), with one of the sweetest, most unique-sounding accents he had known, Nick fell into an easy groove dating Paris.

The upcoming weekend was the play's last. Nick had auditioned steadily for more roles the past three weeks, buoyed by the positive ink he had received. His final callbacks on two leads for plays had gone spectacularly the day before. He would know the following week if he would get either part.

Nick strolled into the theater two hours before showtime on Satur-day night, humming an unapologetically romantic Boyz II Men tune. That evening, after the show, Nick and Paris would go out to cele-brate Valentine's Day. Screw his Cardinal Rules. Despite his earlier reservations about Paris' child, Nick genuinely adored Nicole, and wanted to make his relationship with her mom official. Paris had ever so casually hinted that Nicole would be over at her grandmother's tonight. The timing couldn't be more perfect for making her his girl-friend. The stage was set.

For disaster. Molly sat alone on the edge of the stage, crying a new River Nile. Nick knelt beside her and pryed her hands from her weep-ing face. "Shh, shh, shh," hushed Nick soothingly. "What's wrong?"

The waterworks abated just enough for her to drop the bomb: "I'm pregnant."

Now it was Nick who felt like crying. The back of his throat closed up involuntarily. "Pregnant?" he mangled, wrestling with his voice, his spirit. He sounded as if he had tried to swallow a billiard ball. "Are you sure?"

"Yes," she sobbed. "I was two weeks late, so I took an EPT."

"Those tests are wrong a lot," Nick reassured—himself more than her.

"I know," she cried. "So I went to the doctor yesterday."

A monsoon of a moan came from her gut. "I'm alone, and I'm Catholic, and I'm *pregnant*."

Only one question comes into a guy's mind in a situation like this. To ask it was highly inappropriate, given the emotional state of the woman. But still, it was a necessary question to ask. For the guy. Considering the circumstances of their intercourse, Nick had to ask: "Is it mine?"

Molly slapped the hell out of Nick. All her tears turned into righteous indignation and anger. "How dare you ask me that? *Yes*, it's yours, you bastard!"

*Shit, I had to ask . . .* "So what are you going to do?"

Another slap for his efforts. "I told you, I am Catholic!"

Just great. This slapping stuff had to stop. "So what would you like me to do?" Nick flinched, bracing for a slap.

"Support me. Help me raise this child," she murmured tearfully. Under her blanket of tears, she added, "Our child."

* * *

"**YOU'RE BEING SET** up, dude." This, of course, was Malloy, squawking to Nick over the cell phone right after the show. Nick was on his way to meet Paris for dinner.

"How do you know?"

"What's her proof?"

"She took an EPT and then went to the doctor."

"Oh, come on, player. An at-home pregnancy test and her *saying* she went to the doctor? You need to see more evidence than that. It sounds like you need to do an anal probe. Put on the gloves and fish for something of substance. Like something in writing."

"Look, Johnnie Cochran, this isn't Court TV here. The girl is pregnant and alone and afraid. I wasn't about to cross-examine her on this," said Nick sensitively.

"You wore a condom with this chick, right?"

"Yeah. I think so. I was pretty drunk."

"Well, hell, then. 'If it didn't spit, you must acquit!' " laughed Malloy.

"This isn't funny, Mal. I'm seriously thinking about telling Paris that I'm gonna be a daddy."

"Don't do that, dude, don't do it. Just because that chick *thinks* she's pregnant don't mean that she is by you."

"Gee, Mal, it would be kinda hard to hide it from Paris nine months from now when I have some white chick callin' me up all the time about *our* child," Nick pointed out. "And for Paris to find out then would devastate any kind of relationship I could have with her."

"But that's nine months, dude! A lot can happen in nine months! Just let it ride, playa. Let it ride," Mal advised. "I admire the 'honesty is the best policy' thing, but don't hang yourself by it! Some stuff needs to be kept on a need-to-know, son. And these bitches don't need to know."

Nick sighed heavily. "And that's just it, Malloy. Paris is not a bitch. Tonight, I'm making her my lady."

"EXCUSE ME?" DISBELIEF lived within those three syllables. Never before had Nick heard her lovely, Creole accent sound so harsh and cutting. Conserving words like water in the desert, she uttered coldly, "You did what?"

Nick had not even made it to the meal before he told Paris. Seated in Gordon Biersch Brewery restaurant across from a woman who had gotten pregnant at twenty and had once helped save a bleeding, bullet-ridden woman from certain death, Nick realized that it took a lot to shock Paris. Further verifying his guilt, Nick said simply, "I got Molly pregnant."

"You mean you got some *white bitch* pregnant," she restated rather loudly.

His eyes skirted the room. "Paris, please don't make a scene."

Paris reached out and touched someone. Nick recoiled at the sharpness and sting of the slap. Amid his surprise, she bolted out of the room like a Kentucky Derby thoroughbred.

Nick was not going to let this one get away that easy. Against his better judgment, he ran and caught up to her, steaming full stride toward her car in the vast parking lot.

"Paris, stop. Please. I need to talk to you."

"You've done enough talking for a lifetime," she fired back, not breaking her stride.

"I know. Believe me, I know. I am so incredibly sorry I didn't tell you about this before. I just—"

Paris stopped at her car, swiveled, and looked as if she could hit Nick again. He flinched. "You know what? You *are* incredibly sorry. Here I was, talkin' to you every night on the phone, takin' you and my daughter to the zoo, sittin' around for a month, wondering why we weren't together by now. Now I know the answer. You were out there fuckin' white bitches."

"Look, I'm sorry I didn't—"

"What are you sorry for?" Paris shut him down. "Are you sorry for doing it, or are you sorry for gettin' caught up?"

There was no honest way to answer that question. Nick just let it linger there for a second.

Paris, her senses heightened like an animal ready to attack, sensed his hesitation. A righteous snort. "Or are you just *sorry*?"

There was nothing Nick could say. He hung his head sadly, shamefully, searching for answers in the smooth blackness of the pavement. Besides the woman in front of him, he could imagine another woman who would be very disappointed in him—Mom.

So Paris finished him off. "Whether you're sorry or not, I don't care. I'm sorry for lettin' you into my life. I'm sorry for bringin' you round my daughter. And I'm sorry for puttin' myself in a position where you could've hurt me. So you don't have to worry about bein' sorry. I'm sorry enough for the both of us."

With that, Paris ducked into her car, nearly backed over Nick's foot, and drove out of the parking lot—and out of his life.

**THE NEXT DAY** was the last day of the play. It being Sunday, he had two performances scheduled—one at two o'clock, the other at seven. Still shaken from last night, Nick stumbled his way through the first show, grateful for a two-hour break between shows to recollect himself. Molly, as well, had not been herself during the show, avoiding Nick backstage whenever she could. Mal called Nick up on his cell phone and they met for dinner at a Boston Market in Hillcrest.

During lunch, Malloy wasted no time in setting his boy straight. "That Molly chick set you up."

Nick was not in the mood today. "Whatever."

"No, I'm for real, son. Last night, while you were cryin' in your beer, I hollered at your girl."

"Paris?" Nick asked hopefully. Mal was such a smooth talker, perhaps he could make things right.

"No, Molly," Mal specified as Nick instantly deflated. "I used your cast sheet and called her up. Her roommate said that she had gone to Mr. O's. Since I know this chick who waitresses down there, I call her up and have her put me on the VIP list to get me in free."

"Is there a point to this story coming any time in our future?"

"Just sit tight, dawg. I'm about to make it," continued Mal, undaunted. "So I get to the club, and I see Molly all *over* this one brotha. I mean she's lettin' him smack her on the ass, she's goin' down to the flo' wit' it, she's backin' that thang up. Molly goes off to get a drink or somethin' so I roll up to Ole Dude. I said, 'She's pretty tight, bruh. That your girl?' He gives me this look and says, 'Hell yeah, she my girl.' So I said, 'Good. Cuz I heard she's havin' my boy's baby.' "

Mal leaned in at this point. Nick could not eat another bite of his turkey dinner. "My man's like, 'Naw, nigga! She's pregnant with *my* baby!' I said, 'You wanna put somethin' on that? Your girl's been run up in more times than the LA Marathon.' He went all the way live on that one. I thought we were gonna have to throw down in a second, when Molly came back. Ole Dude wasted no time:

" 'You fuckin' around on me, Molly?'

" 'No!' she says, lookin' all fake and shocked.

" 'Are you fuckin' around on me?' Ole Dude would *not* let up.

" 'I said no. Who's this?' She's pointing at me.

"So I say, 'I'm a friend of your babydaddy Nick.'

" 'That's my child, got-dammit!' my man said.

"I said to Molly, 'Why you tryin' to play out your boy? You didn't tell him you're a whore?' "

Fascinating as it was, Nick interrupted for a second. "You called her a whore?"

"Yes."

"Not a 'ho,' a whore," Nick restated.

"Yes."

"Okay. Continue."

"So I'm talkin' to this *whore* and she says to Ole Dude, 'I am not a whore, and I didn't sleep with anyone else but you.'

"I said to that bitch, 'Look. You tell that lie one more time and I'll slap the taste out ya mouth. Tell him what you told Nick. Tell him the baby's his.'

"I looked at her dead serious, too. She knew better to fuck wit' me. So she came clean. She said that the baby *was* his, but she was tryin' to trap you 'cause he was just a gas station attendant. That trick didn't love either of you, but that still didn't stop her from tryin' to stay with Ole Dude. I don't condone violence against females, but that dude slapped that bitch into next week!"

Nick held a pained, constipated look on his face.

"You alright, dude? You ain't a daddy no more."

That pained constipation started to forge into determined anger.

"C'mon, dawg. Be happy. The kid's not yours."

Nick could feel nothing but anger—anger at Molly, anger at himself, anger at losing Paris because he had reacted off some bullshit. Nick was done eating. He would feed off that anger for the rest of the day—and for a long time to come.

## MARRIAGE MINDED
### *One man's quest to get married in a year*
### *by Anonymous*

Deceit is a dangerous, unnecessary means to an end. When one is dealing with affairs of the heart, deceit undermines the purpose of caring and love. Let me tell you about how deceit ruined my Valentine's Day.

Recently, I have been dating a woman with a kid (let's call her WWK—Woman With Kid). Now, first of all, this breaks one of my Cardinal Rules: Never date a woman with a kid. Right there, I should have known I was in trouble. *Cardinal Rule to Dating No. 12:* **Never get broken by a woman after breaking a Cardinal Rule for her.** If anything bad happens, you have no one but yourself to blame, by breaking the very rules that were set up to save your tail in the first place.

For the record, I am (obviously) not prejudiced against women with kids. I *prefer* dating women without kids because I would like to make a family of my own someday. I am also young, single, and unattached. Dating a woman with a kid immediately brings complications to a new relationship that has enough complications as it is by just being new.

With that disclaimer, let me tell you that we had been dating for a month or so. We were getting close, I had met her kid, and everything was copacetic. Then the wheels fell off.

Remember how I mentioned that women have no rights of ownership to men unless they have been named explicitly as their girlfriend? We had not quite reached that status yet, so information normally privy to a girlfriend was not offered to WWK. Well, needless to say, I finally admitted to her a certain omission, only for her to drive right out of my life—and almost over my right big toe.

What makes this all the more tragic was that my omission was generated by *another woman* as a lie. An out-and-out lie ended my relationship with WWK. I came clean to her about what I had thought was gospel truth from Other Woman, and it turned out to be a lie. So guess who is back to square one?

I would like to give it up to y'all, however. Women can lie like none other. They don't just lie, they make up entire universes of lies. Like Chris Rock once said, "They don't make up little lies, they say things like 'That's your baby!' " There is nothing worse than a *lying* woman scorned.

This has all, of course, left me with a bitter taste in my mouth. While the goal of being engaged to be married is still set for August 14, a mere six months away, the prospects look slim. I remember in the fifth grade wondering in amazement how do people fall in love, much less get married? How did two people come into such a confluence of mind, body, and soul to commit themselves to each other for an eternity?

Now, almost two decades later, that same question baffles me. While my friends around me are falling in love and marrying at epidemic proportions, I cannot even claim a simple girlfriend, let alone marry one. Six months passed, six months to go, and I am alone. On that note, I want to tell you all that I will not be writing this column for a while. Enjoy the hiatus. I certainly will.

# 12

"**OU BROKE YOUR** promise," Craig accused.

"I know." A week had passed since the Molly-Paris debacle. Although distance from that ill-fated Valentine's Day weekend had helped, Nick's soul was still not right. That was why he had quit the column for the moment. "I'm sorry."

"Be sorry. You know you were front-page news in the *Union-Tribune*'s Currents section! We've received five hundred emails a day since your going on 'hiatus.' "

"Were they good or bad?" asked Nick, munching on a chip. They were sprawled out on Nick's futon couch in the living room, watching the Lakers unfortunately dominate the Sonics.

"Confused," answered Craig. "They want to know why the hell you quit the column! They want to know who you are and, better yet, they want to know who Other Woman is. So they can beat her ass. For real."

"I never knew the *Reader*'s crowd was so sketchy."

"It's like a soap opera, kid!" gushed Craig. "They tune in every week by grabbing our paper and reading it. Do you know ad rates are *quadruple* what they were before you got here? You're huge, boi!"

Nick sighed sarcastically. "What a great waste of momentum."

"We've had three dozen arrangements of flowers sent to you from the fans, out of sympathy for what that Molly woman did. Letters, media inquiries are off the hook . . . How can you walk away from this, man?"

Nick casually ate another chip. "Watch me."

---

IN THE IMMORTAL words of Malloy, Game *on*! As the malaise of February slipped into March, Nick went on a dating rampage of the likes not seen since his first year in Chicago, when he was recovering from the heartbreak of a lifetime. With Mal on the loose, they resorted to tag-teaming the females of San Diego County with tactics not exploited since college. Nick's normal, genial self was replaced by a stone-cold charmer, one who had no reservations about using well-thought-out witticisms, making ambiguous observations, or even employing a straight-up line to start a conversation with a woman. Showing no conscience—or originality—they even stooped to an update of the famous *Top Gun* karaoke scene to land Nick a woman. Instead of singing "You've Lost That Loving Feeling," Nick and Malloy butchered a rendition of Boyz II Men's "I'll Make Love to You." And coming home with that woman from the bar, that's exactly what Nick did.

Outwardly, he feigned normalcy. Nick delved into his new job, a complex acting gig as Aaron the Moor in Shakespeare's *Titus Andronicus*. Aaron was a dark, murderous, lecherous, scheming bastard— a perfect role, given Nick's current state of mind. Despite the best of intentions, he had ended up getting played by a woman he never would have had anything to do with had he been sober. It angered him that he had been so easily duped. It angered him that he had been so forthright and honest. It angered him that all that forthrightness and honesty had cost him his lady. Paris was a good woman. She was honest and hardworking, a great person and a great mom. Nick missed her.

The following weekend, Nick and Malloy went to a strip club. Even though the very married Craig and the ought-to-be-married Carlton (as he and Jeannie were now back together) accompanied them, they were determined to show their tied-down brethren a good time.

They could not have picked a better place. Red Velvet was a seedy, no-holds-barred house of sin and ill-repute located a couple of miles from the Mexican border in Imperial Beach. Widely rumored to be owned by a reformed Mexican gangster laundering his money, Red Velvet let anything go—and for cheap. If you had the money, they did the dirty. Under a continuous haze of marijuana smoke and booty-shaking techno music, the women in Red Velvet were largely black and Latina, matching the neighborhood and clientele. And on any given night, the sailors from the nearby Thirty-second Street Naval Base would patronize the establishment, horny and rabid on shore leave.

"I'm glad this place is an all-nude establishment," Mal crowed as they sat down in front of a stark-naked Latina on stage. "That weak-ass titty bar in Kearny Mesa only went topless. What kinda shit is that?"

"I think this place is an anything-goes type of establishment," Nick observed, noticing a scantily clad dancer emerge from the VIP room with one hand on a man and the other wiping her mouth.

"You gotta give 'em some slack, playboy," said Carlton. "Not all cities can be as hype as The ATL."

"Magic City, baby!" enthused Craig. "Man, those women were *hotties*!"

"True that, true that. They don't get much better than that. Well, except Luke dancers," said Mal.

"What the hell you know about Luke dancers, nigga?" challenged Carlton.

"Two words for you: Club Rolex." Mal waved a waitress over. "Eh, pretty lady. Let me get a round of drinks for my boys here. We gettin' *fucked up* tonight!"

Two hours later, that is exactly what happened. With liquor in his system and his boy Luke blaring on the sound system, Mal lost whatever inhibitions he had not already voluntarily given away. Mal jumped onstage with a fistful of bills, gyrating and rump shaking along with the surprised but responsive dancer. At least Mal was a helpful drunk. As more dollars came flying at her G-string, Mal helped collect the money for the dancer and remove her articles of clothing. Soon even the lax security had seen enough, chasing the drunkenly triumphant Mal from the stage and back to the table with his boys.

With Craig as the designated driver, Nick indulged in two rounds of

Midori and Amaretto Sours each. Remembering what had happened the last time he had had *eight* rounds of the tasty, Kool-Aid-flavored drinks, Nick maintained a nice little buzz, one that enabled him to open his mouth and holla at Shorty.

Shorty was actually five-nine, a light-bright type of black woman with a mane of curly dark hair that came to just above her shoulders. She was long, lean, and taut, wearing only a sparkly, silver-sequined bra-and-panty set. Some audacious three-inch heels gave her nicely toned calves their own area code. This woman seemed to carry an air about her, one that was equal parts strong, dominant woman and innocent but whorish schoolgirl. With that same arrogance and innocence, Shorty strutted over to the seated Nick and demanded, "Can I dance for you?"

"Please." Nick pulled over a chair for her. "Have a seat until after this song is through. What's your name, sexy?"

"Missy Delicious."

"No, what's your *real* name?"

She giggled. That schoolgirl innocence. "Melissa."

"I'm Nick."

"I'm sure you are."

"What's that supposed to mean?"

"I'm sure you'll be 'Nick' now, but you won't be later."

"Meaning?"

"Does your wife call you Nick?"

"I'm not married."

"Your girlfriend?"

"I don't have one of those," Nick said, coining a phrase he had first heard from Andrea. He caught an approving head nod from Craig. She was a hottie. C-Nice approved. "And you? Do you have a boyfriend?"

"Look around. You're all my boyfriends tonight," Melissa said flirtatiously.

"I'mma hold you to that," threatened Nick as the music changed. "Time to make that booty hop, girl!"

Hop, bounce, shake she did! Melissa, energized by their brief conversation, gave Nick a striptease for the ages. Flagrantly disobeying posted club rules, she gave and allowed all kinds of contact. Stripping naked, Missy Delicious climbed onto his lap, face forward, rubbing her breasts in his face. When Nick reflexively started licking at them, she squeezed her 34-C's together to fit the nipples in his mouth. All this occurred while her shaved crotch created enough friction to erect a missile silo in his pants. She appreciatively rubbed her clitoris against it while stroking his face. It was the best ten bucks Nick had ever spent.

In a scant five minutes, the song, and the temptation, was over. Disappointed, Nick reluctantly watched Melissa remove herself from his lap. Mal, Craig, and Carlton had long since turned from the main stage to watch, jaw-droppingly, the show Missy Delicious had put on their boy. They had just witnessed sex, just better protected.

Melissa could see the want in Nick's eyes when she came up off him. And, for a change, she had actually been the slightest bit aroused. In the six months she had worked there, she had become pretty immune to arousal by customers. But for some reason, she wanted this one. Leaning in to him, she whispered in his ear, "Come back to the VIP room with me. I'll let you do anything you want to me."

"How much?"

"Forty bucks."

Before the *s* on "bucks" had landed, Nick was up and out of his chair. His boys watched with inebriated amusement as Missy Delicious led Nick by the hand toward the VIP room. More than anything, they were jealous.

Once inside the red-velvet-carpeted and curtained-off VIP room, Nick gave Melissa her soon-to-be-hard-earned twenties. That was as far as his script carried him. He had never been into a VIP room with a paid purveyor of flesh, especially at these rock-bottom prices. "So whassup?"

"You want to see a *real* lap dance?"

"Do your thing."

Melissa gyrated, grinding slowly to the music bumping outside the room. She enjoyed twisting her hips this way and that to a sloweddown bass beat. In no time, her clothes were off again. With more expertise than Nick would have cared to admit, Melissa worked past his belt and unzipped his pants. She reached in and started stroking his shaft, feeling the tissue swell and grow in her very hand. By this point, she was sitting in his lap, caressing his face with her other hand.

She relented, backing off Nick smoothly. Descending to a kneeling position, Melissa slurped Nick into her mouth greedily. She gave him just enough of a taste before sliding a condom on his penis with her mouth. Damn, that was talent.

Just to say something, Nick said, "You weren't kidding when you said I could do anything with you."

"What can I say? It must be your birthday." She grinned, pulling his pants and boxers down to his ankles.

Ascending, Missy Delicious prepared to live up to her nickname by hovering over her willingly helpless prey. She extended her arms, pushing Nick back hard against the cushioned red-velvet couch. Holding him in place, she steadied herself for her descent, not unlike a Harrier fighter jet.

The schoolgirl in her popped out again. "Permission to land, sir?"

"Granted!"

* * *

"**SO MUCH FOR** 'no sex in the champagne room,' " teased Malloy, quoting comedian Chris Rock. Their debrief took place on the way home, with everyone piled into Craig's Jetta.

"That was a slutty thing you did," commented married Craig from behind the wheel. "Even if she was hot."

"Nobody asked you," Nick growled.

"Eh, I ain't hatin' on you, playboy. Go do yo' thang," approved Carlton. "I mean, how many dudes can say they boned a stripper?"

"Did you get her number, too?" asked Mal. "Will there be a repeat performance?"

"And you know this," replied Nick with bravado. "We're going out next week."

"Damn. I gotta hand it to you, Little Dude. You represented tonight," said Mal, almost fatherly. "There may be a drop of a player in you."

Nick raised an unimpressed eyebrow.

"But just a drop."

* * *

**AN INTERESTING DILEMMA** presented itself to Nick. Just where do you take a stripper out on a date? Not only was this woman a stripper, but also he had had sex with her. There was absolutely nothing left to the imagination. He had gone about the whole dating process with her ass-backwards.

Wanting to flip it 180 degrees, Nick kept it simple—coffee. The Borders in Mission Valley had an excellent little adjunct café right off the magazine section. Figuring that since he had already spent fifty dollars on her in the club, he was entitled to a five-dollar date. Missy Delicious—er, Melissa—arrived looking very unstripperlike in a long, gray, loose-fitting sundress. Since they both worked nights, Nick at the theater, Melissa at the club, they met in the early afternoon in the café.

For the most part, Nick listened. He listened to her story unravel and was instantly bored. Born on the East Coast, grew up in Portland, moved down to San Diego to try something new. Trying to find herself. Did not know what she wanted to do in life. Had always liked dancing and wanted to keep buying Prada handbags. If you added it all up, multiplied it, and then exponentiated it, her story still didn't amount to a hill of beans covered in shit. When it came Nick's turn to share, he offered very little, just everything that was topical and surface in his life. No woman now would ever know about his ailing mother.

After an uneventful hour and a half, Nick lied his way out of the date. He went home and immediately deleted her number from his Palm Pilot. Opening night was two weeks away and he did not need the distraction. Also, his time was too valuable to waste. The more he trudged on in life, the more he became lost and deluded.

**SHORTLY AFTER DISMISSING** the stripper, Nick found a new avenue of scandalousness—the Internet. With rehearsals in the evening, his days had become free. With idle hands being the devil's playground, Nick found a whole new, untapped world online. Nick reconnected with NON, Nubian Online Network, the very same on-line service where he had met Maya T. as a penpal almost a decade ago.

All it took was for someone to instant-message him online, and it was on. The woman described herself and emailed him her picture. Her face was nasty and she was looking for sex. Nick stopped talking to her quickly but soon found others. There were not a whole lot of black women to choose from so Nick broadened his search topic to "sex," "San Diego," and "female," which yielded a wealth of results.

The next day, Nick had his picture scanned at a Kinko's and was online in a major way. His sex searches uncovered freaks of all races throughout San Diego County. The names tripped him out: HoneiiBrown, FreakyDeaky, JulieSD69, AsexyHottie4U, etc. Several of these ladies listed sex as a hobby. Jackpot.

After an hour of online chatting with HoneiiBrown and reviewing a picture, Nick left for her apartment in El Cajon. Having described herself as five-nine, 140 pounds, with honey-brown skin (of course), she did not disappoint in person.

Nick never asked her name and she never offered. He called her Honeii while she called him BA, which stood for BlackAct1, his screen name. For two complete strangers who had met each other merely ninety minutes earlier, they had sex like their plane was going down. And as easily as he had met and bedded her, Nick drove home and hopped back on the Internet.

**NICK'S ESCAPADES WITH** Honeii continued for a week. Three more times he went over to her place, and three more times they got sweaty. However busy with his revolving door of chicken-heads, Malloy still noticed a change in Nick but said nothing. Being his best friend, as well as a man, Malloy could sense when Nick was getting some action. Nick was the type to be all clandestine and secretive about it.

*Titus Andronicus* opened to a full house on the last Friday in March. Stripped to his base, carnal instincts, Nick put on a show of pure evil as never before witnessed in San Diego. As Aaron the Moor, Nick plotted, connived, raped, slaughtered, insulted, and brutalized everyone within his demonic touch. Bounding across the stage, Nick slipped entirely into Aaron's dark, diabolical world. Shakespeare may not have written a more evil character, and even if he had, it could not have touched Nick's Aaron the Moor.

Malloy, who had sat in the first row, dapped Nick up as soon as he emerged from backstage. "Way to go, dude. You really scared me up there. Looked like you wanted to kill a nigga. You got skills."

"Thanks."

"You goin' to your cast party?"

"Naw. I've got things to do."

"Cool. Let's bounce."

Once home, Nick headed straight for his laptop and fired up NON. No messages. He dialed up Honeii's phone number. Her answering machine said that she would be out of town until next Tuesday. That *bitch*! They had agreed that she would break him off a little somethin' in celebration of his opening night. Disgusted, angry, and sexually charged, Nick hopped back online again, determined to find himself some little nubile San Diego freak to take her place.

Although he did not know everything that was going on, Mal had seen enough. "Eh, dude. Let's play some bones."

"Bones? Why do you want to play that for?" asked Nick.

"It's been a while, ain't it? Come offa dat 'puter and slap some bones with me, my nig," Malloy invited.

Nick sighed as he turned off the computer. No sex for him tonight. "Aw'ight, man."

Their game of dominoes started off in typical fashion. Both of them came out mouths blazing, trash-talking their jaws to sleep and pounding the table, calling out their scores. Soon, that hard-hitting bravado gave way to a more contemplative atmosphere. As they had hundreds of times since their freshman year, they engaged each other in deep-rooted male conversation that dissected their lives and the world.

"So you been seein' a new shorty?" inquired Mal, saying the word "shorty" with an accent that was clearly from one of New York City's five boroughs.

"Surprised you've even noticed," mumbled Nick, studying his dominoes.

"Man, I've noticed a change in you this past month, and I can't call it. Are you doin' some method-acting bullshit, 'cause you ain't the dude I've known for twelve years. I think that Aaron the Moor done messed with your mind."

"That's just acting and I'm an actor," Nick clarified flaccidly. "Thanks for the compliment, though."

"So how'd you meet Shorty?"

"Through the Internet."

"Is *that* why you be online all the time? To catch some ass?" asked Mal incredulously.

"You'd be surprised how much ass is just *waiting* out there to be tapped," Nick rhapsodized. "And it's all on the Net."

"So you smashed a broad off the Net?"

Nick snorted. "Of course. Wouldn't you?"

"Not some broad I ain't never seen before."

"She sent me a picture ahead of time." Nick whistled. "She's tight."

"A monster, huh?"

"Straight up."

"Tell me something—is it that bad?" asked Mal.

"Huh?"

"Are you having a hard time meeting women, dude? Because this Internet thing . . . it's not your style."

"How the hell would you know? You're too busy whipping women through that revolving door of a bedroom of yours to notice."

"Yeah, but what you're doing is dangerous. When you go out and meet these chicks, you don't know *what* could happen. Yet you keep putting yourself at risk. . . . It's not safe."

"Not any safer than you with your fast ass. We should call you the *Ocean Beach Express* since you only make one stop—the bedroom."

"Am I that bad, dude?" inquired Mal sincerely.

Nick nodded gravely. "Yeah. You're that bad."

Once again, Malloy was all smiles. "Good! That's what I like to hear."

They resumed playing dominoes on the dining room table. Malloy slapped down a bone to collect twenty-five points. "Quarter, bitch!" he howled.

Quietly, Nick said, "You know, Mal, why do you do this? Why do you see all these other women?" Nick hoped for more insight into why he, too, was in an emotional funk. Everything had happened so naturally during his rehearsal to become Aaron the Moor that he had allowed himself this ethical slide. Now Nick sought guidance during this confused and troubled time from his very own in-residence urban poet and prophet. Mal did not disappoint.

"It numbs the pain of not being with the one you love."

# 13

**HE SLIDE CONTINUED** unabated. True to the saying, April brought showers—and continued misbehavior by Nick. He beat down a steady path to Honeii's apartment, as well as to two or three other women he had approached online. Most of his spare time during the day was spent sucked into the laptop, trolling NON for freaky women. Comfortable in the quality—and quantity—of sex he received from his offline encounters, Nick abandoned face-to-face dating altogether.

While Nick continued to slide, others continued to rise. Carlton and Jeannie now shared a sports-talk radio show—or at least an hour of one. This gig was in addition to Carlton's duties at Channel 2. He would come on in the show's final hour and the two would banter playfully about San Diego and national sports news, to critical acclaim. Shortly thereafter, *The Jeannie Rhome Show* went syndicated, picked up by forty affiliates around the country. She and Carlton were in love, life was great, and they could not be happier.

The same went for Robert. He had been, for lack of a better phrase, all up under *his* man for the past couple of months, and, outside of work, MIA since Nick had messed things up with Paris.

Nick, strolling down the open-air walkway in Fashion Valley on a drizzly day, purposefully ignored the Brookstone store to his left. Robert, however, would not allow the store or himself to go ignored.

"Nick! Nick! *Nicolas!*"

Caught, Nick stopped, glanced heavenward, and then succumbed to his summons. Joylessly, he said, "Whassup, Robert."

"Nick . . . I know you didn't think you were going to *slink* past my store while I was working, did you?"

"What's going on," said Nick dispassionately. He really did not feel in the mood for chitchat. He had a hot cyberdate with Pretty-HotAndTempting in half an hour.

"Nothing spectacular. Just life," Robert mused. "I think I will be quitting Brookstone next month."

"Thank God. Working in a retail store never seemed quite like you," commented Nick.

"This is true. Guess what I am doing next?"

Nick did not. He could not spare the energy to guess.

"I'm going to art school!" Robert gushed.

"Art school? Again? For what? I thought you already had a degree," said Nick. It wasn't every day that one of your friends gave up a paying job for art school.

"I do. But I want to brush up on my drawings and paintings. Make some connections so I can make a living at it. I'm going to be a visual artist for real this time!"

The man appeared to be genuinely excited. Nick did not want to burst his emotional bubble, but he had to know some details. "How can you afford to do this? Brookstone giving you a golden parachute or something?"

"Fuck Brookstone," dismissed Robert, immediately lowering his voice as he remembered his environment. "I'm moving in with Antony at the end of this month."

Nick blinked twice. "Pardon? Did you say you're *moving in* with him?"

"Would you like me to repeat?" smiled Robert readily. "Shocked?"

"Hell yes. Unless you two move to Vermont and get hitched, it's the biggest step you two could take."

"I know! I'm thrilled!" Robert could not stop smiling.

Enough of the old Nick broke through his rough, Aaron the Moor exterior to give Robert a hug. Even though he could not find love if he were run over by a truck full of it, Nick still was sincerely happy for his friend. "I'm happy for you, man. Really."

"I have something else to tell you." Robert winced. "Something you might not like."

Nick waved him on. "Bring it."

"I saw your ex-girlfriend in here yesterday."

"Esmerelda was not my girlfriend," Nick stated for the record. "She was damn close, though."

"Not her. The black girl."

"Paris?"

"Yes, that's her name. She was in here yesterday." Robert paused dramatically. "With her fiancé."

Nick wanted to choke on his pride. "Are you kidding me? Her fiancé? It hasn't even been two months since we stopped dating!"

Robert nodded gravely. "She had a ring and everything. They were kissing all over each other. She must've remembered that time we all went out bowling because she came over to me. Mentioned that her and her fiancé had dated back in high school and miraculously found each other again just recently. 'Love at second sight,' she called it. They just knew."

Nick almost collapsed into one of Brookstone's massaging easy chairs; Lord knew he could use one. It took a lot to tame a player. If Robert could find love and happiness, if Paris could, in such short order, why couldn't Nick?

**THE NEWS ABOUT** Paris only spiraled Nick farther down. If subconscious self-loathing were oil, Nick would be OPEC. The man continued to bury his fears and insecurities in sex with Internet tramps and devastating performances onstage. His Aaron the Moor was becoming the talk of the theater community for his savage reality, brutally frank evil, and conniving charm. There was a rumor going around that Nick actually had a police record. A movie producer who just happened to be vacationing in San Diego for the weekend even approached Nick backstage to give him his card. Nick did not realize how lucky he was to have acting as an outlet for his frustrations.

Mom's condition was getting worse. As Nick plowed deeper and deeper into his funk, he cut off calling home. Last report was that she was smoking marijuana, medicinally, to help her cope with the nausea and other side effects of the chemotherapy. The idea of Harrison out on Rainier and Henderson or some side street in the Central District trying to score some weed for his ailing wife was both ludicrous and sad.

Nick was perturbed even more when Mom called on her own, stoned initiative. She was so high, the conversation was a series of Morse code–like giggles rather than a discussion between mother and son.

"Helloooo, there, Handsome!"

"Ma?"

Mom laughed. "It's your poorrrr motherrrr!"

"Are you okay, Mom?"

"Don't you worry about me, Handsome." Giggles. "I'm just going to die before my sixty-second birthday, some thirty years younger than your grandmother, but I am doing grrrrreat!"

Just who was this woman who had abducted his mother and made her sound like an extra from a Cheech and Chong movie? "Mom . . . are you on drugs?"

More giggling. "Define 'drugs,' Handsome."

Mom had never taken any drug stronger than Advil in her entire life, so the prospect of her smoking scared the hell out of Nick.

"Weed. Mary Jane. Herb. Are you smoking marijuana, Mom?"

"Puff, puff, give!" Her voice degraded into laughter. "This is some good shit, man!"

Mom did not curse. Ever. Nick's depression deepened and he secluded himself even further in his stage character and his sexually predatory online persona.

By mid-April, he was through with Honeii. Their sexual flame had extinguished itself, their superficial relationship sucked dry. Ready for new conquests, Nick found a willing participant in the Hillcrest neighborhood. Horny4U, a.k.a. Johnetta, was five-ten and 165 pounds of taut, Caucasian muscle. Or so she said, typed via the computer. The girl didn't have a picture, but she gave her measurements to Nick online: 34B-28-36. Odd proportions, but they were just small enough. Nick was game.

This time, Mal did not blink an eye as Nick scuttled out of the house at 11:40 P.M. on a weekday. He just continued to play video-game golf as his friend went out to handle yet another booty call. *At least I have the decency to bring my women home occasionally,* figured Mal.

Driving for sex was an interesting, even nerve-racking experience. A multitude of thoughts and feelings warred for space inside Nick's conscience. An upbringing by a God-fearing mother that included an entrenched, traditional, Judeo-Christian morality code would always do battle with the needs of the flesh. But overruled by a libido that could consume a city block had it had teeth, Nick would press on to arrive at his booty calls before his conscience stopped him.

Parking this time of night in Hillcrest could be difficult. Nick circled around Johnetta's address a few times before parking a block away. He walked over to the apartment building slowly, quieting his thoughts of dissent. At the entrance, Nick almost ran over Robert.

"Nick! What're you doing here?"

Embarrassed, Nick said nervously, "Visiting a friend."

Robert resisted the urge to check his watch. "At this hour? In *this* building?"

"Yes."

"Are you sure?"

"*Yes.*" Nick wanted to go, badly. "Hey, I'll catch you later."

Quizzically watching him flee the scene into an elevator, Robert said, "Alright. You do that."

Within the safety of the elevator, Nick breathed a sigh of relief. He hadn't bothered to ask himself why Robert was leaving this very same building at midnight.

Here was the moment of truth. Nick walked up to Apartment 511. He rang the doorbell. Waited.

The door opened, revealing a dimly lit living room. Johnetta strutted away with her back to him, outfitted in a sexy little kimono. Nick wandered in eagerly with "How you doin'?"

Inside, she turned around and said in a husky voice, "Just fine."

Only it wasn't a she, it was a *shim*! Underneath a slather of female makeup, there was the bone structure of a male face. What *really* sealed the deal was the Adam's apple. A *goddamn* Adam's apple!

"*What the fuck!*" Nick blurted before he could control it.

"I'm a pre-op transsexual," shim announced grandly. "Do you have a problem with that?"

Nick did not stick around to answer. He was out the door like Michael Johnson running for Olympic gold.

---

**MALLOY STEPPED OFF** the train at the Fashion Valley station and traversed the expansive parking lot. It was Friday evening, and the place was already three-quarters full at five-thirty. On the first level, he walked into a French mini-café and sat down at a table where Carlton waited.

"Whassup, C-Town?" They dapped up. "What's goin' on?"

"It's your world, playboy. I wish I knew myself."

"So why'd you call me on the job to come down here?"

Carlton pointed at Craig, who walked in the door and over to their table. "What's goin' on, fellas?"

Dap was exchanged all around as Craig sat at their table.

"Shoot, we were hopin' you could tell us that, my nigga," said Carlton. He sipped from his cup of hot chocolate. "You call me up on the job and tell me to come down and meet you here at five-thirty about something urgent. You also have me call Malloy and tell him the same. What's the deal?"

Craig smiled thinly and then pointed at the door. In walked Robert, fresh off work.

"Nigga, what? Pssh! I'm outta here," dismissed Malloy, rising up as Robert landed at the table.

"Sit down," said Robert.

"For what? Your gay-ass little meeting? I'm ghost, dawg," Mal proclaimed, turning to leave.

"*Sit down,*" Robert ordered. A hand on Malloy's wrist impeded his progress. Malloy, Crown Heights, Brooklyn, to the fullest, looked down at Robert's hand on his and up to his eyes, then back down again to his hand with that don't-you-know-I-will-jack-you-*up*! look.

Robert gently released his wrist and said, "Look. I know we haven't seen eye-to-eye in the past. I have better things to do with my Friday evening than putting up with a fucking homophobe. But this isn't about you or me. It's about Nick. Now sit down. Please."

Glaring at him all the way, Mal resumed his seat. Robert did likewise. "I called this meeting to order because we have a problem: Nick is in trouble."

Their faces fell serious, with Craig's the most so. "What's wrong with him?"

"Something is not right with our friend," Robert announced. "I have noticed an attitude shift in him in the past couple of months, and not for the better. He's been moody, distant, surly, short, and very un-Nick-like. Has anyone noticed anything like this from him?"

"Are you sure it's not just method acting from that play he's doing? He plays a stone-cold muthafucka in that piece," noted Carlton.

"Naw . . . Nick's always been able to separate fact from fiction," observed Craig quietly. "I think you're right, Robert. Something's wrong with our boy."

Assuming the role of the protective best friend, Malloy challenged with "What *evidence* do you have to support your assertion? I live with the dude. Yeah, he can be a little moody, but I don't know if he's all y'all are makin' him out to be."

"Last night, I saw Nick entering an apartment building that is a notoriously homosexual enclave. In Hillcrest. At midnight. On a Thursday," Robert elucidated.

Mal was ready to spring across the table and beat that fag into an ice cream sundae. "What the fuck you sayin'!"

"I've known Nick ever since high school, like Carlton has. I love the man to death, but one thing he is *not* is a homosexual," clarified Robert coolly. "He exudes heterosexuality. What I want to know is what the hell he was doing marching up into an all-gay apartment complex at that time of night. Something must be wrong."

Carlton whistled in recognition. "My man's right. Those are prime booty-call hours."

Mal grudgingly offered up the truth. "Nick's been meeting a lotta women from the Internet."

Craig squinted. "He crushin'?"

"Like Barry Bonds with an aluminum bat," Mal admitted. "I think Nick's an Internet sex addict."

That sounded just as bad as it truly was. A hush fell over the table until Robert could formulate a question, *the* question. "So how do we bring him out of this?"

"How? How the hell did he fall into it in the first place?" wondered

Carlton. He felt bad. His relationship with Jeannie had knocked him out of the loop.

Craig and Malloy ended up exchanging knowing looks. *Molly.*

"I think Robert's on the right track," piped Craig. "What's going on with him right now is unfortunate, but we all know ways we can bring him out of it. Don't we?"

"Yeah," they all mumbled thoughtfully, simultaneously.

"So then it's up to us, playboys," Carlton declared. "Let's get Nick back."

Their hands piled in on top of one another. Mal exchanged a coded look with Robert as Robert's pale, homosexual hand descended upon Mal's dark, heterosexual one. It was a look of hard-earned respect. Robert loved his best friend and Malloy could not hate on that. *You're aw'ight with me, dude.*

*You, too,* Robert's eyes shined back at him. *Hetero!*

**IMAGINE NICK'S SURPRISE** when Anna showed up at his door. She had the sincerest, most heartwarming smile to match her flipped-up hair, neatly trimmed bangs, and conservative, ankle-length skirt. In fact, she'd worn the very same outfit when Nick first met her. The first words out of her mouth formed a very valid question. "May I come in?"

The woman had traveled from Orange County. Home training took over. "Sure."

As Anna breezed by him, exuding the sweet, fragrant scent of Tommy Girl, Nick instantly wondered just what the hell was her agenda here today. What was she trying to prove? And just what would be accomplished with their little tête-à-tête? Nick was cool on conversation with her. Nevertheless, Anna made a home on the futon couch as Nick sat on the regular couch, a guarded distance away.

"So how've you been?" she started off.

"I've been doing well," Nick lied.

"Yeah. I saw the review of *Titus* in *Backstage West.* Congratulations."

"Thank you." Nick allowed the conversation to slip into suspended animation. The appropriate response would have been to ask how she was doing, but Nick could not spare the effort. *Why, why,*

*why are you here?* his head screamed. He did not want her to know that she affected him in any way. Yet, calmly, he asked anyway.

Joanna Whitley studied the carpet for her response before pushing forward. She had memorized the lines to this scene during the fifty-five-minute car ride down. The actress had to get the words just right.

"I came to see your Aaron the Moor. I also came to see you," she stated primly.

Nick wanted to scream on her, but she gave him very little to work with. "You came all the way down here to see me act?"

"And to take you out to dinner after," she offered hopefully.

Nick stroked the beard he had grown to further villainize Aaron the Moor onstage. *She* wanted to take *him* out to dinner. Was this an inverted universe or something? If nothing else, the woman had balls, to come into the lion's den, months after slitting her own throat with Nick, and trying to dance with the lion.

His hesitation prompted further explanation from her. "I know we haven't had the most stable history in the past. I made some mistakes, you made some mistakes . . . I said some things that I, perhaps, should not have said. But I wanted you to know that it is all water under the bridge." She stole a beat to summon her courage. "Besides . . . I miss you."

By the time Nick had landed on the futon couch beside her, his hardened exterior had crumbled. As delicately as if he were kissing a rose petal, Nick bestowed a kiss on Anna's trembling lips. She sank her head into Nick's chest as he held her. Like manna from heaven, Anna's reemergence in Nick's life was complete.

———

**MALLOY WAS ANNOYED** to find Anna leaving the house that Saturday morning. Apparently, the chick(enhead) had spent the night with Nick. After his meeting at Fashion Valley, he had caught a flick and returned to the house well before Nick and Anna had. Mal was in bed by the time they had returned from the play and dinner afterward.

Exercising more damage control than anything, Mal asked his suddenly smiley roommate in the kitchen, "Tell me you didn't hit that."

"Good morning to you, too, Mal," Nick hummed.

"Please tell me you didn't smash."

"Who? Anna?"

"Was there more than one bitch in your bed last night, nigga? Now tell me you didn't crush that! Please!" Mal begged.

"Alright, Mal. I didn't," appeased Nick.

"Is that the truth?"

"With Anna, yes, it is." Nick began making some breakfast. "Want some eggs?"

"Naw, dude, I'm straight." Mal settled onto a barstool at the counter. "Think she's still carrying her V-Card?"

"A twenty-seven-year-old virgin? Naw, man. She's had her V-Chip pulled. But she is a born-again virgin. She hasn't had any in three years," Nick informed him. "Swears she's waiting until she's engaged."

"Well, that's noble, if unrealistic," Malloy panned. "What I wanna know is how that trick weaseled her way back into your bed."

"She just asked me if she could take me out to dinner."

"*She* asked *you*?"

Nick grinned. "Yup."

Shaking his head, Mal once again said, "You are way too easily impressed."

Nick nearly slammed down the skillet when he heard that. "What the hell are you talking about? I'm sick and tired of hearing that crap from you. You're supposed to be my friend. You're supposed to be happy for me. I don't know if you've noticed, but I haven't exactly been bringin' dimepieces home lately. There are *no quality women out there*. The second I let quality back into my life, you ain't even happy for me! What the fuck is that? Either be my friend or shut the fuck up."

Malloy decided he was going to do both. He knew that this Anna girl was no good for his best friend, but Nick wasn't trying to hear that right now. So Malloy shut up, rolled off the barstool, and trotted off into his room, shutting the door. He made a phone call, a phone call that could hopefully bring his roommate, and best friend, out of all this nonsense.

"I WANNA COME back."

"Thank God, you've come to your senses." Craig embraced Nick with open arms. Nick had come down to Craig's office at the *Reader* to make his pronouncement: His cash cow was back on the team.

"So this is where you work, huh? This is where you make it all happen," mused Nick, looking around at the unglamorous setting of San Diego's largest free weekly newspaper. He had expected it to be a bustling metropolis of journalistic fervor, but everyone seemed to be fairly laid back.

"Naw, kid. *You* make it happen!" said Craig gleefully. "If I get one more email demanding your identity, I'll wig out. Even worse, I just might tell them!"

"It's good to know the readers have missed me."

"I've got an idea to bring you back in style, too, kid."

Nick winced. "Another PR coup of the year?"

"Naw, man. This one will be the PR coup of the *decade*!"

---

**THE DOUBLE DATE** had been Carlton's idea. Since Anna had been making a concerted effort to be in Nick's life during the past week, Carlton figured he could help out his boy by solidifying the relationship.

Talk about the classic double date. Carlton and Jeannie met Nick and Anna for mini-golf at a family amusement center off Clairemont Mesa Boulevard. Scorecards in hand, the foursome took to the golf course.

Everything had started off innocuously enough. Jeannie and Anna politely chatted about their jobs, their friends, the business, and even ridiculed their men. Their men were, of course, challenging each other with blatant displays of machismo on every hole. They couldn't just shoot at a hole—they always had to put something on it.

"You can't make that putt, playboy," sneered Carlton, looking at a hole that was obscured by a windmill and a waterfall.

"Put somethin' on that, trick."

"You put somethin' on that, bitch."

"Then shut your mouth. You talk so damn much, makes me want to be a deaf-mute."

Right when Nick was about to swing, Carlton dared, "You make that putt . . . I'll give you somethin'."

"Oh yeah? Like what?"

"I dunno. *Somethin'*."

"Watch and learn, fake player."

Nick hit the ball, watched it breeze between the windmill slats and over a green felt hill, ricochet off a corner, fly off a ramp and over a waterfall, bounce twice, and then land in the hole. À la Adam Sandler in *Happy Gilmore,* Nick screamed, *"Get in the hooole!"*

And it was on. Childhood rivalries emerged as the duo fired verbal and golfing volleys down the back nine holes, the women fading into the background as Carlton and Nick battled on. Jeannie and Anna watched in sheer awe as the boys acted like, well, *boys.* And, in the end, it all came down to this:

"This is make-or-break, Little Dude," Carlton taunted. "You make this putt, we tie. Miss this putt, you lose."

"I'm well aware of the situation, Dick Enberg," Nick shot back, a reference to NBC's golf commentator. "Will you shut up long enough for me to make this shot?"

"You got it, playboy." Carlton watched with amusement as Nick started to swing, before he stopped him again. "Bet you don't make this shot."

"Put somethin' on that, trick."

"If you make that shot, I'll give you somethin'."

"You already *owe* me *somethin'* from the eighth."

"Aw'ight, then. Make it double-somethin'."

Nick rolled his eyes—before rolling his ball past the cup. He flung his putter at the hole while Carlton erupted into laughter. Nick put on a cursing display that would have made every sailor in San Diego proud, to a soundtrack of Carlton's continuous laughter.

Anna was aghast. Not only had her man lost, but also this friend of his was being awfully rude about it.

When they settled into some of the generic fast food offered at the amusement center, the situation deteriorated. The trash talking continued unabated but this time, Anna stood by her man.

"Aren't you hoarse yet from laughing? You didn't look too pretty on seventeen your damn self," she mouthed off.

Hold up, hold up, *hold up*! Jeannie knew this mouthy New York heffa was *not* talking smack to her man! Jeannie Rhome, known on the radio as the Queen of Smack, got her licks in, too. "At least he knows which end of the club to putt with. You looked so clueless out there, I thought we'd have to call Alicia Silverstone."

"Oh, you wanna talk movies now, huh? Well, I guess all you can do is *talk* about them, since your fat ass won't ever be able to fit in the frame of one," Anna volleyed back.

"Is that the best you got, video ho?"

"Not even warming up, Miss Face-Made-for-Radio!" At this point, Anna was on her feet, fists balled.

Over their respective baskets of fries, Nick and Carlton looked on appalled as their female companions dared to jump over the table at each other. They were horrified. Their trash talk was normal, ritualistic male bonding that went all the way back to the ninth grade and the 989 bus route. These women seriously did not like each other.

"Break it up, ladies, break it up," instructed Carlton with an affable smile. "We just playin', y'all."

As she sat down, Anna's eyes spit fire. *Talk about me again, bitch!*

Who did this chick think she was? Jeannie had made basketballer *Gary Payton,* the godfather of smack, shut the hell up one time on her show. *You don't want none of this,* Jeannie's eyes radiated back.

Carlton gave Nick a look all his own. *Anna needs to settle down.*

Nick shot a look back. *I know.*

---

"I STILL CAN'T believe they were about to throw down," cackled Malloy two days later from the passenger seat of the 4Runner.

"It wasn't that serious," Nick lied.

"Where was I during all this?" sulked Mal.

"Boning one of your biddies."

"No girlfighting? No bitch-hits?"

"Man, for the last time, shut *up*! It was not that serious." Nick piloted the 4Runner into the auditorium parking lot.

"But still, sounds like your girl was a little outta control," commented Mal. "You sure you wanna still mess with her? She doesn't sound quite right in the head."

Nick glared at Malloy as he brought the car to a stop. "No more talk about my lady. Let's walk in here and do this thing."

"Aw'ight, dude. Whatever."

And they did their thing. The male auction had been Craig's idea, sponsored by the Association of African-American Women in Business (AAAWB) as a fundraiser for college scholarships. Advertised heavily in last week's *Reader,* the auction promised one lucky lady a date with Anonymous. Problem was, his identity was not to be revealed. So of the thirty men who signed up to be bid upon, one of them was to be San Diego's most famously anonymous bachelor.

That was the hook. When Nick and Mal arrived at the Ocean Beach High auditorium, the place overflowed with women. A good two hundred stood in line outside the door, itching to get inside to join six hundred others. Like Nick and Mal, who were sharply attired in their best suits, the crowd was elegantly dressed. Women of all flavors were looking *good*! Malloy resisted the urge to holler at them as the pair made their way backstage.

Carlton, their resident local celebrity, was set to emcee the event. He mingled over by the snack table with some of the bachelors who were to be the main event. Mal and Nick rolled over and dapped their boy up.

"C-Town! Whassup, baby?" greeted Nick.

"Just glad to have a job tonight, playboy," smiled Carlton. "What's goin' on, Mal?"

"Loungin', dude. Loungin'."

"So which one of these guys do you think is that Anonymous cat?" Carlton asked Nick. "The ladies out front have been askin' me, buggin' me, *bribing me* to tell them who it is. 'I'm just the host—I'd be the last one to know,' I tell them."

Nick suppressed a smile. "I don't know, bruh. There are a lot of brothas here. I can't call it."

Craig came up behind them. "Gentlemen! Glad to see you all here," he grinned.

Mal dapped him up. "Dude, I gotta hand it to you. There's a whole lotta softlegs out there. The block is hot!"

"Yeah, this was a great idea, kid," Nick agreed.

"I'd love to take credit for it, but it was Robert's brainchild. I just negotiated some of the logistics," Craig responded.

"Where is he?" asked Nick, looking around.

"He's upstairs in the lighting and sound booth, working some things out."

Mal took Craig aside for a moment. "So you can tell me, dawg. We boys. Who is this Anonymous cat? I mean, he must be gettin' mo' ass than a lil bit thanks to that column."

A thin smile. "You know I cannot divulge my sources."

"Can I get a hint, dude?" pleaded Mal.

Craig shook his head.

"I mean, quite honestly, before tonight, I coulda given a rat's ass who this dude was. I thought he would attract nothin' but lonely trolls and transvestites. But the scene here is off the hook, dawg! There are some number-one stunners out there!" Mal admitted. "I just wanna give the boy a pound and be like, 'Keep pimpin'.' "

Craig dapped Malloy up. "Enjoy the show."

And what a show it was. Opening to the edited version of Mystikal's "Shake Ya Ass," the men began their night as sex objects to caterwauling females singing along with the song. The largely African-American roster of men strutted out like a fashion show, first in formal wear, then in sportswear, and then in swimwear. The men showed lots of personality in their time onstage, dancing to the music, letting women close to the stage touch them, and reacting directly with some of the more crazed, expressive women. Malloy enjoyed every bit of this. A room full of women gawking and ogling *him*? It was a player's paradise! Nick, a little tentative at first, was managing to enjoy himself by the swimwear segment. When a woman tossed her panties at him as he came out in his swim trunks, he could not help but loosen up and laugh. Considering the event was part fashion show, part male auction, the women, who had all paid twenty-five dollars each, had gotten more than their money's worth.

Now came the auction. Dressed back up in their formal wear, the men sauntered onstage, one at a time, to find out their physical worth. With a crowd of receptive women this large, most of the men went in the two-hundred-dollar range. Malloy nearly started a fistfight between two aggressive bidders who sat side by side, escalating the bidding to five hundred dollars. Mal stole a glance toward the wings of the stage where Nick awaited his turn for a bid. His look said it all: *This is how* playas *play*.

Once Mal's one-date price was set at a whopping six hundred dollars, Malloy strutted off the stage to the wild cheering of the crowd and his fellow male models. You had to be impressed by that kind of money being spent on a guy a woman had never met.

"This next gentleman is a very special friend of mine, ladies," hyped Carlton into the microphone as Nick made his entrance center stage. "I've had the pleasure of knowing this knucklehead—I mean, man—since the ninth grade. He hails from Seattle, Washington, the Evergreen State. He holds a bachelor's degree in business from Morehouse College, *two* master's degrees from DePaul University, in business administration and acting, and a Ph.D. from the School of Hard Knocks. Let's put your hands together for my friend, my confidant, my *boy* . . . NICK!"

Thanks to an intro like that, the ovation was immense. Carlton walked over to hand the mic to Nick. Moments like this were what Nick lived for. He was the ultimate performer, especially alive when he was onstage. Reaching for his basso-profundo phone voice, Nick spoke clearly, smoothly into the mic, "How y'all doin'?"

The women screamed in delight.

"Are y'all havin' a good time?"

More screams in response. One lady shouted out, "Only if you come home with me, Nick!"

Laughter ensued. Nick flashed some teeth in the direction of Carlton, who shrugged, giving him a look that read, *You the man.*

"Now, that's what I'm talkin' about, ladies. That's a whole lotta love right there. I want *all* of you to take me home tonight."

Squeals of delight prompted Carlton to take back the mic. "Look at this smooth-ass brotha! Gimme this thing back before you seduce the whole damn crowd!" Laughter. "Alright, ladies . . . Bid high and bid hard! Do I hear fifty for this handsome young stud?"

"Fifty!"

"A hundred!"

"I hear one hundred over to the lady in the red dress. One hundred dollars to the lady in the red dress. Do I hear one-twenty-five?"

"One-twenty-five!"

"One-fifty!"

"One-seventy-five!"

"Two hundred!"

"Two hundred dollars for my boy Nick! Two hundred dollars to the lady in the peach blouse. Do I hear two-fifty?"

The crowd murmured among itself, the women balancing their respective checkbooks aloud.

"Come on, ladies! Two-fifty for Nick! That's a steal, ladies! He's worth at least two-fifty-one!" urged Carlton.

"Two-fifty!"

Nick strutted around the stage when he heard that, mugging and waving his arms in the air, pumping up the crowd.

"Three hundred!"

"Three-fifty!"

*"Four hundred dollars!"*

"Four *hundred* dollars for Nick! Four hundred to the woman with the Halle Berry haircut!" Carlton winked at Nick. This was fun.

A voice arose from the crowd. "Girl, you *know* he gotta be Anonymous! Four-fifty!"

The crowd mumbled some more and a new round of bidding ensued.

"Five hundred!"

"Five-fifty!"

Nick hid his astonishment through his onstage prancing, preening, and posing. That was rent money for some that a woman was putting up just to spend an evening out with him. This time it was he who stole a look to the wings, where Mal sweated it out. His record bid was in jeopardy of being broken by *Nick*. How obnoxious would *that* be?

"We have a bid on the floor for Nick at five-fifty. Five hundred and fifty dollars to the woman with the yellow hat," Carlton announced.

Nick took a good look at his bidder. She was a fifty-something white woman with more wrinkles than a road map. He forced a smile at her, and she waved back appreciatively. *It's for a good cause, it's for a good cause,* he reminded himself.

Reading his mind, Carlton exhorted the crowd with "It's for a good cause! Come on, ladies! Only five-fifty for a strapping young specimen like my boy Nick here? Do you know my boy works out? Plays basketball? Is a budding actor with a great new play out? Snores like none other?"

Frantically, Nick gave Carlton the cut sign, slicing his hand in the air by his throat. Carlton just laughed and went back to auctioneering. "For a man of these many talents, you have *got* to bid more than five-fifty! Who's with me, ladies? This man could be Anonymous!"

While that thought re-registered with them, prompting minor, low-voiced discussion, no new bids were raised.

"Sorry, Nick. I guess you're only worth five-fifty," funned Carlton. "But in my book, you're a million bucks! Five-fifty going once, five-fifty going twice . . ."

"A thousand dollars!"

The voice had come from the back. An astonished gasp escaped the auditorium. All heads swiveled back to see a gorgeous, petite Asian woman standing near the crowded entrance in a sleeveless, classy black dress. In the wings, Mal looked as if he were going to fall out.

Carlton stole composure via a throat-clear and repeated somewhat dubiously, "A thousand dollars?"

"One thousand dollars," the woman enunciated clearly.

"Dang. That's a scholarship in itself!" observed Carlton. "Alrighty, then . . . A thousand going once . . . a thousand going twice . . . Hell, just take him! Sold! To the lady in the black dress in the back!"

The crowd clapped politely. The woman in black smiled mildly as she exited the auditorium to go pay for Nick in the foyer. Carlton looked around to verify that everyone had just seen what he had seen. Nick ambled off the stage into the wings. In passing by Malloy, he stopped long enough to utter quietly, with a restrained grin: "Not an ounce, not a speck, not a *drop*."

"**WHERE'VE YOU BEEN?**" Anna asked, via phone.

Nick wriggled out of his jacket and slid onto the futon couch. A bright-red lipstick kiss mark resided on the left side of his face where the woman in black, Jaye, had kissed him. He emptied his pockets, the contents of which included Jaye's business card. They were to have their date the upcoming weekend. "I was at the auction."

"The auction?"

"Yeah. The auction for the black women's business group AAAWB. For college scholarships," Nick refreshed her memory. "Remember I told you about it last week?"

"Oh. I guess. What were they auctioning?"

Nick giggled. "Us."

"Us?"

"Men."

A shift in tone occurred in Anna's voice. "You were in a male auction?"

"Yes," Nick said, ignoring her tone as he turned on *SportsCenter.*

"And I said okay to this?"

"I never asked for your permission," responded Nick delicately. Malloy, who had just changed out of his suit into some sweats, rolled his eyes as he settled onto the adjacent couch. Anna was crazy; Malloy was firmly convinced of this.

"So how much did you go for?" she asked tartly. "One hundred? Two hundred?"

"Well, *Mal* here set the record at six hundred," teased Nick. Eyes glued to the tube, Mal gave Nick the finger.

"Six hundred dollars to date that slug!" Anna was incredulous. She did not find Malloy particularly attractive or charming, especially after the way he had treated her and Tauja on the Frisbee golf course some time back. A married man, although separated, who ran around like a hormone out of control with all these other women not his wife in a different city. She did not trust him. "And how much did you go for?"

"I broke the record at a thousand."

Stone-wall silence.

"Anna? Are you there?"

More silence.

"Anna. Say something."

"A woman paid a thousand dollars for a night with you."

"A date. It's only for a date."

"Are you sure? Are you sure it is only for a date? Sounds like to me you just got involved in the escort business," she accused.

"Escort business? What are you talking about, Anna?"

Mal pried his attention away from a Yankees-Mariners highlight to the contorted expressions generating from his roommate's face. That dizzy broad was at it again.

"I'm talking about you being paid a thousand dollars to sleep with some woman. That's what a lot of those escorts do, you know."

"I'm not going to *sleep* with her, Anna!"

"Well, if I paid a thousand dollars for somebody, I'd be expecting a helluva lot more than just a *date,*" she charged. "Don't be naive, Nick."

"Make *sense,* Anna!" he retorted. "Just because she thought I was worth a thousand dollars a date—and that's a steal, if you ask me—that does not mean I'm going to have sex with her! So get that idea right out of your head."

"What're you doing dating other women anyway?" inquired Anna.

"First of all, it's for a good cause. I do not consider this a real date in the slightest. Second of all, are we official, Anna?" Nick countered. "Because until you are ready to commit for real, one hundred percent and no bullshittin', we are *not* having this conversation."

Mal made faux-boxing swings in the air. "Yeah! You tell her, son!"

"No need to curse at me," Anna said quietly.

Nick waved at Malloy to shut up. "I apologize. But you have been acting out of pocket lately."

"What are you talking about?" she snapped.

"Ever since you came back into my life two weeks ago, your behavior has been erratic and inconsistent," Nick informed her. "Half the time you want to play like you're my girlfriend, but you don't want the commitment. And then you act crazy like you did when we went mini-golfing on Saturday, ready to beat Jeannie up because *Carlton* was trash-talking me, like you were my girlfriend or something. What's the story?"

"The story?"

"Are we together or not? And if not, why the hell not?" Nick demanded.

"Yeah, dawg! Shit or get off the pot!" Malloy cheered from the sidelines. For that, his boy earned Nick's intense glare.

"Don't make me do this, Nick," Anna implored.

"Do *what*? Make a decision? Make a commitment? This is ridiculous," Nick assessed. "You can't have your cake and eat it, too."

"Nick, that's not fair. That's not what's going on here."

"What *is* going on, Anna, because I sure as hell don't know! You have no right to be upset about the auction. *You are not my girlfriend.* You aren't even my fuckbuddy. Hell, I don't even know what to call you besides your name!"

"How 'bout Crazy Bitch?" piped Malloy.

Nick covered the mouthpiece of the phone and warned him with a "Shut it, Mal!"

"You have to give me some more time, Nick. It takes a lot for me to trust people . . ."

"I've given you time, Anna. I've given you the world, and it still isn't enough for you. As much as it pains me to say this, there is something going on with you that I can't help you with," analyzed Nick. "I have tried, Anna. I really have. I have been patient. It's been eight months since I met you and still you can't open yourself up enough to be in a relationship with me. I have listened to you, I have cared for you, I have left you the hell alone. And what has it gotten me? A Hefty bag full of my broken and confused feelings. Either we're going to do this for real or you need to get out of my life. I don't have time for this."

"Is that an ultimatum?" Anna's confrontational sensibilities were slightly raised.

"If that's what you want to call it," answered Nick. "I'm tired of you using me."

"Using you?" she reiterated incredulously. "You live in San Diego, an hour away from me. You're a broke-ass actor just like I am! Using you for what?"

"That's an excellent question, Anna. Just what do you get from spending time with me?" Nick asked. "I would really like to know. It's certainly not about the sex because we haven't had any. It's not about the money because I am a, quote, 'broke-ass actor,' end quote. So what is it? Why do you even hang around me at all? Why do you spend nights here, in my bed, kissing all up on me? Why do you let me serve you breakfast in bed; why do you let me massage your feet; why do you let me hold you when we fall asleep at night? Why? For what reason do you let those things happen when you *know* you are simply wasting my time?"

Mal sat there stunned, fresh out of smartass remarks. He had been cringing ever since hearing Nick's bitter regurgitation of Anna's own words.

Anna, too, was out of comebacks. Her voice turned teary, dramatic. That was the problem with dating actresses: They could be dramatic like none other. "Nick," she sobbed, "I care about you."

"And I care about you, Anna," Nick relented. "But I have done all that I can do for you, and it's still not enough."

Anna's tears released the tension of the conversation, turning the focus, and the energy of it, squarely upon her tortured soul. "But, Nick, it is enough. You have been great to me. You would be great for any woman—"

"But not for you," Nick finished coldly.

"I really do care about you, Nick. Believe me when I say this. But I just cannot be with you now."

Point-blank simple: "Why?"

The tears again. "I don't know."

Nick's torso deflated, like helium escaping a balloon. "You don't know," he repeated flatly, in disbelief. Even Mal winced.

Anna sniffled as she attempted to regulate the tears. "I'm sorry, Nick. Something is wrong with me right now."

*You damn right there is.*

"I don't know how to explain it to you. I've done the best I could."

*Try harder.*

"I wish I could make you understand how hard it is for me to open up to someone, to truly love someone, but I can't. I don't understand it myself."

*You need help.*

"I think I'm going to get some therapy and try to figure this all out."

*Hallelujah.*

"It's unfair to me and it's unfair to you to be with you like this when I know you want more. When I know you are ready for more."

*When you know that I have* deserved *more.*

"I'm sorry to do this to you, Nick."

*Again.*

"But I think I need some space."

*Take Montana, for all I care.*

"I still care for you a lot, Nick. I want us to still be friends."

*Don't they always?*

"I just need some time."

*And a guy stupid enough to put up with this moody shit.*

"I am so sorry, Nick. So sorry."

*Me, too, Anna. More than you know.*

A weighted silence deadened the conversation. Anna had said every-thing she needed to say. Nick could not think of anything he *wanted* to say. The woman he had invested the most time, energy, and emo-tion in had just played him. Again.

"Nick," she whimpered, "are you there? Say something, please."

Nothing.

She had overstayed her welcome. "I'm going to go now, Nick. I really mean it when I say that I want to stay friends. I do."

More nothing.

"Nick . . . baby . . . please say something before I go."

Nick would not.

"Goodbye, Nick," she uttered tearfully.

Nick wordlessly hit the disconnect button. He slowly lowered the cordless to his side. This had been the classic nonbreakup.

Mal, who had sat transfixed throughout the last, silent portion of the conversation, was in awe. "Nick? What happened?"

*Cardinal Rule to Dating No. 13:* **"Never date an actress."**

**MARRIAGE MINDED**
*One man's quest to get married in a year*
*by Anonymous*

All together now: "It's not you, it's me." "I think we need some space." "I want us to still be friends." Sound familiar? Sure they do. All of these are classic female cop-outs used to pull the rip cord on relationships. For all you men out there who have received these incredibly insipid excuses for the truth from women you were involved with, this column is for you.

We welcome the return of Woman with Emotional and Mental Problems. Life has been boring without her. But life has also been cliché-free.

**"It's not you, it's me."** Basically, this woman is inexpressive *and* lying. Saying that everything is all her fault is an easy way to exit a relationship because it makes her the bad guy. And if a woman wants out badly enough, playing the bad guy is not too raw a deal.

She's lying to you because she does not want to tell you that, yes, it truly is you, not her. If any woman wants to salvage a relationship, she is not going to go down without a fight. Saying "It's not you, it's me" puts up about as much of a fight as the Italian Army.

In the case of WEMP, as we shall now call her, this was not a lie. It truly *was* her; she is inexpressive. To descend to a cliché as paper-thin as this one means that she could not put into words what caused her to end our pseudo-relationship. And believe me, it was *pseudo*—inconsistent, unstable, and unconsummated.

"**I think we need some space.**" She can't stand you. No, just kidding. Actually, this is the one cliché that men and women alike can relate to. This is the escape hatch that allows players to play. Needing space is the unofficial breakup mantra that buys the player just enough room to see other people but leaves enough of an out to come back home. It's quite clever, actually, particularly when used by a woman. But it is also the biggest indicator that your relationship is heading toward the rocks, with no lighthouse in sight. When you first get together with Ole Girl, when you two are totally normal and everything is great, there is no other place in the world that you want to be but all up under her. Why the hell would you want space if everything were cool?

And here is my personal favorite: "**I hope we can still be friends.**" Like hell. If we wanted to be friends, we would be just that. Your tongue would not have slipped and ended up in my mouth! Guys do not want to be friends with women they are attracted to, even less so with women they have had relationships with and sex with on the regular. It's not in our genetic or emotional makeup to be friends with our exes. When it's over, it's *over*. We send her back all her stuff, burn every picture, and (finally!) throw out that godawful tie she bought us one Christmas and actually expected us to wear in public. Just like with your platonic female friends, friendship with a woman is a chronic reminder of what you cannot have.

With that said and done, forgive me if I don't want your stinking friendship, WEMP, because I don't. No guy does. Nor do we want your clichés. Say what you mean, mean what you say.

Pissed off, ladies? I'm baaaaaaack!

# 14

THE SLIDE PICKED up where it had left off almost two weeks ago. The latest train wreck with Anna had only given it more steam and purpose. In the next three days, Nick had a new and different Internet hoochie each night. A black woman, a white woman, a Latina. A virtual Benetton commercial for Internet sex.

Malloy observed Nick's activities with a disturbed eye. Everything had gone fine as a result of Robert's little orchestrated meeting two weeks ago until that Anna chick had messed with Nick's mind again. Could his boy's head be so fragile? He would soon find out.

Nick and Malloy ground it out on the video-game football field. Strangely, Mal was silent, playing with the verbal restraint of a monk. Not coincidentally, he was losing as well. But he was up to something, and trash-talking would only distract him from his purpose.

"It's Friday night, dawg. You ain't goin' out?" Malloy finally ventured.

"No."

"Ran out of chickens to hit?"

Nick glared at him. "Are you, of all people, gonna lecture me, Mal?"

"Not at all, player. You're a grown-ass man," Mal demurred. "But I find it odd how you were out just about every night doin' your thang until Anna showed up. Then the second she leaves, you out there again. Whassup, dude? What's the deal?"

"What? You're playing armchair psychiatrist now? Don't worry about me. I let Anna back into my life, so let me deal with the cleanup."

"I have to worry about it. We live in the same house and, more importantly, you're my dawg, dawg. You're my best friend. Talk to me now," Mal urged.

"What can I say? She hurt me," Nick allowed, a few chinks showing in his steely armor.

"And you're feeling sorry for yourself," Mal assessed. "You know what? I feel bad for her."

"Bad for *her*? How you figure?"

"You are you and Anna is stuck with Anna," Mal philosophized. "She's the one who can't get over her own shit and move on. That's the mess she's living with. At least you know for sure that it has nothing to do with you, that you tried your best to connect with that girl and she just wasn't ready. Whatever it is that's hurtin' you is a lot less bad than what's hurtin' her because you *know* what's wrong. She doesn't."

Nick nodded softly. "Now you're talkin' sense."

Malloy snorted. "I always talk sense, dude."

"You have your moments."

"Just stop pitying yourself and let her go, man," advised Mal. "She made you the bitch in the relationship, anyway. She was always callin' the shots. You can't be bendin' over backwards for these bitches. But you do need them. They're essential to survival. I ain't hatin' on your booty calls, dude. If you don't be gettin' you some, then you'll start breakin' shit and things."

"And that moment is gone."

THIS TIME WHEN USA *Today* crossed her desk, an article captured her attention. Again it was about that anonymous writer from some San Diego newspaper who had attracted ten thousand women to a mall parking lot. This past Monday, he'd been the highlight of a sold-out male auction and fashion show that raised $10,000 directly for scholarships, with another $100,000 donated to the host organization by Qualcomm. As the article reported, Anonymous had been in attendance as one of the bachelors bid upon, but his identity had never been revealed.

Before tossing the rest of the paper away and heading to set, she read that the top bachelor at the auction had sold for a thousand bucks. Was there a man alive she would pay a thousand bucks for a date? Hell no—and she could afford it, too. But wait—there was one. There was one guy whom she wouldn't mind paying to see.

**JAYE'S SENTIMENTS EXACTLY.** The woman who had bought Nick met him at the Sky Room, an expensive and classy restaurant at the top of a hotel in upscale La Jolla with an unparalleled ocean view. Aided by the Sky Room's usual accoutrements of privacy, intimacy, and the ability to talk without the distraction of noise, they allowed themselves to begin the getting-to-know-each-other process.

Jaye owned her own printing company, one that printed the programs and handouts for the San Diego Chargers, Padres, and the minor-league hockey team, the Gulls. Her list of corporate clients was impressive as well, which explained her sleek black Mercedes CLK 320 parked in the lot. Jaye lived in a house in the hills above La Jolla and the ocean, and owned an assortment of other houses that she rented out from Carlsbad down to Coronado. All of this wealth was accumulated by the impressive age of thirty-five. With her bronzed Filipina complexion, sparkly dark eyes, and flawlessly smooth skin, Jaye looked more thirteen than thirty-five.

Dinner was excellent as usual at the Sky Room. Jaye's was a funny, distinctive personality. She had opinions on everything—from how you can tell Filipinos from Japanese, to the sorry state of San Diego sports—but still managed to be warm and engaging. Naturally, Nick deflected the anticipated questions of whether he was Anonymous. They got along reasonably well. Nick liked her but still they did not exactly click. That spark, that special something just was not there. He came away thinking that dating her could be a future possibility, but nothing he felt possessed to do at the moment.

After a quick debrief with Mal, who was out the door to meet some girl at Juke Joint, Nick went to bed. Here it was, May 2, and Nick felt as far away from his goal as could be. Even the once promiscuous Robert was more romantically domesticated than Nick, having moved into his partner's apartment the day before. Three months until Mom was closer to her death. Three months until failure. Nick abhorred failure.

Nick was awakened in the morning by a doorbell. He snatched the alarm clock and tried to glare a hole through the plastic face. Any time was too early on a Sunday morning for Nick. Wrapping a sheet around his body to fight the morning cold, Nick waddled into the living room to answer the door. He simply could not believe what he saw.

"Maya T.?" Nick asked rhetorically. As usual, she looked lovely, dressed in a pair of thigh-high shorts, a tank top, and sunglasses. Her hair was straightened and long, swooped over her shoulder to one side. A sports duffle bag was in her hand.

"There ain't none other," she smiled affectionately. "May I come in?"

"You've flown five hundred miles this morning. I suppose so."

Nick would have bet on the return of Jesus Christ before betting on the return of Maya T. Patterson. She had flown down here *again* to surprise him, showing up at his doorstep unannounced. Had the Anna fiasco taught her nothing? After their last, heated conversation almost six months ago, did Maya T. come in war or peace? Nick pondered all this as he set about making some hot chocolate for her while she watched him from the kitchen table. "So what brings you to San Diego?"

"Honestly? You."

"Me? I thought you hated me."

"Hate is a strong word, Nick. I never hated you," Maya T. defused, using that homey, familiar Texan accent of hers to reassure him. "I was mad at you, just like you were mad at me. But when I got the call from Malloy—"

"Mal called you?" Nick interrupted, not sure whether to be irate or ecstatic.

"Yeah. He talked to me for a while two weeks ago. Told me how much you needed me. That you missed me." All of this was news to Nick, but if she said so . . . "Is that true?"

"Pretty much," Nick lied. Of course, he still cared about the girl and did not want to damage her ego. After all, almost on a whim, she had had a ticket to San Diego punched out in no time.

"I hope to stay in San Diego a little longer this time," she joked, winking at Nick playfully.

"Me, too." Mal must have really been worried for him to bring out the big guns. Nick smiled. This was the one woman who had known Nick better than anyone else besides his mother. Malloy knew this. She was here because she loved him. She was here because Mal loved him.

NICK AND MAYA T. did San Diego. Playing tour guide, he sported Maya T. to Fashion Valley, Horton Plaza, Gaslamp Quarter, and even across the bridge to ritzy, upscale Coronado to see how the other half lived. Whatever ax they had to grind had disappeared, their conversation was fun and free-flowing, and it was as if their six-month hiatus from each other had never happened. Nick rediscovered a side to himself he'd always had before Anna, before his Internet tramps, before Molly and Paris. He was *charming*. He was witty and intelligent with a woman who appreciated and reflected both back at him. They had almost ten years of history behind them. Resuming their friendship was like riding a bike.

Going above and beyond the call of duty of a friend, Maya T. accompanied Nick to his two performances of *Titus* that afternoon. The play was some three hours long, with performances at two and six o'clock. On her vacation, Maya T. endured *six hours* of Shakespeare, heroic by anyone's standards. Nick introduced her to the cast simply as "his Maya T." As far as Nick was concerned, everyone should have a Maya T.

After the show, Nick and Maya T. drove back home to scoop Malloy and his girl du jour, Sherika, to go hang out at a poetry open mic at Clair de Lune, an oversized coffeehouse on busy University Avenue in North Park. With two levels, fluffy, plush couches, and several tables and sitting surfaces, Clair de Lune was popular among the eclectic, artistic set from the anything-goes Hillcrest district and the lower-to-middle-income North Park community. On this Sunday night, the place was packed, as local spoken-word artists stepped to the mic with confidence, verbal wizardry, and showmanship.

Nick had driven by Clair de Lune several times before, but took this opportunity to visit thanks to Maya T.: She was a bit of a closet poet herself, and Nick knew she would appreciate the performances. Mal just wanted to appear artsy and deep to his new girl, so that explained their presence at the coffeehouse.

After ordering differing blends of coffee, the foursome settled into a table that had just opened up near the mic stand. Malloy took a gaze around. He nodded his head approvingly at Nick. *A lot of cake in here, dude. A lot of cake.*

For half an hour, they sat through poets of varying degrees of skill. Some were good, even great, but one surfer-dude-looking buffoon embarrassed Clair de Lune and himself by breaking off a ridiculously simplistic and unfunny poem about jellyfish. A lot of the poets carried the aura of the faux-erudite. One woman would shame them all.

She stood about five-seven, a strikingly unique vision in a sarong and sixties-style black-rimmed glasses. Hers was a soft-spoken, natural beauty. She was not the most cosmetically beautiful woman, but she was far from ugly. Her auburn-colored braids were swept back with a hairband and her dark, penetrating eyes seemed at war with their slanted, Asiatic-shaped sockets. A honey-brown-colored complexion that seemed more Latina in origin than African-American added to her eclectic yet exotic vibe. If anyone had any doubt who she was, she let them know real quick.

"My name," she announced with the regality of an African princess, "is Souldance."

Nick winced from the sheer force of her name. Her presence and carriage enhanced the appeal of her attractive looks.

"For those who don't know, my Soul-*dance* is a continuous, harmonious, religious, prestigious, nonlitigious, sometimes monogamous, always on top of this, completely and freely *ridiculous* . . . expression of joy . . . and love." The words just danced off her tongue, tumbled out of her soul, and captivated anyone within their reach. Souldance had the entire crowd in the palm of her hand. Her serious, deep pools of determination that fronted for eyes dared anyone to take their gaze off her, lest she break their ass in two with a razor-sharp verb. She by far transcended Clair de Lune and everyone in it.

And so it was on. Souldance audaciously rocked the mic for a little over an hour. She tried to quit twice, only to be egged on by the raucous and appreciative crowd. Maya T. could not be talked to, she could not be touched—the woman was enthralled. Nick and Malloy like-wise enjoyed the show, dapping each other up repeatedly at some of Souldance's ridiculously placed and voiced adjectives and phrasings. Souldance was the bomb.

After she descended from her invisible throne, Souldance vacated the microphone, which remained untouched. Nobody wanted to fol-low her. As the foursome of Nick, Malloy, Sherika, and Maya T. stag-gered their way back to Nick's 4Runner under the weight of an hour's worth of mystical lyricals, Mal murmured to Nick, "That girl's somethin' special, son. A woman who can spit lyrics like that and still look that *foine*? Now *that's* what I call talent."

**THE NEXT MORNING**, Maya T. and Nick lay in bed, wrapped up in each other. It had been a strange night. After being blown away by Souldance, they had gone straight home and to sleep. Besides the odd kiss, there was no real passion in the way they held each other. And something was on her mind this morning.

"Remember that poem Souldance did called 'Rebound'?" Maya T. asked quietly.

"The one about the guy friend she had who became her man but then they ended back up just as friends again?" said Nick. "Yeah, I re-member that one. Feel like it's speaking to us?"

"Do I," agreed Maya T. She rolled over so that her face, her mouth, was perilously close to his. Her keen eyes studied the smooth melanin of his dark skin, the light, roadlike creases traversing his forehead, and the rough edges of his beard. She took a finger and dragged it along the soft outline of his full lips. "Nick . . . you know I love you."

"I love you, too, Maya," Nick responded easily, honestly.

"Because I love you, I know that we can't ever be together the way you want us to."

This was no big surprise to him. Nick sighed his acceptance. "I know."

"Remember the first time we met? The first time you came out to San Francisco after almost six years of writing and emailing each other?" Maya T. reminisced.

"Like it was yesterday." A chuckle. "I was such a mess."

She poked him in the nose playfully. "Still are."

"Good one, My-T Love."

"That's Maya T. to you. I ain't no kid no more."

"Yeah, whatever." Nick smiled at the woman he had watched metamorphose from an awkward, gawky teenager into a beautiful young woman.

"Remember how we took care of each other like we had known each other all our lives?"

"Yes. And you vowed that you would always be there for me," Nick reminded her. "You promised to always be my friend, no matter what happened."

Maya T. sucked her teeth. "Damn. I did say that, didn't I?"

"I *knew* I should've gotten that in writing!" Nick tickled her mercilessly.

Maya T. screamed bloody murder until Nick relented. Between huffs of catching her breath, she said, "Do you still mean it?"

"Mean what?"

"That we will always take care of each other. That you will always take care of me."

Nick rolled her on top of him so he could address her eyes very, very personally. "Of course I mean it. You're one of the best friends I have."

"Am I better than Malloy?" She grinned.

"I don't rank my friends," Nick evaded. "But you can offer me some things that Malloy can't."

"Punk!" Maya T.'s hands teasingly went down south to retaliate.

"If you didn't look so good in the morning, that would actually hurt instead of turn me on," purred Nick. He kissed her. She responded. Then he turned contemplative. "So what happens now?"

Maya T. sighed. "I think you are looking for more in a woman than I can offer you right now."

"Am I that obvious?" Nick joked.

"I'm also sorry for the way I acted after I came down here the first time," she graciously apologized. "I was not myself."

"You were an entirely different person," commented Nick.

"I am not a jealous woman." Then came a wry smile. "But that doesn't mean I am above *being* jealous."

Nick suppressed a grin. "I understand." Did he ever.

"And I think now that I am the mayor's chief of staff, I won't be able to make these kind of romantic getaways. They've kept me busy since January," Maya T. explained.

"I'm sure they have."

"But I will never be too busy to talk or write to you. Ever," his friend promised. "We are still—and always will be—friends. I sincerely hope you find what you are looking for."

Nick hugged her tight. "I'm glad you came, Maya."

"Me, too."

"When do you have to leave again?"

"Tomorrow night."

A passionate kiss and a smile. "Then let's not waste any time."

SHE LEFT WITH little fanfare or emotion. Nick and Maya T. shared a quick kiss at the gate but that was it. As he began the long walk back to his car, he realized that he would see her again, only it would be under far different circumstances.

The agreement they had arrived at was simple. Their romantic relationship was, for all intents and purposes, over. Still, Nick felt blessed that he had regained the one friend who had saved his soul, if not his life, over the years. She truly was a good friend.

But so was his roommate. When Nick returned from the airport, he and Mal had to have a talk. No PlayStation, no video games, no chatting while watching *SportsCenter*. Just a talk. Player to player.

He found Malloy at the dining room table, hunched over a booklet of some sort. He barely noticed Nick's entrance.

" 'Sup, Mal?"

Mal started. "Oh, what's goin' on, dawg."

"What's that?"

"It's a brochure for National University. I also have one for the University of Phoenix. I've been thinking about going back to school for my MBA or somethin'. This temp shit is gettin' kinda tired."

Nick nodded gravely as he slid into the seat across from him. "I need to talk to you, man."

Slowly, Mal's eyes rose from the brochure to meet his friend's. Mal's eyes lived in fear. "Is everything aw'ight? You not throwin' me out, are you?"

"No. Not that at all, Mal." Nick took a deep breath. "I know what you did."

Mal became instantaneously upset. "Man, don't believe her! That bitch lyin'!"

"I'm not talking about some female, Mal. I realize what you did for me," Nick clarified. "Talking Maya T. into coming to San Diego to straighten out my head. I admit it: I was in a bad place, and you got me out of it. I appreciate that, dawg. For real. You're a good friend."

"Ah, whatever, man. You would've done the same thing for me, too," said Malloy dismissively.

"I did."

"You did what?"

"I called Mia."

Mal's whole face collapsed. "Man, what the hell you do that for?"

"Because you love her. You miss her. You are lost without her," Nick declared.

Mal ignored his observations. Now he was curious. "So what did she say?"

"She didn't say anything."

"Yeah. She's pretty good at that."

"No. I mean I've called her periodically for the past seven months and left messages, but your wife hasn't called me back."

"She be lovin' that Caller ID, bruh. Probably thinks you're me."

"Well, either way, both of y'all are going to deal with this," Nick resolved. "We're going to New York in three weeks."

"What're you talkin' 'bout, dude?"

"I bought us two tickets to New York," Nick informed him. "Mine's round-trip. Yours is one-way."

"What about the play?"

"Closing night is on Sunday."

"Where the hell did you get the money for a trip like that? Acting don't pay that fuckin' well."

"Don't worry about my finances, playa. Just worry about resolving these issues you have with your woman. You two *belong* to each other. You're obviously miserable here without her. You could put ten of these chicks together and they still wouldn't equal half of your Mia."

Malloy's eyes turned hollow as he silently assented to every word Nick said. It was as if his face were a two-way mirror, allowing Nick to see into his tortured, confused, and severely damaged spirit. Mal could count on two fingers how many people could read him like that, who could bypass the bravado and decipher his soul. Now, thanks to Nick, they were going to New York to reconcile with the other one.

"Go get your woman, man."

ONCE *TITUS* HAD closed, Nick did not know what to do with himself. He went on some more auditions, but only sparingly. The roles of the caliber of his last two simply were not there. It had literally been months since Nick had had an LA audition, since his horrific casting-couch experience. Intermittently, Ilene Zimmerman's haunting promise "You'll never work in this town again! *Ever!*" reverberated around his mind, now that there was no Shakespeare, no lines, no Aaron the Moor to occupy it. Thank goodness he still had income coming in from the column, which had now been bumped up to a whopping $750 a week, thanks to Craig's dogged negotiations. Nick would have loved to have been a fly on the wall for that conversation with Craig's prepubescent superior.

One more date with Jaye had sealed her fate. There was just not enough there to go on. He spent a lot of time working out at Bally's and writing on his laptop at the beach. Paris, the woman who fell in love with the speed of a cruise missile, was never at the beach anymore.

This went on for a week until Nick received a phone call from a friend. "Yo, what the deal, B?"

Ayinde! "What's going on, man? Where's your black ass been?"

"You know I've been workin', black! I got back to LA about a month late offa that shoot in Bermuda 'cause Hurricane Nikki wrecked shop for about a week. We had to rebuild sets and everything," Ayinde said.

"Oh yeah. I remember hearing about that hurricane," Nick said vaguely. "She was no joke, was she?"

"Naw, B, naw. When I heard they named the hurricane Nikki,

I shoulda known it was gonna beat our ass. I don't date Nikkis," Ayinde told Nick. "Every Nikki I know is a bitch."

"But what've you been doin' since then? That's been almost two months since you got back *without* callin' a brotha!"

"Well, you know I bounced right to another job after the last one. This one I'm doin' is a Jerry Bruckheimer film. I'm actually gonna be *First* AD on it!" Ayinde damn near squealed.

"*First* AD, kid? Are you kidding me? On a Bruckheimer film?"

"Yeah, dude. And you know once you get in with his production company, they can keep you working forever!"

"How'd you manage that, dawg?"

"It was wild, B! I'm over in Bermuda, wrappin' up this one flick while I'm puttin' out my résumé to some folk back in the States, right? Get this, son. I send out a cover letter that's the standard-issue bull-shit, right? But in the middle of it, I write, 'I am really good at what I do. I guarantee that if you hire me, I will be as good an assistant di-rector as or even better than Norman Moskowitz.'"

Nick was puzzled. "Who's Norman Moskowitz?"

"I made him up!" chortled Ayinde. "It was so tight, man! All these Hollywood assholes are so concerned about bein' left outta the loop that I had people from six of the ten letters I sent out *call me in Bermuda* to hire me! All of them were like, 'Who's Norman Moskowitz?' 'I made him up.' 'Dude! You're hired!' So I had my pick of offers."

Nick shook his head. "You're somethin' else, Ayinde."

"I'm *employed* is what I am, B," Ayinde restated. "So this Bruck-heimer flick is being done by a veteran director who is dealing with a lot of young black actors, so they wanted a young black crew to help out. It's gonna be tight."

"What's it called?"

"*Adrenaline Orgy.*"

Nick laughed. "Stop lying."

"I ain't lyin', black. But that's just a working title," Ayinde said. "Hey. Have you heard the news? Your girl's outta work. *Blackdraft* got canceled."

"No, I didn't." Damned Iowa corn farmers.

"You ain't talkin' to Shana *McAaaaaaaadams* no more?"

"We haven't really spoken since December. I wonder what she's doing," Nick mused.

"Today's *Variety* says she's going to be doing some ensemble flick for scale with Nia Long."

"Nia Long, huh?" The woman that Shana used to complain about competing with was now going to be in a picture with her. Life's little ironies.

"Yeah. Nia Long, Don Cheadle, and Fredo."

*"Fredo?!"* That talentless hack! Nick had seen him on *The Bold and the Beautiful* after his stint on *The Young and the Restless* and was unconvinced Shelby's prized stud was any of "all that." Nick had starred in two very successful plays and had portrayed two very complex and tortured characters. What did he have to show for it? Nothing but his status as yet another unemployed actor in Southern California. What a cliché.

"Yeah. It's a caper flick. Should be wild." Ayinde shifted gears. "Eh, B, I gotta dip. My lady's ready to go."

"Your lady? When did you get a girlfriend? This ain't one of them porno pieces, is it?" snooped Nick.

"Never that! Her name is Travia and she's Bahamian."

"Which means she's tight."

"Word is bond!" Ayinde seconded. "We live together now."

"I see Hurricane Nikki wasn't the only one to wreck shop in Bermuda," quipped Nick.

"Ha-ha. But you right, B."

"Oh, there goes my other line. Thanks for the call, Ayinde. Good lookin' out, brotha."

"Holler at me later, son!"

"Peace!" Nick hit the flash button. "Hello?"

"Hello, Nick."

---

**QUEEN. SHE ALMOST** didn't even look like the woman he had dated in Chicago during his second year of the DePaul MFA Acting Program. While her rich, dark-brown, Nubian complexion was unchanged, her head boasted an anachronistically wavy, flapper-girl hairstyle. Usually, Queen rocked a series of shorter, Halle Berry-type hairstyles or braids. Regardless of her hairstyle, sistagurl was still fine.

High cheekbones, long eyelashes, slim cheeks, a beauty mole on the right cheek, and great genetics had seen to that. And at thirty-five years of age, she didn't look a day over twenty-five. Queen looked fabulous.

"How are you, Nick?" She greeted him with a kiss on the cheek as Nick settled into the booth across from her. Seated at the in-house restaurant of the Downtown Hilton, just on the lip of Mission Bay, they could see the boats cruise and bob in place on the water adjacent to the hotel.

"I'm good, Queen. And you must be fabulous, judging from the way you look."

"I am blessed, thank you," she accepted the compliment graciously. "It's good to see you, Nick."

"So how's New York?"

"Busy and crowded as ever. Same as Chicago, only with three times the traffic."

"So what brings you to San Diego?"

"Work. We're running a show at the La Jolla Playhouse this week."

"What's the name of the show?" inquired Nick.

"*Blues for an Alabama Sky.*" By Pearl Cleage, *Blues* was an exceptionally well-written drama set in the Harlem Renaissance. The play was a showpiece for the role of Angel, revolving around the ambitious exploits of the former Cotton Club showgirl and chanteuse.

"And you're Angel?" guessed Nick.

"That's right," she confirmed with all the complacency of the show's star.

"How's it been received?"

"Wonderfully. Broadway's embraced us." Nick flinched at her mention of Broadway. The Great White Way. The pinnacle of professional theatrical acting. Not even a year out of grad school and Queen was starring in a Broadway play. She was just that good. Modestly, she added, "We're up for some Tonys."

"Tonys? For what?" asked the amazed Nick.

Queen grinned sheepishly, shyly. "Best Performance by a Leading Actress in a Play and Best Play."

"You better go 'head and grab that spotlight, girl!" Nick encouraged.

Queen blushed. "What about you? What have you been up to?"

"I just finished up *Titus Andronicus*," shared Nick.

"Aaron the Moor?"

"Yup."

"I bet you were great." Her eyes sparkled in admiration.

Nick could not understand it. After almost a year away from each other, two years since their relationship, they still fit like hand in glove. The love and support were still there. The mutual admiration and respect for the other's craft were still there. Nick asked the question, affably, that needed to be asked. "Why did we ever break up?"

"Sometimes I wonder that myself," she admitted easily, with a slight giggle. "It had to be the most civil breakup I've ever had."

"And we were such great friends all the way through graduation," Nick recalled.

"Yes, we were. But tell me the truth, Nick: Did you ever get tired of having sex with me?"

Nick blinked in disbelief. "Tired? Of sex with *you*? Are you kidding me? That was the part of our relationship that was *always* good!"

"I know," she concurred wistfully.

They took a pause for the cause and reminisced. No horizontal surface had been safe in either of their North Side apartments. The shower, the chair, the kitchen counter, the walls . . . Even vertical surfaces caught wreck, too. All of these places had been abused with regularity throughout the duration of their intensely physical relationship. They were wild together—perfectly physically matched—and knew it.

"Damn, I'd love to have sex with you again," she mumbled under her breath.

Nick's eyes recoiled back into this dimension. "What'd you say?"

A begrudging smile. "But I can't."

*Why not?* Nick's eyes pleaded with his last true girlfriend.

"I have a boyfriend," she sighed regretfully.

Nick picked up on that. "Is he in New York?"

"Yes."

"Must be lonely out here on tour."

"Hush."

"What does he do? Is he an actor?"

"God, no. You were my last one of those." That made Nick smile. At least he had made some sort of footnote in Queen's love life. "He's a stockbroker."

"Wow. In New York. Imagine that," Nick commented dryly.

"Quit it, Nick. And who have you been dating?" Queen asked evenly.

"I haven't."

"Please. I know you've been terrorizing the women of Southern California," she teased.

"Do you read the *Enquirer*?"

"As in 'enquiring minds want to know'? Hell no," she denied.

*Good.* "Well then, no, I haven't been dating anyone."

Queen looked at him funny, but decided to let it pass. "Well, I'm sure you'll find somebody. You're going to make some woman very happy. Even if for one night."

To fight his embarrassment, Nick rebutted with "Aw'ight now, Madame Corian," teasing Queen about her love of doing it on top of kitchen counters. "Don't start what you can't finish."

Their good-natured ribbing was just like old times. Why *had* they broken up?

"So are you coming to see the show?"

"Are you comping me tickets?"

Queen rolled her eyes. "Yes."

"Then I'm there," Nick beamed.

"Cheapskate . . ."

"Free is my fee, baby," proclaimed Nick proudly. "And you know this!"

"GOTTA LOVE SAN DIEGO," breathed Mal, studying his Frisbee-golf chip shot from twenty feet under a clear blue sky. "Only place in the country that stays seventy degrees year-round. I've knocked twelve strokes off my game."

"And you're still down a shot, too, Herby Dude," jeered Nick.

"Shut up, Trick Fabulous," Mal fired back. "Watch and learn, Cletis."

With a surprisingly light touch, Malloy flicked the flying disc up toward the elevated metal basket and watched it catch nothing but chain. Mal rewarded his efforts with a fist pump. "That's how it's done. Sucka."

Nick tried his own attempt from seventeen feet, only to front-rim the basket. "Damn!" he cursed. He walked over and slammed the Frisbee into the basket. Pulling out the scorecard he muttered, "What'd you get?"

"Three."

"Shit! I got four."

"Dead heat going into the last hole," observed Malloy, sparing no amount of drama.

They walked over to the next tee.

"So tell me somethin', dude. How was it seein' your ex-girlfriend the other day?" asked Malloy.

Nick fired off a long tee throw that eventually hooked left into the bushes. "Kinda weird," he conveyed, stepping aside for Mal to take his tee off throw. "It was as if we had never broken up."

"Did she give you any sign you could run up in there again? Queen's a diamond, fa' sho'," Mal drooled.

"Sort of. She said, 'I wish I could have sex with you again.' "

"Nigga, what?" laughed Mal. He flung his tee throw straight down the fairway toward the hole. "You in there like swimwear, dude!"

"And then she told me she has a boyfriend back in New York," deflated Nick. They began walking to where their discs lay.

"Which don't mean jack or shit because she told you she wanted to fuck you *before* tellin' you about the boyfriend. He's a nonissue," Mal evaluated. "*And* he's in New York? Just the fact that she spoke her subconscious like that is an open invitation to crush her like a grape."

Nick's second shot landed within two feet of the basket. "Maybe. But I know if I got with her, I would want more."

"Why? Because she's a hotshot Broadway actress now?" The pressure was on Mal to come up with a big second shot to stay with Nick.

"No. Because she's Queen," Nick said simply. The fact that they had had a relationship was not an accident. Just her being her had always been enough.

Mal's second shot had a mind of its own. Guided by divine intervention or whatever, the disc floated in the air, hooked left, and then, unbelievably, impossibly, caught the chains inside the metal basket, a good 120 feet away. Birdie.

"Good freakin' *shot*, Mal!" exclaimed a shocked Nick. He slammed his own disc in for a par three on the hole—and his first loss. "Maybe you do have an ounce of player in you. But just a speck. Just a drop."

---

**THAT FRIDAY NIGHT,** Craig accompanied Nick to the La Jolla Playhouse, located on the UCSD campus. This had been their first nonwork-affiliated night out in a while, Nick reflected, as he collected their complimentary tickets at the will call window. What could Craig say? The man loved being married, evidently.

As they settled into their center-section seats, Craig passed Nick a small roll of bills. Even though he was not one to turn down money, Nick still had to ask, "What's this?"

"For your column last week. Seven-fifty. I didn't get a chance to run down to a Bank of America today and put it in your account."

"Aw'ight, then. I appreciate it, kid."

"You know I got you, kid." Craig began to leaf through the program. "So tell me what's up with this ex of yours." He spotted the picture of her and blurted, "Yo, she is a *hottie*!"

"How quickly they forget."

"I mean, forgive me, but Olinda and I haven't kicked it with you and Ole Girl since y'all broke up two years ago. And this is a great picture of her!"

"Isn't it?" admired Nick, gazing at the picture.

"So you hangin' out with her after the show?"

"That's the plan."

"That's cool, then. The wife wants me back home soon anyway. I saw cherry sauce in the fridge," smirked Craig. "It's gonna be *on*."

Nick might never admit it to his boy's face, but he envied what Craig had. Not only did Craig have a hot young wife, but also a *freak*. Women, that is all guys want. They want a lady in public and a freak in the bedroom. Craig had luckily found both in the same woman. He did the smart thing, too, by marrying her. If he had that waiting back at the crib, Nick would hurry home as well.

**QUEEN MET NICK** outside the backstage entrance to the play-house. She was dressed classy but casual in a sleeveless black dress that stopped just above the knee. The second she emerged from the door, Nick applauded her, greeting her with a bouquet of roses for her performance. Queen smiled from ear to ear; he had remembered. Queen loved it when Nick adhered to theater etiquette.

"*Strangé*, girl! *Strangé!*" Nick mock-congratulated, à la Eddie Murphy in *Boomerang*.

"Come here," she said, accepting the roses and giving him a peck on the cheek. "Thanks a lot, babe."

"You were great. No lie," complimented Nick. "I see Broadway has given you nothing but more confidence."

"And isn't *that* a scary thought?" she kidded. "So where to?"

"It's on you, Bee. Whatever you want to do. You're the guest," offered Nick charmingly.

Queen was a little taken aback, but pleasantly so. "Wow. You called me Bee. Haven't heard that name in a while."

"Well, are you or are you not still my Queen Bee?" Nick presented such a wickedly charming smile, she could only submit.

She matched him tooth for tooth. Allowing her hand to graze Nick's now clean-shaven, walnut-brown face, Queen said softly, "Always."

*This feels too good to be just flirting*, thought Nick. He had to make the moment last. "So what do you want to do?"

"I'd like to unwind. Get a drink or something," she suggested hopefully. "The hotel has a good bar. Is that cool?"

"Of course. It would be *my* pleasure to drink with a soon-to-be *Tony* Award–winning actress," Nick said gallantly.

Surprised, Queen asked, "And when did you start drinking?"

"When I discovered that a Midori and Amaretto Sour are the two best things this side of Kool-Aid."

"Well then, lead the way, my brotha!"

**AN HOUR AT** the bar led to an hour upstairs in her room. Down at the bar, they mused over their wildly divergent careers, traded Industry stories, and gossiped about their shallow, two-faced former classmates and teachers. Upstairs in her room, they talked some more, played cards, and watched some TV. By this time, both Nick and Queen were quite tipsy. It was obvious that Nick could not go anywhere for the night.

Feeling herself getting sleepy, Queen sat up in the bed. Nick, halfway between sleep and wakefulness, shook his head crisply. "Whassup?" he asked, startled.

"We're falling asleep."

"My bad," he apologized. "I guess I better get going."

"Do you really mean that? I mean, in your condition."

Nick giggled. "No."

"You're staying with me." Queen stood and walked into the bathroom to change. Nick peeled down to his boxers and wifebeater. Just as he began to set up a makeshift bed out of two chairs, Queen emerged from the bathroom in a long t-shirt. "What are you doing?"

Suddenly, Nick felt stupid, even though he was doing the gentlemanly thing. With no small amount of allure in her voice, she said, "This bed is big enough for the two of us."

Queen crossed the distance between them. She took his hand and began to lead him to the bed. Nick stopped her at the foot of it. There he was, in her room, less than three inches away from her body, invading her personal space as if it still belonged to him. The warm air from Nick's nose tickled her hair. Queen's ample chest stayed in contact with his own. Their emotions were on the brink.

To seduce Queen was easy. He said plainly, "Don't start what you can't finish."

That was all it took for them to engage in wild animal monkey sex. Moving faster than a U.S. Olympic 4 × 100 relay team, Nick and Queen were out of whatever little clothing they had on and into each other. Knowing Queen to still be on the pill, Nick slid inside her like it was his second home. They enjoyed playing. First the table. Against the wall. On the windowsill ledge. The edge of the bed. Queen, upside down, doing a handstand with her feet draped over Nick's shoulders. The wall again, this time Queen facing it. Now the floor felt neglected. *Another* wall. The chair. The dresser. The toilet seat cover. The bathroom floor.

When Nick finally reached his conclusion, Queen had orgasmed so many times, she had just started calling them out. "Number five! Oh, shit! Oh, shit! Number *six*!" It had gotten to the point where she screamed out after number nine, "I . . . can't . . . come . . . any . . . more!" She squeezed her being around his body as Nick lifted her from the shower—where they had ended up—and over to the bed. Underneath the covers and utterly exhausted, her body made a home next to his, as if they had never been apart. Nick and Queen, together again.

"HEY YOU."

Nick groaned out a stretch from beneath the covers. He was still naked. So was she. Last night had not been one intense wet dream. Nick drew her body even closer to his. "Morning, Bee."

"How are you feeling?"

"Sore," confessed Nick.

"Me, too." That brought about a playful smirk. "Thank you."

"No, thank *you*. I've missed that."

She kissed him on the nose. "Me, too."

"Were we always this good?" wondered Nick.

"Yes," she cooed. "Sometimes even better."

Nick shifted himself so that he filled her insides again. "Damn, I've missed that."

"Morning sex?"

"The absolute best," Nick appraised, not doing anything but lying inside her.

"Mmm . . . you feel so good, Nick. . . ."

"Why did we break up?"

Eyes closed, she uttered, "It certainly wasn't over this. . . ."

Nick's hands cupped her breasts, roamed her back, and parked themselves on the mountain range of her butt. Everything was still intact; everything was just as he remembered it. Her body arched appreciatively. "God, it's been so long since I've had this," she whimpered.

"Your boyfriend's not doin' it for you?" Nick whispered in her ear, exuding pure sex.

"Oooo, Nick . . . babe . . . Obviously he can't do it like this. . . ."

Once she started flexing her Kegel muscles, Nick was a prisoner of the poohnanny. "Ahhhh . . . This feels too good to let go, Bee. . . ."

"Call me that again," she ordered.

"*Beeeee,*" Nick elongated, halfway losing his mind.

Her body rewarded him. Nick's toes curled accordingly. He simply could not take it anymore. "I want you in my life, Queen."

"Mmm . . . I *am* in your life . . . right here, right now . . ."

"I mean for good," Nick moaned. "I want you back as my lady."

Queen could not have cooled off any quicker had he put an ice cube in her vagina. Stubbornly, she held on to the part of Nick that was inside her, reluctant to give it up until she had more information. "You aren't serious, are you?"

"Yes, I am, baby. You make me feel way too good not to have you the way we are used to having each other. I want you in my life. I think we can make it work."

Detaching, Queen disgustedly rolled off Nick and onto her back. The ceiling tiles above became her best friend. "It won't work."

"Yes, it will. Forget the distance. We can make it work. *I* can make it work."

"I have a boyfriend."

"You mean the one you are just so in love with you had to cheat on him with your ex? He's expendable," rejected Nick.

Nick was right. But still . . . "I don't want to do it."

"Why not? We have history, we are friends, and we have amazing chemistry. It can work—if you want it to."

"And that's just what I'm saying. I don't want it to work," Queen restated adamantly. "Hell, I don't even want my boyfriend in New York to work out. Relationships take too much time. They're a big distraction to what I'm trying to do."

It all started to come back to Nick.

"All a man wants to do is possess me. *He* wants to possess me. *You* want to possess me. I cannot do that. I cannot be owned by any one man. I am on this earth for a reason, a purpose. My mission is to be the very best professional actress in the field. I can't do that if I have a relationship dragging me down. The only reason why I got into a relationship with my boyfriend was to have a socially acceptable excuse to have sex on the regular. I just can't deal with a boyfriend right now. Obviously if I could, I wouldn't be in bed with you. I have to be free."

This was why they had broken up before. Or, rather, why Queen had dumped him. She had become all consumed with herself, with being "the best actress she could be in the field" and putting every little thing in her life ahead of spending time with Nick. At thirty-five, Queen felt her acting time clock was ticking. Everything she had been working for the past twelve years or so hung in the balance of how she approached the Industry right now. If her man got left out, so be it. And in Queen's quietly self-constructed "me-camp," anyone who detracted from that definitely got the boot. They had broken up because she was a one-woman show. They had broken up because she would always be a one-woman show.

NICK DID NOT have to say a word when he slinked back home later that morning. Mal, sitting on the futon watching the Knicks play Philadelphia in the first round of the NBA playoffs, knew it all. "Did you make wine last night?"

A disheveled and disheartened Nick mumbled, "What?"

"Did you crush her like a grape?" smirked Mal.

Nick did not even deign to answer. He just flopped on the adjacent couch and wordlessly watched the Knicks getting spanked by Philadelphia. Nick admired how Allen Iverson, the lightning-quick Sixers point guard, always attacked the basket, despite his size. He was always attacking, always attacking. Nick could relate to that.

Malloy studied his friend carefully. Only his boy's perturbed face could divert his attention from his beloved New York Knicks at playoff time. He could smell another big-time moody funk coming on. "What happened, dude?"

Turning brittle eyes upon Malloy, Nick's expression almost said it all. "After a perfect night together, Queen reminded me exactly why she dumped me."

"Not the 'possessing me' speech again?" Mal could've rolled a perfect strike with his eyes. "Ditch that old broad. She got issues anyway."

Shaking his head adamantly, Nick said softly, repeatedly, "You don't get it. You just don't get—"

"What, what, what? What don't I get?" interrupted Mal. "That you stuck some ex of yours and she's *still* your ex? What'd you expect? For her simple ass to fall in love with you again? There's a reason why she is an *ex*, whether it's your doing or hers. Did you think a one-night stand was going to *change* any of that? That is how the game is played, son. And when the game is over, you take your toys and go home."

"Did it ever occur to you that maybe I'm tired of playing the game?"

"With as many broads as you've cut through, no, it didn't," replied Mal honestly. "Maybe that was my bad. Maybe I didn't see that you were dating some of these women, looking for something more."

"Isn't that why we date, Mal? In hopes of finding someone we connect with, in search of something more?"

"No. Not all the time" was his answer. "Can you honestly say that all of those—hell, *any* of those Internet tramps you slayed were part of your search for something more?"

Nick dared not answer; Malloy was on a roll. "We are waging a war on these hos, dude! You cannot succumb to her out-of-pocket attitude, her ghetto-fab wardrobe, and her inconsistent logic! You must resist her levels of chickenhead ineptitude! If you take that attitude into dating, then you will be aw'ight. Aw'ight?"

Studying the game on TV in silence, Nick noticed that the Knick defense had begun to shut Iverson down.

"You cannot, and I mean *cannot* let your wig get twisted over any of this, Nick!" Malloy implored. He sucked his teeth before deciding to let it all out. "I know what you're trying to do here."

Ominously, Nick pried his vision from the game. He peered into Mal's serious eyes. He knew about "Marriage Minded"? He knew that Nick was shopping for a wife? He knew that he was driven by his mother's deteriorating medical condition? Just what did Malloy know? "You do?" Nick gulped.

"I do. You want a homie, a lover, a friend. You want a wife. I know it all," revealed Mal gravely.

*How the hell did he find out* . . . "Look, it's not as crazy as you think . . . " started Nick.

"Nick . . . dawg . . . It's not crazy at all. We *all* want a wife. It's natural to want that, especially at our age, when we see all of our friends gettin' married or engaged."

"We do?" Nick could breathe easier. Mal didn't know. He felt better as he allowed Mal to talk in generalities.

"Yeah. It's natural, dawg. I ain't hatin' on that because I had that once . . . maybe I still do. But you've got to be strong. Stay noble in your goal. Don't settle for anything less. Quit messin' with these tired-ass, triflin'-ass back-flappers," Mal advised. "Keep your eyes on the prize and these hos will follow your stare. Keep your eyes on the prize and a good *woman* will follow your stare."

Soaking it all in, Nick nodded, blankly staring at the screen. The Knicks defense had now contained Iverson, and they were well on their way to winning the game. Offense is more exciting, but defense wins championships.

"Nick . . . You, of all people, deserve love," asserted Mal. "But when you don't look for it, it finds you."

**MARRIAGE MINDED**
*One man's quest to get married in a year*
*by Anonymous*

Recently, I met up with an ex. We all have had that happen, I'm sure. When meeting up with an ex, we always want to look flyer than the last time they saw us, right? We prep ourselves as we go into this meeting, typically in a neutral, public setting with plenty of lighting and people around, determined not to show any signs of weakness or remorse or lustful desire. So tell me this: Just how do we end up *sleeping* with them?

Never mind the fact that she was merely visiting San Diego on business. Never mind the fact that she has a boyfriend back home. Never mind the fact that we hadn't spoken in almost a year. There is no explaining—or fighting—the undeniable chemistry that perpetually exists between you and your ex.

Isn't sleeping with an ex almost counterproductive to the **Marriage Minded** mind-set? I am sure you want to know the reason behind my succumbing to the obvious pheromones that still attract me to my ex. Was it weakness? Lust? Sheer habit?

Believe it or not, it was love.

When you love someone, it is hard to ever stop, especially when you both exited on good terms. Throughout my meeting with her, I was constantly asking myself why we ever broke up. The chemistry was still there. We talked in our old relationship code, the one that we alone could understand, as if we had never left each other. As much as we may (or may not) have tried to fight it, we made all the flirtations with each other we used to naturally make. Seeing an ex is like riding a bike—you never forget how easy it is to do.

And that is where the love part comes in. You spend time with her, and you're thinking, *This is crazy. We still play well together. We* fit *together.* You end up a little tipsy, stumble back to her hotel room, things happen, and before you know it, you're thinking reconciliation. It's crazy, I know. The bad thing about ex-sex is that it will never be bad. If it was good once, it will be good a thousand times, whether you two are within or outside of a relationship. That's part of the allure of ex-sex, an allure that hides the dark, other side to sexing the ex:

*She is still your ex.*

This is made abundantly clear the morning after. When the passions have cooled down from wild animal monkey sex, and you two actually have to talk rationally in its aftermath, you are still caught up in the memories of "how it used to be." The key words are "used to be." There is a reason why it does not "be" right now.

I am man enough to admit when I have been dumped. Our relationship ended because she dumped me. Her narcissistic, self-serving, hyper-ambition consumed her, with the first casualty being our relationship. Am I bitter? Of course. It hurts having invested your time in someone, loved someone, only to have her take it away for reasons outside of your control.

The more biting, painful reality is this: It is May 28 and I do not have a girlfriend. Less than three months away from August 14 and, despite my best attempts, I do not have a woman. San Diego . . . I just may not get married.

## 15

NEW YORK, NEW York. The Big Crapple, Maya T. called it. Malloy was visibly nervous about their return to the city, *his* return. All of his San Diego belongings had been stowed in two large suitcases, now buried in the belly of the plane. He hid his nervousness by peering out the cabin window at the urban sprawl that awaited him below.

His friend Nick sat right beside him, placidly asleep. *Figures,* Mal snorted inwardly. The conspirator of this trip to reunite Malloy with his wife *would* be sound asleep.

Chantel Mojica met them at the gate. Mal enjoyed sizing her up. *This may be the last time I can openly ogle a woman again and not feel guilty about it.* Supposedly, she was the woman who had looked out for his boy Nick during some emotionally turbulent times in Chicago. In introducing himself, Malloy smoothly captured her hand, kissed it, and then placed it momentarily against his heart. The look Chantel gave Nick said it all: *I better watch this one.*

The three of them stepped out of the cab after an expensive ride from the airport over to her apartment in the Washington Heights section of Uptown Manhattan. The area was an overwhelmingly ethnic mix of African-American and Latino. Nick welcomed it. Quite the change from the white-majority populace of San Diego.

Nick helped lug Mal's baggage upstairs to the apartment. For $800 a month, Chantel's one-bedroom was downright spacious by New York standards. She was actually able to fit a couch and stereo system/TV stand in her living room. Nick was pleased to see how well Chantel had washed up in New York after her move two months ago.

It was late and Chantel was ready for bed. "I'm sure you boys can make do out here with the couch and floor. Blankets are on the couch." Chantel gave a generous smile to Nick. "Goodnight, homies."

Chantel disappeared into her room, leaving the boys to get ready for bed. Malloy had been noticeably quiet on the entire trip to New York City. All of his customary bluster and bravado had disappeared. These were the only signs of nervousness he would betray, by not showing anything at all. With that in mind, Nick decided it was time to discuss the plan. "You ready for tomorrow?"

"Do I have a choice?" breathed Malloy.

"It's gonna be alright, Mal," Nick assured him. "Trust me."

"I've trusted you this far. I've got no choice."

Lying on his back on the floor, examining the plaster of the ceiling, Nick thoughtfully asked, "Where've your parents been in this whole thing?"

"What do you mean?"

"You haven't mentioned them once in eight months. I mean, you would think that your parents would be concerned about the state of their child's marriage," rationalized Nick. "You didn't receive one phone call from them in San Diego."

"I know." Mal let that statement ride for the moment. "They think it's my fault."

"What?"

"They think that I did something to Mia to break us up," Mal said plainly. "My own parents think that I destroyed my marriage."

"Why?"

Mal snorted. "When I came to them and told them that Mia had cheated on me, they didn't believe me at first. Hell, I couldn't believe it myself; that's why I told them. Then, after some convincing, they believed it, but they didn't believe I was telling them the whole truth."

"Were you?" asked Nick gingerly.

"Of course I was. I told them what I told you—the truth. I never

cheated on Mia to make her go out and do this to me," sulked Malloy.

Nick did not dare say a word. Obviously, all of Mal's San Diego
exploits did not count.

"My own parents doubted me. Do you know what it feels like for
your own *flesh and blood* to turn against you?" The hurt leaked into
Mal's voice. A sniffle in the darkness allowed him to regain control.
"So I turned my back on them. If I'm going to have to do this, to salvage my marriage, I'm going to have to do it alone."

"No, Mal," Nick corrected. "As long as you've got me, you are
never alone."

**NICK AND MAL** took the train to Brooklyn the next morning.
Nick still found New York's complexity and density dizzying. How
could there be this many people in one place outside of China? In almost six years removed from The Apple, Nick had grown used to the
slightly slower pace of Chicago and the altogether sedate lifestyle of
San Diego and Southern California. Nick had no idea just how much
he had mellowed out on the West Coast until being confronted with
the in-your-face audacity of America's largest city. With signs and
placards for everything big and small, New York was an assault on
the senses. Cars honking, garbage cans smelling, lights blinking, people yelling . . . too much, too much. A nice place to visit, but Nick was
glad he no longer lived there.

Mia's boutique existed in the commercially and residentially mixed
Fort Greene neighborhood of Brooklyn. Located just down Lafayette
Street from the Brooklyn Academy of Music, her shop was popular
because it featured unique styles for black women in all sizes. A size 2
could have just as much luck finding a cute outfit as a size 22. Mia, a
Rubenesque size 14 and cute as hell, could fully appreciate the need
for wearing something just as cute as herself.

Around the Way Girl, the name of her shop, beckoned with the
very New York styles of shiny leathers and gators on the mannequins
in the storefront windows. Mal lagged behind as Nick peered past the
mannequins and inside the store. About half a dozen people browsed
the racks at eleven-thirty that morning. Mia stood behind the counter,

crunching numbers in her bookkeeping log between sneaking peeks at the customers. For the most part, the coast was clear. Nick waved Mal on. Showtime.

When the bell to the front door chimed their entrance, Mia's heart nearly skipped a beat: Nick. With her husband. *Her husband.* Subconsciously, she fingered the diamond wedding band that had somehow remained on her hand these past eight, lonely months. Exhaling like Whitney in that silly movie, Mia maintained a thick veneer of composure as Nick approached the counter.

"Hey, Mia," said Nick. He reached to hug her and she recoiled. There was a brief but awkward moment. Mia let down enough of her guard to let the best man at her wedding almost four years ago hug her. It was hard to show love to a man who had helped facilitate her husband's exit. Nick sensed this, so he treaded lightly. "How are you?"

"I'm fine. Still here," Mia answered quietly. Whereas once she had been a boisterous, around-the-way Brooklyn girl, Mia was now a settled, more reserved, business-owning, around-the-way Brooklyn girl. The added weight of losing her husband had also dampened her enthusiasm for life.

She did her best not to steal glances at her husband. Malloy still looked the same in many respects—low haircut, lean and long frame, diamond stud earring in his left ear. But she could tell from his demeanor that the separation had weighed upon him, too.

*Time to step up and be a man.* "Can we talk, Mia?" Malloy asked.

"Not here. Not now. I'm working." Her Brooklyn accent sealed the finality of her decision.

"May I come by the house?" Mal was so sincere and polite. He always was when it came to her.

She noticed. "You may."

Nick silently observed the proceedings not so much out of curiosity but more so as a referee. With these two's mercurial personas, they needed one. So far, so good.

"What time?" Mal requested.

"Eight."

"Thank you."

According to plan, Nick handled the exit. "We won't hold you up from business, Mia. I'll make sure he gets there by eight. Thanks a lot."

"Bye. Nick," she added coldly.

**"SEE? THAT WASN'T** so bad," Nick said over lunch in a busy Manhattan fast-food restaurant.

"She wanted to feed me my penis," muttered Mal miserably.

"She was protecting herself," interpreted Nick, biting into a hot dog. Finally, the roles were reversed, with Nick offering the sound direction and advice that *Mal* needed. Nick knew enough about heartbreak and pain to fill a book. "And you've been gone for eight months. She has that right."

"Am I the one who done wrong here? I never cheated on my wife," protested Malloy.

Nick cleared his throat with a sip of his drink. There was only so much hypocrisy he could take, even from Mal. "Let's be real here, Mal. You've cheated on Mia."

"Like hell I have."

"What do you call messin' with all those women who stayed the night? Jamilla, LaShonda, Sherika, Kammie, Rashida . . ." Nick trailed off. "I could go on, but then I'd sound like a DMX music video."

"Aw'ight, aw'ight. I get the picture. But it's not what you think," objected Mal. "I never hit none of those broads."

"Say what?"

"Hardly even touched 'em. *Maybe* I kissed Jamilla and Kammie, but I ain't never done more than that," Mal revealed. "I ain't never cut none of those girls."

Nick was flabbergasted. Mal and sex went together like Peaches and Herb. "Not even one?"

"Not a one."

"Not even *Rashida*?" whined Nick. Rashida was so freakin' fine, she made *straight women* gawk. When he had seen Malloy come home with her from Mr. O's, Nick had silently made an exception to his disapproval of Mal's extramarital activities.

"Not even Rashida." Mal inhaled half of his drink. "Like I said before: How that look, me cheatin' on my wife? Mia may have cheated on me, but that doesn't mean I don't still love her."

That was sweet. "So what'd these women say when it was time to go to bed and you weren't gonna have sex with them?"

"Some of 'em got mad. No, lemme not tell that lie—*most* of them were mad," admitted Mal. "Notice it was always a different one coming back to the crib with me."

"This is true," nodded Nick at the memory. "And here I was thinking you were just livin' the life of a playa."

"Oh, I'm always livin' that, playa," grinned Mal. "But in this case, I wasn't crushin' like one. You know what I learned, dude?"

"School me," Nick invited dryly. As if he had a choice.

"I always do, young bleed" was Mal's snappy comeback. "Sometimes women have more fragile egos than men."

"I'm listening." *And laughing,* Nick thought at Mal's waxing philosophic.

"Naw, god, for real. It's women. They live in this shitty, male-dominated society, right? And in doing so, we build them up in the most heinous ways possible, devaluing their insides by overrating and glorifying their outsides. After a while, some of them become like the loyal house niggas—they start believin' that shit means something, that outward appearance is their ticket to recognition and appreciation by this fucked-up society that's oppressing them. It's a colonized mentality, dawg," proclaimed Mal, breaking it down. "And when someone with that colonized mind state goes to the oppressor seeking affirmation, having done everything he's asked her to do, only for him to reject her . . . well . . . she gets mad."

"So lemme get this straight, Cornel West," Nick mocked humorously. "So you're the oppressor and women like Rashida are the colonized mind state?"

"If you wanna put it like that." Malloy dove into his fries without a second thought.

Only Mal could come up with a wild analogy like that. And only Mal could, along with the rest of his crazy life, make it all make sense.

**EVENINGS GREW LONG** this time of year. It was the day before June and the sun fought the skyscrapers to the west for room. The smell of smog was pleasantly absent from the warm, mild air. Nick sat on a bench in the middle of the vastness of Central Park, watching the shadows grow long, alone. Mal was on the 5 train at the moment, speeding toward resuming his destiny.

And they were destined for each other. Those two were both re-formed players who had found love. Mal and Mia. Both Brooklyn born and bred. Both HBCU graduates, with Mal from Morehouse, Mia from Hampton. Both loved to talk a lot of shit. Nick could not imagine a better pairing in the universe, not even for himself.

He had, though, once. Returning to New York, even after all these years, still chilled him to the bowels. This very park was an accessory to the crime against his heart. The site of the infamous second date. The holding of hands. The impromptu "I want" speech. The point of no return for his young, formative, naive heart.

Yep, New York would always bear the stigma, and the soul, of the love he had once had—and lost.

---

**MALLOY WALKED DOWN** President Street, the street he had grown up on as a kid, and where his brownstone was located. He found Mia waiting for him on the steps out front. She held a cordless phone in her lap. His wife. *His.* She looked absolutely beautiful.

His head was a mess. A thousand screaming banshees exhorted him to, somehow, know exactly what to do, know exactly what to say. This was impossible. This was unprecedented. This was his wife. She knew every bullshit tactic in the book, in his book. Shoot, she had helped write it. That was what had made him fall in love with her in the first place. As hard as their fronts were, they had been able to penetrate it all to access the purity of the other's soul. Their connection was real and true and thoroughly without pretense—it was a bond. Malloy had no slick opening lines to restore a bond.

So he stopped at the foot of the steps. Her big brown eyes gazed up at him expectantly, waiting for a salve that might never heal her wound. The anguish began to reveal itself plainly on his face. He fought emotions never felt before, emotions so complex they did not have a name. These emotions broke him down before he could even say a word. Malloy's face battled—it blinked, it squinted, it scrunched itself together. His lips contorted. Neck veins struggled and bulged. His face collapsed into itself.

Not willingly, but helplessly, Malloy began to cry. A stream of tears crawled out of the corner of his left eye and forged their way down the side of his face, glistening in the twilight. He could not even bring himself to stop crying.

Similarly, Mia's facade dissolved. Her face softened as she resisted the urge to reach out to her husband. It had been eight months. There were things she needed to know.

"Why did you leave me?"

Malloy could barely form sentences, let alone explain his rationale for the past eight months. "I . . . you . . . you hurt me," he struggled to say.

Mia took that in and allowed herself to process it before responding. "You honestly thought I cheated on you?"

"You didn't deny it," her husband sniffled.

She glared up at the sky, the big, bad, wide, useless sky, channeling her emotions there. When she returned back to earth, she said simply to him, "I didn't say anything." A pause. "I could not believe you could even ask me such a question."

A thread of shame, the fear of being wrong on a globally, universally massive scale, began to creep into Mal's consciousness, enabling him to stop the tearflow. "Then who was that man?"

"Cheat on *you*?"

"Who was that man?"

"The only man I have *ever loved*?"

"Who was that man?"

"You are *my husband*."

"*Who was that man!*" demanded Malloy, now a ball of misdirected energy.

With controlled, contained, accusing eyes, Mia answered, "My father."

Malloy crumpled to the steps. *Her father.* The longtime, missing-in-action, absentee father Mia had never known and never spoken much about. The one who had left her and her mother when she was only six. The father who had "fathered" five children by five different mothers, marrying none of them. The father whose last name Mia had always refused to carry. Malloy was stunned. "Why didn't you tell me?"

"I didn't get a chance to. You had followed me around, drawn your own conclusions, and branded me a slut before I could put two words together." Up until then, Mia had been able to channel her pain into a determined glare. But now the glare failed her as she again reached her gaze up to the heavens to head off the tears. "Now, *that* hurt me."

"Mia . . . you are my wife. I never called you a slut."

"You asked me if I had cheated on you. You didn't have to." She had lost the battle. Tears flowed freely as she accepted defeat graciously. With streaming eyes, she faced her accuser, her lover, her husband. "I took vows, Malloy. I swore before you, my family, and God to love you and give myself *only to you—forever*! When you asked me that, I couldn't say a thing. You hurt me beyond words. I wanted to die."

Mal scrambled for answers. There was no way he could be wrong about this. If he had been wrong about this, he had just wasted eight months of his life, eight months he couldn't get back, nearly jeopardizing eternity with the only woman in the world he truly loved. "But the moodiness . . . you being distant from me . . ."

"I admit that getting my master's and then opening up the shop right after that was too much for me to handle at once. I got tired," she explained. "I'm sorry I made you feel like I was pushing you away."

"But you kissed him twice . . ."

"Both a peck on the lips." Mia sighed. "I've forgiven my father. I am old enough to know now that parents are not perfect. That they are just as real and fallible as both of us. He is not a perfect man. Hell, that fool isn't even a *good* man. But he is still my father, and I have forgiven him."

"And the hotel?" Malloy was grasping at straws.

"I found him in Kansas. He's married with three kids to a white woman who will put up with his shit. I flew him in to see me. I didn't want to tell you at first because when have you ever heard me put two words together about my father? If he didn't come, or didn't act right, or wouldn't be the person I thought he would be, then I didn't want to expose him to my family. To you."

"Why didn't you tell me you were looking for your dad?" Malloy felt slighted. Maybe he could have helped her.

"I was protecting the life we had built from being exposed to a man who had done nothing but ruin every life he has touched," Mia justified. "I was protecting the love we had built. I was protecting you."

"But he looked too young to be your father."

"Add relaxer, a nice suit, and nineteen years to my age, and you have my father." Mia shook her head. "Good-lookin' sonofabitch. And charming. Still quite the player. But thanks to that wife in Kansas, he's completely harmless now. That's why I had to keep him away from you at first, to check him out. You two would have had entirely too much in common."

And there it was. The entire reason behind his eight-month hiatus from his wife had boiled down to a gross assumption that had offended everyone it touched into irrationality. Instead of feeling stupid, Malloy felt sad. He felt sad that he had risked his marriage because of an insecure judgment he had rushed to about the one woman he now knew, more than anyone, was put on this earth to love him.

Saying "sorry" would not be enough. Saying *anything* wouldn't be. So Malloy crawled his head into his wife's lap, the beginnings of a tear starting to form once again. He had been so foolish, so headstrong, so *male,* that he deserved whatever punishment he received. But he was not sure he was ready to hear this next one.

"Malloy . . . I had a miscarriage."

CONFIDENT THAT HIS boy Malloy was in the throes of eight months' worth of make-up sex, Nick was halfway asleep on Chantel's living room couch. That is, until Malloy knocked on the door, awakening him. Despite his sleepiness, Nick wanted to hear how the Showdown on President Street had gone down. They turned Chantel's torchère lamp on low and spoke in quiet tones from the couch and floor as not to awaken her.

Nervous because he was about to find out the fate of his boy's marriage, not to mention whether his expensive, calculated risk had paid off, Nick asked delicately, "What happened?"

Malloy slumped against the couch as he sat dumbfounded on the living room carpet. "Mia had a miscarriage."

"Huh? What're you talking about?"

"We had reconciled and everything. Mia didn't cheat on me. The guy I saw her with was her long-lost father. But then she said—"

"I knew it!" Nick erupted into a stage whisper. He shook a defiant fist at Mal. "I knew it, I knew it! I *knew* she didn't cheat on you! That girl loves you more than life itself!"

"And then she told me about her miscarriage."

"She told you she miscarried?"

"She said that she was six weeks' pregnant when I left. She didn't know for sure until I had been in San Diego for three weeks. Mia said that, had I been there, she wouldn't have been so stressed out and could have had the baby. Crying, throwing up, Valiums . . . Mia was a mess. She was so stressed out, her mother hospitalized her three times. Mia didn't know if I was coming back or not. The thought of being a single mom and struggling like her mother did terrorized her. Mia didn't want to, nor was she ready to, raise a kid on her own." Mal gulped for air. "I killed my child, Nick! I killed my child."

Instinctively, Nick grabbed his skull, crashing to the floor with Mal. "Malloy . . . I can't . . ." Nick couldn't fathom it. He had been kidding back in July when he had bugged Mal about not being a godfather yet.

The totality of it all struck Nick. Mia hadn't cheated, Malloy had jumped to conclusions and left, Mia found out she was pregnant, and then the stress from his leaving killed their seed. Their child. His child.

Tears poured out of Malloy's eyes like rivers. Rivers of emotion Nick hadn't seen from his boy in a decade. Malloy was not the crying type. But here he was, head thrown back against Chantel's couch, crying softly as if his life depended on it. The tears simply would not stop. "It's all been my fault. It's all been my fault."

Nick stretched over to Malloy and encompassed his body in a giant, compassionate hug. "It's over, Mal. It's over. The worst part is over. You're home now. You're home."

---

**FOUR DAYS LATER,** Chantel accompanied Nick to JFK via the train. At that very hour, Mal and Mia were in their second session of marriage counseling. They were going to be alright. In spite of the disturbing news surrounding the reconciliation, Nick's mission had been accomplished.

As they neared the busy security checkpoint area in the airport terminal, Chantel asked him simply, "How did you know it was going to work?"

"What do you mean?"

"Getting Mal and Mia back together. How did you know it was going to work out?"

Nick sighed. "There are some people who you just know were meant to be together. Forever. Maybe it was preordained, or divinely inspired, or whatever, but those two were meant to be together. I didn't want Mal's pride to stand in the way of destiny. And I didn't want to continue as an accessory to preventing his true happiness, which is her."

"Well put, Nicholito."

"What about you, Chantel? Who's your true happiness? Certainly not Jorge, I hope," funned Nick as they stood in line together.

"No way, homie. I killed him off."

Nick clutched his heart. "How could you do that to me? I mean him?"

"Figuratively, *ése,* figuratively. The second I moved to New York, I told them he ran off with a Swedish heiress."

"Swedish?" frowned Nick. "Why she gotta be Swedish?"

"Because I know that's one country my family has absolutely no desire to go to," Chantel smiled. "Otherwise, they'd hound that guy all over the earth for breaking my heart."

"Did I break your heart, Chantel?" Nick fluttered his eyelids at her mock-sincerely.

"You don't break hearts, Nicholito. Just make sure you keep yours from being broken." Chantel ducked to the other side of the cord that formed the security line. She leaned in to give him a kiss on the cheek. Nick could have floated all the way back to California on that alone. "Have a safe trip."

Backing toward the security attendant, Nick said, "You never answered my question, Chantel."

"What's that?"

"Who's your true happiness?"

Chantel transmitted a megawatt smile. "*Myself.*"

**WHEN NICK RETURNED** to San Diego, it was as if the world had turned upside down in the week he had been gone. On the plane ride home, he had read in *The New York Times* that Queen had won her Tony for *Blues* the night before. Good for her. He had also read that in attendance at the awards show was movie and TV actress Shana McAdams, star of the romantic drama *Whisper Softly,* opening next week, with her new boyfriend—*Fredo.* That was just perfect. Nick could not escape him. The meek do not inherit the earth—that was left for the overhyped and talentless.

That was just the beginning. Messages on his machine ranged from the ridiculous to the even more ridiculous. Khalilah called to say that she was engaged to some Saudi Arabian sheik. She would be leaving the country in six months to marry him. Ayinde had proposed to his live-in Bahamian girlfriend. Jeannie and Carlton had run off to Vegas and eloped. The only ones who had not called to announce their nuptials were Robert and Craig. The former could not legally marry and the latter already had. Craig was probably putting cherry sauce on his wife's ass right about now.

After Nick deleted messages from Jaye and Internet tramp Honeii Brown, the worst message was saved for last.

"Nick . . . uh, this is Harrison." The man sounded shaken, positively lost. "It's about your mother."

Nick's legs weakened, buckled, out and out collapsed. He was on all fours on the floor, fearing the worst.

"She's in the hospital again. The medication they had been giving her has weakened. It's now not nearly aggressive enough in fighting the tumor. They're going to try and remove the tumor again. If they are unsuccessful . . ." A huge breath. "If they are unsuccessful, they may have to do a mastectomy."

*No, no, no, no, no. Not. Right. Now.*

From his prone position on the floor, Nick fumbled on the table for the phone.

**SEATTLE SEEMED VERY** forbidding under a veil of clouds. It was as if the Downtown buildings that fingered their way toward the gray, oppressive sky accepted, almost relished, the overcast weather as an opportunity to appear more grandiose and imposing.

Under this ominously foreshadowing weather, Nick drove Harrison to Harborview Medical Center in Seattle's medical hub of First Hill. They breezed through a maze of doctors, patients, orderlies, nurses, and medics to find their girl. Mom lay flat on her back, drugged out. The anesthesia for the upcoming operation had only just begun to kick in.

Harrison whispered some loving, tender words in her ear, gave her an encouraging kiss, and then turned her over to her son.

The first words out of her sedated, smiling mouth were "I am proud of you, son."

"No, Mom. I am proud of *you*," Nick said, trying not to tear up. "You have struggled all your life. You have always been so strong and resilient. Nothing stops you. You just push on, and you do it all with a smile. And now this."

Nick paused to gather himself. "You are everything I have ever wanted to be."

"I know you have been worried about me, about continuing on without me. I don't want you to worry." Her words began to blur into one another. "I have lived a very full life. I have done more and seen more than I had ever thought of or imagined, coming from a Panama farm as a little girl. A very big part of my full life has been watching you grow all your life—and these past few years. You are a man now. Even without any help from your father, somehow, I raised a man. I am very, very proud of . . ."

Mom drifted off into unconsciousness with a smile.

Dr. Karen Willis politely removed Nick from the room as they wheeled his mother out toward the operating room.

Five hours later, a very tired-looking Dr. Willis surfaced from the OR. Smatterings of blood, Mom's blood, clung to her scrubs. Her face was unreadable.

With a stern face, Dr. Willis explained that Mom was okay. They had removed the tumor, but had discovered another tumor that was inoperable. They could remove the breast or keep the breast—it didn't matter. This new tumor was spreading aggressively, playing by its own rules, infecting everything in its environment. Mom was being transferred to Swedish Hospital's Seattle Tumor Institute.

Then Dr. Willis did a very undoctorlike thing: She made a suggestion. Unless Mom received a very expensive, highly experimental gene-therapy, cancer-fighting drug called Pilotaxln, she would not last past October.

Thankfully, Dr. Willis kept everything simple for the medical neophyte Nick. The FDA, she explained, had recently approved Pilotaxln, yet medical insurance companies had been dragging their feet in covering the treatment. At more than $1,500 per infusion per week for a standard year's worth of treatment per patient, Pilotaxln had been enormously effective in those who were able to afford it. While other, more conventional chemotherapies like Herceptin were covered by Mom's insurance, Pilotaxln was not. If only Nick had $78,000 to spare, he could make sure that Mom would keep smiling.

**SUNDAY NIGHT FOUND** Nick back in San Diego, alone and discomfited. The image of the smatterings of blood on Dr. Willis' scrubs as she told him his mother would die by October disturbed him. Mom, anesthesia, surgery, pain. His mother's pain. Pain and loss.

Instead of sitting in his empty home drowning his sorrows in *SportsCenter,* Nick went out to Clair de Lune. Although having coffee would keep him up all night, it still beat being stuck in his empty house all night, haunted by situations of life and love he could not control.

Nick had forgotten it was Open Mic Night. Souldance was in the middle of a rousing set, rhyming, flowing, making words and adverbs dance to the rhythm of her poetic manipulation. Making words turn into soul-healers. The crowd vibed with her, calling and responding to her verbal gymnastics. Nick stood transfixed as Souldance made everyone's soul dance with her. She was *his* soul-healer.

Her final line rocked Nick to his core: "And this man . . . this otha man, this brothaman, this never-seen-outside-the-waters-of-the-Nile, all together, has-my-back-like-none-other-gentle-*man* will love me. Love me with the power that puts eternity on an axis and makes the world spin. Who is that? That's *my* man. Who is he? He's that unknown quantity, that is a part of my serenity, my entity, that independent but not sexist womanist philosophy. My divinely . . . inspired . . .

plan. Do you know him? Neither do I. But still when I find him . . . when we find each other . . . that is *my* man."

Somehow, her eyes came to rest on Nick as she pronounced the last syllable. Nick felt blessed by those eyes, as if kissed by God. For the first time, if but for a brief, fleeting moment in a long while, Nick's heart was at peace. Her lips curled into a smile as she finally unhinged her gaze from his soul, peering around at the wildly excited Clair de Lune crowd. As she stepped away from the mic, adoring fans, new-found and old, mobbed and fanned her up.

Half an hour and two bad poets later, Nick was finally able to break through the sheath of fans to pay homage to the poetess known as Souldance. Almost like a rock star after a set, she sat back in her chair, with her old-school yellow-tinted glasses with big black rims, hair pulled back in a kerchief, long but sexy skirt boasting loud, psychedelic colors, with a slit up the side exposing knee-high black boots and just a hint of honey-brown skin, sipping coolly on a Sprite. Even when she was not performing, Souldance carried this aura, this air of invincibility that repelled the weak but attracted the strong. After the week Nick had had, his demeanor was out of his hands—he could only be strong.

"Souldance," he greeted. "My name's Nick. You were excellent. You *are* excellent."

"That's love. Many blessings. Peace to you, my brotha." Souldance gestured to dap Nick up, but Nick became much more involved. He gave her a hug, a hug as if he had known her all his life. When she broke away, she felt it, too.

"Keep doin' what you're doin'," encouraged Nick. Respect. That was all he wanted to give her.

Nick began walking away when Souldance called out to him: "Nick!" She was up on her feet, closing the distance between them like a stone skipping on a lake. "Where're you going?"

"Home."

"Wrong answer. We're going for ice cream. By the beach?"

Who *was* this sexy, spiritual, sassy, audacious woman? Whatever connection had been made during that hug, Souldance shamelessly exploited it. Hell, Nick had never said no to a woman in his life, and he sure wasn't going to start now. Especially when the woman was as bright and alive as Souldance was.

Playing off his shock with a friendly grin, Nick asked, "Which beach?"

"TELL ME HOW you got the name Souldance."

They straddled a rock wall that separated the beach from the street. Lights illuminated parts of Mission Beach that were otherwise lit only by the moon. With big scoops of ice cream in paper cups, they spooned the milky dessert into their mouths when not talking. Souldance kicked her feet back and forth happily, almost like a little kid.

"Well, my earthbound name is Tabitha Washington. I didn't realize my spiritual name until I went to college, freshman year."

"Where'd you go?"

"Clark Atlanta University."

"You went to CAU? Hey, I went to Morehouse!"

"Oh, that's peace, Nick. That's peace," she approved. "What year did you graduate?"

"After you, I'm sure," Nick dodged. He wasn't sure he wanted to address the age thing just yet.

"I wouldn't be surprised. I just graduated last year."

Nick gagged on his ice cream. "You're only twenty-two?"

"Twenty-three," piped Tabitha proudly.

*Wow. A baby.* "For lack of a better term, how did you get so *deep*? I mean, you've lived all of two minutes in this world. Where does this all come from?"

"And just how old are you, black man?"

"Thirty next month." That was how Nick had chosen to accept it.

"That's it?"

"That's it!" echoed Nick, offended. "Yeah, that's it! What, I look older?"

"I'm kidding, Nick." Impish eyes sparkled in the darkness, lingered on his. He had such beautiful brown eyes, even at night. Those eyes were filled with so much clear-eyed honesty and sadness, they were like puddles of his soul. Tabitha responded well to sadness. "My roommate gave me the name Souldance after she heard me freestyle one night in the cafeteria. She said hearing me recite poetry made her soul *dance*."

"I know the feeling," conceded Nick, eating another spoonful of ice cream. Her poetry was a salve for his spirit. She had such an old soul, such a pageantry to her poetry, such an ability to move the rock of his tortured psyche, he just had to know where it all came from. "So what's your background?"

"What do you mean?"

"Where are your parents from?"

"You mean 'what am I?' " she redirected.

"I guess you get that a lot," conceded Nick. "What can I say? You have very exotic features."

"My father is Dominican and my mother is Cuban."

Souldance's appeal was international. "You speak Spanish?"

"*Sí*. Fluently. And my mother's the light one. She's one of those blond Latinas."

"What do they do?"

"I'm not sure what my father does. I haven't seen him since I was five," she informed. Nick snorted. He could relate to that. "And my mom is a loan officer for Bank of America in LA."

"You're from LA?"

Tabitha squinted in shame. "From the Valley."

Nick laughed. "I just can't see you as a Valley Girl."

"Neither could I. That's why I high-tailed it for Atlanta and never looked back. I couldn't stand growing up in the Valley."

"I imagine it was somewhat like growing up in Seattle."

"Probably. Only with a little Latino flair," she said. "You're from Seattle?"

"The 206 to the fullest, baby!" Nick proudly proclaimed the area code.

"I've never been. Never had a reason to go." Scraping out the last of her ice cream, Tabitha cut her eyes at him. "You a Sonics fan?"

"Is Gary Payton nicknamed The Glove?"

That earned Nick a prodigious roll of her eyes. "It's a shame y'all are gonna get run by us in the Western Conference Finals."

She was a basketball fan, too! The fact that she liked to talk trash as well was not lost on him. "In an inverted universe," Nick taunted back.

"I wouldn't bet on it," she cautioned, snaking her head royally. "The Lakers have Souldance on their side!"

"Stop it. Any more Laker talk and you will 'warp my fragile little mind,' " said Nick in the screechy, whiny voice of *South Park*'s Cart-man.

" 'Omigod! They killed Kenny!' " she hollered.

" 'You bastards!' " finished Nick.

"You watch *South Park,* too, huh?" Luckily for Nick, Tabitha wasn't stingy with her smile around him. When a woman as together as Tabitha smiled at you, you had definitely earned it.

"I'm surprised a woman of your caliber watches a show like *South Park.*"

"A woman of my caliber? You can relax on the love and just talk to me straight up," she invited.

"You know the aura you put out there. You're just so . . . *earthy.*"

"Earthy?" Tabitha wasn't sure she liked that word.

"Like connected. You're very connected, grounded, spiritual," Nick amended. "I have a hard time believing someone so sophisticated could find humor out of Mr. Hanky the Christmas Poo."

"I like to laugh, too, Nick. Just say something funny," she jibed playfully. One word rotated itself in her mind. "Sophisticated, huh?"

"And intelligent. And beautiful. And talented. I could go on," Nick threatened.

"Please do, if you can. We like compliments around here." Tabitha batted her eyelids at him before turning serious. "What attracted you to me?"

"Dang. You really just put it all out on the table, don't you?" smiled Nick. Actually, he rather liked it. Tabitha was a woman who was a straight-up human being, having shaken off and denied playing the game. "It's kinda hard not to be attracted to you."

"That is a very complimentary thing to say to a sista," Tabitha said sweetly, "but such flattery doesn't get you off the hook from answering my question."

For good measure, she added a sweet smile. "Please."

*Cardinal Rule to Dating No. 14:* **Never talk too much about yourself. Listen.** Mal, in his infinite wisdom, once told him, "If you sit back and listen, a woman will tell you everything you need to know."

*Cardinal Rule to Dating No. 15:* **Use the truth sparingly.**

That night, he would break all the rules. "The first time I saw you was a month ago with my friends. I couldn't take my eyes off you, or your performance. You really know how to captivate a crowd."

Tabitha was light enough to blush. "You are a blessing, my brotha."

"Nick. Just call me Nick," he adjusted engagingly. He did not want to be her "brotha." What he saw in Tabitha were the makings of so much more. "But I'm not done."

"My bad. Proceed."

"When I came in tonight, you were just finishing up your set. I've been going through some things recently, things that preoccupy my mind. But the words you speak, the words that you let loose from those lips, soothe me. I feel at home.

"You said something that stirred my soul. Something about finding your man. That you will know when you find him, or when he finds you. That's kind of how I feel.

"I've spent a lot of time recently looking, actively searching for love. I stopped because the harder I'd look, the further away I'd seem to get from it. For some reason, when you looked at me when you spoke those last few words about your man . . . I dunno."

"No, finish. Please."

"I felt that I could be that man."

Internally, Nick cringed. He awaited the inevitable rejection of his statement, his sentiment. Before the words had even tumbled out of his mouth, he had already known he had told a woman too much.

"Would it be too forward of me to kiss you right now?" Tabitha asked politely, if not seductively.

Why the hell not? She had gotten everything else that she had wanted tonight. Quoting *Othello*, Nick said, "My lady, I would deny thee nothing."

With the kiss she bestowed upon him, a fine mixture of sweet, supple lips around soft, tentative, exploratory tongues, denying her was the last thing on his mind.

---

NICK NEEDED A job. Now. As Mom whittled away her life in Seattle without the medicine she needed, Nick took it upon himself to come up with the money to save her life. Harrison meant well but could be of no use. He ran a construction company consulting firm that had just been audited by the IRS. If he wanted to stay in business, he had to come up with an additional twelve thousand himself. Man, when it rained, it poured.

So Nick made that kowtowing phone call to Shelby Townsend. "Shelby . . . I need to work."

"I know, dear. I apologize, but Ilene Zimmerman hasn't made it easy for me to schedule auditions," Shelby intimated.

"I knew it!" cursed Nick. "That vindictive bitch blacklisted me!"

"Well, not anymore. Did you read today's *Variety*?"

"No."

"Gotta get it every day, Nick. I'm telling you. Well, it looks like Ilene Zimmerman's out on her ass. She got fired from her development deal at Fox."

"Stop lying!" Hope sprang eternal. "Why?"

"The real story is she got caught by her husband sucking some young stud's dick at a party two weeks ago," Shelby reported, with no shred of embarrassment. "Her husband, who does his own fair share of screwing around, was publicly humiliated because it was at a Twentieth Century Fox party for top execs at Rupert Murdoch's house. Well, he filed for divorce, talked to his buddy who heads Fox Filmed Entertainment . . . and the rest is front-page *Variety* history."

"So am I in there?"

"You're in there."

"Can you deliver a message to Fredo for me?"

"Fredo? Sure, I guess." She wasn't a messenger, she was an agent, dammit.

"Tell him to treat her right," Nick instructed, almost wistfully. "Tell him to treat her right."

---

"**WELCOME BACK, SAN DIEGO.** It's *The Jeannie Rhome Show* and I am your host, Jeannie Rhome," Jeannie greeted the San Diego airwaves warmly. "I hope you all had a wonderful week last week, because I most certainly did. For those who have missed the show, I hope you enjoyed the opportunity to catch up with *The Best of Jeannie Rhome* during my weeklong hiatus.

"There's a lot going on in the world of sports today. The Western Conference Finals are going on strong, as the Sonics try and dig themselves out of a two-games-to-one hole in the best-of-seven series. The Padres are still in first place, thanks to the hot bat of Perennial Padre Tony Gwynn. I know redwoods younger than Tony Gwynn, but he still keeps chugging along, batting .322 after last night's victory over the hated Dodgers at Dodger Stadium. Roy Jones, Jr., defended his middleweight belt by knocking out another stiff, this one being the pride of Ireland, Sean O'Malley. Which proves that the only Irish worth a damn these days can only be seen on video with Tom Cruise in *Far and Away*. And Arena League football has just gotten underway—and nobody cares.

"And if that's not enough news for you, I have something I would like to share with my listeners in our home base of San Diego and now nationally, as we are officially syndicated in two hundred markets. I, Jeannie Rhome, your Queen of Smack . . . have gotten married!"

Her show producer, Clorox, punched a button that filled the airwaves with a chorus of boos.

"Hey, hey, hey, now!" Jeannie mock-objected. They had scripted this out beforehand. "Just like LL Cool J, I need love!"

Clorox played another audio clip, this one of a crazed Mike Tyson after a fight, threatening to eat some boxer's children.

"Despite Clorox's best attempts to discredit my union, I would like you all to know that my man, my marital partner, my *husband,* is in studio today and will be joining the show permanently. You all have heard him before on these very same airwaves. He is an acclaimed and hardworking sportscaster for Channel 2 News, San Diego, and sure to give me nothing but headaches . . . Carlton Maxey!"

An audio of polite theater clapping was played by Clorox.

"Thank you for that entirely *underwhelming* intro," Carlton ribbed.

"You should expect nothing more," Jeannie retorted good-naturedly. "Now, who do you like in the Western Conference Finals?"

"Do you even have to ask, Jeannie? Sonics all the way!"

An audio cut from the TV show *Martin* with Martin Lawrence as Sheneneh saying "You so cra-zay!" played.

"Careful, Clorox! I think all that bleach in your hair has gone to your head!" laughed Carlton. Clorox ruffled his artificially blond head at Carlton from the other side of the booth's glass. "Seriously, though, Seattle has quick guard play, led by Seattle defensive stalwart Gary Payton, who also spearheads the highest scoring offense in the league, one that should wreak havoc on the Lakers. Combined with the Seattle coach's philosophy to gang-tackle Shaquille O'Neal in the paint and double Kobe on the perimeter . . . Seattle will pull this series out in seven."

"And you're from Seattle," Jeannie added.

"Of course."

Beaming a smile at her husband that sparkled like the three-carat diamond on her ring finger, Jeannie shifted gears with "And with that daily dose of misdirection, let's go to the phones. The number, nationwide, is 1-800-SMACK-ME. That's 1-800-SMACK-ME to call *The Jeannie Rhome Show.* Come hard or don't call at all."

Quickly, Jeannie's eyes darted to the computer screen in front of her. "We're going to . . . Cletis from Seattle. Cletis, you're on the air with Jeannie Rhome and Carlton Maxey on *The Jeannie Rhome Show.*"

"Whaaaaaazzzzuuuuuuuuuuuuuup!" The voice imitated the greeting from those once-popular Budweiser commercials.

Carlton recognized that voice. Tongue flailing, he responded with "Whaaaaaazzzzuuuuuuuuuuuuuup!"

"Whassup, C-Town!"

"Whassup, playboy!"

"For those who don't know, this is Nick, one of Carlton's immature friends from Seattle," interjected Jeannie.

"Congratulations, y'all! I'm really happy for you!" Nick wellwished. "But I'm mad y'all ran off to Vegas to do it."

"Hey, player. I wanted to get it done traditionally, in a church, but there wouldn't be enough room in the pews for all of Jeannie's exboyfriends," Carlton teased. He blew his wife a kiss. They worked so well together, on and off the air.

"They can sit on all your fat-ass girlfriends' laps," Jeannie hollered back.

"Just let me know when I'm gonna be a godfather, so I can spoil the kid rotten."

"True that. We're workin' on it, playboy." Carlton winked at Jeannie.

"I hate to break up this impressive display of male bonding, but we have a little show to do here," Jeannie regulated. "Do you have a sports take, Nick?"

"Sure. Sonics in six," cheered Nick. "The Glove for president!"

Clorox motioned at Jeannie to wrap it up.

"Another poor, deluded Sonics fan. They don't know any better up there. Rains so much, their brains are waterlogged.

"Thanks so much for your call, *Cletis*. Seek help for that Sonics obsession of yours. We'll be right back after selling our souls for the greater glory of perpetuating a consumerist society—and for the greater glory of *my* paycheck. Coming back with Jeannie Rhome on *The Jeannie Rhome Show,* featuring Carlton Maxey."

**IMMEDIATELY, TABITHA INSINUATED** herself into the fabric of Nick's life. He didn't mind it at all; in fact, he welcomed it. Ever since that kiss on the beach Sunday night, their connection had become as tangible as it was cosmic. Nick saw her every day. Tabitha would come over to play, of all things, *video games* with him, even sports games. True, she wasn't very good, but that was beside the point. The woman actually liked playing them, and had made a conscious effort to connect with him on his own terms. Nick felt compelled to do the same, actually sitting by her side for eight hours at the beauty salon as she had her hair unbraided, washed, and then transformed into a web of sprightly auburn curls.

What amazed him more was that he was never bored. He found her personality electric, their conversations exhilarating. They had the whole world in common, from their degrees from black colleges to their fields in the entertainment industry. Tabitha had just landed a book deal with a major publisher. After she won a highly contested poetry slam at the Lower East Side's Nuyorican Cafe, an editor in the audience had been so blown away, he had brought her into the publishing house, where she thrilled the editorial staff with a live performance. She was promptly signed up for a rarity in poetry—a two-book deal. Living off the six-figure advance, Tabitha spent her days honing her craft, reading, eating, and watching her "stories" (soaps).

That night was the fourth consecutive one they had spent in each other's arms, lying on the couch watching *SportsCenter,* equally entranced. They had arrived at this point thanks, in most part, to the assertiveness of Tabitha. Things were moving pretty fast, but naturally fast. Not a thing between them felt forced. It was as if they had known each other in another life. She was passionate and intense, just like her poetry. The woman was a futuristic anomaly, a woman unafraid to play by her own rules and demand what she wanted out of life, out of love. Call it confidence, conceit, connectedness, or courage; whatever it was, it all began from within herself. Nick had simply been lucky enough to be on the receiving end of it right now. It was as if Tabitha had emerged from the drawing studio of his mind; she was so good and so perfect, Nick could only have made her up.

"I'm going to LA tomorrow," Nick announced with little fanfare.

"Okay. For what?"

"Auditions. I'm an out-of-work actor."

Tabitha smiled, cocking her head at an angle to kiss him. "No, you're not. Your job now is to keep me happy." She kissed him again. "Believe me, that's a full-time job, keeping a queen happy."

Damn, she was so playful! Nick loved that. A peck. "Don't I know it."

"So how long are you going to be gone?"

"Through the weekend."

"Can I tag?" Tabitha requested. "I can make life really exciting for you, Nick."

*Really, you already have,* thought Nick happily.

Tabitha was out on a limb. Having thrown out an early test to her romantic interest, she wanted to see if he would react like most men, feeling a bit hemmed up and fighting for a weekend of freedom, or if he would react like *her* man, and invite her along. His answer to her simple appeal would speak volumes about their feelings for each other.

"I'll have to check with my friend I'm staying with," Nick said.

Tabitha's hopes sagged.

"But yeah, that's cool," he smiled.

He was so nonchalant about it, Tabitha kissed him, rewarded him, emotionally exhaling her fears away.

Nick grinned at her. "We'll see just how exciting life can get."

**TABITHA ESTABLISHED HER** worth pretty quickly. In less than a week, the woman was already driving Nick's truck, a distinction that no woman had achieved in more than five years. As Nick studied the sides that had been faxed over to the agency en route to the auditions, Tabitha handled the frustrating LA traffic with all the aplomb of a native. Head buried in paper, Nick read, entirely oblivious, trusting her completely with the care of his 4Runner. Once inside the casting offices, Tabitha additionally prepped him by organizing his pictures and résumés, whispering sample directions a director might ask of him, as well as just offering general love and support.

Nick commanded the audition rooms. Armed with the confidence of a seasoned stage performer, he made the necessary adjustments for the subtler medium of film, toning down his performance without losing the power of his acting choices. There were so many factors involved in who was hired for a film role—budget, comparative height of the principals, if the actor had a look that was commercial enough—besides the most important one of talent. Regardless, he would strut out of the auditions right into the arms of his own poetic little cheerleader, confident he had nailed them. Nick felt like The Man.

With Khalilah over in Saudi Arabia meeting the sheik's family, Nick had Tabitha drive them to Ayinde's townhouse in the Silver Lake area of Los Angeles, in the vicinity of Dodger Stadium. They parked the 4Runner outside a row of identical-looking brownish-colored townhouses on a quiet street in the ethnically eclectic neighborhood. Upon his arrival at Ayinde's front door, Nick was crushed by the man's bear hug.

"Good to see ya, B!" he shouted. "How you feelin', black?"

Smiling easily, Nick said, "I'm doin' alright."

Tabitha, bags in hand, cleared her throat. "I'd say you're doing better than alright."

Ayinde released his friend and glanced instantaneously at Tabitha with a coded look that only fellow males could interpret. "This you, B?" he asked Nick.

"Tabitha, meet my boy Ayinde."

"This is truly a blessing and an honor," she greeted him. "Peace to you, brotha."

Seeing that she truly was with Nick, Ayinde squeezed her into a hug as if he had known her as long as Nick. "What's goin' on, Tabitha!"

Nick broke up the hug, mock-protectively. "Aw'ight, aw'ight, aw'ight. Don't be huggin' her all up."

Tabitha winked at Nick as she slipped past the boys and into the house with the bags.

Once again, Ayinde asked Nick in a stage whisper, "That's you, B?"

"I'm workin' on it."

Ayinde dapped him up royally, displaying his true admiration. "Yo, that girl's the cream butta jones right there! She a butta pecan Rican?"

"Dominican and Cuban."

"*Ai, Papi!*" Ayinde whistled. "You betta hang on to this one, black! She's got a cool vibe that makes Shana McAdams look simple! 'Na mean?"

"I feel you."

"Get on in here and meet Travia. We gonna kick it this weekend, B!"

As Nick entered, he, wrongly, felt pleased. No matter how much outside opinion was *not* supposed to influence your opinion of those you cared about, he still could not help but feel good that Tabitha had passed the first critical, informal test, whether she had known it or not—friend acceptance.

---

**GAME SIX HAD** been a war. Up in Seattle, the SuperSonics had waged a brutal fourth-quarter comeback, rallying from a ten-point deficit to force a decisive, winner-take-all Game Seven. This was to take place on the Los Angeles Lakers' home court, the Staples Center in Downtown LA. And Nick was going.

A call to Wesley had yielded an invitation to his own luxury box he shared with some other actors who were out of town. Now more than ever, Nick was glad he had kept an active telephone dialogue going with Wesley after having left *Blackdraft*. Luxury box seats at the Staples Center for Game Seven of the Western Conference Finals featuring the Seattle Sonics? This was dreamlike for a lifelong Sonics fan.

The dream didn't hit home to reality until Nick arrived at the luxury suite. Free food and drinks flowed abundantly, like catering on a movie set to the third power. About ten or so other people were already present by the time Nick and Tabitha arrived, including Wesley and several lower-tier actors and Industry types.

Wesley dapped him up immediately, giving him a dap-hug for not having seen him in months. Prepping for a role as an undercover narcotics officer in some new movie, Wesley looked a little beefier and had his hair bleached blond à la Dennis Rodman. "Whassup, man! How you feelin'?"

"I'm chillin', doc."

"This here your girl?" Wesley asked Nick of the yellow-tinted-glasses-and-Kobe-Bryant-jersey-wearing Tabitha.

There was an imperceptibly short, awkward pause that Nick smoothly covered. Funny how the most telling questions about one's own life always came from others. "This is my friend Tabitha."

The wind in Tabitha's sails died briefly, but she would never let Nick, or his friend, know it. "Peace to you, Wesley. Your work is on point."

"Thanks a lot! Pleasure to meet you," said Wesley, giving her an Industry kiss on the cheek. The PA system in the jam-packed stadium began to announce the starting lineups. "The game's about to start. Chill, relax, and help yourself to plenty of everything in the room."

"Thanks," said Tabitha, honing in on the platter of crab cakes.

Nick observed his would-be woman make herself a plate wordlessly, as if nothing had happened. Nothing really had happened. But still, unspoken as it was, Nick knew something had.

**THE FOURTH QUARTER** arrived. Fifteen minutes stood in the way of the Seattle SuperSonics from going on to the NBA Finals. Fifteen minutes and a sixteen-point lead stood in the way of the Los Angeles Lakers returning to the Finals to defend their world championship.

Nick, of course, was obnoxious, and let all the Laker fans in the suite (everyone else) know about it. Tabitha, a woman who bled purple and gold, ignored Nick's strutting around the suite hyping the Sonics' alleged greatness, by focusing her energies with mystical concentration on the court below. Eight minutes left in the game and a fourteen-point Sonics lead. Tabitha tried to *will* her team to win.

And that's when destiny took over. The proverbial tide turned, knocking the Sonics out of the water. With agonizing horror, Nick watched his team blow its entire fourteen-point lead to *trail* by one with less than a minute to play!

The atmosphere in the suite—and the stadium—was off the hook. Wesley ran around the suite, dapping people up like he had just hit Kobe's jumper to put the Lake Show up by one. Goading Nick in the spirit of truly rabid Laker fans, Wesley and Tabitha stood directly in front of him, dapping up repeatedly, screaming, "Whut! Whut!" That is until Nick tackled Tabitha lovingly to the couch, tickling her into submission.

He soon released her, as the Sonics had the ball with forty seconds left. Rubbing his defender off on a screen, Gary Payton nailed a three-point jump shot. Sonics by two, twenty-nine seconds to play.

"SAY SOMETHIN'!" cried Nick to the rest of his suitemates. "Say somethin' now, you *suckas*!!!"

When Kobe hit a leaning jumper in traffic to tie the game, the Staples Center came alive again. Tabitha dapped everyone in the room before sticking her tongue out at Nick. God, he loved her spunk.

Game tied, nine seconds left. Emotions were high. The fate of two cities' pride rested on the outcome of this game. The fate of bragging rights for Seattle Nick and his Los Angeles friends rested on the outcome of this game.

Payton, triple-teamed the second the ball touched his hands, passed it off to an open teammate. Only, the ball never got there. Out of nowhere, Kobe Bryant swooped from the wing to steal the ball. Six seconds. Like a bird in flight, Kid Kobe covered thirty feet in four quick strides. Three seconds. Kobe lobbed the ball crosscourt to the streaking Shaquille O'Neal, twenty feet away. One second. The catch and the finish happened with a monster, two-handed dunk. Nick's frantic eyes checked the scoreboard clock even as the horn sounded throughout the arena. Game *over.*

The stadium, the Laker players on the sidelines, and the guests in the suite *erupted*. Pandemonium reigned. Fans overwhelmed security, swarming the court to celebrate, including normally composed movie stars Denzel Washington and Keanu Reeves. As distraught Sonic players scurried off the court, Kobe and Shaq lay in the bottom of a pigpile of purple-and-gold jerseys, mob-celebrated by their victorious teammates.

Tabitha streaked around the suite hugging everybody in sight. The woman was nearly in tears. In spite of his own letdown, Nick was struck dumb. The power that woman carried was remarkable. She lived life fully, intensely, like tomorrow might never come. She played hard, rhymed hard, loved hard, and lived hard. No one extracted more from life than Tabitha Washington. That is why she made *his* soul dance.

Last, she jumped onto Nick, wrapping her legs around his waist, forcing him to hold her in the air as she kissed him feverishly. Tabitha didn't bother to waste the moment trash-talking him; she would rather celebrate with him. Her kisses tasted like sweet white wine, the smell of her sandalwood-scented African oil overwhelmed him. His mind was made up.

When she judiciously let Nick up for air, she peered deep into his eyes. The look he gave her was more serious than just that of a disgruntled, disappointed fan. "What's wrong, Nick?"

Nothing was wrong. Everything was perfectly all right.

"Will you be my lady?"

Tabitha let herself down from her midair perch. Her face was enslaved by emotion. Tabitha said softly . . .

"Yes."

*San Diego Reader*—June 18

## MARRIAGE MINDED
### *One man's quest to get married in a year*
### *by Anonymous*

Do you believe in destiny? Although I am not religious, I like to think of myself as spiritual. I believe in a Creator, but not in any one religion's god. I am far too independent-thinking to buy into the notion that there is this one entity up in the sky pulling the strings of eight billion people's lives in some grand marionette show. It's the American Way to control your own destiny, right? But there are times, events, *people* in your life that make you question that narcissistic view of the very little control we do have over our lives.

We all have met couples who are simply so perfectly matched and happy that we must say, "They are meant for each other." And they are. But as I forge my way through my life, in search of that elusive one who is meant for *me,* I see more and more that "finding" her is a dynamic that defeats the purpose of love. You can "find" fifty-six cents in the seat of your couch, but can you "find" a soulmate?

I recently witnessed the reconciliation of two people who are truly meant to be together. They were married, separated for eight months, and just recently reunited. During their eight-month hiatus, despite allegations of lying and extramarital affairs, they loved each other so much that they couldn't concentrate on the various people buzzing around the fringes of their lives—just on each other.

Tunnel-vision love. Ever had that? The kind of all-consuming love where the world fades to black and the only thing that matters is that other person? Spending seven hours in a mall without buying a thing? Talking on the phone for six hours about absolutely nothing? A love so powerful that even if you two are apart, you want for nothing? That is tunnel-vision love.

Fortunately, tunnel-vision love does not grow on trees. If it did, it would not be special, or be tunnel-vision love. Not everyone is ready for that kind of powerful, all-important love.

When I started this column, I thought I was ready for it. No, I wasn't ready for it. I was ready for the *idea* of it, but not for the actual thing itself. From watching my friends reconcile their marriage, I can see now that, up until then, my head and my heart were not in the right place for this powerful a love. How could I *realistically* expect to manufacture the type of soul-surrendering emotions that fuel tunnel-vision love if I was actively *looking* for it? As hard as I've tried—and you all know that, for ten months now, I have *tried*—to experience it, tunnel-vision love is ultimately out of my control.

This is where destiny steps in. Love comes when you are not looking. Love is not the Easter egg at the end of a hunt. Love is a blessing, a divinely inspired product of the unexpected and the uncontrollable—destiny.

Last week, when I wasn't looking, destiny descended an angel from heaven in the form of woman and placed her in my life. She enriches my life, she makes my soul dance. And the only way I could have experienced her was by, finally, letting go, and becoming less **Marriage Minded**.

## 16

LOVE YOU."

*Cardinal Rule to Dating No. 16:* **Never say Those Three Words—first.**

They had just finished making love for the first time. July 7 was the one-month anniversary of the day they had met, three weeks removed from the day Nick had made their companionship official. Nick lay in Tabitha's bed, her body wrapped around his, holding his smooth, dark brown body within the confines of her creamy, toffee-colored one. Tabitha's beautifully shaped eyes were closed, perhaps awaiting his response.

Nick was scared. He did not know exactly what to say. So far, everything between the two of them had been damn near idyllic. Not a single, solitary ripple on Lake Relationship. This had been achieved, in most part, due to Nick not being so much like, well, *Nick.* He was the king of falling too quickly, too soon. With a war-torn heart scarred by the ravages of failed love, Nick had sworn he would never, *ever* say Those Three Words first. Something happened, some dynamic changed in a relationship when a man, supposedly the less emotional, less expressive member of a couple, said Those Three Words first. He had told Jasmine Those Three Words first, and look where it had gotten him.

Was Tabitha just being young and naive, attaching an emotion to a physical act? Nick chastised himself for even thinking that way. The celebration of their one-month anniversary had been far too special, too spiritual, too heavenly, to be cheapened by describing it as merely a physical act. Their lovemaking was the stuff of legends: three passion-filled hours that had challenged the limits of the flesh, natural dexterity, and, unfortunately, her lease. Tabitha, in having climaxed four times, was part opera singer as well as a poet, chanting and calling for Nick not to stop in French, Spanish, Swahili, and English. The neighbors had banged on the walls once, after Nick had made her climax for the last time, Tabitha having emitted a bloodcurdling scream of ecstasy. So she was a screamer, not a moaner. There was not a thing in life she did without intensity.

Their increasingly connected lives and affections startled Nick. He wondered if this was how it happened, how you fell for the woman you love: that it all happened in a month's time. It seemed too good to be true. Nick didn't want to spoil it by opening up his mouth.

"You don't have to say anything," said Tabitha quietly, eyes still closed. "I just have so much feeling, so much emotion for you that I am running out of hollow adjectives to describe what I really feel for you." A sigh. "I love you."

Nick rolled over to face her. He gently kissed her on the eyelids then peered delicately into those sexy baby browns of hers. The tender fragility of the gesture made her smile hopefully. There was nothing else to hope for. He was hers.

"I love you, too."

---

"**SHE SAID THOSE** Three Words," Nick told Malloy via phone. Nick rested on his porch under the awning on an oddly rainy but warm summer day in San Diego.

Nick anticipated hearing something from Mal along the lines of "Aww, man! Not Those Three Words!" But this time, Malloy surprised him. "And what did you say?"

Maybe marriage counseling had changed his personality. "I said it back."

"Do you mean it?" Malloy relaxed on his brownstone's front

porch in a tank top and shorts, soaking in the sights and sounds of Brooklyn in the summer.

"Believe it or not . . . I do."

"I believe you, dawg, I believe you. That girl's so bad, she shouldn't be called Tabitha. She should be called The Truth!" dubbed Mal righteously. "Finally, you did this one the right way."

"The 'right' way? There is no right way to fall in love," protested Nick.

"But there's somethin' special about this woman. She's got personality, intelligence, ambition, looks damn good in a sarong . . . She's The Truth, son," Malloy appraised. "She's special."

"You don't have to tell me," agreed Nick. "I'm practically living with the girl, we're so all up under each other. Like I went up to LA and shot this commercial last week, right? Her first instinct was to come along with me."

"Does The Truth have a job?" asked Malloy pointedly. "It's cool and all you two are in love, but we don't need no broke-ass women around us. Broke hos is a no-no."

"She's a professional poet, Mal. She goes into poetry slams, wrecks shop, and takes home the loot. She also has a two-book deal with a New York publishing house to print poetry, which is pretty rare, from what I understand. She's working on the second one right now," Nick informed him. "She's for real."

"Well, she sounds like everything you've ever wanted," assented Malloy. "How old is she?"

"Twenty-three."

"Well, she's young, but at least she ain't fifteen like the chicks you normally attract," Mal teased.

"You ain't funny, you herb."

"So what's her problem?" asked Mal.

"Her problem? What're you talking about?"

"Everyone has flaws, *especially* the women you date."

"I mean, tell me what you really think," returned Nick sarcastically.

"But on the real, though. Nobody's perfect. I just wonder what this woman's flaw is."

"Other than an aggressive love of life, I don't think she has one."

"I don't wanna sound like the Grim Reaper or anything, but I suppose time will tell."

"Oh yeah? What's Mia's 'problem'?" challenged Nick.

Malloy smiled. "She's too much like me."

"So, is everything straight between y'all?"

"It's gettin' better. We still take things day by day, but things are gettin' better," testified Mal. "I'm seein' some sides of my wife I ain't never seen before."

"Is that a good thing?"

"No doubt, god. It's reinvigorated our marriage. I feel like we're dating all over again." Mal stretched out along the steps and fixated on the clear, darkening New York skies above. "Minus the game-player bullshit and the chickenhead ineptitude."

Nick was wrong. *Nothing* could change Malloy's personality. And that was precisely what Nick loved about his very best friend.

---

**"I HAVE AN IDEA."**

Famous last words. "Boy, haven't I heard that one before," mumbled Nick. "I'm still reeling from your last 'idea.' "

Craig grinned. "Weren't those t-shirts great?" With some major arm-twisting of his boss, Craig had the *Reader* generate "Marriage Minded" Anonymous t-shirts. On the front was a copy of a "Marriage Minded" column with the *Reader*'s name prominently displayed. On the back of the shirt, printed in bold green neon letters, were the words "Who Am I?" with an exaggerated question mark. They could not keep the thing in stores.

"Fabulous," remarked Nick dryly. On any given day at Fashion Valley, Nick would see fifteen to twenty women wearing the shirts. "I'm glad to see you have appropriately commercialized my search for eternal companionship."

"That's my job," said Craig cheerily. "But I have another idea."

"Bring it."

Once again, stretched out beneath a sun-drenched July sky by Craig's pool in the backyard of his house, the two of them dissected "Marriage Minded" strategy. With a little over a month left until Nick's self-imposed deadline—and the end of one of the most successful stunt columns in San Diego journalism history—the stakes were high for how this whole drama should play out. For Craig, although this truly was his friend's life, professionally, it was just that—drama. He knew about Nick's new girlfriend, but he had never spent any time with the two of them.

"I say we hold a big press conference on August 14 to reveal your identity and report on the failure of the column," plotted Craig.

"Failure? As you keep telling me, the column's a hit. *Kid.*"

"But the point of it was to find you a wife, right? And you're still single, so, in a sense, we've failed."

"Look, Craig, I've got a *great* girlfriend. Everything has gone so well for us this past month, it's ridiculous. And the reason is because I could care less if we get married," Nick explained. "In fact, I refuse to let myself even think that far ahead. For once in my life, *I'm* not going to be the one to jeopardize a relationship's future by thinking past its present. I'm happy, dawg."

"Well, if she's so great and you're so happy, then why haven't *I* met her?" contested Craig.

"This ain't the Westminster Dog Show," Nick fired back. "She doesn't need your seal of approval to be in my life."

"I didn't say all that, kid. If you think you've found someone special in your life then you need to share her with the *other* special people in your life," lobbied Craig. "I'll put it out on the table—I wanna meet her."

"Done."

NICK FELT LIKE a groupie. He milled about backstage with Craig at LA's House of Blues on Sunset, a scant week after their poolside powwow. Backstage before a rap concert was definitely on the left side of ridiculous. Women, who had on about as much clothing as they had respect for themselves, grazed around outside the dressing rooms. While for the most part people just hung out talking and killing time with idle chatter, these relaxations could not be accomplished without heavy supplies of beer and weed. With the distinct smell of Black & Milds in the air, almost everyone was smoking on *something*. Two no-name rappers shot dice in a corner to a small gallery of onlookers. A few music-industry stars from other genres roamed the halls looking glammed out. Just another night at the House of Blues.

Craig, of course, thoroughly enjoyed this cornucopia of cool. A repressed music critic, he was in a Valhalla of his favorite artists. Headlined by Jay-Z, the eclectic concert featured the sprightly New Orleans rapper Mystikal, rhymestress Bahamadia, the perpetually smoked-out-looking Snoop Dogg, and the soulful Jill Scott. Normally, where Nick fit in any of this would be anyone's guess. But tonight, he played the role of supportive boyfriend. Souldance was the very first opening act, set to perform her intelligent and spiritual poetry in front of a dense crowd that had come to hear such uplifting songs as "Shake Ya Ass," "Jigga My Nigga," and "Bitch Please."

Nervous? Hell yes, she was. But the nervousness Tabitha felt as Souldance was all contained in her eyes. Nick could see it when he pumped her up in the backstage area less than two minutes before she was to perform. Her wide pupils gave her away, despite the aura of intelligent placidity she normally radiated when Souldance. In the hallway, Nick cupped her gorgeous, bronzed face in his hands, touching his forehead with hers.

"You alright, Tab?" he asked earnestly.

"No," she nervously laughed.

"Why not?"

"There are few times I get nervous in my life, and one of them is right now."

"Precious, you *are* Souldance," Nick reminded, using his pet name for her. "What you do is recite poetry that is beautiful, intelligent, and inspirational. You *always* rock the mic. How do you think you got your name? You make our souls *dance*."

"Right." She heard the words, but she didn't feel them.

"Knowing all of this, knowing you are going to move the crowd, whenever you feel nervous before a show, don't you always ask yourself afterwards what the hell for?"

Souldance broke into a sexy, confident smile. As she would say whenever Nick did something particularly cute, sweet, or sexy, she purred, "Now that's *my* man."

Nick growled a kiss to her and sent her off with a pat on the butt. "Now get on out there and tell those fools who you be."

She assumed the confident, mystical aura that she habitually carried in her back pocket. "I be Souldance."

Nick mouthed the words "I love you" to her. She winked in response then scurried off toward the stage.

Craig, who had broken out of his living dream long enough to observe their touching little tête-à-tête, walked over the crowded wings area of the stage with Nick. They stood there watching Souldance perform, spellbound like two mummies. As Nick had seen before several times, Souldance captured the imagination of the audience, won them over, and left them wanting more. When she ended her set with "That's *my* man," she spoke the words adoringly, gazing with unbridled love and admiration at Nick. Craig watched Nick's face light up at just her *look*. They shared a connection so personal, so understood, and so deep, Craig felt not privy to even observe it.

"Thank you, LA!" she shouted into the microphone, scampering offstage and into the arms of *her* man. They exchanged some quick congratulatory kisses, Nick gave her an "I told you so," and she trotted off in search of some water.

Craig reached over and gave his boy a pound.

Quizzically, Nick asked of the gesture of respect, "What was that for?"

"That woman has a heart as big as the whole wide world."

"Yeah, she does," Nick concurred dreamily.

What Craig said next snapped him out of that dream. With serious, unflinching eyes, Craig said honestly, "There's something special about her. She's The One, kid. She's The One."

***

"YOU KNOW SHE'S The One, right, playboy?"

Carlton and Jeannie had gone mini-golfing with Nick and Tabitha the day before. This time no fights, verbal or otherwise, had broken out. Just good ole competitive, trash-talking mini-golf. Jeannie had tested the girl's mettle, too. After several of her attempts to bait Tabitha into an argument or missing her shots had failed miserably, the two wound up talking like sisters. It was ridiculous how universally likable Tabitha was.

"Is that right," murmured Nick, just to fill the space. He shifted in his bar seat to catch a better glimpse of Seattle Mariners highlights on one of the several TVs in Seau's sports bar. Carlton had demanded rights to take his boy out for dinner on his birthday. Tabitha could provide dessert later on.

"It's ridiculous how universally likable that girl is," Carlton absently remarked as he pored over his meal.

That startled Nick. "Get outta my head, dawg! I was just thinkin' about that."

"I'm serious, playboy," seconded Carlton. "I mean, you can take her anywhere and she'll fit in. She's got that cool, earth-chick vibe, but then she doesn't take herself too seriously. She'll throw a putter after missing a shot on the eighth hole just as easily as she'll do a cartwheel after a birdie on the eighteenth. She's smart, too, but she's not all stuck up about it."

"I hear you," said Nick, tending to his own food. All this "She's The One" talk was far too premature, especially coming from those who had no idea he was even in the market for a wife.

"She seems like the type who'll play spades with you and your boys, watch a game of ball on TV, and then beat the whole room in some NBA Live on the sticks. I mean, the woman *likes PlayStation*, man!" Carlton emphasized. "You can't beat that with a bat."

"I hear you, playa." *Whatever.*

"I mean, I ain't gonna bullshit ya. You my ni—" Carlton stopped himself.

Nick stopped hacking up his Cajun-style chicken breasts just long enough to toss an inquisitive glance in Carlton's direction. "Whassup?"

"I can't say that word," said Carlton quietly.

"What word?"

"The N-word." The man sounded like a five-year-old boy who knew he was going to get caught by Mommy. Carlton's gold wedding band shone in the overhead light from the bar. "Jeannie won't let me."

While part of him wanted to laugh, Nick decided that this was a good thing. "No, I hear you, dawg. You're thirty-one years old. I just turned thirty today. It's time to give that word up. I'm with you, dawg."

"Glad to hear it, playboy."

It was funny how women could make men change their simplest to their most heinous vices. "Besides, since I've been hangin' around Tabitha and feeling her whole earthy, spiritual vibe, I don't think twice about using it nohow. I'm not ashamed to admit that my woman is a positive influence on my life."

"That's what I'm talkin' about, dude!" encouraged Carlton, relieved. "But you know what? That's not the only thing she is in your life."

"Oh yeah? What else?"

As Nick continued eating, Carlton said, to his chagrin, "She's The One."

---

**"SHE'S THE ONE, NICK."**

"Will you all shut up with that!" yelled Nick.

"Nick . . . settle down. Don't raise your voice in the Cheesecake Factory," Robert advised teasingly. Luckily, they were eating during the lunchtime rush, when the general volume of the place was already cranked up. "Very unbecoming."

"Look, I'm flattered that you like my girlfriend. That *all* of you like my girlfriend. But y'all need to stop saying that shit and jinxing me!" fretted Nick.

"Why not? I could see at her open mic the other night. You two are positively enchanted with each other. Kind of like me and Antony," Robert mused over his Chinese chicken salad.

"'Why not'?" Nick echoed exasperatedly. He had barely touched his blackened chicken pasta, he was so worked up. "*It's been two months.* Or at least it will be next Friday. How can *anyone* know enough about someone to *marry* them?"

"But it's true. She is absolutely delightful," Robert assessed. "I've never seen you look at any of the other women of yours that I've met like that."

Nick snorted. Robert hadn't had the pleasure of seeing him with Jasmine half a decade ago. What blew Nick's mind was that Robert didn't even *know* about "Marriage Minded," and here he was egging him on to marry Tabitha. Was this deeper level of connectedness obvious to everyone else but them? Not once had Nick and Tabitha discussed marriage, and Nick swore that he wouldn't. As far as he was concerned, he had lost in his search to be engaged by August 14. Here it was the first of August, and he had no designs on proposing to Tabitha in the immediate future. Well, at least not in the next two weeks, anyway.

"I'm changing the subject," Nick declared. "So besides hiding out in marital bliss, what else have you been up to?"

"I start art school in September. San Diego Academy of Fine Art. I'm already taking some drawing classes right now. I'm pretty excited."

"So what are you doing for money?" inquired Nick, concerned.

"We manage, thank you very much, *Mother*," Robert said pointedly.

"No, tell me," Nick insisted. "Now you've got my mind going. What does this Antony guy do? Is he some secret dot-com millionaire? Did he invent the Post-it or something? I just want to know what this Antony guy does to be able to support his and your artistic ass."

Robert rolled his eyes and then relented. "He works for Von's."

However inappropriate, Nick chuckled unexpectedly. "You're in love with a bag boy?"

"No. His family *owns* Von's. He used to be on the board of his father's company that bought Von's out. Antony retired shortly after the acquisition. Now, aside from some occasional consulting for them, he's just living and exploring life, trying to find himself, as am I."

"So basically, you've got a sugar daddy."

"I wouldn't put it that way," sniffed Robert.

"No, you wouldn't. That's why I 'put it,' " laughed Nick lightly. "So what do y'all do all day?"

Robert shrugged. "Cook, eat, paint, draw, and make love."

Nick almost choked on his pasta. "Well, there's a visual I didn't need to have while eating. . . ."

Smugly, Robert grinned at him. Waiting until Nick started to eat another bite of pasta, Robert whispered evilly, "She's The One, Nick! She's The One." To his delight, Nick started to choke all over again.

**TRYING SOMETHING NEW,** Nick and Tabitha actually were *not* spending the night together, for the first time in almost a month. Nick suggested it, just as a change of pace, to see how they liked it. Sure if he wasn't on the phone with her anyway, lying flat on his back on his bed in the darkness of midnight, talking easily about everything and nothing. An excerpt:

"You tired yet, precious?" Nick asked.

"I could never get tired of you, babycakes."

*Babycakes.* How positively silly, sweet, and sickening all at the same time. Nick loved it. "Say that again."

"No."

"Please?" Nick pleaded.

"No."

"Why not?"

Tabitha smiled from her reclined position on her living room couch. "Because you want me to."

"So do you have any plans for this weekend?" inquired Nick.

"Other than being with you? No."

"What about your friends? Have I met them all?"

"Pretty much. They've all come to the open mics and stuff. Janice says you have such deep, soulful eyes, they make her toes quiver," Tabitha giggled.

"Poets. Gotta love poets, man," responded Nick appreciatively. "Tell her—and her toes—I said thanks."

"Will do."

"So you're free this weekend?"

"For our two-month anniversary? You better believe I'm free." Sweetly, she added for his benefit, "Babycakes."

---

**AS FAR AS** all-time surprises went, this one had to take the cake. All he had told Tabitha was to "be packed." On Friday, Nick parked outside her Linda Vista apartment and promptly blindfolded her. Once the cab arrived, Nick carefully guided her inside the car. When they arrived at the airport, he placed earphones on her head, loudly playing a slow jams mix tape he had made especially for the trip, shuttling her through the metal detector and to the gate check-in counter. Thankfully, Nick encountered airport and airline employees with a sense of fun and romance, as no one interfered with his carefully plotted plan. Tabitha was a good sport, too, not once daring to remove the blindfold or the headphones even on the airplane, trusting Nick implicitly.

Two and a half hours later, they had arrived. Nick removed the headphones, then the blindfold. Fluttering her eyelids as she adjusted to sight for the first time in four hours, Tabitha gasped.

From the Kerry Park lookout point on Queen Anne Hill, all of Downtown Seattle at twilight was laid out before her. Orange, pink, and light purple remains of the sunset backlit the majestic Olympic Mountains to the west. Individual house lights flickered on in residential Alki Point to the south. The varying architectural beauty of Seattle skyscrapers formed the heart of Downtown to the east. Elliott Bay bridged the east, west, and south with its lightly lapping waves. A lone ferry chugged out toward the waters of the Puget Sound. The Space Needle. Safeco Field. The Columbia Tower. For the first time in her life, Tabitha was in Seattle.

What a bold display of romance. That was *her man*.

---

**AFTER INTRODUCING THEM,** Nick left Tabitha to chat with Mom in her room while he and Harrison discussed business. The outlook was not good. Mom spent a lot of time in her room in bed. She had already started losing her hair. Vanity, which ran in the family, caused her to wear a bandanna around her head. Harrison flirted with the idea of taking up a second job, any job, to help afford the Pilotaxln treatments. Nick had already donated more than half of his checks from the two commercials he had shot in the last month. Although one of the commercials was slated to be a national one, the residuals from it depended upon how often it would run. Ordinarily, one national commercial for a principal actor could net him more than $50,000 a year easily—but the residuals would be paid out over the course of the year. Mom didn't have a year. She had until October. It had been decided that Harrison would start financing the Pilotaxln treatments with his dwindling life savings with additional help from Nick when he could. Without Malloy splitting the bills with him anymore, Nick's financial contribution would be almost nonexistent in the short term. Realistically, Harrison only had about a month's worth of money to pay for Pilotaxln, since the IRS had cleaned him out. Hopes for keeping Mom alive kept slipping away like the sands in the hourglass of Time.

When Nick had surfaced from his sobering discussion with Harrison, he ran into Tabitha on his way to Mom's bedroom. His girlfriend's eyes had water in them.

"Your mom is an amazing woman," Tabitha uttered. "Amazing . . . simply amazing . . ."

"What did she say to you?"

Tabitha just kept shaking her head as she gave Nick a quick hug. "She's just amazing. . . ."

Nick regarded his girlfriend quizzically as she wandered off, still shaking her head and muttering. Determined to find out just what his mother had said to bring tears to Tabitha's eyes, Nick entered Mom's room with a gentle knock. "Mom?"

"Enter, Handsome."

She was such a mom. Nick entered tentatively, gauging her expression to see if this truly was a good time to talk.

Not only was she a mom but also a mind reader. "It's okay, Nicholas. I'm up."

"How're you feeling?"

A tired smile. "This is one of my better days."

Nick sat on the edge of the bed and gave his fatigued mother a kiss. Gingerly, he smoothed some of the bangs peeking out from under the red bandanna, taking care of her as a good son should. "What's on your mind?" she asked.

*Everything and nothing,* he did not say. These trips to Seattle depressed the hell out of him. Who could take seeing his mother dying in front of his very own eyes? "What did you say to Tabitha?"

"That soon she will have my job." Mom transmitted a warm, motherly smile. "I told her to take care of my baby."

Nick could have cried right then and there.

"She's The One, Handsome. She's The One."

---

**NICK AND TABITHA** returned to San Diego on Sunday just in time to drive up to Los Angeles for Ayinde's wedding. All of Ayinde's friends and family had flown out for the somewhat impromptu affair. Both anxious to start their eternity forever, Travia and Ayinde had hired wedding organizer to the stars Dez Tucker to plot out the wedding on the fly, within their minuscule, two-month window. Thanks to a good word from Nicolas Cage, with whom Ayinde had become quite buddy-buddy on the set of *Adrenaline Orgy,* Dez Tucker took the job seriously. She briefly shuttered most of her other advance matrimonial projects in order to concentrate fully on Ayinde's nuptials. Since Travia's father was a high-ranking official in the Bahamian government, the father of the bride could afford to foot Dez Tucker's quite substantial fee.

How did the saying go? You could take black folk outta the ghetto, but not the ghetto outta black folk. Despite being richly decorated and held in quite possibly the only Southern Baptist church in Beverly Hills, the proceedings started forty-five minutes late. Although everyone was decked out in their Sunday best—men with their lightly wet curls and alligator shoes, women with their freeze-dried hairstyles and lavish neck jewelry—that still did not repress certain ghetto tendencies. When the minister asked brotherman to please remove his hat in the house of God, brotherman called the minister a "rat bastard." One of the featured songs before the processional march was the R&B group Next's "Wifey." After the ceremony, many of the guests, including Ayinde's best man, had to make a run to the liquor store before coming to the reception. One of the groomsmen poured beer on the ground for the homies that were unable to be there with them.

In spite of the outrageous displays of ghetto fabulousness at this wedding, Nick and Tabitha had a ball. Not even a catfight over the bridal bouquet between two maids of honor could spoil the reception, held at a local hotel ballroom. Bubbles were still blown, food was still consumed, and pictures were still taken. Ayinde and Travia made a strikingly beautiful couple. There Ayinde was, all tuxed out and handsome with his reddish-brown skin and sienna-brown braids down to his shoulders, while the darkskin Travia with her short, jet-black haircut proudly represented the other end of the Nubian spectrum. Tabitha seemed glossy-eyed over the whole affair, soaking everything in with her wonderfully intelligent eyes.

As the newlyweds fed cake to each other joyously at the head table, Nick sighed wistfully from his seat at a regular ballroom table. *August 9.* Like dominoes stacked up against each other, everyone around him was getting married. This had gone on for too long to merely be a fad. It had all started a year ago with Craig and Olinda. Then Loq and Desiree. Mal and Mia had reconciled. Khalilah was prepping to marry some sheik. Robert was practically married to his man. Chantel had married herself. And Nick . . . Was Nick married to being single? Instead of hating on his friends, he congratulated them. Satisfied with his developing relationship with Tabitha, Nick settled on this one realization about his own wedding: *It is just not my time.* A quirky smile arose. That didn't mean that he still didn't want one.

Having scrutinized her boyfriend's face for the past few minutes while he had been staring off into the distance, Tabitha tapped him gently. "Let's dance, babycakes."

"Yes, precious."

Within the comfort of his arms, Tabitha asked softly, "What're you thinking?"

"About how much I love weddings."

"Mmm." She let that remark resonate within her soul.

"Is this your first one, precious?" Nick asked.

"Believe it or not," she confessed.

"Trust me; calling the minister a 'rat bastard' is *not* standard wedding procedure."

Tabitha gave a little laugh. "It's very beautiful. I'm quite impressed."

"Start getting used to it. You're entering that age bracket where everyone else around you starts getting married," Nick warned.

She raised an eyebrow. "How long does it last?"

Nick smiled. "I don't know. I'll tell you when I find out."

They danced in silence for a minute, enjoying the warmth of each other's touch, the scent of the other's breath. Tabitha breached the silence with "Doesn't it ever get lonely?"

"You mean seeing all of your friends get married instead of you?" restated Nick.

"Yes."

"It does," he admitted, shrugging. Then, optimistically: "I guess it's not my time yet."

Some more dancing to the music. Babyface crooned how he was a bit old-fashioned and didn't mind being that way.

"I have a question for you," Tabitha announced brightly.

"Okay."

"This is one of those questions you have to answer without think-ing. Just say the first thing that pops into your head," she instructed him.

"Sure."

"Will you marry me?"

"Yes."

## MARRIAGE MINDED
*One man's quest to get married in a year*
*by Anonymous*

*Press conference at the San Diego Marriott, Mission Valley, at 2 P.M. this Friday, August 14! Come MEET the man behind "Marriage Minded"!*

Call me Virginia Slims because we've come a long way, baby. It seems like just yesterday that I made this brash, bold statement: "All you need to know, dear San Diegans, is that I am on a mission and I will *not* be denied." And that was just the beginning of the most arduous year of my entire love life.

I want to thank you for being there for me, San Diego. I want to thank you for helping me get through all this. I want to thank you for helping me survive my first column offering, Miss "Dinner-and-a-Movie" date. You all were there for me during the entire WEMP (Woman with Emotional and Mental Problems) ordeal. San Diego also helped me out during my movie-star miscues. I would also like to apologize for having stood y'all up back in December. But I'll make it up to you—this Friday.

I'm keeping this last column short and sweet. We all know about the journey we have taken together. Hopefully, you have enjoyed, as I have, reading this column, and grown with me as I have pursued marital bliss and happiness. This is my last "Marriage Minded." For all of you who can't make it on Friday—I'm getting married, y'all!

# 17

ABITHA WAS MORE stunned than Nick—and she had asked the question. They had stopped dancing at this point.

"Did you hear the question?"

"Yes."

"And what's your answer?"

"Still yes," beamed Nick.

The emotional person she was, Tabitha started to cry. Nick reassuringly wiped her tears away and kissed her. Positioning her head, he created some eye contact.

"Look at me, now—I *love* you," Nick professed. "I would be damn proud to spend the rest of my life loving you."

Tearing again, she managed, "Me, too."

Nick kissed her tears away. "Save them. We've got an announcement to make."

Whisking her away to the head table, Nick bogarded his way to the mini-mic stand in front of Ayinde. Before Ayinde or anyone could stop him, Nick snatched up the microphone and turned it on.

"I have an announcement to make," Nick proclaimed over the music. "DJ, stop the music, please. Stop the music."

Figuring Nick was someone of importance, the DJ stopped the music.

Ayinde looked expectantly up at Nick from his seated position. More interested than perturbed, he assumed that whatever Nick had to say must be pretty damn important to be interrupting *his* wedding.

"I'm sorry to interrupt the festivities, but I have an announcement to make." Nick gazed adoringly at his fiancée. "Tabitha and I are getting *married*!"

Collectively, the room gasped. Then they cheered—wildly. Nick put down the microphone and gave his wife-to-be a huge, face-engulfing kiss. The ovation was stronger than that for a UCLA touchdown in the Rose Bowl.

When he finally released his fiancée, Nick received a dap-hug from Ayinde.

"Yo, I'm so happy for you, B!" he gushed. "Congratulations, son!"

Happily, exuberantly, Nick finally came to terms with what he had known all along. "You know what, Ayinde? She's The One."

---

**EVERY OTHER MAJOR** news outlet in North America ran Nick's last "Marriage Minded" once the Associated Press picked up the short, final article in its entirety.

Including *USA Today*. Headlining its Living section was "MARRIAGE MINDED" MYSTERY TO END, featuring a centerpiece color photo of one of the "Marriage Minded" t-shirts with a great big question mark stamped on it.

Sitting in the makeup chair, she read the article with interest as the makeup woman buzzed about.

She read about San Diego's obsession with finding out the identity of Anonymous. She read about the t-shirt craze surrounding the column, noting with chagrin that her own assistant makeup artist wore a black "Marriage Minded" t-shirt. She read about the editor brainchild behind "Marriage Minded," some white-looking mixed guy named Craig Donnelly. Craig called "Marriage Minded" "the perfect marriage, so to speak, of money and matrimony." She read about how the *Reader,* a free weekly newspaper in San Diego, at times had *tripled* its circulation, thanks to the "Marriage Minded" phenomenon. She read how more than fifty press credentials had been issued *overnight* in anticipation of Anonymous revealing his true identity

at the press conference. TV crews had descended upon San Diego
County in advance. A media village camped outside the *Reader* offices, hoping for a glimpse of Anonymous walking in with Craig to
pick up a check or something. She read about how San Diego, in general, was on fire, with everyone wanting to be the first to find Anonymous. An Internet search revealed 135 fan sites devoted to "Marriage
Minded."

For the convenience of people like her, *USA Today* provided a
"Marriage Minded" timeline, chronicling the history of San Diego's
most popular newspaper column in history. Hmm. Started last August, huh? The latest hot rumor was that either R&B singer Beyoncé,
dancer/choreographer Fatima Robinson, or actress Sanaa Lathan
would be at his side to announce her engagement to Anonymous, a
report that all three wildly divergent camps denied.

She shook her head. The whole thing sounded pathetic. This
reality-TV mentality America had been locked into for the past few
years was way too much. As she always did, she tossed the paper into
the trash before darting off to set.

**FRIDAY HAD ARRIVED.** The piqued interest of an entire city
centered around two in the afternoon in a Mission Valley hotel.
About a dozen media trucks lined the edge of Hazard Center Drive,
representing all the major networks and cable news outlets. A swarm
of about five hundred people, Nick estimated, milled about outside
the Marriott, generally disrupting traffic. Craig unobtrusively turned
his Jetta in to the parking lot. No one knew who they were or what
they were about to do.

They chose not to wade through the crowd of interested onlookers
who jammed the entrance to the hotel in a vain attempt to try and
shoehorn into the packed conference room. Didn't these people have
jobs? Craig guided Nick through a side entrance for kitchen deliver-
ies that was heavily monitored by beefy hotel-security personnel. Their
names were on a list one of the men carried of newspaper staff and
guests. Besides, they both looked harmless enough. Nick was dressed
summer business casual in a collared polo shirt and khakis while
Craig wore a shirt and tie. This was his big national moment.

Once Craig reached the conference room, he motioned for Nick to hang in the back of the room until the stroke of two. The editor delighted in dragging out the drama for the ludicrous turnout, and in the media interest in what he would call the ultimate PR coup of San Diego history.

As Craig made his way toward the elevated podium at the front of the jam-packed room, Nick surveyed the environment. Insisting upon getting front-row seats for this event that would finally illuminate who it was their friend worked with, Robert (plus Antony), Carlton, and Jeannie sat next to Tabitha, who was also in the dark. She had observed San Diego's infatuation with Anonymous from afar for the past month or so as the hype had built, but she had no clue who he was. Having accepted the offer from Nick as a show of support for Craig, Tabitha was merely along for the ride. Nick smiled. Boy, would she be in for a shock. As would be Olinda, who sat behind Tabitha. Not even Craig's *wife* knew the identity of Anonymous, despite her months and months of pleading. Filing this factoid away for later, Nick realized that Craig sure knew how to keep a secret. A chair even sat empty next to Tabitha, to give the impression that Nick would be joining them in finding out who Anonymous was.

At the stroke of two, Craig began. He warmly greeted the members of the media and all interested parties. Nick watched with horror as a cavalcade of flashing lights intermittently brightened the room. Several camera crews jockeyed for space. Craig spoke into a bank of at least a dozen microphones.

Nick had had no idea that anyone outside of San Diego would care whether he found love or not. In that moment, a truism of life crystallized for him: People love *love*. They spent all their lives craving it, looking for it, reveling in it. Love was one of the most fundamental human needs. That was the one thing Nick had in common with everyone in the room, everyone who had read the column, and everyone else who didn't: They'd all had their own experiences with the ups and downs of finding love. Nick had just happened to share his with them, celebrating the one main thing that humanized them all.

"And so without further ado," Craig concluded, "I would like to introduce the man you have *all* been waiting for . . . Anonymous!"

With Craig's outstretched hand pointing to Nick at the back of the room, everyone's head swiveled. Nick made his way down the center aisle to the deafening sound of shutters clicking and shocked mur-

murs. Robert elbowed Antony. "I knew it all along," he smirked, lying.

Standing behind the podium, Nick released a huge gulp of air. His friends, in the front row below, stared up at him with sheer and utter amazement. Even the normally unflappable Tabitha held her mouth agape. With a subtle gesture to his chin, Nick motioned for her to close her mouth. Now he turned his attention to the media, who exploded flashbulbs at him with nonstop regularity. Squinting into the glare, he said simply, "Hi. I'm Nick."

**NOTHING ELSE BUT** a cliché would do. "Well, I'll be damned."

Shana sat in her trailer on the Sony Pictures lot, watching the press conference live on CNN. Although somewhat trivial, this was still news. Thanks to the *LA Times* reprinting the column during the last three months, "Marriage Minded" had become a bit of a Thursday-morning staple for Shana. She thought the guy who had just *so* many women problems and beefs was too funny to be true. She just never thought that guy could be Nick.

*Well,* shrugged Shana, *that explains a lot.*

**NICK REALLY HADN'T** prepared much to say. He hadn't wanted to appear pretentious or self-important, especially if nobody showed up. "Do you have any questions for me?"

Reporters fired off questions like a hailstorm. Nick picked one and went with that. "What do I do?" he repeated.

**"I'M AN ACTOR,"** Nick answered, from inside Shelby's TV screen in her office.

Shelby shook her head, marveling at her client. Could he ever keep a secret and lie his ass off or what! Eyes steadily on the screen, Shelby picked up the phone and started dialing. "Yes, you are, baby. Yes, you are."

**"WHY'D YOU DO IT?"**

"Why did I start writing 'Marriage Minded'?" Nick specified.

"Yes. Why did you give yourself until today to find a wife?"

---

**"WELL, I WOULD** like to keep the specific reasons for the deadline to myself," said Nick on a TV in a boutique in Brooklyn. Mia hid out in the back room, eyes transfixed, while her assistant minded the counter up front. Her hand was already dialing a familiar number.

"Morgan Stanley. This is Malloy."

"Baby, turn on the TV to MSNBC. Quick!" she ordered.

From his old office that had waited for him during his eight-month combination of personal leave and vacation time, Mal changed the channel from Headline News to MSNBC. Damned if it wasn't Nick, his brownskin mug filling up the screen. The caption below the face read "'Marriage Minded's' Anonymous—Revealed!" almost like a *Jerry Springer* caption.

"You see it?" she asked.

"Yeah, I see it." Mal was a little more than disturbed. *Nick* was Anonymous?!? For eight months, Mal had been that dude's roommate and *he hadn't even known*! Malloy did not know whether to be angry or feel stupid. That was okay—he felt both.

---

**"BUT I WOULD** like to say that everyone wants love, and many of us who are single would like to be married," Nick added. More flashbulbs and lights.

---

**FROM HER LIVING** room couch, sick, Chantel observed Nick with an amused eye. Such a stunt like this did not surprise her. "Not me, homie!" she shouted at her friend onscreen.

"I was just a little more aggressive than others in looking for it," Nick replied from her TV.

Chantel blew her nose at him.

**"NEXT QUESTION."**

Some guy from *USA Today* won the shouting match. "What are your future plans?"

**"WELL, I PLAN** on continuing to pursue my acting career and maybe even dabble a bit in some writing," replied Nick from Asanti's computer screen. The press conference was being webcast simultaneously over CNN's website. Thanks to her high-speed connection from her new job at the Chicago Mercantile Exchange, she watched the whole scene unfold in next-to-real time.

Astounded, the now-married Asanti mumbled, "Sonofabitch." Judging from the amount of media there, she figured that Nick had to be rich and famous now. As bad as the thought was, she selfishly began to wonder if she had married the wrong guy.

**"ONE LAST QUESTION,"** Craig refereed, briefly appearing and departing from the podium.

Finally a reporter had the pipes to shout out the most obvious question: "Nick, who's going to be your wife?"

Nick bit his lip excitedly. Leaning in to the podium mic, he said smoothly, "The wedding is set for September nineteenth. I would like to introduce you all to my fiancée—and nationally acclaimed poet—Souldance." He offered his hand out for Tabitha to join him onstage.

**SITTING IN THE** mayor's empty war room with the elevated TV turned on, Maya T., who had been shaking her head in disbelief throughout the press conference, frowned, a tad disappointed. True, this Souldance woman was cute, but Maya T. had been expecting to see either Beyoncé, Fatima, or Sanaa.

Maya T. watched Souldance ascend to the stage cautiously, into the outstretched arms of her husband-to-be. They looked so right for each other. As it had so many times before, Maya T.'s spirit embraced secondhand joy for someone, which manifested on her face in the form of a smile. To no one in particular, Maya. T. said, "Yep. She's The One."

**SOULDANCE'S ELEVATION TO** the stage released a whole new flood of questions. While hugging Nick, she asked him, "Should I answer them?"

"When have you ever asked me for permission to do anything?" smirked Nick. "Go attend to your public."

"Peace and love to everyone," Souldance said in a somewhat shaky voice into the bank of microphones. Remembering what her fiancé—wow, she could *really* call him that now—had said about nervousness, she found her inner composure quickly. "My name . . . *is* . . . Souldance."

"Why are you called 'Souldance'?" a brotha from Associated Press called out.

Out of her peripheral vision, Souldance stole a look at Nick, who smiled. They had walked right into her carefully laid trap. As she had before almost every other poetry slam or open mic she had been to since college, Souldance smoothly recited, "For those who don't know, my Soul-*dance* is a continuous, harmonious, religious, prestigious, nonlitigious, *happily* monogamous, always on top of this, completely and freely *ridiculous* . . . expression of joy . . . and love."

Nick beamed at the subtle change in Souldance's intro from "sometimes monogamous" to "*happily* monogamous." His fiancée winked at him. As usual, they acted as if they were the only two in the room. They were in love.

"Drop a rhyme on us, Souldance!" cheered Associated Press Brotha.

Not exactly looking for permission, Souldance glanced over at Nick. After all, it was *his* press conference. Nick gave a shrug that read, "Dowhatchalike."

Souldance liberated the hotel cordless microphone from its stand and began to pace the stage to a beat in her own head. "I'd like to perform a piece for you called . . ." She stopped dramatically, gazing across the stage at . . . "*'My Man.'*"

**AN EIGHTEEN-WHEELER COULD** have driven through her mouth during the whole proceedings, she was just that shocked. Now a fixture on the morning shows, she was free in the evenings to watch amazing events on TV like this. This Souldance woman, who was proclaimed the *fiancée* of Nick, stalked the stage as if she were at a spoken-word concert instead of a nationally televised press conference.

What made it worst of all was that the little bitch was actually good. Souldance closed out the set by saying her last line forehead to forehead with her fiancé. It was clear to all that this Anonymous guy, Nick, was *her man*.

She reached for the phone and made a mental note. *Buy a USA Today on Monday.*

"**. . . THAT IS MY** *man*." Tabitha lowered the microphone and gave Nick a peck on the lips. Holding hands, they turned out to the rest of the media, who were on their feet, clapping enthusiastically. Nick's informal cheering section of Carlton, Jeannie, Craig, Olinda, Robert, and Antony cheered the loudest.

Tabitha kissed the back of Nick's hand before going back to replace the microphone on the podium. She returned, grasping his hands and pulling him close to her, once again forehead to forehead. They grinned fiercely at each other. Two stars were born.

"**YOU COULD'VE TOLD** a brotha." Malloy was hot. Literally and figuratively. The temperature was a ninety-five-degree Brooklyn heat. Not that sorry Cali heat, always dehumidified by a cool ocean breeze, but a muggy, urban, inner-city, *Brooklyn* heat. Malloy stalked the area of sidewalk in front of his brownstone with his shirt off. Not only was it just that hot, but also he had been working out ever since returning from California. Nick's workout ethic had shown him the way. "I mean, how could you keep a secret from ya boy?"

"You know it was business never personal, baby." Nick shuffled around his apartment, packing for a trip up to LA for work. Within hours of his press conference, Shelby had work for him. Not auditions, *work*. Shelby had booked him for two national commercials on consecutive days and an interview with the producers of *Naval Crossing* for their next major feature film. This would be a $100 million summer-movie behemoth called *Sand Adventures*. And, no, Ilene

Zimmerman would not be present. He would leave late that Sunday night and stay at Khalilah's, who had just returned from Saudi Arabia. His fiancée would accompany him to scout houses in the Los Angeles area. With her agent having arranged recording-contract talks with three major record companies for the two days Nick would be on set, Tabitha felt they were on the verge of something big. Funny how it had taken so long for them to get the attention of the Industry, but how quickly it acted once they had.

"I guess I underestimated your ability to keep a secret," joked Mal.

"Well, now the secret's out and you've got a month to get your shit together for this wedding."

"No doubt," Mal approved. "I know why you did it all, too. I mean the 'Marriage Minded' joint. Your moms must be stupid proud."

"She always is," Nick responded.

Malloy grew solemn for a moment. "I know I don't tell you stuff like this too often but . . . *I'm* proud of you, son. I mean that."

Nick stopped packing, curious. "What I done did now?"

"You're pullin' it all together. Got the phat job, the phat wifey . . . Future's lookin' bright, dawg," Mal appraised. "I'm proud of you. On the real."

Coming from Mal, that meant a lot. "Thanks a lot, man."

"Now get offa my phone, *Cletis*!"

---

**NICK'S 4RUNNER SPED** north up Interstate 5 toward Los Angeles under the cover of darkness. They had left late enough not to be bothered by the solid stream of vacation traffic San Diego experienced every weekend. To his left, past fenced portions of highway and signs forbidding fleeing Mexican families from crossing the highway, the Pacific lay dark and expansive, lit only by a full moon.

As she did more often than Nick did these days, Tabitha drove. Peacefully, Nick observed the woman he was to marry. His eyes enjoyed traversing the curves of her even, light brown skin. Her short African-bead earrings dangled freely from her earlobes. The tight, colorful sundress she wore flattered her small, taut B cups. Nick wondered how he could be so lucky. He wondered how *any* man could be so lucky.

"There were lots of guys at Clair de Lune. Why did you choose me?" Nick asked quietly.

"I didn't choose you. We chose each other."

"But you asked me out first. What was it that made you ask me out?"

Tabitha continued to focus on the road as she prepared her answer. "When you hugged me when we met, it just felt *right*. Like I had known you all my life. Like we were chosen to be together in some way. And I have based all of my actions in relation to you, to us, just off that one hug."

They rode in silence for a moment as Nick absorbed her presence. Even silence between them was never dull, never awkward, and always natural. In so many ways, he was *her man*. "Do you ever watch the show *Friends*?"

"You mean that white rip-off of *Living Single*? No," Tabitha responded pointedly.

That was funny. Undaunted, Nick continued with "Well, there's this one episode where Phoebe has this theory about lobsters."

"Uh-huh." Tabitha seemed quite unimpressed.

"She said that it's a known fact that lobsters fall in love and mate for life."

"Is that right?"

"No, it's not," said Nick truthfully. "I looked it up and lobsters actually engage in a bunch of serial monogamies, one after the other. Kind of how I was back in college. But I always liked the idea behind what Phoebe said, even if it was wrong."

"How lobsters fall in love and mate for life?"

"That's right. That somehow, they just *know* who's The One." Nick gave her his eyes adoringly. Softly and sweetly he said, "You're my lobster, Tab."

BIG CHANGES OCCURRED in the next month. On the strength of the media that the press conference had generated, Craig finally ousted his pimple-popping boss as entertainment editor. He enjoyed the position for a full week before being lured away as the editor of the music section for the *San Diego Union-Tribune*. Doubling his pay helped, too. Ayinde wrapped production on *Adrenaline Orgy* and took a three-week honeymoon with Travia in Aruba. Wesley's new film debuted at number one at the box office a week after the press conference. On the set of his new undercover-cop film, Wesley was riding high as production offers and deals rolled in with the congratulatory back-slapping. That is, until his newly released film lost 70 percent of its first-weekend gross the next weekend and the offers promptly dried up. Hollywood was quite a fickle mistress. Carlton and Jeannie received a national-TV deal to do a half-hour banterfest with guests from the sports world for Fox Sports. Naturally, Carlton had to ditch his sideline-reporter role for Channel 2 News, even though they offered him the sports-anchor position. In an amazing display of his humility, deference, and love, as with the radio show, the show for Fox, set to debut in October, was to be called *The Jeannie Rhome Show Featuring Carlton Maxey.* Another one of their stipulations was that it be filmed in San Diego, using San Diego sets and crew members. Carlton refused to move to a city like Los Angeles that did not have a pro football team.

As the big day drew near, Tabitha's mother, Blanca, set up camp at Tabitha's apartment to help coordinate arrangements for the wedding. In all honesty, she *commandeered* the wedding, using a week's vacation time from the bank to concentrate fully on the event. That was a relief because Tabitha was far too busy to worry about the minutiae of the most important day of her life. When she wasn't driving up to LA to take meetings associated with her recording contract with Warner Bros., she was assisting Nick in coordinating his auditions and shoots.

Nick had landed the lead role in *Sand Adventures,* touching off a series of randomly important meetings from wardrobe fittings to blue screen test shots for the special effects–laden flick. Principal photography was scheduled for early October. Nick's compensation for this role, reported to the trades as a million dollars, was more like $500,000, with box office bonuses, even less after taxes.

Five major New York publishers wanted Nick to write a book on the "Marriage Minded" experience. Numbers being bandied about by Nick's brand-new literary agent ran in the high six figures to million-dollar range. An auction would be set up among the interested parties after Nick's honeymoon.

Nick had hired Loq back in Atlanta to be his financial manager.

It would be a couple of weeks before Nick himself saw any of the money, as Loq set up legal and financial devices that would reduce Nick's tax burden. But once Loq did, Nick and Tabitha would be able to buy the modest three-bedroom, two-bath house they had been eyeing in the oceanfront Playa del Rey area of LA and move in together after their honeymoon in the Bahamas. Travia had promised that her people would take care of them real proper. Nick looked forward to receiving the money as soon as possible so he could start Mom's Pilotaxln treatments.

Despite her weakened condition, Mom, along with Harrison, made the flight down to San Diego the day before the wedding, insisting upon staying in the Mission Valley hotel where the reception was being held. They were not too far from the church in University Heights where Tabitha occasionally attended. Both she and Nick were more spiritual than openly religious, yet they preferred having a traditional church wedding with all the trimmings. Malloy and Mia had also flown in, opting for a hotel as well. Loq and Desiree stayed at Nick's house.

Arranged by Craig, the bachelor party took place at the strip club Pacers. This one was geared more toward white men, but ass was ass. There was certainly plenty of it to go around here. For Nick, the man of honor, a gorgeous lightskin sista stripper emerged from the VIP room with a mask on. The dozen or so men at Nick's table whooped and hollered as she strutted her sexy self past them.

"This here is my boy Nick!" crowed a buzzed Malloy, rum and Coke in hand. "He's gettin' married tomorrah! This is his bachelor party. Like I said back in the VIP room, I'll give you a *Benjamin* if you can *keep* this fool a bachelor!"

"Oh, he ain't gettin' married tomorrow," she promised. As she gave Nick the lapdance of his life, she would repeatedly, lightly slap away his hand when he would try to remove the mask.

At the end of the song, she said to Nick in a voice that sounded vaguely familiar, "You sure you still wanna get married tomorrow?"

With a few drinks in his system himself—all Midori Sours, of course—Nick said with a bemused grin, "You damn right."

The sista smiled beneath her mask. "Well, congratulations. She's one very lucky woman, Nick."

With that, she removed her mask. Missy Delicious! Melissa bent over to kiss him on the cheek. In his ear, she whispered, "Trust me. I know."

Nick shot Malloy an "I'm gonna get you" look. Mal played it off with a raise of his glass. "A toast, gentlemen, to the groom . . . to our boy . . . to our muthafuckin' *friend*, Nick!"

Glasses clinked and Nick smiled unabashedly. Ready or not, after several stops and starts in his life, he was finally getting married. What made it all perfect was that his friends and family—especially his mother—would be there to see it.

**THROUGH NO FAULT** of Craig's own, the press had found out where the wedding was being held. By the time Nick arrived, a small cadre of local-news trucks and camera crews had camped outside of New Bethlehem Baptist Church. More disgusted than angry, Nick was just glad that they had been barred admittance to the inside of the church and kept from potentially ruining his wedding. As he passed by the camera crews and bounded up the church steps, a goofy smile took hold of his face. *Welcome to the life of a famous actor, Nick.*

The hardest part of this whole thing was the waiting. Nick was a good three hours early, sequestered from the rest of the world down in the church basement. Already nattily attired in a gray tux with tails, looking like a Gingiss model, Nick passed the time playing black-jack with the similarly dressed Malloy.

"You got the ring?" Nick asked his best man.

"Hell yeah, nigga."

"Please don't use that word around me anymore," Nick requested politely.

Amused more than anything, Malloy retorted with "Nigga, please!"

"I'm serious, dawg. Both Carlton and I have given it up. It's a tired and contradictory word that may have served its purpose for us in our younger, more rebellious days, but we are men now. *Married* men, with children to raise someday."

Nick began shuffling the cards, effectively ending the subject. That last remark reverberated in Malloy's heart. "Can I tell you somethin', Nick?"

"Whassup?"

Mal formed a smile. "You're gonna be a godfather after all."

Nick's eyes widened. He stopped shuffling. "Mia's pregnant?"

"Three months," acknowledged Mal with a smile.

"Yo, congratulations, player!" Nick dropped the cards, reached over the table, and embraced Mal with a dap-hug. "Y'all didn't waste *no* time, huh!"

"After we were back on the right track, we wanted to make up for lost time and the . . . well . . . you know," alluded Malloy.

"Damn! I'm gonna be a godfather!" cheesed Nick, sitting back down.

"Another player comes down the pipe," Mal said, puffing up his chest.

"You already know it's a boy?"

"Naw. I can just feel it. He's gonna be a boy. A player, just like his father, and his father before him," prophesized Malloy. "I can just see it."

Grinning himself, Nick said, "Well, coming from you and Mia, he's gotta have at least an ounce of player in him."

Mal concurred. "More than an ounce, more than a speck, more than a drop!"

"**WE ARE GATHERED** here today to celebrate one of life's greatest moments, to give recognition to the worth and beauty of love, and to add our best wishes to the words which shall unite Nicholas Andre and Rosa Tabitha in holy matrimony."

Finally, the moment Nick had been waiting for all his life. Only his nervousness at standing before a church full of people was able to rein in the emotions that threatened to leak out of his eyes. He found strength in Tabitha's big, beautiful, brown, feline-shaped eyes, through which her preternaturally calming spirit prevailed.

Nick was all too aware of Tabitha's mostly Cuban- and Dominican-American family members mixed among his African-American ones. Three hundred people's attention was firmly fixed upon the anticipated drama at the altar. Blanca kept nodding softly to herself throughout the proceedings. Craig, holding his wife's hand, looked on, grinning.

Maya T. had tears in her eyes. At Nick's side, Malloy beamed like a proud father. Seated, Mia projected pure happiness. Ayinde and Travia leaned against each other, examining another couple about to enter into marital bliss. Robert and Antony, two white blips on an all-black radar, scrutinized the festivities as if plotting their own wedding someday. Harrison looked on fondly while Mom—Nick's whole reason for being—smiled like the proud parent she truly was. No matter what the future might hold for her, she had lived long enough to see her one and only child, her Handsome, her Number One Son, get married.

Nick sighed. His already full life was about to be totally complete.

"Should there be anyone who has cause why this couple should not be united in marriage," began the minister, "they must speak now or forever hold their peace."

"I do!"

Gasping, the crowd turned to look back down the aisle. So did the groom and bride. The church doors had been flung open to admit a panting, out-of-breath, professionally dressed woman. Her eyes were afire with determination. Nick had seen that woman before. That woman was Jasmine.

Tabitha looked perplexed. Mom's face soured. Malloy's eyes rolled back into the nether regions of his skull in disgust. Nick feared the worst.

"He doesn't love her!" Jasmine declared emphatically.

Malloy, unfortunately, had to get ghetto in the house of the Lord in order to save his friend's wedding. "Jasmine, go sit down, shut up, and let the boy get married!"

"No, I will not!" Jasmine yelled back, striding down the aisle now. "I have cause why this couple should not be united in marriage!"

Tabitha's eyes radiated terror. *Do something or else I will!*

Nick squeezed her hands reassuringly before he stepped down from the altar to handle the situation. If he had any homicidal tendencies, he did his best to repress them now. Face-to-face with the woman he had proposed to six years ago—only for her to say *no*—Nick, through gritted teeth, threatened her in a low, guttural voice. "Jasmine, what are you doing here?" Translation: *Jasmine, what the fuck are you doing here!*

"I need to talk to you," she asserted urgently. "In private."

"This is not a good time." *And there never will be if you're involved.*

"This is the *only time* I have left to talk to you."

Nick had seen that look of resolve in Jasmine's stubborn eyes before. She would not be denied.

*Jesus!* He requested a moment from his bride with his index finger. Grabbing Jasmine by her elbow, Nick practically hurled her into the minister's chambers and shut the door behind them.

Nick paced around like a freight train out of control. This was the only way he could manage his emotions on what was supposed to be his most very special day. "You wanted to talk, so *talk!*" Nick barked. *Before you make a criminal out of me, woman!*

Jasmine held out a copy of *USA Today*'s Living section's front page from a month ago. Smack dab in the center was a picture of Nick and Tabitha, bearing the headline ANONYMOUS—REVEALED! She waggled it at Nick. "Nick . . . She's not The One."

"And you are?" sneered Nick.

"Yes, I am. I love you, Nick," she expressed with gut-wrenching honesty.

"Jasmine, give it up. It's over. It's *been* over!" hissed Nick. "We've had this conversation before. Showing up at my *wedding* is not going to change the fact that it's *been over* for *six years!*"

"But you love me, Nick. I know you do!"

"Really, I don't!" Nick replied.

"Say it, then," she demanded.

"Say what?"

"Say you don't love me!" Jasmine shouted.

"Saying it won't accomplish anything, Jasmine."

"Say it!" she demanded.

"No."

"Say it!"

"Saying it won't prove a damn thing other than you can boss me around on my wedding day!"

"I wanna hear you say it!" Jasmine cried.

There was a knock on the door. "Is everything aw'ight, dawg?" came Malloy's muffled voice through the door.

"Yeah. Go away!" Nick answered gruffly.

"Say you don't love me, Nick! Say it!" Jasmine stalked around him swimmingly, like a shark after its prey. "That's right, you *won't* say it! And why not? Because you love me!"

"I don't!"

"*You . . . love . . . me!*"

Nick had heard enough. He snatched the paper out of her hand abruptly, crumpling it up and hurling it at a wastebasket. "*I don't love you!*"

He screamed it with such force, time seemed to stop. Jasmine was stunned into stillness. It was then that Nick could finally focus on the woman before him. If it were possible, Jasmine looked far more incredible than even he had remembered. Her caramel-coated face—a face that featured preciously plucked eyebrows, full, soft lips, and slanted, Asiatic eyes—was flawless. The high cheekbones were still there. So were the shy dimples. Every crevice and curve on her face that he had once claimed for his own was still there. Jasmine's dark hair was fashioned into her signature, professional-looking bob. At five-nine, her legs went on forever underneath her baby-blue skirt, accentuated by a pair of pumps.

Taking the high road, Nick slumped into a chair and asked while rubbing his eyes tiredly, "Jasmine . . . what are you doing here?"

"I love you." When Nick started to protest, Jasmine stopped him with a hand. "Hear me out. When you talked to me right before you left Chicago, when you rejected me like I had rejected you . . . it got me to thinking. I evaluated my life and decided that I was not happy with it, with what I was doing. I gave the station director an ultimatum to put me on the air or to fire me. After some reporter work, she put me on as coanchor of the morning shows. Jasmine Selene is now the anchor of the six and seven A.M. shows on WAGA on weekdays and sometimes Saturdays."

"Jasmine Selene? Why're you using your middle name for a last name?"

"It's show business, baby. I'm sure you know a little something about that," Jasmine Selene explained. "Whatever it is, it's working. Now, I'm the Atlanta Journalist Society's New Television Anchor of the Year."

"Congrats." *What, you want a cookie?*

"I'm not telling you this to brag. I'm telling you this because, once again, you've saved my life, influencing it for the better. And I love you for that."

"Why are you at my *wedding*, Jasmine? You could've put this on a postcard or somethin'," Nick groused miserably.

"After the Anonymous press conference, I hired a private investigator." Nick was fully present after hearing that someone had dug into his life. "I found out a lot of things. I found out about that fiancée of yours. I'm sure there are some things about her you'd like to know before you say 'I do' to the girl."

"Shut your mouth," Nick told her.

"I also found out about your mother being sick with breast cancer, with not a whole lot of time left to live. I hear that she needs some pretty expensive medication and I'm prepared to help."

"I don't want your help, thanks," denied Nick.

"Well, I'm here to help, regardless," she offered. "I also found out where and when your wedding was. I had to hustle to get here in time after doing the morning show in Atlanta today, but I made it."

"Lemme guess: You snooped because you cared?" Nick tossed at her sarcastically. "You're no longer a part of my life, Jasmine. Accept it."

"But I love you, Babyluv." Jasmine said it so plainly and simply, its pure honesty threatened to defuse Nick's protestations.

*Babyluv.* That was a name he hadn't heard in many moons. There was a time when that name had meant everything to him. There was a time when this woman in front of him had meant everything to him. "I don't love you."

"I love you, Babyluv."

"I don't love you." Nick was on his feet now.

"I love you, Babyluv."

"I *don't* love you." The more vehement he was, the more Jasmine knew he straddled that thin line between love and rejection. *He doth protest too much.* As much energy as it took to deny her accusations was as much love that lurked there beneath it all.

Without another word, Jasmine flew to Nick's face, forcing a kiss upon him that would have toppled Rome. Nick tried fighting it, only to ultimately submit to the thirty-second kiss. Feeling her tongue inside his mouth was like slipping into a nice, warm bubble bath on a cold and rainy Sunday night. It felt like home.

When Jasmine let Nick up for air, she peered at him hopefully. He had to have felt that, he *had to*! Nick's face was incapable of forming an expression right then, even though he *had* felt something. Jasmine looked at Nick expectantly. *Well?*

In the heat of their verbal battle, neither Nick nor Jasmine had heard a furious Tabitha enter the chambers. She had been there long enough to see some heffa *kiss* her man. *Her* man. Tabitha spun Jasmine around and decked her, a right cross upside Jasmine's head. Jasmine tumbled clumsily to the floor.

"What the fuck are you doing here, you triflin'-ass bitch!" Tabitha howled, house of God be damned. "You heard him say he don't love your sorry ass, you dumb bitch! Don't you *ever* fuck with me or my man!"

All of this was said by Tabitha as she rained blows upon the fallen Jasmine. At first, Nick had been shocked into a statue. A totally different side of his fiancée had emerged, a side that was, at the moment, kicking the shit out of his ex-girlfriend/almost-fiancée. Mal had been right. This was Tabitha's flaw: a seriously hot temper. Who could blame her, though? Some whiny ex-girlfriend had come to disrupt her wedding. *Tabitha is just far more physical in expressing her anger than others?* Talk about your failed rationalizations. This wasn't a garden-variety girlfight. This was ugly. Souldance was about to *dance* on Jasmine's soul.

When Nick snapped out of it, he pulled Tabitha, fluffy white wedding dress and all, away from stomping on Jasmine. She kicked and swung in Jasmine's general direction as Nick carried her off to the farthest corner of the room. After heading off a few more charges, Nick cautiously drifted toward the center of the room. Jasmine, not known to be a fighter, collected herself as best she could, glaring pure hatred over at Tabitha's corner. Nick, eyeing both women closely, kept his head on a swivel.

"Everybody just try and calm down," he pathetically tried to referee.

"You don't love her, Babyluv!" pleaded Jasmine with Nick.

"You don't love *her*, babycakes!" Tabitha threatened Jasmine.

"I love you!"

"No, *I* love you!"

Jasmine ran over and kissed Nick again—until Tabitha smacked her silly with an open hand. His fiancée returned fire by planting a kiss on him as well. Anything Jasmine could do, Tabitha could do it better.

Nick's head was spinning. This was surreal. He had just been kissed by the first person he had ever loved and the person he loved now and couldn't fathom living without.

"What's it gonna be, Nick?" spat Tabitha. "Her or me?"

"We were meant to be, Nick!" Jasmine lobbied. "You're my Baby-luv!"

"No, *we* were meant to be!" challenged Tabitha. "You're my lob-ster!"

In unison, both women hollered at Nick: *"CHOOSE!"*

For the first time in his life . . . Nick could not.

*To be continued . . .*

## ACKNOWLEDGMENTS

This could easily be the beginning of another book, I have just so many people to thank.

First and foremost, I would like to thank all of the readers, booksellers, book clubs, media, and friends who have helped spread the word about *Ever After* and supported me on my tours. You all know who you are. I appreciate you more than you will ever know.

I give special thanks, including but not limited to: my business partner for life, Curtis Midkiff, Jr., of JCM; mother-agent extraordinaire Janell Walden Agyeman of Marie Brown Associates; my manager, Trevor Engelson, and producer, Nick Osborne of Mission Films; the role model of publicists, L. Peggy Hicks, for her professionalism, enthusiasm, and dedication; the dynamic, super-talented, and inspirational A. Ryan Leslie and the whole NextSelection camp; screenwriter/baller/cultural critic at large Greg Colleton; Stanford and Brooklyn's finest, Tawanna Browne; my personal editor/story gladiator, Desiree Tucker (couldn't have written this without you, girl!); Industry hustler and entrepreneur Kevin Wyatt; the lovely and talented TJJ; mentors Drs. Jocelyn Jackson and Melvin Rahming of Morehouse College; my Atlanta fam, including Elvin Sutton, Jr., Esq., Kimberly Swan-Sutton, and the whole GQ Lounge (we incorporated now, baby!); my real fam in New York, Aunt Pearl; author/salsa dancer Trisha R. Thomas; my imprint-mates at Villard/Strivers Row Parry "EbonySatin" Brown, Travis Hunter, C. Kelly Robinson, and Tracy Price-Thompson; the city of Atlanta for being a home away from home; the city of Los Angeles for supplying an endless stream of ridiculousness; and the city of San Diego for being everything that LA is not.

And last, as always, now and forever, I thank my mother, to whom I owe everything, absolutely everything. *Everything.* And then a little bit more. Love, Mom. Love.

If I missed anyone, my bad! But enjoy the book anyway!

*Edwardo Jackson*
*nevahafta@aol.com*